As Good as a Fire

A Novel

Sharon O. Lightholder

ALBEDO PRESS

As Good as a Fire

Also by the Author

Fiction

The English Rendition

The Baldwin Portolano

The Paris Draft – The Road Back from Dementia

Jefferson's Chef – James Hemings From Slavery to Freedom

Nonfiction

Vietnam: The War Zone Dictionary In Their Own Words

Dedication

Maureen O'Bryan Shanahan
Wife, mother, and military spouse

CONTENTS

PART I

1947

CHAPTER 1

The June heat in D.C. melted Grace's makeup and ambition as she trudged alongside the old Treasury Building toward her past. Just another two blocks to the new headquarters of whatever the hell they were now calling the Office of Strategic Services. At least they air-conditioned the basement to protect the documents.

Her task was simple: make order of the jumble of paper the OSS generated in the China Burma India Theater during the war. They said the assignment was because she'd been there for the whole show, but the guys from Ceylon were upstairs. She ran the radio and managed the logistics of rescues in northern China. When they were shorthanded, she bucked orders to stay put and went into the field. First China, then Japan, the work camp at Nagasaki. Dutch and Aussies, but a few Americans got singed in the blast too. The OSS got there before the Army or the Red Cross.

The ass-chewing hadn't been all that bad. What could they do? Just words. The post-war reorganization of the OSS provided the perfect excuse for the new Central Intelligence Agency to forget the women. Most of the gals from the Asia gang were gone. Some married the OSS guys from Ivy League schools and lived on Park Avenue or in Georgetown. Law, finance, politics. Others used their technical skills at small radio stations or simply vanished rather than becoming overpaid file clerks with ridiculous titles.

A skinny security guard held out his hand. "ID, Grace,"

"Come on! I'm dying out here." She flashed her card at him and hurried through the lobby to the stairs. No need to run into any of the fellows from the Asia postings who were taking the elevator up. Maybe when the files were in order and sent to the National Archives, she could escape the cave and find light again. If not in the CIA, she'd find a home somewhere else.

Mildew and flickering fluorescent lights greeted Grace. The basement file room was a maze of battered file cabinets and mounds of rotting cardboard boxes piled on and under long wooden worktables. She let the heavy door slam behind her.

Susan called from several rows away, "Grace?"

"In the flesh!" Grace dropped her purse, balanced her hat on the coat rack, and loosened the belt on her suit jacket. *Really, what is the point? I could be nude for all the attention the file room got. Heels for filing? Really?* She traded her heels for slippers.

Rounding the corner to the second row, Grace asked, "Where's Molly?"

"Just us chickens. She took maternity leave early."

Grace chuckled. "One more escapee."

Half an hour later, Susan shouted from three rows away, "Lunch at the drugstore today?"

"No. I brought a ham on rye."

Susan came around the corner. "Crap. I ran late."

"Okay. I'll split it with you. If you bring the beer to the party."

Susan frowned. "What party?"

"Next week! Independence Day is the same every year. Where is your head?"

"Heat never hit me like this when we were in Ceylon."

Grace hoisted a water-stained box onto the table. "We didn't have to wear heels and stockings there, just whatever we wanted or as little as we could."

"Remember how we smoked like chimneys to keep the bugs away?"

Grace laughed. "That and a river of gin." *And Teddy, until he left for his father's law firm and his never-mentioned fiancée. A lot of things went unmentioned.*

Susan looked at the mountain of work. "Where do you want to start today? Assemble or file the completed ones?" Without answering, Grace pulled out a drawer and began finding homes for the files they had recovered the prior afternoon. By mid-morning, Susan started sneezing, and Grace's fingers were cramping.

Susan laughed. "Trade?"

Silently, Grace attacked a fresh box. Burma this time. She frowned. The files were still sealed in the burlap used for the eyes-only confidential dispatches. Unopened. Unread. All that fieldwork for nothing. "Susan! Got another sealed pack."

"Maybe it'll still have something useful when they unwrap it upstairs."

Before Grace could reply, the squawk box on the pillar by the worktable hissed. Both women looked up, hoping for a reprieve. Sometimes, they had to hand-deliver a file to a new hire above their pay grade and explain the abbreviations used in the field. New guys, half of them full of FBI smarts in new Sears suits, and all of them greener than goose-shit. It would be a long summer.

The intercom clicked. "Grace McPeters. Report to HQ. Repeat. Grace."

Abandoning her file, she tapped the button on the top of the squawk box. "What's the file name?"

"Just you."

"On my way."

Susan called across the room, "You might see Virginia Hall. Grapevine says they gave her a desk upstairs. You knew her—"

Grace hurried to add the last few pages to the fresh jacket and bent the prongs. "Met her in passing. She should be the director by now. Ran the best field network in France. They have already promoted half the guys she trained."

"Heard she'd be in line for director if she wore pants and didn't have a wooden leg."

Grace slid the file into an open drawer, then slammed it. "You mean the same leg she had the whole time she was in France? The one she had when she climbed over the Pyrenees in winter—chest high in snow-drifts—leading our guys into Spain? The head of intelligence in London, Smith-Cumming, has a wooden leg too! Don't get me started."

Susan laughed. "Should I make a check-out card for you? Pretend you are a file?"

Grace slipped on her heels. "Hilarious."

After being escorted in, Grace stood in front of a massive desk and watched the Assistant Director flip through a thick personnel folder. Pipe smoke haloed him. Without glancing up, he motioned for her to sit.

"What did you do for your college newspaper?"

"Some reporting and backup photography. Mostly editorial work."

He flipped to the next page. "You didn't list typing on your application."

"My father said I'd end up in the typing pool if I did. But I type well."

He drew on his pipe and frowned. "Think you could pass for a reporter?"

She tensed. "Yes."

"Your file indicates prior postings in Ceylon, then Burma, a bit in northern China." He paused. "I see you went to Japan for the recovery mission."

"Yes, sir." A slow, deep breath. "Our boys weren't in the best of shape. We were the closest. As much as they needed the food and medicine that we parachuted in, they needed to know they were not forgotten. The war ended so suddenly."

"You were a preacher's kid, weren't you?" Not asking. Asserting a truth.

She chuckled, "I *am* a PK."

He made a note on a legal pad. "Were all the exchange students who lived with your family from China?"

"No, sir. We had a boy from Java. But only for one semester."

He flipped a page. "Elite university, full scholarship. Junior year in

Paris. How's your French?"

"*C'est superbe.*"

"Kept up on your Chinese?"

She smiled. "My Mandarin is excellent in multiple regional accents. Cantonese is functional. I can read books and get the drift of documents. But I'm not a technical translator."

He leaned back in his chair. "We need eyes and ears aboard a transport ship of military dependents. Wives and brats. See if there are any dissidents, anyone overly sympathetic to the ideals of communism. Seems the ladies wrote letters to Congress and the Secretary of the Navy about missing their hubbies. Some genius at the War Department is reuniting them with servicemen in Tsingtao, China. Since Pearl Harbor, most of these ladies have moved three to eight times. A couple of different duty stations before their husbands went overseas again. Then they scattered like quail. FBI couldn't find most of them and focused on other security clearances. They never got the vetting they should have."

He gauged her reaction, decided never to play poker with her, then continued. "We'll want you to stay in Tsingtao to see if you find anything interesting in town or with the military, if you can cozy up. Stuff that the embassy fellas or intelligence there wouldn't catch. Trends, crimes, the usual."

"Any ex-pats of interest?"

"A few business executives. I'll send a list. Some French and White Russians. Soviets have a quiet presence. International city, Navy, Marines, flyboys, and their gals. Should be interesting."

She paused long enough for him to frown before she said, "I'm missing the angle. What kind of reporter am I? The usual invisible woman in the back row at the press briefing?"

"No! Flashy. Feature writer for *Ladies' Home Journal* with credentials to travel on a military transport ship. Think Rita Hayworth. Henna your hair. See wardrobe for your outfit and props. Get clothes made there for the nightlife. Interview everybody from bigwigs to homemakers."

"Communication?"

"Use mail for stories and pictures, expect inspection. The boys will fix you up with a transmitter. No human drops."

"I'm in a rental here."

"Consider the posting indefinite. You'll be sailing with them from San Francisco next week. Ingratiate yourself with the wives. Fit in as a pal now. See what they're thinking."

"How's flashy going to work with a bunch of housewives?" She held in a smile. *For once, being a woman is in my favor.*

"You'll find a way. Let them soak up a little glamour from a journalist for a magazine they all read. Remember its slogan: 'Never underestimate the power of a woman.' Once you land, spread that glamour around town. Besides being a strategic port, Tsingtao used to be called the Riviera of the Orient. It's still classy. Get noticed at the nightclubs, military and civilian. Play Brenda Starr, girl reporter. Meet with the resident press guys. Embassy briefings, for starters."

"As me?"

He smirked. "You need a new name. Think fast."

She smiled. "Claire Peters. Mom's first name and close enough to my last to get my attention."

He made a note on a form and handed it to her. She ran her finger down the paper and laughed. "Passport application. I live in New York. Journalist! Now I get credit after all those propaganda dispatches that I wrote."

"You were a freelancer for third-rate rags in New York. All defunct now. You will file stories with the *Journal*. That's all arranged. They'll edit as needed to make you look good."

"They'll already be good. Any of the old Asia gang there?"

"Not officially."

"Where's the parachute?"

"If things go upside down, the embassy can offer safe harbor. But they won't know about you in advance."

"And the military?"

"Will treat you like any other civilian."

"Housing? Recommended areas?"

"We'll set you up at the Edgewater Mansions Hotel. Upper floor with a bay view. Paid for by the *Journal* if anyone inquires. Stone's throw from the Officers' Club at the marina." She thought: *Clubs! Bay view! Hell of a lot better than my two months sitting in a jungle watching for Japanese destroyers.*

She smiled. "Sounds swell."

"Afraid the digs will be spartan. The hotel's still recovering, but it's a real crossroads. Lots of ex-pats, families, and entrepreneurs. Bar is up and running."

"Always a must."

That afternoon, Grace canceled her Fourth of July party. Over the next two days, she became Claire. She memorized her briefing book, and completed a crash course in the latest slang, military terminology, and the political situation in China. She rated outstanding on Morse proficiency and Chinese. Issued only one suitcase and one trunk, she packed her trunk with a basic summer and fall wardrobe, a cocktail dress and heels, a battered Smith Corona, spare typewriter ribbons, binoculars, a Kodak, and a guide to Chinese coastal birds. She set aside a scuffed Rolleiflex twin-lens reflex camera and travel clothes for her suitcase.

The day before her cross-country flight, the lab called her to pick up her radio. A white-coated technician looked up from a workbench when his door opened. "Claire?"

She smiled at her new name.

"Come in." He led her to the rear of the electronics workshop and pulled out the high stool for her at his workbench. He patted a sturdy black case. "We began with a Zenith Trans-Oceanic Clipper. The latest 1947 model. It looks like a good shortwave receiver that anyone can buy for a hundred bucks. Popular with foreign service and soldiers overseas and shortwave hobbyists here at home. I suspect you'll play it often to make it a part of your new persona. The battery should last a year."

"Only one battery? The prior model had two."

She frowned when he ignored her, unsnapped the front, and twisted the two small dials. She strained to see any signs of alteration.

He fiddled with the knobs. "Standard on-off and volume, and buttons for band selection. Stunning reception, even with none of its three antennas out."

In painful detail, he showed each of the several functions of the radio. "All standard so far. The company's founder was a yachtsman who wanted his music, news, sporting scores, and weather reports while at sea, so his lads at Zenith came up with this gem. But we've done it one better. We kept the outer shell of the second battery and gave it new insides. You can transmit."

She found her keying finger tapping against her knee. "Great. How?"

"There are two small knobs on the front."

She sighed and wondered if he thought her dense.

He placed the radio on its back. "In the off position, depress and turn the left knob to lock it down and tap the right as if it were a Morse key. It will be silent. If you wish to listen to your outgoing or engage in a two-way exchange, use the standard Zenith earpiece as if you were listening to the radio."

"Range?"

"Morse is about fifty miles. It's already tuned to a receiver on a ship." She waited for him to name it. "No need to stare. I don't know which one. Ears on twenty-four a day. If it goes to sea, our man transfers ears to the embassy, but they won't know who is sending. Your transmissions should be from several locations. Don't be predictable."

"Of course, to avoid any direction finding."

"Right. But a pretty girl at a picnic or at the beach club enjoying her radio shouldn't garner much attention." He blushed. "The radio, I mean." *Beach? I'll need a car during monsoon season or winter if the assignment lasts that long.*

"Is there a set transmission time or a code?"

"Not my department."

Latching the cover and patting it twice, he pushed it toward her and put two spare batteries beside the radio. "If ever you need to obscure its use, remove the battery like giblets from a turkey and plug in the real one. Undetectable. The operational element is useless to anyone else."

"Brilliant. Simply brilliant. Thank you."

He paused as if surrendering his puppy.

She thought to reassure him. "I've got a special place in my trunk. I'll take good care of it."

CHAPTER 2

The fog lifted by noon, yet the day remained San Francisco chilly. Peg and Beth, her seven-year-old daughter, stepped back when the approaching taxi nicked the curb as it stopped at the Saint Francis Hotel. Peg's father said his goodbyes and hugged them both. After helping them into the taxi, he handed their two suitcases to the cabbie, who asked, "Where are they going? Train station?"

"Fort Mason."

The driver made the trip a roller-coaster ride through San Francisco. Peg grabbed for her field bag when it slid to the floor, then pinned it between her feet as she held Beth against her.

The cab jolted to a stop behind three other cabs at the guard station. Peg pulled her military ID, travel orders, and passport from her purse and had them ready for the sentry, who directed them to the terminal for the USS *General A. E. Anderson*.

Once the cab snaked past the rows of barracks, three wharves came into view. Each had a massive terminal, but there was only one ship. Peg tried to gauge its size. Two smokestacks. Maybe two football fields long and a hundred feet across. Lots of decks. The brochure from the Navy had its actual dimensions, but what she remembered was that it took five hundred men to operate it and had carried four thousand troops at a time during World War II.

A pair of covered gangplanks connected the huge gray ship to the terminal building. A steady stream of sailors with seabags on their shoulders crossed from the terminal on the upper one.

"There it is! That's our boat." Beth pointed.

The driver stopped at the entrance of the terminal and pulled their suitcases from the trunk. When he saw Beth's frown as she looked at the massive ship, he said, "Lady, you're gonna have a great ride. The *Andy* is a solid ship. My boy sailed on it to Yokohama." Peg paid him and nodded her thanks.

At the terminal building, Peg handed the boarding officer the full packet of paperwork. After he inspected her military ID, the passport with both mother and daughter in the same photo, a visa from the Chinese government, travel orders in triplicate, duplicate luggage tags with their cabin assignment, and the receipt for the steamer trunk that was loaded the prior day, he motioned her through to the first-floor seating area.

There was a double click on the public address system speakers. "All dependents and civilian passengers, prepare to board in alphabetical order. I will announce a letter and then call names. When your name is called, proceed into the ship's quarterdeck."

After most of the passengers had boarded, and Beth had eaten half of the crackers from Peg's bag, their name was finally called. Peg took her daughter's hand and walked across the level gangplank. Unlike the starkness of the gray paint and insulated pipes, the deck of the entry area was painted with an ornate marine compass five feet in diameter.

The ship's captain, who was wearing a crisp white uniform, greeted them. A sailor gave Peg a booklet about the ship's operation and rules and a map with directions to their cabin. Finding their cabin, Peg opened the door which hit a suitcase. Fresh paint, old oil, something sharp, like a hospital disinfectant, filled the room. Beth went to each of the four suitcases jammed against the wall and examined the luggage tags.

"Beth! Don't be a nosy bee. You know the tan Samsonites are ours. Not the other two!"

"Where's the trunk with my books and toys?"

"In the hold below. The ship's basement."

Looking over the two sets of bunk beds, Beth pointed at the upper bunk nearest the porthole. "I want that one."

"We'll see who gets what once the others arrive. Meanwhile, sit on that lower one."

The door banged open and a slim bleached blonde with a movie star page boy hairdo came in, glanced around, and smiled. "Hey. My name is Gerri. Hated Geraldine! Guess we're bunking together." Orange blossom perfume filled the cabin.

"I'm Peg Ryan. This is Beth."

"Good to meet you. I hope nobody snores. My hubby saws logs like a lumberjack. Bet they can hear him halfway across China." She punched the lower mattress. "Jesus, scrambling in and outta these is gonna be a mess."

When the door opened again, a tall brunette said, "Hi, everyone." She pointed to her chest. "LaVerne."

Gerri snickered. "What'd you name the other one? That's my husband's joke."

Peg smiled and introduced herself and Beth, who squirmed while the women put away their suitcases. Gerri scrambled to the top bunk against the wall and announced that she intended to sleep as late as possible and didn't want the light from the porthole waking her. LaVerne took the bunk under her, saying she was an early riser.

Peg dug into her bag, pulled out a small camera, and took Beth's hand. "We're going to explore, and maybe take a picture of the Golden Gate before we go under it. Anyone else want to come?"

Gerri waved her off. LaVerne smiled and bounded up from the bottom bunk, clipping her shoulder. The communal bathroom was the source of the strong disinfectant smell, but mercifully close. A dozen white porcelain washbowls lined both walls. They painted the industrial piping below the sinks the same off-white as the entire room. Past the sinks, there were a dozen toilets in stalls. They located the shower room further down the corridor.

LaVerne chuckled, "Looks like I'm going to keep my bathrobe on my bunk at all times." Peg wondered how many midnight trips she and Beth were going to be making during the next several weeks.

Peg asked, "Ready to go up?"

Once at the rail, they felt the vibration of the engine change and watched as a rusted Chevy drive onto the dock and stop near the lower gangplank. Two men in civilian suits emerged. The driver hurried to the car's trunk and pulled out a motion picture camera on a huge wooden tripod. The other man dug into the trunk and got out something resembling an oversized lunchbox. They hurried to the foot of the gangplank as a small bus stopped at the foot of the dock and unloaded a few women and children.

LaVerne nudged Peg. "What on earth? Latecomers?"

"Beats me. Looks like they're setting up to film something. Beth? Can you see what it says on the side of that case?"

"'Movie' something. 'Movietone,' I think. Is that a word?"

"They make the newsreels we see before a movie starts."

A sentry ushered the men away from the gangplank. The cameraman hoisted the tripod and rushed after the reporter. They set up halfway between the bus and the sentry. The reporter motioned for the camera to roll, grabbed a microphone as big as an all-day sucker, and faced the camera with the bus in the background. He struck a pose and exclaimed, "Here they come! Ready to join their husbands, those gallant Marines who are defending China against communism."

A redhead carried two suitcases behind a woman struggling to keep a squirming three-year-old on her hip. Beth pointed. "How come she has two suitcases? We just got one each."

LaVerne put her hand on Beth's shoulder. "I bet one belongs to the lady in front of her with the kid."

As the women hurried toward the gangplank, the newsman stopped a chubby blonde in a shirtwaist dress and motioned her aside. "How long's your husband been in China?"

She tilted over the microphone. "Two years now. He's a pilot. I am extremely grateful to the Secretary of the Navy for arranging our journey.

It is the patriotic thing to do. Going over there and showing them what democracy looks like."

"What's your name?"

"Eleanor."

"Thanks a lot."

The man blocked the woman with the child on her hip. "Movietone news. Tell me, why are you going to China? Seems a long way to take a kid?" The redhead stalled behind her, leaning over to adjust the strap on a high heel. The woman, in sandals and a housedress, grinned at the camera while her son chewed on a cracker. "He hasn't seen his father in a long time." She smiled and shifted the toddler on her hip. "Sandy, wave to your daddy. Maybe he'll see you in a movie."

He grinned and shouted, "Hi, Daddy!"

Shrugging at his cameraman, the reporter asked if that was enough footage.

When the redhead straightened and hurried toward the gangplank, the cameraman pointed. The man shoved a microphone in her face. "And what about you, young lady? Why are you joining your Marine in China?"

She tipped her head toward him and purred, "Sex. I think we all missed the sex." She winked at him and walked to the gangplank.

The cameraman put the lens cap on the camera. "Well, that ain't gonna make it past the Hays Office. Too bad. Got a great shot. Kinda looks like Rita Hayworth."

The redhead handed the young mother's battered suitcase to a sailor and hurried to the pay phone at the end of the dock.

"Yes. Operator. I need to place a collect call to Washington, D.C. The number is Capital Five." She whispered the remaining numbers. In a moment, she sucked in a deep breath and held it. "It's your 'Claire.' I'm about to board. No time to chat, but some joker from Movietone had a camera on the dock. Hit me for an interview while I was boarding. I tried to make it unprintable. Better grab the film anyway."

She glanced at the line. "Yeah. Okay. Sorry, but you wanted flashy." She chuckled. "Sure! Now I get to go be Brenda Starr, girl reporter. Wish me luck." She let out a throaty laugh. "Bon voyage, yourself, Chief."

Once the last passengers boarded, the vibration in the ship changed as the sailors brought the engines up, then backed them down to check pressures.

Beth covered her ears when the *Anderson*'s horn sounded. After four blasts, tugs eased the ship from the dock. Peg and Beth stayed at the rail until the Golden Gate Bridge filled the viewing screen of the small Kodak, and they took the photo.

When Peg woke the first morning aboard the ship, only the deep throb of the engines gave proof of their movement. She looked out the porthole. Calm. Flat sea. Bright, cloudless sky with fog in the distance. Squinting at her watch, she saw it was six-thirty. The first breakfast seating would be at seven. If they hurried, she could have Beth dressed before the others woke and needed the limited space to maneuver. When leaving the upper bunk, she hit her head on the ceiling while negotiating the ladder.

She nudged Beth and whispered, "Let's go before it gets crowded in here." The girl nodded and struggled to get over the tall side of the bunk. Once again in their boarding clothes, Peg grabbed her field bag. They hurried through the stuffy corridor to the bathroom, where Peg did Beth's hair into braids as the girl wiggled. The morning air on the promenade deck was bracing.

Peg glanced through the dining room window as the stewards carried the last of the steam trays to the buffet table. She looked at Beth's hair. The braids were lopsided and the rubber band on one had already escaped. She sighed. She leaned over to her daughter. "The booklet said breakfast and lunch are going to be buffet style."

"Like a line?"

"Right. Let me order today. Tell me what you want."

Peg stopped at the door to the dining room to fix her daughter's loose braid. A woman with a child Beth's age stopped beside her. "We saw you yesterday but never had time to say hi. I'm Trudy and this is Sally, my daughter. We're the Franklins."

Beth said, "I'm Beth."

"Peg Ryan. Glad to meet you both." She leaned down to her daughter. "Stay behind me."

"Okay. Can I have scrambled eggs and toast?"

Peg scanned the serving trays. "And ham. And some milk."

Trudy smoothed Sally's curly red hair and tugged at the sleeve of her pullover top. "Did you hear her?"

She smiled at her mother. "Can I have the same things?"

"Sure."

The large dining room had a dozen tables for six arranged in neat rows. Along the window, there were a few tables for two. The stewards had set all with white tablecloths and silverware. A carafe of water and stubby glasses were at the center of each table.

The new foursome sat together at a table for six. A few minutes later, LaVerne came in and asked to join them. All smiled agreement. As LaVerne took her first bite of toast, the familiar static and clicks preceded the announcement and interrupted breakfast.

"This is a drill. Go to your Abandon Ship Station immediately. I repeat. This is a drill. Go to your Abandon Ship Station immediately." The clatter of silverware against plates replaced the low hum of early-morning conversations. Chairs scuffed back. A few women raised their voices as they hurried for the exits.

Peg forced a smile as she grabbed Beth's hand. "Let's go! It's practice. Remember what the booklet said about lifeboat practice? We need to get our life jackets." Peg bolted for their cabin and pulled their bulky orange jackets off the hooks on the back of the door. She saw Gerri in her bunk, yelled for her to get dressed, and hurried away while holding Beth's hand.

Once on the assigned deck, under six lifeboats, Peg slipped the bulky jacket over her daughter's head and tied the front ties. She laughed and pointed behind Beth. "Looks like you have a tail."

The woman beside her helped Peg pass the two long straps under Beth's skirt. "That's so the kids don't slip out."

She smiled at the woman. "Thanks. I'm Peg. This is Beth."

"Hi, I'm Silvia. He's Jimmy. How far are you going?"

Beth grinned. "China!"

"Wow. We're jumping off in Hawaii."

Peg shook her head at the jumble of attire, nightgowns, slacks, dresses, a bathrobe or two. A few garters showed. Some tottered in high heels. Others were barefoot. She whispered to Silvia, "I think I'm going to switch to slacks for the rest of the trip."

"You gals pack shorts?"

"Yes."

"Good. We lived in Hawaii. Gonna get hot soon." Beth and Jimmy fussed with the ties on their jackets. Sylvia whispered, "We were there for Pearl. Danny made me go live with my folks on the mainland. Then he got transferred all over hell and gone. But finally, we're going home. He's got a year left on his hitch, so I hope we don't get bumped again. I love Hawaii."

Peg said, "It's lovely from what I hear."

The women made a ragged line and were late in their execution of the task. The captain watched the drill on both sides of the ship and sighed.

When Beth wiggled out of her life jacket, she made a face. "It's stinky."

"More like dusty. We can fix that."

Beth waited in the corridor for her mother to bang the jackets together and fan away the dust cloud. When Peg opened the door to hang up the jackets, Gerri was still in bed, reading a magazine.

In the early afternoon, the PA system squawked again.

The captain's voice boomed. "This is an announcement for all civilian passengers of all ages. All are to be present in the dining room at eighteen hundred hours. That's six p.m. This is a mandatory assembly."

Peg and Beth went to dinner early. Gerri and LaVerne joined them. They were halfway through their meals when the captain came into the dining room with a sailor holding a life jacket. "Ladies, let me make this brief. Today was an excellent drill. It showed us what we can do better."

The captain had a sailor show how to pre-tie the leg straps on the lifejacket and step in. After fielding their questions and concerns, the captain smiled. "These are excellent considerations. Please let me know of other issues so I can address them to make your journey safe and comfortable. Now enjoy your dinner and tonight's speaker."

Twenty minutes later, Beth had finished her meatloaf and swirled the remaining brown gravy into her mashed potatoes. Peg asked, "Do you want to hear about China or go to the playroom with other kids?"

"I'll stay here."

As the messmen cleared the plates from the tables, Peg lingered over her coffee. The captain introduced the woman who sat beside him during dinner as Professor Lowe from the Department of State. As he rattled off her credentials, Peg reached into her bag for a notepad and pen. She glanced at Lowe and thought her too young to be an expert, then wondered how often others might have thought that of her own husband. The speaker was thirty, slim, dark hair pulled back, and glasses suggestive of a librarian.

Lowe approached the small lectern and invited everyone to get comfortable before she began. A few women left with their children. Peg watched them and noticed the redhead, sitting with several women at a table without children. After some scraping of chairs, the professor started. A few women smoked.

The speaker adjusted the microphone. "Tonight, I'll summarize the political scene in China to assist you in your dealings with the allies you will meet on your arrival. I'll be with you until Hawaii, so if you have questions after tonight, please ask."

She glanced at her notes. "Ladies, you are going to China as a part of our support of our Chinese friends fighting communism. Mao Tse-tung is threatening their way of life, so our government is assisting Chiang Kai-shek to keep his nation democratic. First, how do you pronounce your city? Forget what it looks like on paper and listen. It's SING Tao. Tsingtao is a major city in China, on the Yellow Sea, at the base of the Shandong peninsula. It was a treaty port and a German colony for almost a century. They controlled all trade, in and out. The Siege of Tsingtao in 1914 is how the Germans lost the port. It is a battle of World War I often omitted in history classes. Fortunately, much of the city remained untouched. Some liken it to the French Riviera."

Gerri finished her coffee and let the cup clatter on the saucer. Undaunted, the speaker continued, "To understand China today, you need to look at the China of yesterday. Generations lived in feudal conditions like Europe of the Middle Ages. Europe had kings, and China had an emperor."

Gerri slid her chair back. "Well, your kid's tougher than me."

LaVerne gave Peg an embarrassed smile.

Watching her leave, Lowe continued, "Through the first decade of this century, Sun Yat-sen worked in China, Europe, and the United States for support of a revolution that ultimately replaced the emperor with a democratic government, now called the Nationalists or Kuomintang. The KMT for short. Chiang Kai-shek was a student of the founder, Sun, and now leads the KMT. You might be interested to know that the current First Lady of China is the younger sister of Sun's wife. Both sisters have had significant influence in Chinese politics."

Peg made notes as Beth nodded off.

"In a challenge to the Nationalist Party, the communist or People's Party emerged. For decades, Mao Tse-tung has been their leader. Now I don't want you to think I am being familiar or disrespectful when I call these leaders by 'Sun' or 'Chiang' or 'Mao.' In China, the family name is first, so Mister Chiang and Mister Mao are the leaders of the two most important factions in China today."

Several women at the side of the room left quietly.

"The tension between these two groups has been active for decades, with Mao gaining support in the rural areas and the KMT in the cities. Only during the Second World War did the internal civil war pause and the Chinese unite against the common enemy of Japan. We tried to help negotiate an ongoing peace, but the parties could not reconcile."

She gestured theatrically. "Today, our Navy and Marines remain in Tsingtao to serve three functions: to prevent the Soviets from gaining a foothold at that strategic port, to protect the Americans still in China, mostly in Tsingtao and Shanghai, and to support the Nationalists while our diplomats continue to work to find a peace agreement between the two."

LaVerne fled when Lowe asked for questions.

Beth had fallen asleep, tucked under Peg's left arm. After the questions, Lowe came to Peg's table. She whispered, "I often have this impact. I should have spiced it up with tales of the intrigue when Sun married his secretary without divorcing his wife."

"Ching-ling Soon, right?"

Lowe smiled. "You've been doing your reading! I hope we can talk again. Goodnight."

Peg then roused Beth and took her hand. The cool night air was a relief from the stuffy room. As Peg walked Beth toward their cabin, the girl saw Gerri on a deck chair. A sailor leaned over as if to kiss her.

When Peg opened the cabin door, LaVerne put her book aside and said, "Oh. I figured you were Gerri since we both ducked the lecture."

Beth mumbled something that Peg ignored. She pulled off her daughter's top and slipped her nightgown over her head. "Stand up. Let me get your slacks off, then we'll go to the potty."

Beth mumbled, "On deck."

"What, Honey?"

Beth sniffed. "Is that sailor her boyfriend?"

The next morning, Beth and two women bumped into each other when they all tried to dress at the same time. LaVerne escaped to the bathroom while Beth and Peg dressed. Gerri slept through the commotion.

Professor Lowe saw Peg at lunch and nodded. Once Beth had finished, they walked by her table. Peg said, "Just wanted to let you know once again that I enjoyed your lecture."

She chuckled. "Thanks for listening. I'm used to students, a captive audience."

"We're going to the snack bar. Join us?"

While Beth ate her strawberry ice cream, Peg said, "I was trying to fit the part about the Soong sisters into the time frame. Sun and his wife seemed a generation apart."

Lowe caught a drip of her vanilla cone before it escaped. "They were. Sun was born in 1866. Ching-ling was born in 1915, so he was fifty years her senior when they married."

Peg blanched at the age difference. "What? That's like marrying your father . . . grandfather almost. Is Madam Chiang closer to her husband's age?"

Chuckling, Lowe said, "Mei-ling is slightly closer to his age. *Only* a forty-year difference. But older men have more power than younger ones. And their father, Mister Soong, was an exceptionally powerful man. These were like the arranged marriages of the European royalty."

Peg laughed. "Now if there's a third sister to marry Mao, they'd have all the political bases covered."

"They did better than that. The oldest sister, Ai-ling, is married to the richest man in China, H. H. Kung, a banker. Besides, Mao is already married."

"Where'd Mister Soon get his money? I thought he was a minister."

She raised her eyebrows. "Educated at a Methodist college in the States and returned as a missionary. He figured it was cheaper to print Bibles in China than to bring them from the States, so he started a publishing house, got rich, went into banking, and his girls married very well."

Peg asked, "You do this talk for all the dependent transports?"

"No. This is a first. I teach at Berkeley when I am not consulting with the government, but I got an offer to do this lecture. Dance for my supper. After some work in Hawaii, I'm going on to Shanghai to finish some interviews and then back home."

"We're stationed in Tsingtao, so if you get up north, call us."

"Sorry, I won't get up there."

"Me too."

CHAPTER 3

Peg and Beth were finishing a spelling drill in the library when the double clicks and static on the ship's PA speaker jolted Peg. *Another lifeboat drill? So soon?* Peg had visions of ship fires, floating mines, and sunken destroyers.

"Attention. This is a notification for all dependents. This is Captain Floyd. We have sighted a pod of humpback whales forward of the ship and will adjust our course to give them safe passage. Expect a change in the engines' sound and a slight movement as we turn. This is normal. If you wish to see the whales, come to the starboard side of the ship."

"Can we go?"

"You bet!" Peg shoved the lessons into her field bag. Pushing aside her journal, the pencil case, and a writing tablet, she found the leather-cased binoculars and Beth's camera. Once they were at the rail of the promenade deck, Beth leaned into the netting above the waist-high metal railing and poked the binoculars through a gap. With her glasses pressed into her eyes and the leather strap around her neck, Beth pointed. "See it, Mommy? The whale just jumped up and blew water!"

She kept her hand on Beth's shoulder. "Breached. That's what they call it when they come out of the water like that. They need to blow any water from their spout first, so they only get air, not any water."

Beth giggled. "So, their spout is like a nose? On the top of their head?" She handed the binoculars to her mother. "They're all gone."

Peg stood on tiptoe to see over the netting. "Not quite. I bet if we hurried to the top deck, we could see them a little longer. Want to try?"

When her daughter took off at a run, Peg called after her. "Slow down! You know the rule."

Beth skidded to a stop, then scrambled up the outer iron stairway like a monkey. Passengers rarely visited the upper deck because of its sun exposure and lack of protective netting. Peg kept her hand on Beth's shoulder as they left the stairway.

The wind tugged at the girl's pullover shirt. Only a waist-high metal rail and a knee-high band of wire kept them from the sea.

Beth pointed. "He shot water in the air again. Like Old Faithful!" She started for the rail, but Peg took her by the shoulders and marched her away from the edge until her back was against the base of the bridge. "We can see fine from here."

"Mommy?"

"Nope. Here or below."

"Okay. Can I have them?"

Peg took the strap off her neck but held it. "How should you ask?"

"May I?"

Once Beth's attention locked on the pod of whales, Peg kept her hand on her daughter and glanced up at the bridge, wondering if anyone up there was watching the whales too.

Against the dull gray paint came a flash of orange behind a sailor in working blues, his dark denim trousers and light blue shirt covering most of the bright fabric. A sundress. The skirt fluttered. Her back was against the bulkhead under the window of the bridge. The sailor pressed against her. His hand moving up from her waist, whispering to her, hiding her face. She bent her head. He pulled back. She glanced in Peg's direction. Pushing the sailor away, she said something and made a show of smoothing her hair. He hurried away.

"Mommy!"

Peg leaned down to her daughter. "Sorry, Honey. I didn't hear you."

"Do they eat little fish, or could they eat us too? Like Jonah got eaten?"

Captain Floyd joined them. "Mrs. Ryan, isn't it?"

"Yes. Thank you for the announcement. We are really enjoying this."

"Pity more aren't watching."

Beth still held the glasses to her eyes. "That's a big herd of 'em."

"Pod, they call them. Those are humpbacks. They're about forty feet long, but the way they swim, we can only see a little bit of them at a time."

Beth asked, "Do they live here?"

"More like a vacation. When it's too cold up in Alaska, they come down here. Then they go back and spend all summer eating up near Alaska and Russia. They migrate for better food and warmer weather."

"Like ducks go south in winter?"

"Right. Some are going to stay around Hawaii and have their babies there. These are some stragglers. Some go to the Philippines and even China, so we might see others."

Beth lowered the binoculars. "I wish you could drive closer so I could watch them longer, since we're going the same way."

"It wouldn't be safe for them."

Peg touched Beth's shoulder. "Can you thank the captain for telling us about them?"

"Thank you." She grinned. "My father is a captain, too. He has his own plane. We're going to China."

"Tsingtao. Beautiful city. I've been there before. You can see whales from the mountain outside town this winter and into spring."

Beth grinned. "Really?"

"They're fin whales. They are about twice as long as the humpbacks. Shaped like a torpedo. They can outrun us." He knelt beside her. "Bet your mom and dad will take you up to the hills outside town to look for the fin whales this winter if you asked nicely."

"Oh, okay. Can I ask you something?"

"Sure."

"How far to Hawaii?"

"We're about three days out."

She frowned. "Okay, thanks."

Peg gave the captain a nod and tapped Beth's shoulder. "Lessons!

Then we can look up all about whales in the *Britannica*."

After an hour in the library, they finished the spelling drill and read the entry for whales.

Peg checked her watch. "About ready for lunch?"

Beth slammed the book shut and slid off her chair.

"Why the attitude?"

Beth frowned. "He didn't answer my question."

"Then ask *me*."

"I wanted to know how *far* to Hawaii. He told me *how long*."

"Let's solve it right now. Get the atlas. The big one from that stand."

Soon Beth learned how to use the scale on a map and estimated the distances, which she wrote on an index card: San Francisco to Hawaii - 2,400 miles. Hawaii to Guam - 4,000 miles. Guam to China - 3,500 miles. Peg thought her husband could have done a better job explaining maps and distances. Beth returned the atlas to its stand, folded the index card, and put it in her pocket.

At lunch, they joined Trudy and Sally. Beth fussed with her sandwich.

Peg asked, "What's the matter now?"

"I don't see why I have lessons when the other kids get to watch cartoon movies and play."

Trudy said, "Sally has lessons too." Sally made a face at Beth and picked up her sandwich.

"Well, most of the kids don't."

Peg glanced around. "Those little kids aren't in school yet. You will not miss a grade."

Beth rolled her eyes.

"Attitude, young lady!"

Beth sat straighter and drank the powdered milk she hated.

Peg took a slow sip of her iced tea. "What if we did your lessons in the morning and then went to the rec room for checkers or ping-pong in the afternoon?" Beth nodded quickly.

Trudy said, "That's a great idea." Her slow smile grew into a grin.

"Look, the girls are in the same grade. Why not teach together?"

Eyes wide, Peg said, "Maybe even trade off teaching days if our lesson plans match."

"Oh, I am certain they will." She dug into her large purse and put a book on the table near Peg. "Before I forget, thanks for the loan. It's interesting."

Gerri came into the dining room and straightened the skirt of her orange sundress. She smiled when she saw Peg.

Noticing that both girls had finished lunch, Peg asked, "You two want to get dessert now? You may eat them by the big window."

The girls rushed past Gerri toward the dessert table. Peg motioned for Trudy to watch the girls. After a questioning glance, Trudy asked, "Everything okay?"

"It will be."

Gerri smiled as she passed Trudy and joined Peg while balancing a fruit salad and an iced tea on her tray.

Peg stared at Gerri. "I think we need to talk."

Gerry ran her finger over the rim of her glass. "Sorry if I offended your sensibilities today."

"It's not a good idea to talk to sailors or get involved. It's putting them at risk of discipline. Think of your reputation."

"Got it, Mom."

Beth ran up to the table as Gerri said, "I'm just going buggy on this floating henhouse."

"Mommy, what's a henhouse?"

Gerri laughed. "It's where the lady chickens live. Like here. Not a daddy in sight. They are all in China."

"So, are they the roosters?"

Peg answered before Gerri could. "That's right."

Trudy was a step behind Beth. "Want me to take the girls for the afternoon?"

She gave a crooked grin. "Mind reader. I'd love to have a shower and wash out some underthings."

"I got 'em. Library until they get squirmy. After several laps around the promenade deck, we'll be in the lounge. No rush."

Trudy motioned for Sally. "Okay girls, we are off like a . . ."

Sally and Beth yelled in unison, "Herd of turtles!"

Once the girls left, Peg addressed Gerri. "Beth's seven, not seventeen or twenty-seven. And I want to keep it that way. Am I clear?"

"Sure. She's a kid. I get it."

Peg slid the book into her field bag. "I hope so."

"I can't see traveling with one."

Peg paused before saying, "I don't know if I'd be making this trip if it weren't for my daughter. Bill has only been home for two of her seven years. He was in the South Pacific with his fighter squadron. He's been in China almost eight months now. That's a long time for a child. We need to be together since we're a family."

Gerri laughed. "That's choice. I've had enough of family. I just got away from working in a mill job and slaving in my dad's store on weekends. Johnny's flying over. He's gonna get us an apartment in town. Says I'm even gonna get a servant. Can you imagine that?"

"It's hard to imagine that I'm even here now."

"What's the book?"

"*Thunder Out of China.* Trudy and I are reading it together. We finished *The Good Earth* by Pearl S. Buck, if you want to borrow it."

"No thanks. Johnny sent it to me, but who wants to read about a Chinese farmer and his sad wife going bust like some Dust Bowl story?"

"It shows rural life and helped me understand the current conflict there. The other book is about the war years in China."

"Why'd you want to read that sad stuff?"

"The men are going to talk about the war and strategy and history, so I can understand what's going on."

"Thank God we're going to a resort town on the ocean, not a missionary dirt patch."

CHAPTER 4

Lieutenant John David Summers pressed against the window of the C-54 transport plane as dawn painted the high cirrus clouds a light peach. When they left Guam, he was the only living thing at the ass end of the freight transport. For the past eight hours he had tried to stay warm and find a comfortable place to sleep among the bins of potatoes, racks of fresh eggs, crates of sundry crap for the Post Exchange, fifty-gallon drums of cooking oil, and sides of beef in an ice chest the size of a field morgue.

He gave up trying to rearrange the makeshift bed he had made of the life jackets and went to pee, then snaked his way forward, hoping the pilot and co-pilot would welcome some company. He pulled the curtain aside. "Morning, fellas. Can I spell either of you?"

The Navy pilot scowled at him and shoved his earphones back. "I wouldn't trust this craft to a skinny Marine flyboy any more than I'd trust you with my sister."

"Wouldn't worry if she's as ugly as you." He flashed a gold band at the pilot. "Besides, I'm a newly married man. Even though I'll be bunking in the Bachelor Officers' Quarters for a while."

"Still a Marine." He chuckled. "Even worse, you're gonna end up one of those gung-ho China Marines, all piss and vinegar and itching for combat."

Summers jerked both thumbs toward his flight jacket. "Enough of a pilot that they held the plane for me."

The co-pilot stretched. "If you two are gonna keep comparing dicks, I'm gonna hit the head and grab a breakfast box. Why don't you let him take the second seat?"

The pilot laughed. "Sure. He might learn a thing or two. Still wouldn't trust him with my sister if I had one."

The co-pilot handed his earphones to Summers, who hot-seated in and adjusted the microphone.

The pilot asked, "Where'd you learn to fly? Some traveling circus air show?"

"P-cola."

"Pensacola. At least you learned the Navy way."

Summers glanced back at the empty navigator's seat. "Want me to check bearings?"

"Nah, we got it. Certified in the C-54?"

"No."

"Then I gotta wait for my number two before I can go do number one." Summers slid out of the seat when the co-pilot returned. The pilot said, "Here, take my seat. We'll see if the baby-flyboy can hold our heading."

The pilot grinned at Summers as he squeezed past him into the chilly hold. A few minutes later, the pilot brought a box for Summers. "Looks like you are enjoying driving the bus. Wanna eat up here and let me catch a few winks?"

"Sure, thanks." He held out his hand. "John Summers."

The pilot nodded. "Chuck Sims, and that's Paul White."

Two hours later, when the coast of China appeared, the pilot took the controls. Summers asked if he could strap into the navigator's jump seat for the landing and got a nod.

The pilot asked, "So, Marine, been here before?"

"Nope. Not even briefed, just hustled over."

After the pilot moved the radio dial to the frequency for the Tsingtao field and announced his entry into the controlled airspace, he shouted back at Summers, "Welcome to the Sin City of the Orient."

As the small islands off the coast became visible, Summers saw the lush green terraces on the hillsides. Then his pilot's eye took over.

Modern city, not some village. High mountains to the north, nav hazard. Open bay. Two Navy ships docked in the harbor. Lots of wide beaches, a golf course, plenty of places to ditch.

He shouted, "Is that a racetrack?"

"It was. That's where the local Japs surrendered. No races now. Big barracks and parade grounds there. See the pier with the red pagoda at the end? Most of the HQ stuff is near where the pier meets Pacific Road. Field's ahead, about a twenty-minute Jeep ride back to town."

"Thanks. You boys spending over? Be pleased to buy you a drink."

"Sorry, but we're on a turnaround early tomorrow morning."

Summers half-expected a crude landing strip that the Seabees scraped out of a jungle. Instead, he saw a well-maintained air base with a legitimate tower, hangars, barracks, and offices. A smaller civilian airstrip huddled to the west.

They made a textbook-perfect landing and taxied toward the tower. Summers glanced across the runway at a dozen Corsairs on the apron and smiled. Their gunmetal blue and gull wing design should terrify anyone unlucky enough to be in their path even before they heard their roar.

He grabbed his flight bag and two-suiter and followed the pilot down the aircraft stairs. The heat and humidity hit him like a steam room. "Thanks for the ride, fellas. Never seen a better landing."

"Navy way!" Sims laughed.

Summers headed for the operations building, still surrounded by the stink of hot rubber and exhaust. He looked at the hills. Terraced and a vivid green.

After checking in, he hitched a ride, got his room at the BOQ near the center of town, grabbed a shower, and put on civvies. His light tan slacks and Hawaiian shirt marked him as off-duty military. He found the Officers' Club by the Pagoda Pier and took off his sunglasses as he walked into the dim bar.

Two men in sports shirts and light trousers were at the bar. The taller one asked, "New guy?"

"Just landed."

He looked at the sunglasses. "Marine aviation?"

Summers paused, waiting for another crack from some Navy hot-shot. "Yeah. Heard you had some Corsairs out here that needed flying."

The tall blond man shot out his hand. "Phil Wilson, Ryan's our skipper. And this guy is Red Franklin."

He grabbed Wilson's hand and grinned. "John Summers. Looks like we'll be flying together."

Franklin said, "It's George, unless I'm in the air." He pointed to his copper-penny hair. "Not very creative."

"Good to meet you, George. Usual rule? New guy buys the first round?"

Both grinned. Over a bourbon and water, they traded who-do-you-knows and where'd-you-train.

Franklin asked, "So you're straight from P-cola?"

"Finished and got asked to help train the next class, so I got my hours in."

"But no combat."

"Not yet." He watched the men for their reaction.

Franklin said, "Well, you couldn't ask for a better skipper than Captain Ryan. He's done it all but won't tell you half of it. Listen up be-cause he won't say it twice. If you fly with him, you are in elite company."

"Any combat time before here?"

Franklin chuckled. "He was all over the Pacific Theater. Different stories about him. One was that he flew nonstop for twenty-four hours. Some said thirty-five. Only came in when he needed gas, ammo, or a sandwich."

Summers felt his butt contract to a pucker factor of five. "But the book limits—"

Franklin laughed. "He's by the book. *His* book. It's harder than the manual. But you won't get killed if you do like he says."

When the evening ended, Wilson gave Summers a lift to the BOQ and offered him a ride to the airfield in the morning an hour before the briefing.

Summers hopped into the Jeep at zero six hundred hours and dropped his flight bag into the footwell. "Appreciate you going out so early."

"Skipper usually wants some time with new guys before the briefing at seven. Glad you got your flight suit on. He's a get-to-business guy."

During the ride to the airfield, Summers sweated through the back of his flight suit. "Always this hot?"

"Wait until August! They say it's not the heat but the humidity. It's a lie. It's both."

Summers stared at the terraced hillsides, which shimmered like green silk in the early light. "What're they growing up there?"

"Tea. Some vegetables."

Once they cleared both the Nationalist and Marine guard stations at the gate, they drove to headquarters, passing close to the fighter planes before the anthill of activity began. *Two dozen Corsairs. Some dinged. Some paint thinning in spots. Props look sharp enough to shave with. Canopies clear. No oil drips. Good maintenance crew.*

He followed Wilson into the ready room, past a worn couch and a cluster of old school desks facing a wall of maps. At the hallway Wilson said, "Showers and lockers to the left. Offices to the right." He tapped on the first door before opening it. "Skipper?"

Captain William Ryan, in his flight suit with the sleeves rolled up, closed a manila file. Summers entered and snapped a salute. After returning it and extending his hand, Ryan said, "Welcome aboard, Lieutenant Summers. I go by Skipper unless there's brass nearby."

Summers shook his hand over the desk, noting Ryan's solid grip, roped forearms, broader shoulders than most pilots, but slim. Balanced like a boxer. Regulation white sidewalls but longer on top. A comma of chestnut hair fell forward. His blue eyes were pale against his tanned face. "Yes, sir. I go by John."

Ryan frowned. "We already have a John. You're John Two until we get a better call sign for you. Have a seat." He provided the radio frequencies and cautioned Summers to memorize them and never write them in his flight notes.

For the next thirty minutes, Ryan briefed Summers on the current strategy: no massive flights of a dozen fighters swarming over a target. Missions were strategic. Surgical. Squad split into small teams. Short hops, a handful of planes out for a few hours. Home for dinner, most nights. Good rotation schedule so you can get eight hours of rack time before you fly. Ryan took a breath and smiled. "That's the official poop. I need your full attention topside, so if you don't get the required sleep or you're sick, tell me. You might have a quick hop, and clean sheets, but it's an actual war out there." Summers nodded. Ryan pointed to the door. "Go meet the guys. I'll be out in five."

Summers returned to the ready room, now filled with the stench of burned coffee. Wilson introduced him to the cluster of other pilots. Quick handshakes and blurted names blended into a swirl of unfamiliar names to put to new faces: Mack, Andy, John, Arturo, and others that he missed when someone at the back of the room called, "Skipper on deck!" Chatter stopped. The pilots came to attention.

"As you were," said Ryan, and handed a stack of small maps to a pilot, who passed them out to the others.

Summers slid into the battered school desk that Ryan pointed to and pulled his knee board out of his flight bag, strapped it on his right thigh, and took a ballpoint pen from under its clip. The other pilots all took their usual seats and clicked their pens.

Ryan said, "Good morning, Breakfast Clubbers. Quick announcement. Navy is hosting the Independence Day party at Officers' Beach, details on the handout pinned to the bulletin board, but check the duty roster the day before. Okay then, I hope you all have met our new guy. John Summers."

A theatrical whine came from the back row. "We already have one.

Send him back."

Ryan laughed. "He's gonna be John Two until we get a better call sign."

Someone muttered, "Sounds Biblical."

Pointing to the large man squeezed into the desk beside Summers until the chatter stopped, Ryan said, "Arturo Sanchez is a pro, so ask him if you need anything and I'm not around. The Nationalists issue these maps on a mission-specific basis with the latest troop locations. There's an after-action burn bag for the mission maps and flight notes. Deposit them right after we land. We can't let even old flight information get out."

Ryan used the blackboard like a coach, noting the weather and their respective positions in formation for each of the two flights. The first was an observation flight to photograph the troop movement far to the west. The briefing was routine and fast. As the pilots on the recon flight departed, Summers watched Phil and Andy leave with the others as calm as if they were going to drive a bus.

When Ryan launched into a more detailed description of their mission, Summers felt a trickle of sweat crawl down his spine. "John Two. On my starboard wing, observing. Aerial defense mode only unless otherwise requested. Rare that we find a dangerous bird in the air, but it happens. Arm both your Brownings, no bombs. Art, Red, and I are hauling two 500-pounders each. We're taking out a bridge and then an ammo dump. I want full magazines all around. Expect some ground resistance."

The silence in the room spoke to their focus.

Ryan continued, "Weather's good for this run up north. We'll form up at angels' fourteen. Their flak has been topping out at thirteen thousand feet. We'll break into two formations. At the bridge, John Two and I will soften up any defenses of the bridge with our Brownings. Sanchez, follow us and drop your two eggs on the bridge. Red, stay upstairs. Then we go east to the ammo dump, drop the rest of the bombs, then regroup at angels' fourteen and head home. John Two, you'll be topside watching the sky for us on that run."

Sanchez asked, "Standard, side by side, over the dump?"

Ryan said, "Roger that. Summers! Stay at least eight hundred feet above the target. I don't want you catching any blowback. Come up and get the turn points off the board."

After they marked their maps, Ryan erased the blackboard. "You boys know the sector, an hour up over land. Back over water, so Mae West preservers and G suits. Anyone in need of a pre-flight dump, avail yourself now. Sanchez, swing by the silk shack and get him a new rig while I watch his pre-flight inspection."

"Sure thing, Skipper."

On the field, Ryan shadowed Summers through the pre-flight protocol of his Corsair's inspection and nodded approval. Sweat beaded on their foreheads when they finished. Ryan took a deep drink from his canteen. "Might want to take some water up. It's gonna be hot until we get some altitude. Secure it so it won't bounce around. I clip it to my harness. But do what you want."

Half an hour later, pre-flight checks were over. Suited up in the survival gear, the other pilots jogged to their planes, their chutes already in their cockpits.

With their G suit leggings and yellow Mae West inflatable life preservers on, the men were dripping before they mounted their planes. Today, they were going to defy gravity. They expected to come close to the nine Gs it took to rip the wings off their Corsair. When they were green, most of them thought they could manage a six-G pullout of a bombing run, but most only remembered their faces deforming like a gargoyle, their balls flattening on their reserve chutes, and their feet being too heavy to manage the rudders.

Most of them had experienced a full blackout, but most passed off that gap in their memory as a grayout, the type of almost-fainting that accompanied the flu. But they were wrong. Only God in his goodness let the design of the Corsair fly itself until they regained their senses.

The bitching about the G suits stopped after Ryan reminded them that a third of the casualties for pilots in the First World War were not from enemy fire. The fatalities were from blacking out. Every fighter pilot had gone gray. Now the suit's pressure on their legs and gut held their blood north so their brain could keep working, so their vision didn't fail, so they didn't faint like Southern belles. Too hot at sea level, but just fine when you were at altitude in a tight turn or dive, if it kept you from blacking out and burying yourself in China dirt.

Sanchez helped Summers into his parachute. He climbed onto the wing, the reserve chute flapping at his butt.

Sanchez nudged Ryan. "Looks like a kid with a load in his diapers."

Summers slid into the cockpit and cranked the seat until his line of vision was barely above the gunsight.

Ryan wondered aloud what the kid could do with two thousand horsepower. "He's got the swagger, now we'll see if he's got the stuff. Let's go."

Captain Ryan suppressed a smile as he thought back to the Philippines when he flew a combat mission in his pajamas, looking much worse than this new kid. They strafed the field at sunrise. That's how the Zeros worked it. He made five runs that day. The manual said two at the most. Take a piss and inhale a sandwich while the pit crew loaded new armaments and fuel.

Ryan's tent mate, friend, and wingman, Jackson, flew in boxers and shower sandals that day. They were the first up. Dogfights all day and into the next. Crazy SOB. Lucky he never had to walk home. After they cleared the Zeros, Jackson took up a case of beer to chill it at altitude. A month later, his luck ran dry. Another brother who would never come home.

On the way to his plane, Ryan grinned at his men, all climbing aboard his fleet of gull-wing Corsairs. The Navy called the paint job Sea Blue. In some light, it looked more like the gunmetal blue of his old Smith & Wesson strapped to his right ankle. When he and the machine became one, he felt like he broke the laws of physics, of time and space, and owned the sky.

"What's funny, Skipper?" Sanchez shouted.

"Gonna be a good day. We're up to full strength again. Weather is with us."

Sanchez muttered, "From your mouth to God's ear."

Take off went perfectly. The blue exhaust filled the calm sky over the runway. They formed up and flew over the city, reminding them that there was still a war outside the redline separating the city from Mao's China. During the run on the bridge, John Two held on Ryan's wing, even when he altered altitude or course.

At the bridge Ryan and John Two did a clean sweep, Brownings open, strafing the bunker in six-second bursts. Chaos created. They pulled away, opening the door for Sanchez's Corsair to scream in and unload two 500-pounders. By the time the men on the ground heard the shrill whistles of air passing into vents on the leading edges of the wings to cool the eighteen-cylinder engines, the bridge and half of the northern hillside were rubble. No wonder the Japanese called the Corsair the "Whistling Death" during the war.

The ammo dump was ten minutes north. As they approached, Sanchez came on the radio. "Skipper? Defenses seem light to you?" They were chatting, moving past radio protocol. They knew each other's voices and patterns.

"Yeah. Musta moved the big guns since yesterday's intel. Abort!" He pulled the stick, and the others followed his path.

Ryan clicked on. "There's another dump north of here. Sanchez, see if they moved it all there."

They flew above the layer of clouds. Sanchez ducked under the cover for a recon run, his call back announced the expansion and heavy guns.

Ryan got on the horn. "I'm calling an audible. New target, larger one. Red on my port wing. Sanchez, since you dropped your eggs, stay on my starboard and man the Brownings. We have one shot at this, and I don't want any of us picking up debris when it blows. Arm your Brownings and ordinance. Guns on full. Reserve a quarter. John Two, ammo status?"

"Less than a quarter down."

"Good. We'll meet you at angels' fourteen after the party."

"Roger that. Over and out."

Ryan said, "Steep dive. Speed should be close to 400 when we level to strafe and drop."

The three planes ripped down through the cloud cover as one. Ryan's navigation was perfect. A half a mile shy of the ammo dump, they speared down, almost weightless, then pulled more Gs than allowed when they tugged back on the stick to level off. They fired their Brownings on the way in, unloaded the eggs, and climbed. The clouds went orange when the dump exploded below them.

As Summers flew over the brilliance, he shouted, "*Jesús, Dios!*"

Once over the water, returning to the base, Sanchez chuckled. "Sanchez to Skipper. Over."

"Skipper here. What's on your mind?"

"John Two got a new name. Think his new call sign's JD!"

Summers clicked into the conversation. "How'd you know my middle name's David?"

"Didn't. Got it from you yelling, '*Jesús, Dios.*' Thought of calling you 'God,' but that seemed presumptuous."

Once they had completed the paperwork on the mission and secured the maps and notes in the burn bag, they showered and changed into khakis. Ryan saw Summers lingering in the ready room, pretending to read a magazine, his foot tapping of its own volition. "Hey, JD! Good work up there today."

"Thanks, Skipper."

"But I got a question. How come you're yelling '*Jesús, Dios*' in Spanish?"

"Guess I picked it up from my flight instructor. His parents were from Mexico."

Ryan saw JD's hand shaking despite being pressed against his knee. "It's okay. It takes a while to unwind. You're gonna be flying several times a week, so get used to it. Get your mind on something else. I'm heading into town. It's market day. Want to come along and stretch your legs before we fly tomorrow?"

CHAPTER 5

The three Corsairs finished the photo recon run and were climbing on the way home. Ryan leading. Sanchez was on his right wing. JD on his left. Ryan entered the cotton-ball cover of the spotty stratocumulus at seven thousand feet when he saw the flak flowering ahead of him and shouted, "Star spread high!" The planes scattered left and right, climbing fast. Ryan went high and left. As he leveled at fourteen thousand, flak ripped into his left wing, peeling off a blue steel plate. The Corsair pitched.

"Flak at angels' fourteen, climb." In his peripheral vision, he saw another blue steel plate ripping free from the center of his left wing, spinning away as his craft dipped. Instinctively, he corrected. Shocked when the plane responded, he glanced at the wing. The leading edge was still intact. Flaps moved. Connectors seemed unharmed. Hydraulics intact. *Fucking miracle.* He wanted a hard climb, but feared the wing would shred. On a good day, the Corsair could climb to forty thousand, but this wasn't a good day.

A burst of mushrooming iron exploded in front of him. Pull left, minimize stress on the wounded wing. Another wall of flak bloomed ahead and high. Don't trust a hard stick up. Roll left. Drop. Don't fly into the sizzling iron. Level again, fly under the raining shit. A shell blossomed dead ahead. No choice now. Stick back, throttle up. *Wonder if the wing's gonna hold when the torque of the engine spins me clockwise.*

More hot iron spread to his right and ahead. Pull left and pray. Small frags dinged off his prop and chipped the windscreen. Fist-size chunks of Chinese iron kicked the Corsair's underbelly like sledgehammers. The plane pitched and yawed. He jammed the stick to the right, his harness cutting into his neck, his head ringing off the canopy. More hits to the belly, like some asshole was throwing gravel at him. Pull up again. Hit again. Jammed left. Shoulder numb. Check instruments. Everything was cherry.

A blur. Start of a grayout? The stench was acrid, smothering like burning hair or melting nylon, canvas, rust.

Smoke swirled inside the cockpit, then cleared, sucked through the new holes in the underbelly. When he reached for the small extinguisher under his left knee, it was trapped in a tangle of wires then he knew the path the flak had taken. The belly shot passed through the corner of his seat, clipping his parachute. It cracked the canopy at eleven-o'clock high and fell into the cockpit.

Fucker's still in here waiting to bounce around and cut a wire or worse.

Still searching the sky ahead of him, he emptied his canteen on the smoldering edge of his seat's reserve chute. Now he sat in a puddle and laughed. He had seen other puddles from other guys. But not like this. Oh, what the fuck, he was sweat-soaked now, anyway. Who's gonna notice? Or have the balls to say anything?

When he checked that the chute fire was out, he saw a new oil-dark smear on his left thigh, but all the oil lines were below his knee. He leaned to his left to check the line, then saw the torn shoulder of his flight suit. Flapping. Bloody. The sharp twinge when he moved. More blood dripping on his thigh. Shit. Oh, shit. Hit. Stings like a hot poker. But the arm's still working.

JD maintained his circling protocol. When his boss popped above the clouds, he dove to give him cover and shouted, "Oh, fuck! He's shot up." He sang soprano. "Skipper's hit! Skipper's hit." He moved to a high overhead, head on a swivel.

Sanchez emerged from the clouds and moved to Ryan's right. "Five minutes to water. Need a May Day, Skipper?"

"Negative!" Ryan shouted over the wind shriek off the damaged wing and the belly hole. "Negative, she's still flying! Nice work, fellas."

The others joined up and went into formation, undamaged. Once they were over water and ten minutes from the turn inland, Ryan radioed, "Sanchez, get ahead of us. Take the lead going in. JD? Look at my belly, check the landing gear hatches for damage. Let me know before we get over the city."

"Roger that, Skipper."

Sanchez cut in, "Gonna add a lot of drag to that busted wing when you drop your wheels. You sure you don't want to go in on your belly?"

Ryan shouted, "Nope, but need to test the landing gear! Don't want crap falling off over the city."

JD dropped to Ryan's right. "Skipper, starboard wing looks fine. Front gear hatches look good. Half the tail hatch is gone."

Ryan gave him a thumbs-up. On the mission radio, he reported. "Lowering landing gear now." He recited the ditching protocol under his breath like a rosary as he pulled the lever. "Looks like hydraulics are holding fine. Increasing speed to compensate for the rough damage. Keep up." JD did another pass beneath Ryan. He pulled under the port side, and saw sky through the gap in the wing, shook his head, then pulled slightly higher than his commander. "Struts look fine, but you're missing your rear tire. Got a big fuckin' hole through the middle of your left wing. Should have failed."

"Failure's not an option today. We're going home."

JD glanced over to look at his boss and the raw meat on the crest of his shoulder.

Together, they flew south in silence. Ryan couldn't ignore the pain. Shrugging his shoulder, he pretended it was a Sunday drive. He rotated his arm to find relief, like he did after his matches with Swede. It was still the Great Depression, even if the newspaper said it was over. He and Swede Larson were boxers in college. The Nugget Saloon just outside Fargo paid them each a silver dollar for a bare-knuckle fight. A five-rounder on Saturday nights. Others bet on them. They beat the crap out of each other and stayed best buddies. But that was the shoulder Swede used to pummel, trying to wear down Ryan's left jab. Those Sunday mornings were like this.

When they were five miles out and about to start the turn for the field, Ryan got on the radio. "Sanchez! Take us in."

Ryan brought it in barely over the stall point of seventy-three knots, balanced on the two struts like the plane walked on its hands, until it stalled, then the tail plopped to the runway, offering sparks and a piercing screech. Ryan stayed in the cockpit while the ground crew got a wagon under her butt and his men put their Corsairs to rest.

Sanchez ran back and hopped up on the wagon as Ryan leaned over to look for the shrapnel. Not seeing it, he ran his hands under his seat, where he found it wedged into the base of the electrical panel. He had freed it when Sanchez vaulted up on the wing.

"Need a hand, Skipper?"

"If you take this, I can manage." He handed the jagged chunk of Chinese iron to Sanchez, who tossed it in the air. "Crap, it's still warm. Gonna be a swell paperweight."

"Not until I read the after-action report. A guy I knew in Tientsin got a court martial for damaging his plane. The brass said he fired high, then flew under his own spray of bullets." He made an arcing motion with his right hand. "Leave it in my middle drawer. The metallurgy lab in D.C. cleared him. So, yeah, I hope it is just a paperweight."

"You ought to get a medal for bringing her in."

The crew chief yelled, "Ready to move her, sir!"

Ryan eased out of the seat. After a deep breath, he dismounted slowly, finding the toe insets in the plane's side, then to the dip in the gull wing. The quick hop to the ground inflamed his shoulder. He patted the wing. She brought him home.

Two medics flanked him as he walked to the locker room. After they cut away the part of his flight suit that had matted to the wound, Ryan shrugged away from the top of his flight suit. The stench of sweat and burned fabric combined. After easing the charred flap away, the first medic stepped back, scissors still in hand. "Sir, I gotta tell you, I've never seen such a clean wound."

The second medic, holding a compress, paused at the oozing shoulder. "Looks like it cauterized itself. But I still want to clean and dress it." He held a four-by-four gauze pad and a bottle of something that was going to sting.

"Can I get a shower first? Meet you in my office?"

The medics glanced at each other before the older one said, "Yes, sir."

"Thanks." Alone in the row of lockers, Ryan slumped on the bench, still catching his breath. He overheard JD in the shower. "Skipper made a hell of a landing."

Sanchez bellowed, "No shit!"

CHAPTER 6

The excited buzz began two days before the *Anderson's* arrival in Hawaii. On landing day, Peg and Trudy met early. As the room filled, Peg saw many of the younger women carrying address books and pens like autograph seekers. They exchanged addresses, destinations, and hugs. She had already captured the information from new friends in the prior days. She knew not to wait.

Peg watched as they exchanged addresses of parents and sisters, in case they lost track of each other, thinking only of transfers or temporary duty assignments. Not knowing there might be another use. She remembered each of the times she sat with a new widow after the chaplain left, drove someone to the hospital while they held their kid in their lap, made casseroles, found a black dress for someone, or called their parents when they couldn't find the words. But there were also the celebrations, weddings, births, baptisms, promotions, birthday balls, and Christmas cards with new addresses to update in her book.

Beth tugged at her sleeve. "Look, there's Frankie and his mom. They're staying in Hawaii. Can I have my camera now?"

"Think there is enough light in here?"

Pointing, Beth said, "Mom! They're by the window. Bright sun. See the shadows!"

Trudy watched Beth maneuver her camera with skill and direct other children into groups by the window. "She's like those picture girls in nightclubs."

Peg watched her with the other children, knowing they would part and someday meet again. Peg had learned to use ink for names and pencil for the addresses and ranks. She treasured each of her own eight addresses penned inside the back cover for when they needed to list all residences for some governmental form or rental agreement. Their homes. The addresses in parentheses showed her father's address when Bill was overseas or on temporary duty. Looking at the number of addresses, it amazed her how often he was away. Reunions had been joyful. Sometimes his return was rocky, and they had difficulty getting back to deciding things together. It was so easy to make a decision when you were alone. Bill was right when he said she needed to let him back into the family when he returned.

The men had their slogans: Duty. Honor. Country. First to fight. They shall not pass. Semper Fi. She held close the invisible knowledge of purpose and pride. Somehow, the links stayed strong in the invisible chain, with or without the men, and these small moments were how new links were forged. The sisterhood of Marine wives was growing stronger.

The din subsided when the captain entered and announced that information sheets were in each cabin detailing the departure procedure for those staying in Hawaii and the protocol for those returning to the ship from sightseeing. He raised his voice. "Navy ships do not wait for latecomers on departure day. Ever." Sparks of anxious laughter and anticipation filled the room as the captain moved from table to table offering farewells to those leaving the ship. The commotion offered a welcome relief from Gerri's stone silence for the past several days.

Trudy motioned for Peg to lean closer. "I have a friend who's a nurse at Tripler. She's been tracking our arrival date and will meet us at the dock. I'm sure she'd love to have you and Beth join us. We go way back."

"I'd better not excite Beth until we are sure we'd be welcome."

Picking up her coffee but not sipping, Trudy stared at their girls. "Don't you wish we could bottle that energy?"

"Love it. It's frightening some days."

"And others, I'd like to drop her overboard. How about you?"

Peg laughed. "No comment."

Trudy motioned toward the girls, whispering together. "It's great how they are getting on. I hope we can stay in touch once we get there."

"We better!" Peg got a crooked grin. "How would you feel about bunking with us? LaVerne is staying in Hawaii. If Gerri moved, it would be a relief."

Trudy smiled. "Sure, if you can pull it off."

When the captain came near their table, Peg asked if he had a moment for a brief chat.

Captain Floyd smiled. "I'm about to take a walk on deck if you'd care to join me. I'll be a minute."

Trudy stood. "I've got the girls. Don't worry."

Once on the empty promenade deck, Captain Floyd stopped where Peg waited at the rail. "Yes, Mrs. Ryan?"

"A request. One of our cabin-mates, LaVerne, is staying in Hawaii, and Trudy's girl and mine have become fast friends."

He smiled. "Say no more. I think we can have Mrs. Summers moved to a more suitable berth with other singles." He laughed. "There are some nurses who might give her a run for her money. I appreciate your patience. She has been a . . . concern."

"Putting it mildly! Thank you again for teaching Beth about the whales."

"My pleasure. She's a firecracker. So, her father is a captain as well?" He laughed.

"Marine aviation, not a Navy captain. I explained the difference. Now she understands you are the same as a Marine general." She paused. "You might find it humorous that the War Department sent us two sets of travel orders. One to Captain Ryan, USMC, and the other to Captain Ryan, USN."

After a deep belly laugh, he said, "You would have had your own stateroom, if you had only been less honest. RHIP."

She smiled. "Rank has its privileges."

"But so does honesty. And your husband outranks hers if you need an explanation for her transfer."

After lunch, Peg and Trudy returned to the rail, their daughters standing in front of them. Someone said, "That's Tripler Hospital, just below the peak of the island." It glowed Pepto Bismol pink against the lush greenery. Bill had told her that the same architect who did the Royal Hawaiian Hotel designed it, and that's why both were the same color.

Bill had friends who had gone to the burn ward at Tripler. Some made their way back to the States. She remembered Tripler began the death registry and identification of the remains of those lost in the war and whispered to Beth to take a quick picture of the pink building for her dad. She put her hand over her heart, giving the hospital and all who served there her own salute of gratitude.

As the ship entered the bay, passing Hickam Field and approaching Pearl Harbor, conversations stopped. Peg held Beth's shoulders a little tighter. She was just a toddler then. Six years ago. A Sunday. The women at the rail all knew this was where and why America had entered the war. The silence on deck lingered as the oil slick around the *Arizona* glistened rainbows under a clear azure sky.

Her throat tightened as she understood what the newspapers had tried to explain in the weeks following the attack. The Japanese planes came over the hill, strafed everything in their path, engulfed Hickam Field in flames, and torpedoed ships. She caught her breath, remembering how sanitary the account had been. Type on newsprint failed to fully capture the horror. Over two thousand in uniform killed, another thousand wounded. Four battleships sunk, a dozen other ships, cruisers, battleships, and destroyers damaged. Two hundred planes demolished. The field shot to tatters. Scores of civilians who were in the path of the planes died while they were hanging up laundry or walking their dog.

Beth watched her mother and wondered why some ladies were crying.

Within minutes, tugboats brought the ship to dockside. Without a terminal, the ship deployed its own uncovered gangplank. Beth leaned as far over the rail as she could to watch the free end of the gangplank move away from the ship and lower to the dock. The passengers who were staying in Hawaii left first. Beth watched the commotion on the dock with interest.

She pointed. "Look, some of 'em have flower necklaces."

Peg said, "That's a Hawaiian greeting. They are called leis. I'll get you one when we get off the ship."

Trudy waved both arms over her head. A stocky woman on the dock did the same and held two leis that were several strands of tight ivory blooms strung like pearls. "That's Diane!"

Peg took her arm. "My God! Is that Diane de Mayo?"

Trudy pulled back. "Yeah."

"Any word on Cinco?"

Trudy whispered, "Changed from missing, to presumed dead." She stood taller to avoid the children's interest. "How'd you know her?"

"We met in Corpus Christi. Diane's a Southern gal and he was from the Midwest, so they didn't know that the fifth of May was a Mexican celebration down by the border, Cinco de Mayo. The boys started calling her husband 'Cinco' after that." Peg took a deep breath and whispered. "My condolence letter came back, with 'no forwarding address' stamped on it." She looked at Trudy and knew that she felt it too. Almost half of the pilots never came home from the war. Diane reminded them of their luck and something close to guilt.

As soon as they signed off the ship, Trudy took Sally's hand and hurried to Diane. After a hug, Diane draped the leis around their necks and motioned for Peg and Beth to join them.

Diane gave Peg a long hug. "Haven't seen you in forever, girl." She pointed to Beth as Trudy put her lei around Beth's neck. "And who is this beauty?"

After an introduction, Diane laughed. "You gals got bathing suits?"

Peg said, "Sure. Back there." A crowd still filled the gangplank. "I'm afraid it's gonna take forever to get 'em."

Diane opened the back door of her car. "Pile in. We'll find you cheap ones in town. The stores here sell cute cover-ups too. I know just the place. And I've got tons of towels in the trunk. After all, it's Hawaii."

Peg said, "We need to be back by five."

"That's fine. I'm not on tonight until eight."

The heady sweetness of the leis filled the car, even with the windows down. Trudy said, "I've never seen a flower like this. It's amazing."

Diane laughed. "Don't grow 'em back home in Georgia. Call it *pikake*. Means peacock in Hawaiian. It's a jasmine."

"It's so rich. Almost overwhelming."

Diane drove toward the center of Honolulu. After finding bathing suits and muumuus at a local store, she asked the girls, "Want to see the inside of a real volcano before going to the beach?"

"For real?" Sally gasped.

"Yup. But it's safe. No boiling rocks." After ten minutes of snaking up a single-lane road, they found a pullout that overlooked the city, the shore, and in the distance Diamond Head.

"Bail out! We're on an old volcano."

Looking at the lush foliage beside the road, Peg said, "I thought it would be bare rock."

"Honey! This is Hawaii. Stuff can grow on a pane of glass." Diane kicked at the grass beside the car and a tuft flew away, exposing dark pebbles and pumice. "There ya go. That's volcanic soil." She grinned at the girls. "Who wants to race me?" Diane struck out for the top. The girls tried to keep up on the steep incline, but their legs were still wobbly from time on the ship. In a few minutes, Diane stood at the top of a steep mound. She waited for the others to catch up.

Beth won by a few feet. Both girls plopped on the long grass beside Diane, who taunted their mothers, "Come on, slowpokes!"

Trudy glanced at Peg. "Don't fall for it. Keep walking. I didn't think she'd try to kill us."

As they approached Diane, she pointed. "Look down there. That is an extinct crater. This is where the melted lava rock came out of the volcano and blew off the top. See how it is like the inside of a big bowl?"

Both girls nodded as their mothers joined them.

Diane spread her arms. "This is called the punchbowl. Know what that is?" Both girls were silent. "It's like a huge salad bowl, but they put punch in it. That's Kool-Aid for grown-ups. Y'all want to run around down there to where it's flat while I talk to your moms?"

Both girls raced downhill, arms windmilling to keep their balance. At the bottom of the crater, Beth and Sally flopped on the ground like they were going to make snow angels in the lush grass.

Diane sat cross-legged and motioned for the others to sit beside her. They laughed at the girls racing around and their antics. Then the women were silent. The breeze rustling the grass. Diane flicked her gold wedding band with her thumb. "This is where priests sacrificed Hawaiians in the long ago to appease their gods. I thought that might be too much for the kids."

From the crater, Beth pointed at the three women seated at the edge of the crater. Diane's hands covered her face. Their mothers sat on either side of her. Beth nudged Sally.

Sally squinted. "I can't tell if they are laughing or crying."

"Crying. Mom wouldn't hug her like that if she was laughing. Why'd you think she's sad?"

"Grown-ups are weird."

Diane wiped her eyes and threw back her head. "Wow. Don't know what hit me. Sorry."

Trudy said, "For what? Being human? You had a long row to hoe. Look, you still are the great gal I met years ago, so don't be so hard on yourself."

In the silence that followed, Peg wondered if the wives of policemen or firemen also held their breath some nights when there was a knock on the door and if their parents had told them not to marry the cop or fireman. Peg closed her eyes. *Dad shouting, "You can't marry him! Flying is too damn dangerous!" My shouting back, "I'd rather be his widow than another man's wife!" Then the long silence between us.*

Diane watched the girls climbing the opposite wall of the crater. "Hope they remember being here. It got designated as a military cemetery, but Congress hasn't funded it. They need to be honored. Here is where we hope it'll be." Fleeced clouds floated in a deep blue sky. "I don't know of another place this close to God."

Beth and Sally were sweaty after racing around the volcano's caldera and climbed slowly to where the three women sat. Returning to the city after their hike, Diane drove to the main beach near the Royal Hawaiian, parked, and led them a few doors away to a hole-in-the-wall restaurant. They slid into a circular booth of red vinyl. Peg and Trudy stared at the menu, then glanced at Diane for help. She laughed. "How about the Hawaiian plate lunch? I'll ask them for some Kalua pork and chicken katsu. This place also adds a slab of fried Spam. It's a thing here. Trust me, it's better than it looks." Peg and Trudy opted for a mixed plate. Beth and Sally only wanted chicken.

When the plates arrived, Diane waved her fork over all in a benediction. "Eat up." Peg and Diane traded addresses written on flimsy paper napkins while waiting for the check.

They changed and walked down to the beach. Trudy and Diane laughed, enjoying their reunion, sitting near the water. The surf at the shoreline was ankle high and warm as Peg waded beside the splashing girls. The sand was grainy and snow white. Not at all like the sugar sand on the Gulf Coast when Bill was at Pensacola or Corpus Christi or the darker Atlantic sand when he was in Norfolk with the Navy transferring aircraft. Or La Jolla's narrow beach by the steep cliffs sheltering the baby seals in the cove when he was at Miramar.

After the girls exhausted themselves in the water, Diane dusted everyone off and they piled into the car in wet bathing suits. As they passed a slower gray bus filled with women, Diane sped forward. "Looks like you're gonna get some fresh faces on board." She maneuvered past several trucks loading crates onto the dock and dropped them off near the gangplank. She hopped out and gave the girls a hug. "Nice to meet you both."

Peg thanked her and took the girls toward the ship. Diane called after them, "You better let me know if you come through here again. I'm gonna want to hear all about China." She hugged Trudy. "Good to see you again, girl. Been too long."

"I can't tell you how much it means to me to see how well you're doing." Trudy held her friend's shoulders. "Please remember, I pray for you every day."

"Day-by-day. The hospital is keeping me sane, sort of." She slid into the car and white-knuckled the steering wheel.

The bus arrived behind them with a noisy release of the airbrake.

Diane laughed. "He woulda said, 'The bus farted,' then we'd all pretend we didn't hear him."

"I miss his laugh."

"Me too! Better get on board before the herd cuts you off. Write. And come again."

Back aboard the ship, Trudy took Sally to shower and get ready for dinner, leaving Peg and Beth in the cabin. Perched on the upper bunk, Beth flopped on her stomach and hung over the edge, watching her mother sorting their clothes. "Mom?"

"What is it, Honey?"

"Why was Diane sad today?"

"Why do you think that?"

"When Sally and I were down in the volcano hole, she was crying. I saw her."

"Come here." Peg pushed their clothes aside. They sat on the lower bunk. "She misses her husband."

"Like we miss Dad?"

Peg pulled Beth closer to her. "Remember your father coming home from the war and how happy we were to see him?"

"Kinda."

"Her husband didn't come home. You know in war that sometimes people die."

"Yeah. They get a telegram, and there is a funeral. Then everyone's sad."

Peg paused before saying, "But sometimes, soldiers get lost in a jungle or their ship sinks, so your brain understands they are gone but your heart still hopes they might be okay."

"Mom? Is she still married or a widow like Sally's gramma?"

"I think she's a widow, but she still hopes."

"Could he come home?"

"I don't think so. Maybe that's why she stayed here and is a nurse, trying to help other people get home to their families."

Trudy and Sally returned in robes. Their hair was wet, and they were laughing.

Peg hugged Beth. "Ready to get clean?"

"Sure."

When the foursome arrived for dinner, a redhead they recognized was sitting at their usual table. Her back was to them.

Sally pointed. "Hey, that's our . . ."

Trudy leaned down. "Shush. There's still room there."

The redhead looked up and smiled. "Is this your table? I've been eating with the same gals since we left San Francisco, but they had friends come onboard in Hawaii." She stood.

Peg said, "You're fine. Join us."

Beth spotted the Rolleiflex. "What kind of camera is that?"

Peg pulled out a chair. "Why don't we all sit down? We ought to introduce ourselves before you get nosey."

Claire shook Peg's hand. "Claire Peters. I'm reporting for the *Ladies' Home Journal*."

Beth clambered into the chair closest to the boxy camera and grinned.

CHAPTER 7

After departing Hawaii and the mandatory lifeboat drill, the routine smoothed. Sally and Beth played well together. Peg and Trudy had similar parenting styles and enjoyed each other's children. Both women found a new freedom when they traded teaching days and met the women who boarded in Hawaii with news that the Navy omitted from their ship-board newsletter.

Hawaii also brought new movies. Tuesday and Thursday night offered children's films. Both mothers vetoed the death-themed *Bambi*. *Fantasia*, at an hour and a half, left the younger viewers squirming or asleep. But *Make Mine Music*, an animated version of popular songs, found its way into the rotation weekly and became a sing-along favorite.

Nights when the weather was marginal, the showing was in the dining room. When the weather permitted, the screening was on the stern deck. They lashed the movie screen between two steel poles, so it looked like something trapped in the center of a spider web. The rows of wood benches with straight backs were less inviting for a film than the briefer church services held there in fair weather.

Peg and Trudy exchanged glances when Captain Floyd bounded onto the small stage, delaying the start of *Snow White*.

After tapping the microphone, he said, "Sometime tomorrow we will cross the International Date Line. And I have it on good authority that King Neptune will join us for a ceremony, so stay alert for announcements. Now for the movie." He hopped off the stage.

Both mothers watched the girls snug into the front row as the film sputtered across the screen.

Trudy pointed at them. "Why do they insist on sitting in the front row? They can't see it properly."

"Doesn't matter. It's the third time they've seen the darn thing."

Trudy chuckled. "Maybe they're trying to ditch us."

"Probably. Bill told me the Date Line crossing was a big deal when he sailed across it for the first time. Lots of hoopla. There's even a rumor that Senator McCarthy broke his leg during the shenanigans and passed it off as a war injury. Got a purple heart for it."

Trudy spoke softly, "George just hates him. Calls him Tail-Gunner Joe. Knows a guy that flew with him. He could not hit his targets. Dumped his ammo on the way back. Once he unloaded on some palm trees along the runway. Scared the you-know-what out of the ground crew. Can't imagine what the antics were to bust a leg."

"Whatever they were, I suspect they'll need to tone it down a bit because of all the children."

Peg shrugged. "Guess lessons are off tomorrow morning."

"Good luck competing with King Neptune. Maybe after the ceremony?"

Before going to breakfast the next morning, Peg slipped Beth's camera and several rolls of film into her field bag. Peg and Trudy intentionally kept the girls on the promenade deck after breakfast, rather than going to the playroom, lounge, or retreating to the library for lessons. Over the PA, the crackle brought the usual silence, followed by a few groans from those expecting yet another lifeboat drill. "This is your captain speaking. This is an announcement for all cabin passengers."

His voice was melodramatic. "In approximately thirty minutes, we will cross the antimeridian, known to some of you *landlubbers* as the International Date Line. It is the place where we will have a day drop out of our lives. But! Fear not! It will be restored when you return to the United States of America, reversing today's course. And if you believe this to be a silly announcement, let me assure you it will become much sillier when we have the initiation ceremony on the stern deck. King

Neptune is about to depart the briny deep and join us."

Peg tapped Beth's shoulder. "Do you remember what your father's letter said about the Golden Dragon ceremony?"

"That it's silly and fun?"

Trudy called to them. "Hey, you landlubbers! Let's get a good seat!"

When Peg smiled, the girls sped off with their mothers in hot pursuit.

In his most formal manner, the captain took center-stage and tapped the microphone, which squealed. "As we enter the Domain of King Neptune, let me introduce him to you."

Stepping aside, a junior officer arrived wearing a sheet wrapped like a toga over his uniform and a white cloth wrapped around his head. He held a gold-painted broomstick as a scepter. 'King Neptune' directed everyone to stand. "Know ye this, all you chit-signers, goldbrickers, sad sacks, fish-eaters, and sons of the briny deep. You baby fish and tadpoles. Arise! On your feet! All follow my commands!"

He raised his golden scepter as if it were a sword and he was about to knight someone.

Beth watched how Claire positioned herself at the edge of the audience before leaning over her Rolleiflex. She took a picture and laughed. When Peg handed Beth her camera, Beth planted her feet like Claire before taking the picture.

The man in the sheet pointed. "Look to the east, where you have left your land. Look to the west, where again you shall be landlubbers. Now look all around you for as far as you can see. This is my kingdom. I am King Neptune! I am Poseidon. I am the ruler of all oceans! Today, I invite you to become my subjects."

He waved the golden scepter over their heads. "Harken ye all sculpins, whales, dolphins, sea otters, finny denizens of the deep, and mermaids! There appear before us those wishing to join our mythic and majestic domain. Shall we accept them?"

He paused and placed his hand to his ear and balanced precariously on the stage, waiting for the ocean to answer. "Yes! I hear your calls. They say, if you give up a day, you may become members. What say you all?"

Led by the captain, a few well-placed sailors, and several women in cahoots with them, there rose a shout of agreement.

King Neptune made some vague hand gestures. Beth took the shot as he grandly declared, "All present company are now welcomed into the Domain of the Golden Dragon and are required to give honors to all other members of this elite community wherever they may meet on land, at sea, or in the air or to suffer the displeasure of the Ruler of the 180th Meridian."

In his last melodramatic burst, he threw his arms open wide and shouted, "You are hereby inducted into the Mystic Order of the Golden Dragon!"

He led a cheer for all new members as the captain took the microphone and said, "Thank you, King Neptune. I know you must get back to running all the seven seas, but I will be happy to give each of your new subjects their yellow membership cards."

Beth tugged at Peg. "We get a card?"

"Looks like it. Let's get in line with Sally."

That afternoon, Trudy attempted to teach a math lesson in the library. She asked, "If there were seven horses at Mister Brown's farm and the next two farmers also had seven horses each, how many horses would there be?"

Sally fussed with her paper and wrote the equation correctly. "It's three times seven."

Before Trudy could comment, Beth chimed in. "It would be the same if they were three fishermen, and they had seven silver finny-fishes. Then it would be twenty-one silver finny-fishes." After they dissolved in laughter, Trudy took the girls to the snack bar. Trudy sprang for three root beer floats in paper cups and the trio carried them up to the promenade deck. Once in deck chairs, the girls sipped as though they were royalty. Peg saw them parade past the lounge and caught up with them. Trudy waited at the rail holding the root beer float.

Peg sidled up beside her. "What gives?"

"Here! I brought this for you so you wouldn't ask."

"Thanks for the bribe. But I still want to know."

"I surrendered when any of the word problems in the workbook somehow related to Neptune's finny denizens and they dissolved into giggles."

At dinner, Sally and Beth compared their cards, which had their names in blue ink. Sally asked, "Did you believe that if you always went one way, you would never get older?"

"That's silly. We gotta come back this way to get our day back."

Trudy listened to the exchange. She and Peg traded shrugs and silently agreed to leave well enough alone.

Claire joined them as they were about to finish their spaghetti and meatballs. "Hi. Got your cards?"

Both girls dug into their pockets and showed them as if they were passports.

Claire flashed her card, too. "Did I see you taking pictures today?"

Beth grinned. "With my Hawkeye. It's a proto."

Peg dabbed some tomato sauce from Beth's chin. "Prototype for a new Brownie. My father works for Kodak."

"Wish he'd talk to the stuffed shirts at my magazine. They made me take the Rollei. Great portrait camera, but a pain for fast shooting and candid shots."

Beth abandoned her meal. "Why?"

"Look down into this little glass screen. Everything looks right side up, but it's backwards left to right."

"You want to see my camera tomorrow? Nothing is backwards."

"Really? I'd love to see it. You going to early breakfast?"

Peg said, "It's a date."

Claire asked, "Could I interview you both for some background? I'm trying to get an idea of who Marine wives are. So far, I've only met the ones without children during meals and bridge games. I don't want to interrupt."

Trudy smiled, "Go right ahead."

"Maybe I could start with a couple of general questions for both of you."

They smiled agreement.

"Your husbands both fly?"

Trudy said, "Same squadron in China. Bill's the skipper."

"And moves. Most of the gals I've talked to have moved a lot. How about you?"

Peg said, "When we needed to. Sure. Mobility is one of their strengths, so I guess it must be ours as well."

Claire paused. "Mind if I write that down? No names, just what you said."

When Peg paused, Trudy glanced up from fixing Sally's hair clip. "Go on. I'll be in the game room with the kids."

Peg said, "Here or do you want to walk?"

"Walk! If all the meals are like this, I think I'm going to put on five pounds before we get to China."

Peg laughed and picked up her field bag. Once on deck, Claire set a brisk pace. Peg matched her, even with the heavy bag over her shoulder. "No notebook?"

"Nope. Ready?"

Peg said, "Shoot."

"Your background?"

"Born and raised in Rochester, New York."

"Where'd you stay while he's been in China?"

"With my father. Same as during the war. Lucky to have him. Bill's folks are older with health problems, and Dad loves our company."

"Was he in the service when you met?"

"No, in college. He was studying to be an architect. I fell for Bill right away, we got married, and had Beth. He joined up right after Pearl. Bet that's the story of half the gals here."

"Got a place there already?"

Peg grinned. "In the old German district called Badaguan. Bill said it is a big house with a high wall and cherry trees along the street. The owner is going to live in the guest house and manage the day-help. I begged for snapshots, but he said I had to wait and see it in person."

"Transferred often?"

Claire stopped to catch her breath. Peg put down the bag with a thud and glanced at the horizon. "It comes with the territory."

"Some stories I've heard are truly amazing. Packing up four kids and a household in three days to go across the country. And the moving disasters! Packers moved three full trash cans from Hawaii to Florida in the summer. The loss, or theft, of valuables or family keepsakes."

Peg told her about Bill's jazz records melting in a moving van parked in Dallas while the driver visited his brother for a weekend in August. She wouldn't tell Claire the hurt wasn't losing things; it was losing the friendships that were only starting, of disrupting schools, or leaving a job you finally got.

Claire continued, "I have to say, their resilience in turning these disasters into stories, not tears, really amazes me."

Peg said, "Three moves are as good as a fire. That's what we say. We expect change. Most civilians don't."

Claire looked at her. No bitterness, but resignation, commitment. "You have any more of those stories?"

"Sure. Bill got transferred from Pensacola to Santa Barbara. Florida to California. He bought a map book and blue-penciled the whole route. Come moving day, they packed the map book and his car keys and took off before we found out."

They shared a laugh and relaxed.

"New topic. Friendships. How long have you and Trudy been friends? I thought the transfers didn't make for long-term friendships, but clearly you have one."

Peg laughed. "We met here, on the *Anderson*, first day. Our backgrounds are similar, our girls get on famously, and we'll be home-schooling them in China. We trade times and subjects already. They're both supposed to be in the third grade."

"How do your parents feel about you going to China?"

She paused. "My mother passed away months before Beth was born. Now Dad tries to be both mother and father to us."

Peg recalled when Bill's telegram arrived. *"Bill says Tsingtao is called the Riviera of China. All the Western conveniences and even diplomatic dinners for the senior instructors."*

He waved that away. "Hooey! They don't send ace fighter pilots to scribble on a blackboard like he's a coach chalking out some football play. There's a damn civil war there."

"Claire, my father is very protective of us. Maybe overly so. It was hard for him to see us go, but he supported my decision. Even flew with us to San Francisco on TWA. Had a couple of days of sightseeing." She motioned to her field bag. "Even reconditioned this for me. He'd carried it all over the world, testing Kodak cameras and film. Might seem silly lugging it around, but we're not running back to the cabin every ten minutes for something."

That night, both girls wanted to put their yellow cards under their pillows. Peg refused, seeing the potential for tears if the cards became damaged. She offered to put Beth's card in the back of the passport for safekeeping. Trudy followed suit, hoping the hilarity would subside. The girls were in their bunks and the lights out when one, probably Beth, started imitating King Neptune's decrees under the covers. The muffled rendition sent Sally into the giggles. Soon, the mothers were laughing as well.

When the laughter subsided, Peg could not get to sleep and watched the moonlight flutter on the ocean. *Only a few more days to Guam.* Was this what Bill had called "channel fever," the unsettled anticipation of the landing? Or maybe the uproar of transferring to the USS *Jefferson*? Soon Guam. Then ten days to China. Then they would be a family again.

CHAPTER 8

The announcements began before breakfast. "Before docking at Guam, those transferring to the *Jefferson*, see the quartermaster for your transfer tags for suitcases to move to your new quarters. We will transfer all stowed trunks. Those disembarking in Guam must confirm your departure with the quartermaster. Docking will be at ten hundred hours. Passengers remaining in Guam may disembark at eleven hundred hours. Passengers transferring to the *Jefferson* will disembark at noon."

At breakfast, the chatter centered on who was going to China on the *Jefferson* and who was staying in Guam. Women speculated about accommodations on the next ship and exchanged addresses.

As they were finishing their coffee, Peg asked Trudy, "Want to pack first? Beth and I can wander."

"Go ahead. I want to catch up with a couple of gals who are staying."

Once packed, Peg and Beth went for a walk around the deck. She saw Claire taking a picture of the harbor as they approached Guam. Beth ran up to her. "Are you going over to the *Jefferson* like us?"

"Yup! All the way to China, so we can talk more about cameras." She took the strap from her neck and put it around Beth's neck as she offered the girl the Rolleiflex. "Look how to sight it in the bright light. Then tell me if yours is easier."

Beth fiddled with the knobs and squinted down at the screen. "I think mine is better, but it's packed until we get to the other boat."

When Trudy and Sally joined Peg at the rail a little later, Trudy was breathless. "I can barely believe we'll be there in just ten days."

Peg lowered her voice. "Closer to twelve if we hit the storm. I overheard the crew talking about a monsoon. Rain and high seas."

"Yikes."

Peg motioned Beth to join them. "What do you say to one last ice cream while we wait our turn to get off the ship?" Peg looked at Claire and called, "Care to join us?"

"No thanks. I want to watch the silliness when we dock."

Shortly before ordering, a slim woman Peg had seen at dinner stood beside her in line. "I don't mean to intrude, but I wanted to say how much I admire how you and your friend are with your daughters."

Speechless, Peg finally said, "Thank you. I'll tell Trudy. I'm Peg."

"Maxine."

"You have children?"

"Not yet. But Andy and I are hoping."

"I haven't seen you much on the ship."

"Guess moms have a different schedule."

Laughing, Peg said, "That's the truth."

Static on the PA system caused Trudy to giggle. "He can't be pulling another drill, can he?"

"This is Captain Floyd. This is an announcement for those of you transferring to the *Jefferson*. There are a few seats available on a military transport going to Tsingtao. It is a twelve-hour flight with a brief layover in Japan. Any interested dependent should sign up in the dining room immediately. First come, first to board. Anyone allowed to go by plane should carry their suitcase from the ship. Trunks are going on the *Jefferson* and will arrive in China as scheduled."

Peg whispered, "We'd duck the storm."

"It's going to be a long flight for the girls."

"We can make it work."

Peg and Trudy grinned, grabbed their daughters, and sprinted to the dining room.

Once signed up and assured that the Navy would notify their husbands of their early arrival, Peg smiled at Beth. "Let's go figure out what we'll need for the flight. Twelve hours is a long time. Comfy clothes, don't you think?"

Beth scowled and said, "I want to wear my new dress like we planned when Daddy meets us."

"Honey, you can wear it after we get there. You'll be more comfortable and warmer in your play clothes."

Pouting, Beth nodded.

Peg said, "Guess we better unpack our sweaters."

"Is it cold in China?"

"No, it's summer there too, but planes can be chilly."

After several delays, the bus arrived to take them to the airfield. Peg and Trudy led the line of twelve women and six children toward the dual-prop aircraft. Several of the women had dressed as though they were arriving in an hour. Peg shook her head, grateful that she and Trudy were wearing slacks.

Walking to the plane, Peg said, "It's an R4D, the Navy's version of the DC-3. Should be a sweet flight. Solid plane. Bill says the only way to wreck it is to crash." The starboard engine sputtered and belched blue smoke. Over the roar, Trudy shouted, "Where do you want to sit?"

"Just behind the wings, kids at the windows, so they can look out and we can talk."

At the narrow stairs that extended from the plane, Peg told Beth to go ahead of her, holding on to her daughter's waist as she maneuvered up the steep steps.

At first glance, Peg shook her head. *This certainly wasn't TWA.* Canvas covered the thinly padded seats. A hint of dust lingered under the smell of oil.

Once seated, they watched the other women board. Most greeted each other with a nod or a quick hello. Claire sat in the second row. A slim man emerged from the cockpit and stood at the front of the plane, watching the women getting settled. Peg expected to see a flight suit, not Navy khakis. She smiled. Bill always called them "bus drivers" in jest but admired their skill.

"Welcome to your ride to Tsingtao, China. If you think this flight is going to Chicago, please exit now." After the obligatory chuckle, he explained the seatbelt operation, where the latrine was located, and that they had put a cooler of drinks and sandwiches on board, which he would distribute in a few hours. As he finished, the port engine caught. The plane vibrated and grumbled until the engines warmed and smoothed. He checked the seatbelts and redid a few.

He stopped at the door to the cockpit and faced the passengers. "Our first stop is Midway, for fuel. Then about midnight, we will refuel and re-supply the plane in Japan. You can stretch your legs and use the facilities. We'll be there a couple of hours, then we'll get you to China on Friday in time for dinner. If you have questions, ask me now or when I come by in an hour. And don't worry if I'm back here. I'm not flying the plane. I'm the radio operator. Call me Sparks."

Once in the cockpit, he buckled in and was about to slide on his earphones when the pilot asked, "Why'd you say dinner? I'm shooting for noon."

"Want to be a hero for getting in early, or a bum for missing noon?"

The pilot checked the panel and said, "Saddle up. We're up to pressures and temps."

Once in the air, the excited buzz from the women diminished. Fatigue and boredom soon silenced most who fanned through magazines or napped. Both girls, however, required continual attention. Peg exhausted all her tricks from pointing out cloud formations, to drawing pictures, and reading from her history of China to Beth. Only when the lights dimmed did her daughter fall asleep.

Landing at Midway was a brief interruption for fuel. As soon as they were up in the air again, the cabin darkened, and the groggy passengers slept.

Close to midnight, the radioman called out several times to waken all the passengers to announce that they would land in Japan in half an hour.

Peg and Trudy took the girls to the restroom in the terminal and walked its length twice before returning to the plane. On their way back to the plane, Claire passed them and smiled.

They were two hours into the last leg of the flight when the co-pilot asked, "Want some company up here?"

"What're you thinking?"

"How about a little educational opportunity for the Marine wives?"

The pilot frowned. "How about a court martial?"

"Naw. Invite 'em up one at a time to sit in the second seat. Imagine them telling their hubbies they 'flew' a plane."

"Oh! I get it. Grab a clipboard. Get a list of who is interested when you make the breakfast chow announcement. Not now."

Peg left her window shade up overnight so the dawn would wake her. She was reading by seven. Most of the passengers were still sleeping when Sparks shouted, "Good morning! Morning, ladies." He called several times over the engines before everyone woke. "Before I give out the breakfast boxes and juice, I need a show of hands. Any of you ladies want to come into the cockpit after breakfast?" Several hands went up. "Okay, I'll take names after you eat to be sure you all get a chance."

Peg leaned over the aisle. "You ought to go up. I'll watch Sally."

Trudy laughed. "Really? Where's she going? I don't think even she can get into trouble in these tight quarters."

After Trudy wrote her name, Sparks smiled at Peg. "And how about you? Want to sit in the co-pilot's seat?"

"Oh, I have before. Not like this, but with my husband. A Piper. But if you still have time after everyone else has gone up, maybe you could let me take Beth up, just to have a peek."

"Write her name. I'll ask the Skipper and get back to you."

One by one, the women went into the cockpit. Some stayed only a few minutes to look around, not wanting to squirm into the co-pilot's seat in a dress. Others were there for ten to fifteen minutes.

The radioman motioned for Peg and Beth after everyone else had had their turn.

Peg made her way forward, hand on Beth's shoulder, bracing against a seat back for balance.

The pilot slid his earphones down and smiled at Beth. "Hi, Beth. Does your daddy fly Corsairs?"

Beth shouted her answer. "Yes! Daddy let me sit in his seat and wiggle the stick of his plane."

Peg said, "Family Day at the base."

"Any chance he's Wild Bill Ryan?"

Peg laughed. "At home he's just Bill. You know him?"

"We met in the Solomons at about fifteen thousand feet. He provided cover for the troop transport I was driving. Never met in person. Tell him Frank Mulholland owes him a beer and would like to shake his hand."

Peg asked, "Are you on a turnaround?"

"No. Laying over for a couple of days."

She grinned at him. "He's meeting the plane. I'll introduce you."

"Look forward to that." He turned to Beth. "Well, little lady, what do you think of all this?"

The instrument panel had rows of switches. She craned her neck to look past the co-pilot to see the controls at his right hand. She looked at the colored levers between the pilot and co-pilot. "What do those do?"

"That's the throttle. Makes it go faster or slower."

Pointing to the co-pilot's hands firmly on the yoke, she asked, "Why don't you have a stick to make it turn?"

"This is called a yoke. It's like the stick in smaller planes or a steering wheel in a car."

"Oh. Okay."

Peg leaned down. "Ready to go back, Honey? Thank you, gentlemen."

Beth said, "Yeah. That was neat. Thanks."

Once again buckled in and settled, Peg opened a book and read with her daughter for a while. It startled her when the co-pilot stopped at her seat. "Skipper wants to know if you want to co-pilot for a bit. Thinks your husband might get a kick out of it."

Trudy motioned to shoo her out.

For the next thirty minutes, Peg took the second seat, but unlike the other women who had merely warmed it, she followed Mulholland's direction and flew the plane. At first, she focused on the yoke and measuring the sensitivity of the control. Her smile became a grin. *Bill won't believe this!*

Half an hour before landing, she thanked the crew for their generosity and returned to her seat with a huge grin. Trudy had both girls seated together, reading to each other. Peg leaned down to Trudy and whispered, "Be there in about thirty minutes. Time for a potty run before they make the announcement and there's a line."

Once in their seats again, Peg redid Beth's braids, dug in her purse, and tipped her head to screw on an earring.

Trudy capped her lipstick. "Fancy! Hadn't seen those earrings on the ship. Ivory?"

She fingered the delicate flower. "Lily. Wedding present from Bill."

When Peg slid her bag under her seat, Trudy said, "Peg! You didn't put on your other earring."

She laughed. "Bill has it. When he goes overseas, he takes the left one."

As the transport flew over the islands guarding the large bay, a hum rose. Women on the right side were pointing out the waterfront hotels in the distance. Peg leaned past Beth and motioned to the red pagoda at the end of a long pier. "Your dad says we can walk out to it."

Trudy called, "Peg, come look." Trudy glanced out the window, Sally on her lap. Peg leaned over them. "There. Those red roofs. I think it's the villas. I've been memorizing the map the whole trip!"

Peg laughed. "Me too."

Sparks called from the cockpit doorway, "Landing soon. Everyone back to your seats. Stow your gear. Buckle in!"

CHAPTER 9

Bill honked the Buick's horn once and glared at the door to George's house. *Come on. Come on!* Then he chuckled to himself. It wasn't George he was urging on, but the plane with Peg and Beth. Once at the base, Bill and George paced in the ready room, listening to the chatter in the tower on the squawk box. Both were in crisp khakis, their ties loose. Bill muttered, "Don't know how they put up with waiting for us."

"They're saints. Jesus, can it get any hotter? I'm sweating through my shirt."

When the tower's final landing instructions came over the box, both men tightened their ties.

They paused in the meager shade beside the tower until the plane landed. Bill listened to the growl of the engines, then the squeal as the tires touched down. As much by sound as sight, Bill rated it a perfect landing. The transport taxied off the runway to the apron. Once the roar of the engines stopped with their usual sputter and whine, the ground crew braced the chocks under the wheels. Bill and George hurried onto the apron as the crew opened the side door and unfolded the short ladder.

Bill tensed. George stood taller.

Women without children exited first. Several stumbled and grabbed the handrail, stiff from the long flight. Sparks exited next and lifted the smaller children over the steps. Families reunited in small clusters and slowly migrated toward the tail of the plane.

George spotted his daughter's curly red hair and called her name. She ran to him as Trudy hurried after her.

Peg leaned over to Beth at the bottom of the ladder. "That's your dad!" Beth sprinted to him. Bill scooped her up as though she were still

73

five and parked her on his hip.

Peg hurried after her and gasped when the humid air wrapped around her like a shower curtain. For a moment, the smells collided: scorched rubber, oil, exhaust, and rotting canvas.

She grinned as she heard Bill ask their daughter, "How'd you get so big and pretty? Mom been feeding you spinach like Popeye?" Beth giggled and pushed her head into his shoulder. Bill took Peg's waist, kissed her, and handed her something from his shirt pocket. "Hey, Beautiful."

As she screwed on the matching earring, she grinned. "Hey, yourself."

Bill said, "I brought the car so we can take George's family too."

"You'll like Trudy, she's a peach."

"We figured you two would get on fine."

Mulholland clambered down the metal steps and stood a few feet away while they greeted one another.

Peg motioned to Mulholland to join them. "Bill, our pilot wanted to say a quick hello."

Extending a hand, he said, "Frank Mulholland. You saved my, er, bacon one day over the Solomons. I was flying a . . ."

"Med evac transport, wasn't it?" Bill returned a firm handshake.

Mulholland grinned. "Still owe you a beer. Anytime. Anyplace."

"There's a gathering tonight at the marina club. It's the best prime rib in town. We might be there. If I miss you, I'll call you."

Claire was the last woman to exit. She pulled her sunglasses from her purse, put them on, and immediately yanked them off, glaring at the condensation that fogged them. *Tropics again*, she thought and walked to the rear of the plane. The crew pulled luggage from the hatch. She held her glasses casually and stood back as the families found their bags. Once her glasses warmed, she wiped the lenses and slipped them on again. She hoisted her suitcase and walked toward the gate, looking around to get her bearings.

As she passed Claire on the way to find their bags, Peg asked, "Is someone picking you up?"

She gave a throaty laugh. "Thought I'd grab a cab. Never considered we'd land out in the sticks. Silly me."

"Bill, meet Claire. She's a writer for *Ladies' Home Journal*. Do we have room in the car?"

"If you don't mind crowding. Where're you staying?"

"The Edgewater Mansions Hotel. Know it?"

"Sure. It's on the way." The Franklin family waited by the Buick. "That's our car."

Beth broke away and raced to Sally. Bill turned to Peg. "Are they pals?"

"Thick as thieves."

They piled into the Buick, Bill driving, Beth beside him and Peg at the window. George held Sally on his lap and Trudy snuggled up to him while Claire sat at the other window, her red mane flying.

The ride from the airport began in the pungent air, passing stagnant canals and abandoned fields. As they passed mud huts on the edge of town, the acrid charcoal smoke of cooking fires smudged the air and competed with hints of latrine.

Beth struggled to see out the front window. Peg pulled her daughter onto her lap. Refugees living shoulder to shoulder in mud huts looked like drawings of China a century ago. Boney old women squatted by black pots balanced over charcoal fires. Small children, clad only in ragged tops, walked along the road as though looking for something.

Peg asked, "Where are the men?"

"The Nationalists conscripted the able-bodied ones if they made it this far without joining Mao. Those too old or too sick scramble for jobs here. Pull rickshaws, load ships." He veered around a donkey cart, then continued, "They help fishermen at the docks do whatever. Hand to mouth. Lots of them hire out their kids as servants."

Beth pointed at a boy pissing by the road. "Why don't they have pants?"

"I don't know, Honey."

Soon the shantytown gave way to the edge of the city. Older wooden two-story buildings, some homes and shops emerged with an orderliness Peg expected from the photos Bill had sent. "Is this the old town?"

Bill said, "Yes. Remember, this was a German colony for a century. They leveled the firetrap wood buildings downtown and built their European city here as a resort and their trading and shipping center. Had to before they could build the sewers, electrical power plant, rail station, and all the other trimmings of a modern city. Improved the harbor as well. Navy's command ship, warehouses, and the hospital ship are to your right."

When he crested the hill on Chungshan Road and started downhill toward the center of town, the fresh sea breeze replaced the stench of the shacks. He drove slowly past the open-air market along the edge of the road. Older Chinese women carrying cloth bags wove between stacks of cabbages, celery, and bok choy displayed on sheets of canvas on the ground, bordered by baskets of onions and garlic.

Halfway down the hill, a city policeman on a white platform whistled for traffic to stop and held up his hand to allow cross traffic.

Bill pointed to a Chinese woman, round as a dumpling, shaking her finger in the face of a vendor standing next to a mound of melons. "Watch their dance. She's already set her mind to it. She wants that melon. He named his price. They'll haggle. Both feign disgust." She tapped the melon a couple times, suggesting it was inferior. "Now watch the sly nods and agreement. That's the game we need to play here. Lots of our new boys are getting taken for a ride, paying full price, which is usually twice what the local sellers would go for."

Ignoring the vendors, Peg peered down a narrow alley of weathered wood buildings jammed with shops with what looked like apartments above them. Two men with bamboo poles on each shoulder carried a small refrigerator on straps down an alley.

George said, "If you don't bargain here, the street vendors lose face because you are a stupid customer. It's all diplomacy. Probably more sub-tle than Truman in D.C."

The policeman whistled again and waved for Bill to proceed. After the market, there were modern buildings, churches, banks, commercial offices, glass-fronted stores, and hotels. A stark yellow building inter-rupted the somber grays and creams of the commercial buildings. Peg looked for a sign but found none. The sea ahead of them glimmered em-erald. A lazy surf foamed pearled arches on sandy beaches. A long pier shot into the bay with a blood-red pagoda at the end. Trudy gasped and pointed. "This is gorgeous!"

Bill said, "I wanted to come this way to show you the grand view rather than going the back way over Signal Hill."

Beth pointed. "Can we go to the beach tomorrow?"

Glancing at his daughter, Bill said, "We'll see. There are three differ-ent beaches here. That one's too rocky. Another one is by Claire's hotel, but the best one is by our house. The Navy dropped a bunch of boulders offshore and put up a rope with cork floats around the swimming area. If you stay inside the rope, it is the safest beach in all of China."

Bill stopped at Pacific Road, waiting for the city policeman to halt through traffic. "That's the Grand Hotel there. MP headquarters and YMCA are over there, too. There's always a cab or rickshaw in front. City police are there too." He looked back at Claire. "You'll need to regis-ter with them. I think it's within three days of arrival for civilians."

"Thanks for the tip. I'll do it today."

Peg asked, "Do we need to?"

"I asked Major Moretti. He's the head MP. Said since he'll have the ship's manifest to show the local cops who's here, all we need to do is check in with him by Wednesday."

Claire asked, "Any idea where I go to retrieve my trunk from the ship when it arrives?"

George said, "They'll deliver it, if you had your hotel's name on it. If not, they'll hold it at the dock's warehouse."

Claire smiled. "Lucky me, I had the address. Now, that's what I call service!" She sat back. *Wonder how the boys in D.C. are going to like my first report once I get the radio set up. Gals without kids just talked about nightclubs, bridge, and their fellas. Married ones went on and on about setting up house and caring for their kids. Not a Red in the bunch. Batting zero, which is good news.*

Beth leaned out the window to watch men at the base of the pier who were sitting on stools by small fires, cooking fish on steel plates or stirring something in a pan that looked like an enormous metal bowl. The aromas of street food and restaurants along the waterfront blended. Garlic and ginger. Braised pork and fish. She pointed toward the Grand Hotel where drivers in Western suits were smoking in the shade of a doorway, watching their limousines while a dozen men clad in ragged shorts, faded tops, and straw sandals squatted by their rickshaws. "Can we ride in one of those carts?"

"Rickshaws. Someday."

Once the policeman blew his whistle and pointed, Bill turned left onto Pacific Road. "Claire, that's the Edgewater Mansions."

She stared at the Art Deco structure on a rocky outcropping overlooking the water.

"Seriously? I didn't think my magazine would pop for a swell place like that."

Turning around, Beth said, "But you're a reporter and you have a neat camera."

Claire laughed. "Your daughter's some shutterbug! She said she even developed film in the States."

Peg chuckled. "True, but I mix the chemicals and do the trays. I let her run the enlarger. Safer that way."

"First thing, I need to find a photofinisher and get my film developed to send to the *Journal*."

George said, "There are several good ones in town. The hotel knows 'em."

Bill pulled into the driveway of the Edgewater and went to unlock the trunk as Claire said her goodbyes. When the bellman arrived, Bill handed him Claire's suitcase. She noticed Bill's Old Spice aftershave. Her father's favorite, no matter what she gave him for Christmas. A taxi edged close to them. The driver wore sunglasses that were taped at the hinge. Claire hopped to the curb and called to Peg as Bill got in the car, "Thanks!"

Bill put the Buick in gear and waited for a rickshaw to move. Several Chinese men in traditional attire walked in front of the car. Beth stared at their ankle-length gowns. "It looks like he's wearing a nightgown."

"George? Do you know what that's called?"

"I call 'em robes."

More men in long dark robes and others in Western suits and snap-brimmed hats walked with purpose into the hotel. The few women with them were older and wore ankle-length sheath dresses with high collars that fastened at the shoulder.

Peg pointed. "Those are lovely dresses."

George said, "That I know. *Qipao*, that's what they call them. Some younger ladies have knee-length hems and even split up the sides for cocktail dresses."

Trudy elbowed him. "How do you know all that?"

George chuckled at her teasing. "I was going to surprise you with one but got talked out of it. Some of the nurses from the hospital ship wear them to dances at the club. If you want one, there are great tailors here."

Bill followed the cab out to Pacific Road, and drove along the coast, slowing when they came upon a donkey cart until traffic cleared and they passed it. Rickshaw-coolies maintained a steady trot, their straw sandals slapping close to the edge of the road. Rusted Chevys or Fords from the late thirties and open Jeeps competed with carts and rickshaws. Ragged beggars near the water were digging for clams.

In a few minutes, Bill pointed. "That's our beach. When we have parties, HQ sends out Shore Patrol. I'll show you posted hours when a lifeguard is on duty."

Peg asked, "Chinese?"

"No. Enlisted guys do it for extra pay. I'll tell you all about the rules later."

He slowed to allow an oncoming bus to pass some rickshaws. "I came the long way because I want the girls to see how to get home from anywhere. But you are never, I repeat never, to go out alone." He asked Beth, "Do you remember which beach this is?"

"The lifeguard stand is here. Then there is the rocky one by the hotel where Mom's friend is staying and the one by the pier."

"That's my girl." He drove inland. "This is our street. Shaoguan Road. It's the one with the cherry trees."

Peg gasped at the deep green canopy over the road. "It's beautiful."

"Wait until you see it in spring! Ours is only one of a couple of streets going directly up from the beach. Got it, Beth?"

"Yup."

"Good, now let's get our friends to their new home. Their street is one block before ours and over two blocks."

"Do they have cherry trees?"

George said, "Nope. We have ginkgo trees."

Both girls laughed at the new word. Trudy asked, "What?"

George said, "You'll see in a minute. The leaf looks like a green fan. In a few months, the leaves are going to be bright yellow."

As they passed streets with the different trees, Peg decided that a leaf-collecting science project would be an easy addition to their lessons.

Bill passed a tall, whitewashed wall and stopped at an iron gate. A stout woman in a black dress came through the gate as the Franklins got out of the car.

George made the introductions. "Giselle, meet Mrs. Franklin and our daughter, Sally." He turned to his wife. "She's our housekeeper and cook. Born here. Folks were Swiss."

Two thin Chinese men came to the trunk of the car and took their suitcases.

Sally waved as the car pulled away.

"Okay, ladies, let's go home. What's our address, Beth?"

"Fifty-two Shaoguan."

As he drove slowly past walled mansions, he asked, "See our number yet?"

"There it is." The address plate on the high whitewashed wall was not in Chinese characters but as the Germans had left it, with eggshell-white numbers on a light blue background of enameled metal. Impervious to the sea air, it had outlasted their colonial empire. Shards of glass as big as an angry fist topped the imposing wall.

"Should have seen it in May. Cherry blossoms were like a pink cloud over the entire street. They imported all the trees to remind them of Germany. There are eight streets here, each named for a gate through the Great Wall."

Stains of cherries the crows had missed still dotted the street and sidewalk.

Bill stopped at the iron gate across the driveway and tapped the horn.

Looking past the iron bars, Peg put her hand to her mouth. The creamy stucco, red tile roof, and heavy oak door of the two-story mansion could have graced a postcard from a Bavarian resort a century ago. The only hint of China was in the upturned tiles at the corners of the roof, for good luck.

A stocky Chinese man dressed in gray slacks and a matching overblouse hurried from the front door to the gate. He could have been anywhere from thirty to fifty. He opened the large iron gate and then shut it after Bill stopped the car. Handing him the car keys, Bill helped Peg out of the car. "So? Does that mean you like it?"

Peg put her hand on his shoulder. "I'm stunned."

He motioned for Beth to crawl over the seat to him.

"Leon, I would like to introduce my wife, Mrs. Ryan, and our daughter, Beth."

Peg extended her hand.

Leon shook it once and offered a nod. "Welcome to your home, Madam. And Miss Beth."

He hurried to lock the gate and carry the suitcases to the front stoop. Holding the car keys for Bill, he asked, "Will you be using the car later tonight, sir?"

"Not sure. Better lock it up."

Peg held Beth's hand and took a few steps into the living room. The clean scents of furniture polish and lemons welcomed her. She stopped. "Oh, Bill, this is even more elegant than your letters said. It looks like a Bavarian castle, with Chinese antiques." Peg let her fingers run over the wood mantel. Lovingly polished for over a century. They built this home for generations, not like those one-bedroom places the War Department slapped together.

He laughed. "Come on, I'll give you the three-dollar tour."

Bill walked through the spacious living room and held Beth's hand when they went upstairs, where it was warmer, despite the open windows. While looking over the rear of the villa's grounds, Bill pointed out Madam Tong's bungalow, which was almost hidden by evergreens. Beth was more interested in the tennis court under the window of the guest room. She led the way downstairs. At the billiard room, she asked, "Can I play this?"

"Let's get settled, then we'll see." After sweeping through the bedrooms and den, Peg stopped at the door to the dining room and stared at the crystal chandelier which looked like an upside-down wedding cake, the pale wall covering she thought might be silk. A massive mahogany table with ten chairs was flanked by side tables topped with pale marble with crimson streaks. Bill smiled, took his family to the kitchen, and poured glasses of lemonade.

Peg sniffed and looked to the side hallway. A laundry room: deep sink, folding table, and an ironing board. A hint of lavender. The clean smell of a hot iron on cotton.

Bill asked, "Want to see outside now?" Beth jumped up and down. He laughed. "Finish up." She gulped down the last of her drink and bolted out the kitchen door. Her parents followed, still holding their glasses.

"Bill, this is fabulous! The house. The grounds. A tennis court!"

He put his arm around her waist. "That cinched it for me, knowing how much you enjoy tennis. And there's plenty of room for her to roller skate on the court."

While Beth explored the tennis court, the bungalow door opened. Madam Tong emerged wearing black linen slacks and a cream silk blouse. She waited for Bill to come to her. After introductions, Madam Tong said to Peg, "If there is anything you need, day or night, please ask. Leon has a room here. I am pleased you arrived early but must apologize that the amah won't be here for another few days. We must chat soon."

Peg tipped her head as Madam Tong retreated into her home.

Bill said, "The amah helps with Beth and does the laundry." Peg smiled as if it all made sense to her.

Sorting the suitcase contents between rooms consumed most of the afternoon. After showering, Peg dressed Beth in the outfit she had wanted to wear on the plane and selected white slacks and a blouse with a floral print for herself.

"Hey, Beautiful. What's your pleasure? Dinner here or roast beef at the club?"

"Oh, Bill. I'd love to stay home tonight. Beth's going to crash soon."

He grinned. "Let me tell Leon. We thought you'd want to eat here."

Over a dinner of fried chicken, mashed potatoes, and a salad, Beth regaled her father with shipboard antics, the discovery of whales, and the Golden Dragon ceremony. Bill invented a secret handshake involving the interlocking of little fingers before shaking seven times, once for each sea. Beth dissolved into giggles. Leon presented a cherry pie for dessert, boasting that the cherries were from the trees right outside the window.

He said they filled an entire shelf in the basement with cherries in glass jars and other carefully preserved fruit.

After half of one storybook, Beth fell asleep. Peg hugged Bill once the two were alone in their bedroom. "Thank you. This was a perfect welcome home."

"Not over yet." His finger brushed an earring. "I kept staring at them over dinner."

"I noticed. Were you thinking of the first time I took them off? I was."

She unbuttoned his shirt. He pulled back when she took off her earrings. She frowned.

"Just wanted to look at you."

"I'm not going anywhere."

He closed the adjoining door to Beth's room and locked it. That night, their lovemaking was slow and tender, a homecoming, a celebration that was unlike the fierceness of their goodbye so many months ago.

CHAPTER 10

Saturday breakfast featured Leon's perfect pancakes with maple syrup. The overnight rain stopped after they sat in the dining room to eat. Peg finished her pancakes and sipped her juice. "Trudy and I are going to the commissary on Monday. See what's there. Anything special you'd like for dinner next week?"

Bill cut the last of his sausage without looking at her. "A roast? Ask Leon what kind he cooks best."

"Fine." Bill caught the crispness in her tone.

As though listening, Leon knocked softly on the door before entering the dining room. He balanced an envelope on a silver tray and held it next to Peg. She took it with some awkwardness. "Thank you."

After he left, she opened the envelope. Beth reached for it, but Peg held onto it. "What is it?"

"Madam Tong has invited us, just Beth and me, to tea tomorrow afternoon."

Bill wiped his mouth and grinned. "Answer it and go. She's the closest thing to royalty we'll ever meet. Fascinating old woman."

"She is so imposing."

"Only at first. She's really a lamb."

Beth watched her parents over a forkful of pancake.

He said, "Go. You'll both enjoy her."

"I suppose this takes a written response."

"Yes, and a gift when you visit her home for the first time."

Peg crumpled her napkin. "We live in her *home!*"

"Her residence. She calls that bungalow her home now." Bill motioned for his wife to wait and clapped his hands twice.

The door opened, but Leon remained in the doorframe. "Sir?"

"What would you suggest as a tea present for Madam Tong? What would she like?"

"Confection is very hard to find. Chocolate, she like."

"Thank you. Mrs. Ryan will have a reply later in the day."

After a tip of his head, he closed the door.

Beth jumped out of her chair and took the invitation from her mother. "Are we going to a tea party?"

"Yes. Bill? Can you take Beth with you to the base this morning and find a *confection*?"

Beth tugged at her father's arm. "What's a confection?"

"Something fancy and sweet. Like your mother. Come here and let her finish her juice."

She scowled. "Why doesn't she just buy candy at a store like we do?"

"Sugar is scarce. There are so many refugees that it's everything the shops can do to keep regular food for people."

"What's a refugee?"

He looked at Peg for help. She shrugged.

Clearing his throat, he said, "You know those people we saw living outside town? To be safe, they had to leave their homes."

"And their stuff? Like candy?"

"Yes."

Beth stirred the remains of the syrup on her plate. "Then why can we get candy?"

"Because we are very, very lucky."

Peg rescued Bill. "If you're finished, go wash up."

"I didn't get sticky."

Bill laughed. "Wash your face and hands before the ants get you."

Their daughter glared at them before stomping away. Peg waved the invitation in the air.

Bill stacked the dishes on the table. "What's on your mind, Peg?"

"Write an acceptance! Bill! I can as easily shout out the kitchen window or walk over there."

"Or do the proper thing. She may be there, but we're guests in her country and . . ."

"So, instead of going to the beach today, it looks like you're taking Beth with you to get a confection, and I'm writing a note to someone in the backyard." Peg stormed out of the room after Beth. Bill drank the last of his coffee and sighed, wondering what happened to his happy child and unflappable wife.

Saturday afternoon, Peg glared at the Whitman's Sampler of assorted chocolates perched above open copies of *The Navy Wife* and *Emily Post's Etiquette*. On her desk sat a draft acceptance, cobbled together from both books. When Bill and Beth passed by the door to the den, she called, "Come in here, you two." She handed the draft to Bill.

He grinned as he read it. "Elegantly done."

"Thanks. Now let me copy it."

"I know this seems silly, but it's only once. You'll see, she is very nice, kinda grandmotherly once you get to know her. This is the first impression, and it is formal." He stared at Beth. "Think you can show your best manners for your mother?"

"Church manners?"

"Exactly!"

Peg looked at her watch. "Bill? Is there still time for a swim?"

He grinned. "Sure, if Beth can get changed in time and help me get our beach stuff in the car."

Without a word, Beth scampered toward her room.

Peg laughed and shook her head. "I'll finish this and walk it over."

"Leon will take it, Peg."

"Of course, he will."

"Oh, and he asked if you would prefer Beth to have juice or tea."

Pushing away from the desk, Peg then gave her husband a hug, and said, "Tea is fine. Sorry about earlier. Guess I'm used to managing our home. I don't know how you found this wonderful house, but I love it.

And I love you even more."

Once Leon departed with the reply, they left for a late afternoon at the beach. The water was tepid and the sand warm. While Peg cinched the leg straps on Beth's life jacket, the girl pulled away. "Mom! I can swim."

"In a lake or a pool. Until we get used to the ocean, you need to wear this." Bill made a racing dive into the water, did a fast crawl toward the floating platform, swam around it, and sped back to shore. Breathing hard, he joined Peg and Beth, who were splashing in knee-high water. "How about we go out to the float?"

Beth looked at it. "I don't think I can swim that far."

"Your mom can. She's a superb swimmer. What if I towed you?"

"Okay. And back too?"

"It's a deal."

By four, Beth was burning. After Beth showered and Peg smoothed Noxzema on her shoulders, Bill called into the bathroom, "How about dinner at the club?"

Peg added, "And catch up with that Navy pilot?"

"I'll call the BOQ and see if he's still around. How about I call George and we make it a foursome?" Peg gestured toward Beth. Bill said, "Uh, a sixsome for an early dinner at the club in town. It's quieter."

"I thought you liked the marina one."

"I do, but the one in town is near the Provost Marshal's Office. Nobody in their right mind is going to get liquored up next to a police station. Better for families."

Mulholland's Navy uniform identified him easily in the dining room. He was just finishing dinner and smiled when he saw Bill. After Bill got his group seated, he joined Mulholland, who laughed as he pointed to his iced tea. "Need a raincheck. Moved up the flight, but happy to buy you that beer."

"No need. Good to meet you."

"Maybe next time I'm in town."

"Anytime. Call the field. They'll know where I am."

Bill glanced across the room at Peg. She and Trudy were chatting. George was still asking the girls about their adventures on the *Anderson*.

"Better get over there if you know what's good for you."

"Thanks. Should be good flying weather tomorrow."

Sunday morning, Beth dawdled through breakfast. Peg left the table to dress for church.

Bill nudged his daughter. "Finish up, Kiddo! We can't be late."

She twisted in her chair. "I don't know anybody there."

Laughing, he said, "You just got here! We'll fix that. There are a couple of ladies who want to meet your mom and plenty of kids your age. They have great cookies and juice. Scoot!"

When they returned from church, Beth changed into shorts and a light top to play inside. That afternoon, she changed back into her blue church dress and asked her father to polish her Mary Janes.

Bill escorted his wife and daughter to the bungalow, which was a single-story replica of the mansion, down to the same brick-red roof tiles and creamy stucco.

As they neared the bungalow, the lean older woman opened the door. Her ankle-length silk brocade dress was a deep blue and perfectly tailored to her petite frame. Her hair glistened like polished onyx. As she moved, the jewels along the edge of the comb in her chignon sparkled.

"Madam Tong, I would like to introduce you to my family, Peg and Beth."

She motioned for them to enter. Bill winked at Peg before he left.

The living room smelled of sandalwood and something sweeter, possibly jasmine or rose.

After Beth presented the chocolates, saying they were her favorites, Madam Tong motioned them to sit on a leather-covered Craftsman sofa and sank into a matching chair with a small table beside it. Silently, Leon entered through a back door, placed a tea service on the longer table in front of the sofa, and retreated.

After minor pleasantries, she poured tea and handed Peg a cup before offering Beth a slightly under-filled cup. Beth balanced the cup with care before mimicking her mother and placing it on the table in front of the sofa. Pointing to the unopened box of chocolates beside their cups, Beth said, "My father and I didn't know if you'd want this, or the box of chocolate-covered cherries."

Madam Tong opened the Sampler box and offered a piece to Peg, then Beth. "Both are wonderful. Why did you decide on this?"

Beth hovered over the box before making her selection. "You can have choices. I like choices."

"As do I." Madam Tong selected a chocolate and let her hand fall over the armrest. The sun glistened off the gold setting of her large jade ring.

Beth carefully picked up her teacup and sipped. "This is pretty good. We usually have Lipton, it's brown. In San Francisco, we had little cups of tea made from flowers."

"Jasmine?"

Beth looked at her mother, who nodded.

"This is a green tea. They grow it on terraces just above the city. I could take you and your parents up to see how it is grown. Would you like that?"

Beth grinned quickly as Peg said, "There is so much to learn about tea, and about the city. We would be delighted to accompany you."

Madam Tong looked at Beth and lowered her voice as though sharing a secret. "There are three thousand teas in the world. But all are of a general type, like green tea, black tea like your Lipton, white tea, and oolong."

"Oolong?" Beth laughed. "That's a funny word."

"It is. But if your mother is interested in tea, we can have a new kind every time we take tea together. Would you both like that?"

Peg smiled. "Yes. I love learning new things."

Beth leaned forward, dangled her hand over the edge of the sofa, enchanted by the elegant woman, and announced, "As do I."

That night, Peg slid into bed beside Bill. He pulled her close, saying, "I have to tell you something."

"Am I gonna like it, or is it more about the tea party and confections?"

He lowered his voice. "I know it's hard to adjust to having servants when you are so capable, but that's the way they do it here."

"How am I supposed to spend my time?"

"You'll find something important and challenging here as soon as Beth settles in."

"What would you think about my volunteering at the orphanage? Your friend at church gave me a real sales pitch and seemed to find it rewarding."

He paused, then said, "Worth looking into. But remember that there are folks out there willing to pay for any drop of information about us, military moves, any hint of political stuff they can get. Madam Tong got cleared, but things change here. Leon hires helpers from the missionary school who aren't screened by the embassy, but still—"

She pulled back on one elbow. "So, not only can't I cook for my family, but I also need to censor what I say in my home?"

"No. Only where and how loud. And what we say around Beth that might get repeated."

"Really!"

He grimaced. "Same at the Officers' Clubs, church, and at any of the embassy dinners."

"Why at our embassy?"

"We'll get invited to other ones too. Usually for large receptions."

She shook her head and recalled the slogan from the war posters: "Loose lips sink ships!"

He chuckled. "Right."

"Is it even safe to whisper here?"

"Sorry you came?"

She snuggled into his chest. "Never."

CHAPTER 11

Toweling her damp hair, Claire opened the door to her balcony to test the August morning. It was barely past seven. The Monday briefing at the American Embassy started at ten. The high cloud cover and cooling breeze off the water seemed promising. She selected her beige linen skirt and a light blouse. Once dressed, she typed up a few notes for her "first impression" story, ignoring the wobble in the table. At the front desk, she asked, "Do you have a city map for tourists? You know, in both languages?"

"Certainly. Do you need me to write an address for the taxi?"

"How far to the American Embassy?"

He opened the map and showed her. "Thanks."

After walking for two minutes in the heat, she returned to the hotel for a taxi. The driver wore sunglasses with a strip of dirty adhesive tape over the left hinge. The same glasses she saw when she arrived. *Coincidence, a regular here, or a plant?*

The cab stopped at the embassy far too early. She paid the driver and strolled through the shaded neighborhood of elegant mansions. Some remained as private residences, but others had flags of their respective nations flying at their embassy or consulate, a bright burst of color against the deep green of pine trees.

The Marine guards at the gate examined Claire's purse, passport, and police registration card before allowing her entry. Once inside, the framed portrait of President Truman above the reception desk flanked by her flag reassured her she was magically on American soil. She chuckled to herself. *At least that was the theory.* She smiled as she relaxed. She was home.

Claire heard the start of a briefing in a small reception room. Several men in tropical-weight slacks and shirtsleeves clustered in the front two rows. She slipped into the back row and arranged her skirt, hoping that any air from the humming fan in the corner might reach her.

A slim man in a tan suit stood on an elevated platform at the front of the room, leaning on a lectern. He delivered the account of troop movement as though reading the telephone book. This unit to that sector. Nationalists holding that city, leaving another. She needed to consult a larger map to get this in perspective and create a mental battle map for herself. She made notes quickly. The speaker's dull monotone recitation of statistics on the number of trucks here or tanks there became a jumble without meaning.

The men in the front row took notes. He droned on as they slouched in the metal chairs. When he finally closed his notebook and braced for questions, a short Chinese reporter asked about inflation.

The speaker offered a reassuring smile. "Inflation is now under control. The Nationalist government created tight restrictions to stabilize the terrible inflationary pressure on Chinese currency. In 1940, a hundred yuan could buy a pig. By 1943, a chicken. In 1945, a fish, while in 1946, it would buy only an egg. Earlier this year, it couldn't even fetch a pack of matches. But now, they are stabilizing it." Claire suppressed a smirk. *Some answer! Ignore the fact that this was driving all but the wealthiest into poverty and starvation.*

As the speaker hurried from the lectern, a rail-thin man with collar-length black hair shouted after him, "Will the occupation of several of the northern cities by the communists this week change the face of the American campaign here?" *Sharp question for someone who looks like he came off a bender: greasy hair, wrinkled light blue sports shirt.*

Claire listened intently and pretended to take notes as the representative deflected the question of national policy and spoke only of the larger goals of the Nationalist Chinese.

When the speaker left the platform, most of the men departed. The thin man stood and argued with a stocky fellow with close-cropped graying hair. They stopped when they saw her; both walked toward her. The slim man asked, "New to us?" *Accent—not quite French. Tall. A year or two my senior. Sharp features, nose longer than most, three-day scruff, and smelling like a goat from a smokehouse.*

She smiled her best smile. "Yes. Still getting my land legs."

He continued, "Who are you with?"

"Oh, I'm just doing features for an American magazine. I thought I'd sit in for background."

The large man shot out his hand. "Childe of *The Times*. Sebastian Childe. He's Jean-Claude DuPont. French wire service." *Brit, colonial manners, white linen suit, wrinkled, open collar, hair short enough to be ex-military, pushing forty. At least he bathed. Is that the German 4711 cologne? Citrus, lavender, and rosemary all point to it.*

She took his hand. "Claire Peters."

Sebastian grinned. "What a welcome fresh face. Tiring of these usual mugs."

"*The Times?* Wow! Maybe I could pick your brain on what the briefing left out today. Sometimes that longer look can really spice up my copy."

"Of course, but I'm off to an appointment. You might find a meeting with the three of us may offer a broader perspective, as we disagree on most things."

Seeing only two men, Claire glanced around.

Sebastian laughed. "Our third is a White Russian. Pukka chap. Not press, but a long-time local with an interesting perspective." He tapped the other man's arm. "Must run. Fill her in, will you?"

Jean-Claude smiled at her. "*Avec plaisir.* We have a perpetual cocktail appointment at the Grand Hotel. Mondays at five. Come and meet Mikhail Karpov."

"Cocktails? Tonight? Sounds lovely. Thank you."

"Our pleasure."

She glanced around. "Could I ask you a question?"

"Of course."

She whispered, "What's a pukka chap?"

"Sebastian takes pleasure in using words from his time in India to confound others. Means a good person. Trustworthy. Not everyone here rates such an accolade."

Claire returned to her hotel after the briefing. Despite the once-elegant entrance, the Edgewater Mansions Hotel showed the scars of war. The ruby carpet had stains large enough and dark enough not to ask about and a general need for maintenance. Once, this had been a world-renowned resort, an international playground for tycoons and film stars, but it had not recovered from the privations of Japanese occupation. But as her mother might have said, its bones were good. It was redeemable. She chuckled. *Wonder what Mother would make of my own chances for redemption after Ceylon?*

Returning to her room to get her notes in order, she kicked off her shoes and tried to type on the flimsy nightstand while sitting on the bed. She abandoned the effort as the continual shimmy of the table made typing impossible, went into the bathroom, and filled a glass with water. Pausing, she then recalled that Tsingtao was a modern city with safe water. She drank, stood in the doorway, and surveyed her room. Spartan, best suited for a brief stay, a day or two at the most, not a working space. Several items were not quite where she had left them. Too soon for housekeeping to have dusted. She smiled. The inspection by someone was exactly what she expected. But it was amateurish. Sloppy. Easily detected.

She took inventory: two double beds, a nightstand, and a serviceable reading lamp between. Two straight-back chairs with frayed fabric seats flanking a small table. Mercifully, the carpet was gone, leaving a well-polished oak floor. The closet was spacious enough to be her pantry and wardrobe. Two rods, drawers, and shelves. The bathroom was in excellent condition. Two windows flanked the door to the balcony, which was a tangle of spider webs and dead leaves.

Marching to the elevator, she adjusted her attitude on the ride down. She smiled at the manager. "If you have a moment, I have a question."

"Certainly, Madam Peters."

"I wanted to check on something. My magazine should have sent you a substantial advance payment for my room, as I will work out of it the whole time I am here."

"Thank you for your inquiry. You are correct. And there is an open invoice for a month-to-month billing after that." He looked concerned and frowned. "Is there an issue with the room? Would you prefer a city view?"

She laid her hand on his arm. "No. The room is grand, and the furnishings are fine for a brief visit. But it must serve as my office as well." She glanced around the lobby and pointed to a well-worn leather club chair. "I need a reading chair like that one, not straight-back chairs and some silly little table. I'll need a desk, or a table and a chair for it. And remove one bed, please." She laughed. "There is only one of me."

"Of course, we can explore our storage room in the basement. I am certain we can find more suitable items for your extended stay."

"That would be just wonderful. Perhaps if I joined you, I could help make the selections. I'd hate to put you to any more trouble than is necessary."

He thought for a moment, considering his schedule. "When could you join me?"

"As soon as it is convenient for you."

He glanced at the clock behind the reception desk. "I'll be free in a few minutes."

"That would be perfect." She smiled and waited in the club chair.

By three, they had delivered the replacements: a small dining table, a scuffed bentwood chair, a bookcase, and the club chair she had admired in the lobby.

Soon the accouterments of a reporter graced the table that she had pushed against the wall under the window: a fresh ream of paper beside the typewriter, random pencils, and her Waterman pen in the blue-glazed jar she bought that morning. The reading chair beside the bookcase holding her Zenith radio, binoculars, the birder book, and her new "journal," a cheap cloth-bound ledger book that had been on sale. Inspecting the stage setting of a life, she smiled. Now she would make routine journal entries and leave half-written articles on her desk for whoever was visiting her room when she was out.

She opened the blank journal and made her first notation. *Tsingtao August '47. Summer is hot and humid. Registered with police as required. Found a beautiful, blue-glazed pencil jar at a shop near the pier. It will adorn my desk forever. Office all set up. Wonderful view of the sea. Met two report-ers at the embassy briefing, a thin, messy French fellow and Sebastian—a tidy Brit reporting for the Times. Cocktails at the Grand tonight.*

Closing the journal, Claire aimed its spine at a black dot, the flaw in the jar's glaze. If Mao had planted someone who could read English on the cleaning staff, it would disappoint them that her journal held only her silly ramblings.

Buoyed with the success of the renovation, she made her official calls on all the city and military offices in town, leaving a calling card an-nouncing herself as a reporter for an American magazine. Before pre-senting her card, she made a show of penciling the hotel phone number on the back and handing it to each person, as though they alone had it. With a broad smile, she invited them to leave a message for her with the desk if they had news that might interest an American reader.

On her walk back to the hotel, she discovered a liquor store and bought a bottle of Scotch for her room and one of Courvoisier, recall-ing that a good cognac was better than cash in Ceylon. Seeing the hotel manager at the desk, she asked if they could speak in his office.

Standing just inside the door, Claire said softly, "While the desk phone is sufficient for most visitors, I fear I may become a burden.

Would it be possible to have a direct line installed in my room?"

"Of course. But we will charge it to your room."

"Certainly! And another thing, could you recommend where I could buy a car? Just for puttering around town." He offered to ask on her behalf. She thanked him for his help and presented the Courvoisier. From the smile on his face, she had correctly guessed his weakness.

After her second shower of the day, Claire dressed for cocktails. *Jean-Claude and Sebastian.* She reminded herself of their names. As she approached the hotel minutes before five, she decided the hotel was the least Chinese thing she had seen since her arrival. It could have been in any of the European capitals she had toured during her junior year abroad. She quickly put that thought away as the low-tide stench brought her back to the Orient.

She smiled her professional smile as she started up the hotel steps. The lobby had the inviting aroma of what her father called "old money," like the hotel bars in D.C. where handshake deals soon emerged as law, and missionary fundraisers smoothed rough edges. Claire had never quite decoded that carefully curated mixture of lavender and lemon that masked competing perfumes and cigar smoke. At least it was air-conditioned.

The bar was intimate, appointed with mahogany and plum-colored upholstery, and modestly lighted. Well-dressed patrons were having cocktails and impressing each other. A quick inventory. Western suits on both Chinese and American men sporting gold cuff links and tie bars. Business. Women in silks—some traditional sheaths, others in Western cocktail dresses—joined several of the older men. Maybe business. A pudgy couple. The older man smiled as a woman his age opened a bracelet box. An anniversary. Claire was glad she broke out her high heels and her little black dress. Cocktails at the Grand, indeed.

The desk clerk glanced at her. She smiled and walked through the lobby, inspected the garden in back, and returned to the bar. They were still missing. She checked her small gold watch. The bartender appeared at her side, a white towel over the arm of his crisp white tuxedo shirt. His black vest was silk. Chinese, mid-thirties, ebony hair slicked back Valentino style.

"May I seat you, miss?" She tipped her head ever so slightly. Once she was seated at a table near the door, he asked, "What may I bring you, miss?" *Crisp British English, interesting.* He continued, "The Singapore Sling is a current favorite of hotel guests."

"Is an old fashioned possible?"

"Of course." He paused. "As you are a new guest, I should mention that we use our local cherries, darker and richer than the usual maraschino. But if you prefer, it would please me to make it in the more traditional manner. But I believe the Grand's are superior."

Claire tipped her head. "The Grand's, please."

He retreated to the bar, made her cocktail efficiently, and presented it on a silver tray. A small dish of nuts accompanied her drink. The cherry was a deep red, not neon. The orange slice was perfect. After a sip or two, Claire wondered if their invitation had been a prank. An initiation of the new journalist if she could call herself that. She checked her watch again. Twenty after.

It startled her when Jean-Claude arrived at her side. *Tan suit, burgundy tie, shaved, quite an improvement. Lime and sandalwood aftershave? No, a richer scent, a cologne.*

"Ah. There you are. *Pardonne-moi.* I should have told you this morning that we meet back there." He pointed to a closed door at the rear of the bar.

She stood and reached for her drink. He motioned for her to stop. "No. David gets sulky if you break his protocol. Only he may carry a drink in here." *The accent? Not Parisian, but French. Sentence structure was British. Was his use of the occasional French phrase intentional, a flag for an adopted persona, or legitimate? Educated where?*

While they waited for David to notice her departure, he asked, "Did you register?"

"With the police? Yes. The embassy checked that."

"*Ah, bien.*"

She shook her head. "Interesting organization. City police, Nationalist military, American Shore Patrol and Military Police."

Jean-Claude added, "You may hear it called the Jo-Sap in the briefings. It is an abbreviation for Joint Operations Sino-American Police."

"Do they cooperate?"

His smile was sly as he said, "Rarely."

She took his offered arm and walked to the private room after David had nodded to Jean-Claude. Sebastian sat in a large circular booth at the end of the room. Several smaller booths lined both walls. The dance floor glistened.

As she approached, Sebastian smiled. Jean-Claude motioned Claire to enter the booth before him. As she arranged her skirt, David arrived with her drink.

Sebastian motioned with a swirl of his hand. "Another round, and please put hers on the tab." She glanced at the table. An empty brandy snifter sat unattended at the edge of the table. The remnants of a gin and tonic rested by Sebastian. Jean-Claude spun a melting ice cube in his glass.

Claire said, "Interesting clubhouse. Only journalists?"

Sebastian's voice boomed a deep bass. "Once. But our numbers dwindled over the past few years. When it came down to only the Frenchie and me, we found Mikhail. Local business owner whose companionship we enjoy. Knows most everyone worth knowing. Been here since Methuselah was a lad. And he is a great gossip, bright as a button, lovely chap. He's making a call but should return in a moment."

When the door opened, an elegantly attired man marched to the booth but stood facing Claire. *Pushing fifty. Military bearing. Mahogany hair cropped short. High widow's peak. A thick mustache and a crisply trimmed goatee. Oatmeal-colored linen suit. Pale blue shirt. Silk tie, dark blue, large but loose knot. Gold tack, higher than usual. Musky and cedar scents. Perhaps camphor.*

Jean-Claude said, "Claire, may I introduce our good friend, Mikhail Karpov?"

She extended her hand. Mikhail offered a crisp nod before he took her hand for a formal shake. *Diplomatic. Cultured. Reserved. Monied?* "A pleasure."

Sebastian slid to the center of the booth, his girth meriting two seats.

Chuckling, Mikhail sat beside him. "What lies have they told you about me?"

"Just that you've been here longer than these rogues." She smiled, knowing that a good-natured insult can break the ice.

Mikhail smiled. "Seems forever ago that I came." She took a second look. *Russian by name and regal by bearing. Small signet ring. Comfortable.* She paused, trying to find the balance between an intelligence probe and the conversation of a normal journalist. She settled on the conversation. "For business or pleasure?"

"Both, it seems. Initially, it was only an import-export firm. Fabrics and woven rugs. High quality. I was in my twenties in Shanghai, thinking I was the only one who could make this my living. What do you know at twenty?" He leaned toward Claire. Laugh lines crinkled. "I was wrong."

She laughed. "So, what did you do next?"

"My best decision ever. I married Arina. But on the business, I opened small shops, bought a building in Shanghai. One here when Arina wanted to leave the big city. I only rent in Australia, mostly for a presence."

Claire frowned. "I thought you said selling rugs wasn't—"

He grinned, teasing, and said, "Oh, did I forget to mention that I became a factor?"

She put her finger to her temple, as if pondering. "Which is?"

"I am the go-between that makes business happen between the Chinese and the rest of the world. I translate and negotiate. My stores are a convenient place to meet. I was lucky enough as a child in Russia to have parents who traveled widely and enjoyed languages. My father spoke five well enough to translate novels into Russian and order food in seven others." *That was it. Other languages blur his Russian accent.*

Claire feigned innocence. "Oh my. I struggled through my high school Latin."

"At home we spoke Chinese, French, English, and German before I knew they were different languages. Absorbed them at home. In school I discovered their backbones. The grammar and all that."

Claire wanted to know more, but David arrived with fresh drinks. He deftly delivered her old fashioned, a brandy for Karpov, a gin and tonic for Sebastian, and something on the rocks for Jean-Claude.

Claire asked, "What're you drinking?"

"Bourbon. Your Marines introduced me to it. Generous lads."

Sebastian watched her inspecting the room. "Nice, isn't it? Private parties used to be all the rage here. Since money's gotten tighter, we can have this room to ourselves at the cocktail hour."

Jean-Claude laughed. "And well into some evenings."

She tipped her head. "As lovely as it is, why here?"

Sebastian dropped his gaze. "To be frank, they expelled us from the bar when some Aussie reporter relieved himself into an ice bucket. It was late and there were few to witness the event, but the hotel management didn't trust any of us after that."

She laughed. "Have I spoiled my reputation by coming here?"

Sebastian shook his head. "Mikhail will redeem it. He's well respected all over the city. But to business. After the embassy briefing, you said you wanted the long view."

"I need an angle for a women's magazine. Here's what I know. Charlie Soong had money from printing Bibles. Sun Yat-sen had ideas. Both were Christian and spoke English. Sun married one of Soong's daughters, and Chiang Kai-shek married another. I don't know if Mao is married or not. Is he?"

Sebastian shook his head in disappointment. "Spoken like a feature writer. Let me start with a gift." He extended a tattered book to her. "Who among us has read the Red Book in Chinese? No one, that's who. That's why I asked Mik to get me a readable translation for you, one he trusted since he speaks the lingo. This is all you need to know about Mao, in his own words."

She fanned its pages. "It's poetry."

Mikhail pointed at it. "And social commentary. It's all there if you read it carefully. Mao's plan to reform the China he sees as corrupt."

"As a communist?"

"It's more complicated than that. I look forward to your thoughts on it."

Claire chuckled. "We'll never have a poet as president."

Sebastian tapped the table. "Come on. Truman's not that bad."

She tossed out a seed of dissent to open herself for information. "Some of my readers view him as a guy who ran a small-town men's clothing store."

Sebastian shrugged. "Not everyone can be an aristocrat like your late president, FDR."

Claire pushed her character as a disaffected writer. "Heir-ocracy, you mean. Inherited wealth. Nobody makes that kind of money anymore."

Sebastian leaned closer to Claire. "You know where the Roosevelt family money came from, I assume."

She frowned.

"Opium. Seriously, his grandfather played diplomat here and ran an opium trade on the sly. Blind eye from the rich. Just like the American oil companies are getting free security from the military."

"Really?"

"Really!" He downed the rest of his drink. "Who's hungry? I am getting peckish."

Claire said, "I hear the food at the Grand is excellent."

Sebastian wrinkled his nose. "European fare. Do you know about Chinese cuisine?"

She grimaced. "Just from Chinatown in New York when I worked there. Afraid I've been slow getting my courage up."

Sebastian puffed out his chest. "Look no further, my dear. We are here to guide you."

She looked at Jean-Claude for assurance. He nodded.

Claire took a long pull on her old fashion. "Okay. Where do I start?"

Sebastian beamed and began. "With us. No better excuse to dine together. The specialty cuisine here in Shandong Provence is a style called *Lu Cai*. As we are coastal, there is more seafood, often steamed, and light sauces. Inland, you find heartier dishes. Deep-fried chicken or pork and richer sauces." He patted his belly. "I can attest to its merits from having lived there for a bit. It's a temperate climate here, so there are apples, pears, Western-style spinach, sweet potatoes, bok choy, cabbages, and many other vegetables you would know."

"You're making me hungry already."

"Sauces usually feature green onion, garlic, and ginger. Soy sauce in some."

"With lots of rice?"

He shook his head. "We have more steamed breads, small fold-over buns. Some resemble your American biscuits, while others are like French crepes. Filled with shredded meat and sauce, they are grand. But there is rice as well."

"Where have you men been all my life?"

Jean-Claude nudged her. "Here. Waiting for you."

Sebastian eased out of the booth and shouted, "Back in a flash!"

Mikhail finished his drink and motioned for the others to do the same.

Claire frowned. "Why? What's up?"

Jean-Claude grinned. "He's got a plan. Let's see what it is."

When Sebastian returned, he motioned for the others to follow. "Green Dragon in twenty minutes. Get a wiggle on."

Mikhail chuckled. "Enjoy yourselves. Our daughter, Katia, is back from the university in Shanghai. Dinner with her tonight."

In the cab on the way to the Green Dragon, Jean-Claude laughed as Sebastian peppered Claire with what he called "Chinese courtesies" and she called etiquette.

"Where to sit? The guest of honor, you, sits farthest from the door. The one paying, which would be me, sits closest to the door with my back to it. You pour tea for others and acknowledge with a thank you or a tap on the table with two fingers." He used the back of his left hand as a table and tapped it with both his index and middle fingers curved.

"Why that gesture?"

"Many stories. Seems the Emperor wanted to go among his people and disguised himself as a cook. His guards acted like customers. One always bows to an emperor. But they could not, as that would reveal him. So, as he was served tea, they made their fingers bow to him. Double tap."

She said, "Tap for thanks. Clever."

"Never flip over a fish: eat the top half and remove the bone to eat the rest. To turn it over is like a boat flipping over. Bad luck. To pay the check, you need to offer before allowing the host to pay, but not until quibbling back and forth several times. Chopsticks. Serve only with the big ones on the platter, not the ones you are eating with. I will be sure they have silverware and chopsticks. But only for tonight. And plates, not only bowls. And about the tea. Never ask for more, simply leave the lid ajar, and they will refill it. And—"

She put her hand to her throat. "I'll never remember all that."

Jean-Claude laughed. "That is why we booked a private room. Your lessons begin tonight."

It was after midnight when she pulled her chair up to the desk. Her journal appeared to be where she left it, until she sighted down its spine and saw that it no longer lined up with the flaw in the pencil jar, that darker dot in the glaze. She made the entry in her journal with care, adding laborious details of the food and drinks and the name and address of the restaurant and the jazz club they haunted after dinner. Smothering intelligence notes in fluff is a classic ploy. She chuckled. *Maybe my secret reader might enjoy the restaurant review.*

CHAPTER 12

During their first few weeks in China, Peg and Trudy suspended lessons to get their households in order and explore the city with their girls. Peg met with the director of the orphanage and agreed to volunteer one day a week, starting that afternoon. Beth and Madam Tong were inseparable. Sally joined them for tea one afternoon and was enchanted by the older woman who made them use simple Chinese words—*shì* for yes and *bù* for no—in response to her questions. After three short afternoon events during which Madam Tong entertained the girls, Peg asked if she would consider watching both girls some evening so she and Bill could go to dinner.

On Saturday morning, Bill invited Trudy and George to join them at the club for dinner. Trudy dropped Sally off at three and went home to change. Madam Tong entertained both girls, teaching them how to use chopsticks and play dominoes between stories of old China.

On the drive to pick up Trudy and George, Bill reached for Peg's hand.

"When was the last time we were alone, except in bed?" she asked.

He laughed in the deep roar she loved. "I don't know. Maybe we should mark tonight on the calendar."

Trudy and George were giddy during the drive, snuggling together in the back seat.

Bill turned into the driveway for the marina.

Peg asked, "Here? I thought we were going downtown."

He grinned at her. "We're going to the grown-up one tonight."

She laughed. "Getting rowdy?"

"Never know."

Bill squeezed into a slot near the head of the dock. The watchman, speaking on the telephone, ignored him. The lines of several sailboats softly tapped against their masts. Rope bumpers from a few small cabin cruisers rubbed and groaned against the dock as the tide shifted.

Bill took Peg's arm as they walked to the entrance. Two old life rings painted white hung on posts on either side of the door. Once inside, Peg glanced at the usual black-and-white photos of aircraft and squadron pictures of a dozen guys in flight suits standing in front of a plane. Three flags on poles in the lobby. American, Marine Corps, and Navy.

As they passed through the bar area, the swag of fishnet behind the bar was all that distinguished the decor from the sedate club in town. Red booths for four lined the far wall. They had scattered tables for four or six throughout the room. Bill led them to the only available table for four and ordered a Manhattan for Peg and a Canadian Club and Seven for himself.

George told the server, "Ditto for us."

Peg smiled. This could have been the Officers' Club at Pensacola, Corpus Christi, or Santa Barbara offering the same hint of stale beer, floor wax, low tide, and something just shy of mildew.

Halfway through their dinner of prime rib and a shared bottle of French Burgundy, a four-piece band came onto a small stage and played slow dance numbers. While Bill and Peg had a coffee, George and Trudy danced.

Finally, returning to the table, Trudy winked at Peg. "Nightcap? I saw Claire at the bar with a Navy guy, drinking something green in a thimble-size glass. Looked interesting."

George looked at Trudy and grimaced. "Green? You sure you don't want a brandy?"

Trudy shrugged. "Surprise us."

When both men went to the bar, Trudy leaned close to Peg. "We're having a ball! George is dancing close tonight, whispering in my ear. Thanks for offering Madam Tong and keeping Sally there."

Peg gave her a nudge. "I'll take her to church with us in the morning. She can wear one of Beth's dresses. I'll drop her off at your place about eleven. I'll give you a buzz first if it's going to be earlier."

"Bless you. I'll return the favor. It feels like we turned a corner tonight. It's been a rocky week."

"That first week usually is. Changing roles isn't any easier for them than it is for us."

Trudy watched George as she nodded. "Some days he's proud of all I do. Then, other days, he seems resentful if I decide something he wanted to."

"Is he okay with how we've set up the school schedule?"

"That's fine. But it's like he thinks I don't need him. That we could get by just fine without—"

Peg watched their husbands returning from the bar. "Did I tell you Madam Tong is teaching Beth a few words in Chinese, as a part of learning tai chi exercise. Words like 'stop,' 'go,' 'left,' and 'right'? She says it's practice for some martial arts. Sorta looks like a slow ballet to me. She recommended it when Beth was getting fussy one afternoon when Bill and I were trying to play tennis. She loves tai chi and, I swear, it calms her down."

The men handed absurdly small glasses with shimmering green liquid to their wives. George said, "Good luck."

Peg sniffed it and waited for Trudy to take a sip.

Eyes wide, Trudy said, "Wow. That's . . . interesting."

Peg sipped and let the taste linger. Anise, apple, minty, and perhaps sage. "Strong, but nice. Herbal."

George snickered. "Smells like cough medicine to me."

Trudy pushed the glass toward him, laughing, teasing. "Here, try it." George pulled back.

When Claire walked toward them, both men stood. Claire had done her hair up in a tight chignon. Her sheath was a deep emerald. She held an empty glass. "Don't let me interrupt. I wanted to see who else on the planet drank Chartreuse."

Trudy said, "Just trying it."

"Would you mind if I joined you for a moment? The rest of the gang is about to go barhopping at the Prime Club then to Flosset's, but I wanted to say hi."

Bill pulled a chair over from the adjoining table. "Nice to see you again. Can I get you a refill?"

She laughed. "No, thanks. I've been nursing this glass, listening to pilots one-up each other long enough."

Bill theatrically examined his watch. "Yup, it turns into the liar's club about this time."

She laughed. "This is much more civilized than most of the publishing parties I went to in New York."

"We're looking forward to reading your articles," Trudy said.

"Wish I could say I've written anything that they found interesting enough to publish. Embassy briefings are deadly dull, and politics is not their cup of tea, even with the refugee and Displaced Persons angle. They want more personal stories. Happier. Heartwarming."

Trudy nudged Peg. "You ought to tell her about the orphanage."

"What orphanage? Where? Sounds like a story."

"In town. On the main street, the one that ends at the pagoda. I just started, but I could ask next week if they'd give you an interview."

Bill noticed JD, his back against the bar, staring at him. He excused himself. "Hey, JD."

"I gotta problem, Skipper," he slurred slightly.

"Can it wait?"

"Not really. Ya know that nice walk-up I got for me and Deena? Problem is the sombitch that rented it to me didn't own it. He rented it and then ran off with all my money."

"I'm sure you can—"

"See. That's the problem with all the refugees and crooks in town. Never know who to trust."

"JD! Monday."

He pawed drunkenly at Bill's arm. "Now I'm screwed. My savings is shot, what with the rent and now I gotta get a hotel when she gets here. City cops just laughed."

Bill glanced over at Peg, watching them. "That's rough."

"Heard that you found your place through someone at your church, so I was wondering if you could ask around tomorrow and see if anyone had an apartment or would split the rent."

"Sure. Why don't you get some fresh air? See you Monday."

JD hung his head. "Sure, Skipper."

When Bill returned, Peg motioned to JD. "What's that all about?"

"He's up a creek. His apartment in town fell through. Got swindled. Now he and his wife are going to need a hotel he can't afford. You might know her. Wife is Deena."

"Deena? Doesn't ring a bell." She looked at Trudy, who shook her head.

Bill said, "I'll ask at church tomorrow and see if anyone knows of a cheap place. He says the *Jefferson* is on track for arrival next Friday or Saturday."

"Hey!" Peg said, "Why couldn't they stay upstairs for a few days until he gets it sorted out? We've got plenty of space."

Peg dropped off Beth at Trudy's and drove the Buick toward town. The overnight rain had cleaned the city. When she stopped at the entrance to the hotel, Claire was at the curb dressed in sturdy shoes, loose linen slacks, and a long-sleeved blouse suitable for an outing with the children from the orphanage.

Claire slid into the car, putting her oversized purse and a wide-brimmed sun hat on the seat beside her. "This is so kind of you, Peg."

"Not at all. They are desperate for volunteers. I really appreciate you helping us take some kids down to the beach for the morning. If your article could gin up some donations, that would be fantastic."

Claire dug a slim reporter's notepad out of her purse. "Mind if I take notes? No names, just for background, unless I check with you for an okay."

"Sure."

"How'd you get roped into this?"

"Church. One of Bill's friends recruited me. I've just started. Makes sense since I have Leon to manage the house, and Trudy and I trade off schooling the girls."

"How do you split it up?"

"She's a wizard at teaching geography, spelling, and reading. I'm better at math and science. But since we had similar lesson plans, we get by." Peg chuckled. "And we plan to do field trips for music and art."

"I thought the military had schools for the kids."

Peg waited for a break in traffic on Pacific Road. "Better for high school. The elementary grades are marginal."

She slid the Buick into an opening, then braked suddenly as a donkey cart pulled onto the main road. Claire gasped. "Wow! I figured he was a goner."

"Bill warned me that the carts and rickshaws, let alone the refugees, dart into traffic almost like they want to get hit. And the swarms of bicycles! They are the biggest challenge. At least, this was a German colony, so they drive on the same side as us. Someone in Bill's squadron visited Hong Kong and said it was the opposite there."

"British colony?"

"Right. Nearly had a head-on collision. Never drove there again."

Claire said, "It was nice of the War Department to reunite your families."

Peg scowled and gave her a quick glance. "Nice! From what I heard, congressmen got tired of getting piles of letters begging them to either bring the servicemen home or let their families join them in China."

"Are you saying this was to placate the complainers?"

Peg sighed. "Look. The Corps puts up with us for morale, but make no mistake, the men and their mission will always come first." She laughed. "There's an old saying that if the Corps wanted you to have a wife, they would have issued you one in basic training."

"How do you feel playing second fiddle to the Corps?"

Peg gave her a quick smile. "It comes with the job, Claire. They don't call it 'the service' for nothing." She paused, wondering how much to trust her, then took a chance. "Duty comes in a lot of forms. To God, country, those you love, yourself. In the best of times, they overlap."

"I don't know if I could be that strong. Staying alone—"

"That's just the beginning. Being flexible is harder. Go wherever and whenever. Do everything, decide everything when they are gone and magically reunite when they return and readjust your relationship. It's like being promoted and demoted repeatedly."

Claire chuckled, fussing with her notepad. "My readers might be interested in how it is having servants."

Peg shot her a side glance. "I don't have *servants*. Leon manages people to run Madam Tong's house, not wait on me. They need jobs, like everyone else. His cook, Charlie, went to the mission school after he left the orphanage."

Claire flipped the page in her notebook. "How old are the kids at the orphanage?"

"Newborns to twelve-year-olds. I'd guess maybe thirty-five to forty of them. There's a trade school for teenage boys and another for girls on the edge of town. They won't get adopted at that age, or at any age if they are mixed race."

"Financed by?"

"Mostly church-funded with some help from the city and, of course, private donations."

"Where do they come from? Refugees coming into the city dumping their kids?"

"Some. Others die and the police find the children with them or wandering. They are easier to place. The mixed-race kids aren't. Some of the older ones were from the comfort women the Japanese kept here. Basically, sex slaves for the soldiers. Some have colored fathers." Peg drove up the hill. "That's it. The bright yellow building."

"God! It's a daffodil."

Peg laughed. "They said they painted it that way so it wouldn't get bombed during the war."

Claire dropped her notebook into her purse and took a deep breath as she followed Peg into the orphanage. The huge open room could have been a gym in any American high school, except for the kitchen at the rear, the bunk beds to the right, and several small tables where children were doing schoolwork. At the tables, about thirty children wore shorts, sandals, and loose tops.

A hum filled the room: lessons, children reading to each other, teachers asking questions, children answering, laughter. Every table had a Chinese woman in a simple blue cotton *qipao* who guided their studies. They corralled toddlers in play groups on the polished floor.

Claire watched the nun at the back of the room, beads around her waist swinging as she moved easily between the tables, leaning over to brush a lock of hair out of a girl's eyes or straightening a shirt slipping off a boy's shoulder. Each correction had a lingering moment of touching, of valuing. These children were not her charges, Claire thought, but her mission.

Peg nudged the reporter. "Sister Francine. She's the ringleader. If she gives an order, jump. She's Swiss. Amazing how she can calm the new ones. Nuns bring in the abandoned babies left most mornings near Saint Michaels. City police and MPs deliver the ones they find wandering or lying beside a parent who died overnight on the street."

Claire knew tears were gathering. She needed to brush back memories of other abandoned children. She cleared her throat. "Do many of the Navy or Marine wives volunteer here?"

"A few. Most are women in the ex-pat community who have lived here for years." Peg laughed. "Even though I haven't been here very long, from what I can tell, it's a regular League of Nations some days. We've got volunteers who are German, French, Chinese, of course, Americans, Australians, Swiss, a few Russians. Some days, we go through two translators to get a message across." She pointed to a cluster of older women in comfortable slacks and blouses preparing food. "That's the English gang. Some days we resort to gestures. Amazing what you can do if you all have the same intent."

"And what is that?"

"To get them fed, or bathed, or stay with them during a doctor's visit. Or do a field trip."

After a deep breath, Claire said, "They look pretty good. Toddlers are engaged. These second-graders look great."

Peg put her hand on Claire's arm. "Most of these kids were skin and bones when they got here. Their country's been in one war after another their whole lives. Those 'second-graders' are mostly ten or twelve."

"But they're so small!"

"I know. Malnutrition." Peg whispered. A group was forming by the door. "Come on. The kids are ready for the beach."

Sister Francine led the way with a child on each side, followed by ten volunteers holding the hands of twenty more children. Three nuns carried picnic baskets and a soccer ball.

Play at the beach was subdued. The boys practiced passing the ball while the girls waded with volunteers in the warm water. A light breeze tugged at Claire's hat. Returning to the orphanage, a small girl slowed their progress.

Claire motioned to Peg. "Can I pick her up?"

"If she lets you." As Peg followed them, she saw Claire kneel. The little girl smiled and reached for Claire's hat. Once placed on the child's head, they both laughed, and the girl hopped onto Claire's back. When the girl began stroking Claire's red hair, the reporter did not stop her.

When they arrived at the orphanage, Peg said, "I'll see if Sister is available for an interview."

"Let's wait until I get a better handle on what's going on, so my questions make sense. Maybe interview a couple of long-term volunteers this afternoon."

"How about I show you the rest of the building?"

Claire nodded and followed Peg down a hallway. She opened the door. "Bathing, dressing, and toilet area." Claire jolted, then regained her balance. The astringency of institutional cleaners accosted her. Ceylon. The evacuation centers. The futile attempt to hide the stench of poverty and privation.

When they stopped at a door marked with a red cross, Peg tapped on the door and said, "The Navy gives us a doc and nurse as part of a local aid program. Twice a week. There's also a Chinese doctor just down the street and the city hospital if needed."

A woman called, "Come in!"

Peg said, "Anna. This is Claire. She's a reporter. Got a minute for us?" Claire glanced at her name tag to get the spelling for her article. "Rosetti," it said. Navy nurse.

Anna stood. "Sorry, I have three exams to do before I leave, and I'm late now. But Doctor Stein is in this afternoon." *Italian with a hint of New York in her speech.* A thin boy holding a nun's hand arrived at the doorway. Anna smiled, walked over, and took his hand.

Back in the hallway, Peg asked, "Can you stay for the meal?"

Claire's voice fell to a whisper. "No, not today. I have lunch plans."

"Free after that?"

"Why?"

"Hang on a second while I check on something."

A few minutes later, Peg found Claire waiting by the front door. "Doctor Stein is due in about two."

Once on the street, Peg offered to give Claire a ride to her lunch appointment. "No thanks. The walk will do me good. Need to think about how to write up what I saw in there." *And manage what I felt. Pretending not to know what a starving child looks like.*

"You sure?"

Claire waved as she walked downhill. "Thank you, though."

Once Peg's car was out of sight, Claire leaned against a rock pillar at the entrance of the small park near the orphanage. What the hell? She had faced armed men in a jungle and held prisoners of war in her arms, but those kids got to her. She couldn't eat a bite, saddened by the memory of the orphans in Ceylon.

After checking on several of her city contacts, Claire talked herself into going back for the story, half-hoping to miss the doctor. A middle-age Chinese woman led her down a hallway to the medical office and knocked.

A Navy officer with a stethoscope around his neck opened the door so quickly that Claire recoiled. He stuck out his hand. "Sorry if I startled you. Jacob Stein. You must be Claire Peters." His smile was bright against his lightly tanned face and black hair.

"Right. You're one of the volunteer doctors?"

"*The* doctor now. Others rotated stateside. We still have three nurses and volunteers, so the children always have a chaperone. Come in. We can have some privacy here."

He motioned to the side chair beside his desk, wedged against the small examination table. Claire struggled to get into it.

He laughed. "So much for chivalry. Look, I've got a break now. We could go down to the snack bar at the YMCA, grab a bite, and talk."

On their way past the children at the tables, he stopped to look at a bandage or pat a child on the head. He seemed to linger, looking at a young woman who was giving an English lesson. *Twenty-something European. Dark hair and eyes. Braids pinned into a crown atop her head, eyebrows looking sculpted, full, and well arched. No jewelry. Simply dressed, a white blouse and brown cotton skirt. Sandals. Watching him.*

He stopped and smiled at her. "Nice to see you today, Katia. Are you staying for dinner?"

"Yes."

"I'll be back soon. See you then."

Claire smiled at the woman. "Katia Karpov?"

"Yes."

"Mikhail's daughter?"

She frowned. Claire laughed and extended her hand. "I took a wild guess. It's such a beautiful name, I remembered it. I'm Claire Peters. American journalist. Your father welcomed me when I arrived by telling me about the city."

"And the work we do here?"

"No. That came from a friend of mine, Peg Ryan."

"Oh, I love Peg and her daughter. She's come here several times with her mother. Beth is a scamp."

"Is she now?"

On her way back to her hotel, Claire struggled with what to add to her journal. Memories of the street urchins in Ceylon: scars from burning huts, undersized from malnutrition, legs bowed from rickets. New faces with the same horrors. She stopped at the window of a tobacconist, pretending to examine the glass jars of pipe tobacco offerings: Latika, Cavendish, Perique, and Virginia. She laughed and went inside, looking for Camels, hoping they didn't carry them. When they didn't, she pointed to a blue pack of Gauloises.

The yearning for a smoke on dream-tossed nights had returned. She spoke in Chinese, then corrected herself. She shrugged and gestured her way through the transaction to hide her fluency.

Later, she wrote: *Faces of want. City is changing.* Claire thought of her secret reader: *Will he understand the change was the influx of refugees and the exit of wealth?*

That night, the dreams of Ceylon woke her. Small faces, twisted bodies, fire.

On the balcony, she ripped open the pack of Gauloises, lit the cigarette, and let the rough smoke try to overtake the memories.

CHAPTER 13

The USS *Jefferson* docked Sunday afternoon after steaming through two tropical storms. Bill drove the Buick downtown to pick up JD from the BOQ and Deena from the ship. Peg took a last look upstairs and made sure new towels were in the bathroom. Bedroom and sitting room, dusted. Perfect for houseguests.

When she heard the gate open, she rushed downstairs to greet them. What was it Bill said, JD and Deena? New faces, but a Marine and his wife. Simple courtesy. Just a few days or a couple of weeks, Bill said. Let him get a few paychecks in the bank, so he could rent a new place.

When Deena got out of the Buick, Peg gasped. Her smile faded. *It can't be! This is some cruel joke. How the hell could Deena be Gerri?* Then it hit her. The name on their cabin door that first day on the ship. Geraldine! And JD was her Johnny. Well, as far as she was concerned, it would not be a long visit. She walked toward the car and forced a smile. "Welcome, Gerri."

JD looked at her. "It's Deena. Her name's Deena."

Gerri gave him a playful punch to the arm. "Decided that Gerri was a better fit on the boat ride. New name. New me. Kinda like Bill calling you JD."

He gave her a look like she could tell him to walk over broken glass and he'd ask how far or fast. "Gerri! I love it!"

Bill carried several suitcases upstairs and had Leon send up a pitcher of iced tea.

Peg motioned Bill into their bedroom. "What the hell? She's the nightmare I told you about. In our cabin before Hawaii. Flirting with sailors! Potty mouth!"

Bill ran his hands through his hair. "Jesus! Is she the one you got thrown out of your cabin?"

"Yes." She scowled. "Before Trudy joined us."

"Want me to kick 'em out now?"

"Yes. But how would that look? He's in your squadron."

"I know. But I promise I'll try to get them out ASAP."

"Good. I better be the one to pick Beth up from Sally's and break the news to her. Wish me luck."

Over the next week, Peg decided that her efforts to unify her household were pointless. She focused her attention on helping the newly arrived Marine wives get settled, then established a phone tree that webbed the spouses of Bill's pilots together. She once told Bill that he had a chain of command, but the women had a chain of caring by sharing. They spread squadron news, invitations to parties, emergency notifications, and occasionally gossip. Usually, Peg started the call to Trudy and Maxine, who then called two others and so on until everyone had the same information. But unlike the military, Peg expected any of the women to start a call, up or down the chain, in an emergency.

Gerri and JD were discovering new single friends and a seemingly endless number of nightclubs and bars. As much as she tried, Peg could not ignore the taxi's brakes shrieking at two in the morning and the couple's raucous laughter as they slammed the front door and clattered up the stairs. She couldn't decide if she was grateful or envious that both Bill and Beth slept through the disruptions.

Peg visited Trudy's as often as possible when she wasn't giving the girls their lessons at her house.

Saturday morning became a whirl. Bill and JD had a baseball game, so Peg and Trudy escaped to the beach. After the usual chaos of setting up the beach umbrella and two folding chairs, Trudy and the girls splashed in the knee-high surf while Peg set up lunch. After they ate, Peg sent the girls to build sandcastles.

Trudy frowned at the abruptness. "What's chewing on you, Peg?"

"That woman!"

"What now?"

"Came downstairs in her underwear this morning, strolls into the kitchen while Leon and the cook are cleaning up after breakfast. Bill had gone. She wanted a cup of coffee to take upstairs while she got ready. Imagine."

Trudy repressed a smile. "I can't."

"The new cook, Charlie, froze. He's from the mission school. Leon, bless him, stared at the kitchen clock, then fussed with his watch. The amah quit."

"Did Gerri apologize?"

"Nope. Just before I left, she was lounging in the living room in a robe."

"Let me guess. You told her off."

"Just told her they called it underwear for a reason and that in the future she needed to be covered or not come downstairs. I don't know what to do about her anymore. I don't want her around Beth or Sally. Talks like the guys in the squadron when they don't think ladies are around. Even calls her husband JD now. She's a handful."

Trudy said, "I see your point. She's young and hasn't had the advantages we have."

Peg scowled. "Anyway, do you think we could do all the classes at your house? I'd still teach on my days like we do now."

"Sounds fine. I'll check with George."

Peg patted Trudy's arm. "You are a dear."

"It's not a problem. Oh, I heard that the exchange was getting a shipment of winter clothes on Monday. Want to go?"

Peg laughed. "This is pure China logic. We're sweating to death but talking about winter clothes."

"I'll have Giselle babysit the girls. Add this to her cooking and cleaning duties. Maybe we could hit the commissary for some good meat after the exchange?"

"I'll drive."

After Peg backed the Buick out onto Shaoguan, Beth waved to Leon, who locked the gate. As Peg turned toward Trudy's house, Beth asked, "Mommy? Can you see if they have another box of chocolates for Madam Tong? She really liked the one we gave her when we got here."

"I'm sure she did. Any idea what you and Sally are going to be doing today?"

"Cookies. Sally said Miss Giselle is going to teach us how to make real gingerbread cookies. Do I like gingerbread?"

"I think so. It's like a spicy chocolate cake. I like it, but your father isn't fond of it, so I guess I don't make it often. Are you going to eat all the cookies and not want dinner?"

Beth giggled. "No!"

"You can bring some home for Leon and Madam Tong."

"What if she doesn't like gingerbread cookies?"

"We'll find out. I think they would be nice with tea. She'd appreciate you making something for her, don't you think?"

"I guess."

Peg walked Beth to Trudy's front door. Giselle smiled at her as Trudy hurried out to Peg's car. She sank into the seat and slumped.

Peg laughed as she drove away. "Hard day?"

"It would have been easier to make the damn cookies myself than get everything ready for Giselle."

"What? It's just a few ingredients: mix, make a log of dough, let both girls cut slices off the log, and bake them. What's hard?"

Trudy adopted a Germanic accent. "Vee must have bake stations! Each girl to have her own bowl to mix. To make. Start to finish. That is the only vay to learn!"

Peg laughed. "Good to know! Think the kids are going to make her crazy?"

"It should be a fair fight."

"How'd you hear about the clothes shipment?"

"From a nurse on the *Repose*."

"Is there a problem?"

"Just went for a refill on her cough medicine. She keeps getting this juicy cough at night. Allergies."

Peg asked, "Looking for anything for yourself today?"

"I'll see what came in. I really want to get a couple of sweaters and warm slacks for Sally before it gets cold. She's growing so fast. I'm afraid the stuff I brought over won't make it past Christmas."

Peg said, "Hand-me-downs? We need to find a kid bigger than ours who is still growing."

Trudy laughed. "Good idea. We already know the moms of younger kids we can pass stuff on to. Or donate to the orphanage?"

"Good news! I was going to the darkroom at our house and snooped in the basement. Honestly, I was looking at all the preserved fruit and vegetables down there, and saw an old sewing machine shoved in a corner. Must be one of the first Singers."

Trudy whooped. "Tell me it's a treadle machine."

"It is! I asked Leon to get it dusted and brought upstairs. There's room in one of those empty bedrooms off the laundry. We can make our own alterations now. Other gals might like to use it as well."

"My God! The memories I have of running the foot pedal for my mother when I was about Sally's age. I'd be on the floor like a puppy dog and pump it with my arms until I got tired, then she'd take over."

Fall was late. The heat and humidity lingered. The monsoons seemed to come and go at will. Claire twisted in bed and tangled in her thin nightgown. Just shy of midnight, she knew it was going to be one of those nights that lasted too long. The dull rumble of heat lightning jumping from cloud to cloud rubbed against her skin like a feral cat. She sat up and reached for her water glass on the side table. Tepid.

The distant flashes cast pale shadows of the Scotch bottle on her desk against the far wall like some Halloween dream. She threw back the sheet, stomped toward the window, grabbed the curtain to draw it against the light, then stopped. The sea was luminescent. The low lapping water foamed a pale green, like a glass of Chartreuse.

She stood on the small balcony and pulled her hair up from the damp nape. The breeze smelled of rot and beached seaweed. She pulled on shorts and a light top. Pocketing her room key and smokes, she took the elevator to the lobby.

"Madam?" She waved away the desk clerk's concern.

She hurried down the slate steps to the beach, crossed the sand, and perched on the rock outcropping. The red tide had a rotten-egg stink she tried to ignore as she struck a match and fired her cigarette.

The breeze picked up. She scanned the sea for boats, relaxed, and watched the clouds sliding over the moon. She finished her cigarette and flipped it toward the sea. Falling short, it sent a spray of sparks across the rocks below her. Then she saw him. A man swimming toward shore. She froze and watched him stand and take easy steps, kicking the ankle-deep water, making it glow brighter. The rail-thin man in dark bathing trunks rescued a dark shirt crumpled on the sand. Jean-Claude.

"Good morning, Claire," he said as he passed her, brushing sand from his shirt.

She stood and scrambled after him. The moonlight slashed bright ribbons across his back, from his right shoulder to his waist.

She struggled for something to say. "Couldn't sleep either?"

"Wanted a swim."

She hurried to join him. *Those are scars.* She cleared her throat. "How'd you see me?"

"Didn't. Saw your cigarette."

"Thought you hated the water. That's what you said."

"Thought you didn't smoke. That's what *you* said."

She stared at him. "So, we all have our little secrets."

He pushed back his wet hair. "Love to swim. But . . ." He shrugged in that practiced manner of the French.

"I won't ask. Come up for a Scotch? No ice."

"Thanks, but I need a shower. I smell like bad eggs."

Claire paused. "I have a shower."

He glanced at her. "Do you?"

They rode the elevator to the top floor in silence, both trying to ignore the stench from the red tide. She opened the door to her room and flipped the light switch.

She lifted the bottle. He nodded. She poured a double shot into each glass and handed him his. He took a sip and shivered.

"You're chilled. There's a robe on the back of the door. Leave your trunks to dry."

He emptied the glass and went into the bathroom. While he showered, she tossed her nightgown into the closet and retrieved an open can of Planter's peanuts that she put by their glasses.

When the shower stopped, she refreshed their glasses. He opened the door, knotting the belt of her terrycloth bathrobe. "This is nice. I had a fear it would be short and silk."

They both laughed. He sat in the leather chair beside the desk.

"Sorry it's not bourbon. Seriously, a Frenchman liking bourbon. How'd you connect with the GIs?"

He stood, watching her eyes. "Why do you ask what you already know?"

"I don't always believe what people tell me. There's usually another story."

"The camp at Wei-Hsien. I was there until your GIs liberated us and brought me here."

She listened, motionless, then gave a small nod.

"After the war, I returned to France. Just long enough to settle some family matters and get my job back. They thought I had died, like my parents. I had to leave."

"Why?"

He shrugged. "I tell people there wasn't enough food. Rationing, you see. But I was useless there. My family was gone. There were too many memories." He took another sip. "The day I decided, it was in October. The sun blazed all day. Late in the afternoon, I crossed Pont Neuf. You know Paris?"

"No," she lied.

"I crossed from the Left Bank toward the Louvre. The sun was behind me. People coming toward me held their hands up over their eyes, against the sun, but like saluting, like I was a hero when we all were just survivors. I had to come back."

"We were the lucky ones. Safe in America." She took a deep drink, hoping to wash away her lies. His hand shook.

She let the silence fill the room.

His shoulders relaxed. He stretched out his legs and crossed his ankles. He examined the glass. "This is a fine Scotch, thank you. I still like bourbon, but you are better company." He took a small sip. "It is nice to see you without the others."

"Interesting group."

He chuckled, taking a few peanuts. "Ever the diplomat. We are not all, how you say, boy scouts."

"Why?"

He laughed. "You're the reporter. Find out."

"What was your first impression when you arrived here? Right after the war ended."

"The freedom of the air. The freshness. No latrines. The sea smell and apples. Food was scarce. A bowl of apples sat in the lobby for anyone to take. Many held theirs for days, not trusting there would be a next meal."

"But there was."

"Food . . . it's still a communion, you know, *une chose sacrée*."

"A sacred thing. A sacrament."

"Oui."

Her tears came. The POWs who she had evacuated still visited her dreams as ghosts brought down to mere bone and hope.

He held her, she in her damp shorts and wrinkled shirt, he in her bathrobe.

In the morning, she woke with a start. He was washing the glasses in the bathroom. She sat up—shocked to still be in her clothes—watching him pulling on his overshirt. "Leaving?"

He tipped his head. "Is that what you want?"

"Was it a mistake to invite you up for a drink?"

"You were not the mistake. This hotel was. It made memories too strong."

She almost asked, then stopped herself, went into the bathroom to get a drink of water. She expected to hear the door close. When she came out, he was sitting on top of the sheets. His back was against the wall. He patted the bed. "Sit."

She sat at the foot of the bed, cross-legged, watching him.

"You didn't ask."

"I thought you didn't answer questions. Just ask them."

He laughed. "True, but I must be honest with you if you want to know me."

"I don't need to know a thing more to still want to know you."

"But, I need to tell you. As French as you think I am, Indochina was my home. My family owned a farm, a plantation. My mother was English, my father was French. After university in France, I found a job as, how you say, a stringer for a paper, and came to China."

"Before the war?"

"*Exactement*. I was here in Tsingtao when the Japanese came in thirty-eight. At first it was armbands, mine was F for French, and house confinement. That changed in forty-one."

She silently leaned forward, elbows on her knees, hands clasped under her chin, barely breathing.

"They put us in trucks and drove us to a place called Wei-Hsien. It's about a hundred and twenty kilometers west. The Australian kids sang all the way there, making a joke of 'we-sang.' But once we arrived, it was not funny. It was a deserted missionary training center. Bandits had used it. It was in ruins. It had a church and dormitories and two-story houses inside a high wall. Single men lived in a dormitory. Families and the few single women gathered into small quarters together. We were two thousand in a place planned for two or three hundred."

His hands shook as he spoke. She knew she needed to remain invisible. Sympathy made it harder. She watched his eyes. "Soon we formed committees to make it into a city. Cooks and doctors trained helpers. I taught English and French in the school. Some old military men designed a way to operate. Schedules and duties. We all worked together to make what we had go as far as it could, but there was never enough. The latrine was a long trench outside. In the summer, coolies used the slops to fertilize their crops. In the winter, we used pots inside, and the slops stayed in a frozen pile outside until spring."

He leaned forward. "The Americans parachuted in to liberate the camp and bring food. They had bourbon. Imagine."

Claire didn't know she was weeping until he brushed his hands across her cheeks.

"It's past, Claire. The trucks brought us back here, some to the Iltis Hydro Hotel, out on Iltis Hook, but I came here. I was here for a week until I got my strength and found transport back to Indochina. I wasn't here as a reporter. I was a refugee. I didn't think I could ever come here again."

"But you did."

"Yes." He paused and watched her eyes. "You didn't ask about the scars on my back."

"I don't need to."

"Anything people could give me, I traded with the slop-coolies for food. I smuggled messages out with the coolies and got war news. I bribed a guard." He shrugged. "They discovered." He stood, took off his shirt, and turned away from her. Scars silvered in the light of morning.

She stood, walked around to face him, and held him.

CHAPTER 14

B ill Ryan rode shotgun in Sanchez's Jeep to the airfield. *Sun should hold long enough for what we need today. A quick in and out before the rain.*

When he came into the briefing room with Sanchez, JD and Phil grew silent. "Good morning, gentlemen. It's just us today. The others are giving a navigation class to the KMT pilots, one-on-one. We'll be taking snapshots of a rail depot. Standard diamond formation." Ryan paused briefly and looked at his pilots. This was what he lived for. Flying with talented men, not the political dance of the weekly advisory meetings with the Nationalists or the squabbling when there were conflicting reports on troop movements or strength.

As Ryan outlined the mission, each pilot noted the coordinates and altitudes for the tactical approach on his map.

The photo-recon mission out of Tsingtao started like any other. Ryan was in the lead with the movie camera. Covered by JD on his left wing and Phil on his right. Sanchez flew at the rear of the diamond with the higher resolution still picture camera to capture the changes to the railway to the northwest. The intelligence staff in G-2 and the Nationalists only had informants reporting that Mao was transporting tanks to the north of the city for a new offensive. Ryan's job was to put a stamp of true or false on it and not get his men killed.

Take off was by the book. The sky was inviting. Stratocumulus clouds on the way north yielded to a blue sky about the shade of their underbelly paint. Sweet flying.

Radio chatter as they approached was also by the book. Low, slow, and controlled as they formed into a tight diamond that swept over the installation, filming it.

The new warehouse was unpainted, its roof made of tar paper and batten. Not a permanent installation, but it had space for supplies. But something was off. No cannons. A spur, not a major line. The rails didn't catch the sun.

Ryan got on the horn. "Sanchez, did you catch any glint off the rails when we made the sweep? Looks like they aren't using it to me. Rust or dirt on 'em."

"Roger that, Skipper."

"JD? Phil? Rails look new to anyone?"

In order, both reported, "Negative."

"Okay, let's do it again to be sure, lining up to get a reflection. Low sweep at a thousand and up to angels' fifteen."

The four fighters swept over the station with precision. No interdiction. Nobody was trying to kill them today.

After they reached altitude and headed for the coast, Ryan reported their impression to the tower to pass to the Intelligence Officers in G-2. Along the coast, the clouds were building. They flew under the cloud ceiling, heading home after a simple mission. The film would validate their radio report. It was a milk run.

Two minutes later, they were over the coast. Phil spotted them and yelled into the mike, "Bogey! Eleven high!"

They pulled into a starburst pattern. Phil and Sanchez spun down to the right, evasion. JD and Ryan up and left, offensive covering the others. Four Japanese Zeros. Hand-me-downs from the war the Russians had graciously left for Mao.

JD shouted, "Fucking Zeros!"

Ryan countered, "Power up past them, go high and work down."

The superior speed of the Corsairs and tight maneuverability was no match for the older planes or the skill of the pilots. Sanchez and Phil gained altitude. Then it was a dogfight with the Zeros being snapped at by the stronger, faster Corsairs. The older planes were spitting machine-gun fire. Thrashing like tuna surrounded by sharks.

Three Zeros took hits and one spun off, going high for home. Two flamed when they slammed into the earth. One hit the water. Hard.

JD whooped, "*Jesús, Dios!*"

Phil shouted, "Skipper, I think I'm hit!"

Ryan's body went steel-cold for a second. "Clarify!"

"Needle on the fuel gauge pegged zero. Oil pressure dropping."

In half a heartbeat, Ryan knew that fuel wasn't the worst problem. There was a small reserve under the empty mark. But without oil, the eighteen pistons would melt into a solid block of iron. He had to move fast. "You hurt?"

"Negative."

The sun caught the leaking fuel, spreading behind the plane like the tail feathers of a peacock.

The beach was a slender thread of rocks and sand, over a mile off. Ryan knew he was looking at a deep-water ditch. They were all on fumes after the dogfight. "JD! Sanchez! Head home."

Phil yelled, "The beach! I could make it!"

"Negative. Stay over water." Ryan ground his teeth at the thought of Phil smashing into a pile of rocks, blue steel folding around him. As they hurtled south, he saw three small sampans and a rowboat in a cove. "Go for the boats." Silence. Ryan called, "Phil?"

Silence.

Ryan shouted into the mike, "Wilson! Start your ditch list."

"I can't find the fucking list." Phil's voice was climbing, his words jamming together, adrenaline taking control. Ryan needed to pull him back to his training. That's when he saw the oil covering the windscreen. Phil was flying blind.

"No sweat. I'll talk you down. There's a sheltered cove that's per-fect." Without waiting for a reply, Ryan gave him a new heading and sighed when Phil responded. Ryan figured the engine would seize up close enough to the fishermen below to give them a story to tell their grandkids. "Phil! Secure classified and loose items. Shove your map in your flight suit. You got this. You're looking cherry." Ryan read the angle of the chop.

"Sunglasses off. Don't inflate your Mae West until you're out. Run down the wing. If she sinks fast, you don't want to get sucked under."

He heard Phil muttering, perhaps praying.

"Your angle's good coming in flat. Canopy back. Look out the side. Check your altitude."

"Roger!"

"Take a piss so you won't rip up your bladder."

"Done."

The plane skimmed a few feet above the water. Ryan shouted, "Pull a carrier approach, ass down before the prop hits, so you don't cartwheel. It'll bust the tail and flood, but you'll get out easier."

"Tell Ellie—"

"Tell her yourself. Full flaps now! Hands off the stick. Grab harness."

A sound like crumpling newspaper filled Ryan's headphones before the silence.

Ryan pulled a tight turn to circle the position. The plane was level in the water, like a stingray off Pensacola sunning in the Gulf. As the twelve-thousand-pound Corsair sank, Phil was going down with it. He had to get free of the harness right away. *Where is he?*

After the longest minute there ever was, Ryan exhaled when he saw Phil bob up. Mae West inflated a bright yellow against the green sea. Phil raised his arm. The man in the rowboat pulled the cord on the outboard motor. A cloud of blue exhaust belched as the boat went toward Phil.

Ryan scanned his gauges, tipped his wings, and turned toward home. He never heard Phil gasp for air, scream in terror when he popped above the water, or sob when the fisherman pulled him aboard.

Ryan flew solo to the base. The rain was sheeting over the city when he made his approach to the field. Sanchez and JD were in the briefing room, waiting for him. Sanchez tried to read Ryan's stony face. "Skipper, we heard your transmissions. Reported his position to the Navy. They don't have anyone close. Did the sampans pick him up?"

"Not sure, but he was alive, and a small boat was heading for him."

"Friendlies?"

"Not military. Fishermen. That's all I can say. You closed out the books on the mission?"

"All but your notes and map, sir."

"Right."

Sanchez asked, "Need a ride, Skipper?"

"Yes. Thanks."

Major Moretti was buckling his trench coat outside the door of the Provost Marshal's Office as Bill jumped out of the Jeep and ran up the steps, his flight suit drenched. He smiled. "Here to report a lost umbrella, Captain Ryan?"

"Wish it was that simple, Major. One of my guys is down over the redline."

The Major's face went flat as he motioned for Ryan to follow him into his office.

Ryan ran his hands through his wet hair. "Ditched close to shore, about five miles up the coast. Waved me off, so I know he made it out of the plane. Fishing boat nearby started for him. Think they picked him up. Phil Wilson. You might have seen him at the club, tall blond guy."

"Yeah. I remember him. Easy smile." He paused. "With that light hair, he'd stand out."

"We talked about it. He carried a black knit cap in his flight suit. I wanted your guys on the alert in case they hear anything about a ransom demand or see him coming in on his own."

Moretti pushed a pad of paper toward him. "Gimmie his full name. I'll get his ID info out at the shift-change briefing." Ryan wrote carefully and handed back the pad. "Lemme walk this over, spread the word in case they hear anything from their black-market contacts or drug informants. Wait here."

"Can I use your phone?"

Moretti nodded as he left.

Peg answered on the second ring. Hearing Bill's voice, she teased, "Don't tell me you're going to be late, and you met a guy from . . . ."

"Peg! It's Phil Wilson. He's alive but had to ditch today. I'm going to Eleanor's."

The chill hit her. She braced against the trembling. "I'll go with you. How soon?"

"Leaving downtown now."

"I'll have the car out front."

Bill slowly placed the handset in its cradle, glanced around the office, and noticed the deep-water rod and reel leaning against the wall. When Moretti returned, Ryan said, "Thanks. Now I gotta tell his wife. Thank God Peg's coming with me."

"I'll give you a ride."

Once on Pacific Road, Ryan broke the silence, needing to clear his mind. "That was a huge fishing rig in your office."

"Ever been deep-sea fishing?"

"Once. On a half-day boat in the Gulf."

"Deep-sea fishing is kinda like my job here." Ryan tipped his head, puzzled, but Moretti continued, "Just need some patience and sometimes the right bait and you can get 'em. No matter how deep the sea."

"Wish trout were as obliging. Got to outsmart them."

Moretti chuckled. "That's the other part of my job." He slowed when a three-inch wave of water swept over the street. "How's the family settling in?"

"Good. Peg likes the house. I'm loving Beth's stories about the trip over. You know, they saw a pod of whales and she swears they migrate here."

"She's right. In winter, folks drive up the mountain to see them. Take picnics. They clog the turnouts."

"That'd be something to see. Can you let me know when?"

"Sure thing."

Bill saw the Buick at the curb. "Thank God she's going to Phil's house with me. I don't know his wife very well."

Moretti pulled to a stop. Through the rain, Bill saw Peg at the steering wheel with someone from her monthly bridge group beside her. Bill crawled into the back seat.

Peg looked back at him. "Madam Tong and Leon are looking after Beth. Maxine's going to spend over with Ellie after we leave."

Maxine softly said, "Peg called me. She knew I was free tonight. In the morning, we'll call around and see who'll stay with her tomorrow."

It was after eight when Bill and Peg returned home. They sat in the driveway in silence for a moment. Once inside the kitchen, Peg hung up her raincoat. Bill stood, rain dripping on the floor.

Leon looked at them and started for the refrigerator. "Let me heat something for you."

Bill looked at Peg. "Just toast and a scrambled egg?"

She said, "Fine."

When Bill went to change into dry clothes, Leon reported that Beth had been fussy during dinner and wanted to go to bed early. Peg hurried to the bedroom and saw Beth, still in her play clothes, on top of her bed, Golden Books strewn around her. She tugged at her ear and sniffed as she sat up.

Peg took a hard look. "What's going on?"

"My ear feels funny."

Peg gathered the books, put them on the desk, and sat beside her, teasing, "Did you read *all* these while we were gone?"

"Leon read to me. He changes voices."

Peg looked at Beth's ear, had her open her mouth, and inspected her throat. Fine. But a red ear called for warmed eardrops. Peg grabbed the bottle from the bathroom, hurried to the kitchen, pulled out a small saucepan, and started heating water.

Bill looked up from his plate. "Ear again?"

She took a bite of her toast. "Looks like it. The drops usually help. Go on. I'll be a while."

After Bill left, she touched Leon's arm. "Thank you for looking after her. Did she beg for a book?"

"She ask. Good to practice Eng-rish." He started to wash their dishes.

"It's late. I'll do them while the oil heats."

After they were in bed, Bill asked, "Is she okay?"

"Sleeping." She tugged at the sheet and collapsed. "Night."

When Peg checked on Beth at two, a low fever had bloomed, and her ear had reddened. Peg found her robe and returned to the kitchen to heat the bottle of eardrops again. As she stood by the cupboard, pulling out a small saucepan, she heard the lock on the back door rattle as Leon entered.

"You scared the daylights out of me."

"So sorry, Madam." He wore his gray trousers and boxy jacket as usual. The only hint of the hour was a tuft of hair standing like an oil gusher from the crown of his head.

"Don't you ever sleep?"

"I see light and think maybe I needed. Someone hungry? House problem?"

Her shoulders relaxed. "Beth's ear is getting worse. I'm going to warm her eardrops again and see if that helps."

He took the pan from her. "I heat water for you."

"Thanks." As he filled the pan, she sat at the table. Leon remained at the stove.

"You want to boil or just body hot? Like baby bottle?"

She held up a dark brown bottle with a rubber stopper on top. "A little warmer than a baby bottle."

After the water came to temperature, she held the bottle in it by the rubber dropper. "Thanks. I got it from here. I won't need it again until morning."

"Good night, Madam."

Minutes later, Beth fussed at being ministered to then settled down when Peg slid into the narrow bed and held her. "I know, baby. But it's going to help."

"Read to me?"

"The story Leon was reading?"

"Okay. He did it good. Like the Sunday funnies on the radio."

Peg frowned. "Like when we were with your grandfather in New York?"

Beth nodded slowly. "He made different voices like that radio man."

"Fiorello LaGuardia? The mayor?"

"Yeah, that guy."

"How'd you ever remember that? You were only five when the newspapermen went on strike, and he read the Sunday funnies."

She drifted now. "Little Orphan Annie was my favorite."

Peg eased out of the bed and pulled the sheet to her sleeping daughter's chin. "Mine too, baby."

The next morning, as Bill shaved, Peg said she might take Beth to the hospital ship if her ear didn't clear by mid-morning.

"Good idea. That was nice of Leon to help."

"Yes, but . . ."

He splashed the remnants of lather and toweled off. "But what?"

"Do you think he's a spy?"

Bill laughed. "Why? Because he helped you?"

"He's always where he needs to be. Underfoot, but he's not, really."

"Come on, Sweetheart. We're just not used to having servants."

"Staff! Can we call them staff?"

He reached for his flight suit. "Sorry."

"And."

"Okay. What is it?"

Peg said, "He knows more English than he's letting on. Better English."

"So? That makes him a spy?"

"Maybe not, but can you think about it?"

He gave her a hug and finished dressing. "Sure, but let's figure out Beth's ear first."

Bill was relieved that he only had to fly a mission, not deal with his daughter's earache. He often told young pilots that their wives had the toughest job in the Corps. They did what they needed to do. Peg going to comfort Eleanor. Maxine staying with her until the next replacement arrived. Packing up and traipsing anywhere at a moment's notice while making it look easier than it was and quietly supporting each other.

She stared at Leon as he served breakfast. When he returned to the kitchen and Beth had gone to her room, Peg whispered to Bill. "You trust Madam Tong, right?"

He answered quietly. "The embassy cleared her before I made the deal with her. Why?"

"I want to ask her about Leon. Something's not right."

Bill held his voice to a whisper, his fists clenched. "You think he's a danger to Beth?"

"No. He's been nothing but wonderful."

"You are not his boss. She is. Protocol is a big deal here. You could get him fired if she thought you were unhappy with him."

"What if I said that we think he is great, but ask why he seems like different people?"

Bill finished his coffee in silence, then asked, "Want me to talk to her?"

"No. It's my concern."

Bill got up and kissed her. "Thanks."

"Let me know if you hear about Phil."

Later in the day, Peg knocked on Madam Tong's door and stood back as the door opened. "Yes, Mrs. Ryan?"

She smiled. "I have a question, if you have a moment."

She remained at the door. "Yes, how may I assist you?"

Peg paused, wanting her meaning to be clear. "Bill has the greatest respect for you and your selection of Leon for our household. As I do. We think he is wonderful, but I have a question?"

"Yes? Something about his duties or how he manages the help? A problem with the cook?"

Peg shook her head quickly. "No. He manages the house perfectly and Beth adores him. But. His English seems so basic and accented sometimes. Yet he read a story to Beth the other night that seemed in perfect English."

Madam Tong laughed. "Come in." Once seated, she said, "And you wonder who he really is? Have we put a spy in your home?" She paused when Peg did not answer and weighed her words with care. "He learned pidgin English from dockworkers. Many Americans expected it. It offended some if he spoke well, so he learned to hide his ability."

Peg's cheeks flushed. "I can assure you that he need not hide his accomplishment with us."

After the slightest nod of her head, Madam Tong asked, "Would you join me in a cup of tea? The summer harvest of green tea."

Peg's shoulders relaxed. She sighed before she smiled, knowing the conversation was over.

That night, she told Bill how pleased she was with her discussion and Madam Tong's explanation, then after he was asleep, she wondered if she really believed it. Bill's tugging on the top sheet woke her before the alarm went off. She expected to see his usual smile. Instead, he was in a dream, jerking, mumbling. She held him until the alarm rang and she went to check on Beth, who was sleeping comfortably.

CHAPTER 15

They were well into their drinks when Claire arrived, only five minutes late. Sebastian had just shredded some poor writer's dispatch with a critique that had Jean-Claude in tears of laughter.

Mikhail frowned. "Don't be so harsh."

Claire shook off her raincoat and slid into the booth beside Jean-Claude. "How can it be this hot and rain at the same time?"

Sebastian gave a sly smile. "Secrets of the Orient. Speaking of that, what did you think of Mao as a poet?"

"Interesting. The link from his poetry to the tenets of his movement seems shaky to me. Peach trees to land reform. Turning farms over to the sharecroppers doesn't sound lyrical."

Sebastian clutched his hand to his mouth. "My God! You sound like the Algonquin Round Table."

Jean-Claude asked, "What is this table thing?"

Claire said, "Some bigwigs in the New York theater used to meet for lunch at this hotel before the war. The Algonquin. Supposedly the brightest conversation in town."

He leaned back and spread his arms over the top of the booth. "Like us!"

She chuckled. "Exactly."

David entered and placed his perfectly made old fashioned on the table. She nodded to him. "Thank you, David." He departed in his usual silence.

Sebastian lifted a glass to her. "And I suppose you fancy yourself our Dorothy Parker."

She threw her head back and gave a throaty laugh. "How do you know about them?"

"Covered a New York desk for a brief time after India. Too cold there for my liking. That's why I came here."

She took a deep drink. "For the sun?"

"Ah, that Parker sense of snappy irony."

"I'm not that sharp a wit. I'm more the Harpo Marx type."

Jean-Claude gave a half-smile. "The comic man in films?"

She laughed. "Yup. Most of the Algonquin crowd were playwrights: Benchley, Woollcott, and Kaufman. All too serious for me." She glanced at Sebastian. "What'd you cover there?"

"Plays. Worst assignment of my life. Your American wit escapes me. Or is it a matter of taste?"

She took a sip. "Speaking of taste, who has found a new spot to eat? I really enjoyed that small place you recommended, Sebastian."

He grinned. "I have a new find for tonight. Well, new for you."

Jean-Claude shook his head dramatically. "Don't trust him! Yesterday we went to a small bar after an interview at the tennis club. Promised me food. But it was all raw, unidentifiable things."

Laughing, Sebastian said, "But tasty."

Claire tugged on her raincoat. "I'll get the bill."

Sebastian said, "No, my dear. David runs a tab for our esteemed group. Anyone who wanders in *alone* for a drink is on their own, but two or more goes on the tab, which we split at the end of the month."

Claire said, "My God! Are you three fellas a club?"

Sebastian extended both arms. "We are now. I dub us knights and lady of the Booth Club."

Claire drained her drink and saw Jean-Claude sulking. "Come on. Snap out of it. Let's go."

He moaned. "It's raining."

She thought of offering to drive, then reconsidered. "On and off. We'll take a taxi."

Sebastian rose from the booth. "Then we are away! To the Palace

Restaurant on the water." Glancing at Mikhail, who was still sipping his brandy, he asked, "Coming?"

He shook his head. "No. Family dinner tonight."

Jean-Claude slipped into his raincoat and walked toward the door. Over his shoulder, he said, "Need to make a phone call. Meet you there."

Sebastian motioned for Claire to remain seated. "Relax while I use the bar phone to call ahead for a table."

Mikhail shook his head after the other two had departed. "They need such silliness. Some days, they both seem my age, but I'm old enough to be their father. Those boys have seen more than they should have for as young as they are."

"What do you mean? Here?"

"Yes, here. And before. Sebastian was a fighter pilot in North Africa."

Claire tipped her head as though she had not understood him. "What?"

"He was fit in the past. Well decorated, as I understand it. But cashed out, is that how you say it? For vision."

"Vision?"

"Virtually blind in one eye after a crash. Went into the army's press unit immediately, thence to India. Only if swimmingly drunk will he tell you how occasionally he forgot he was unarmed and got in and out of several pickles during the war. If well oiled, he might say that he was 'half the man I am now' and pat his girth. It's all a joke to him."

"Then this 'correspondent for *The Times*' is all a lie?"

"Oh, my dear, no. *The Times* is a paper in some obscure village in Scotland, and his pieces get picked up by other papers in the Commonwealth. But no. He is not writing for the one in London."

Claire paused before saying, "I would not have guessed that from his cavalier manner. He never seems pressed for cash."

"Disability pension and a little income from his writing. Travel articles mostly."

"Isn't anybody who they seem here?" She blanched at her own deceptions.

"No. This is China."

Sebastian called from the door. "Our taxi awaits!"

Once at the Palace Restaurant, Sebastian gave Claire his arm as they followed a waiter to a table overlooking the sea. He steered her into the seat with the view. Now that the rain had become a drizzle, the twilight let the slow surf and easy swells glimmer. Close to shore, fishermen in sampans dangled their oil lamps over the water.

Sebastian spotted Jean-Claude and motioned to him. "Into the breach once more. I was waiting for you all to celebrate. My treat."

Jean-Claude chuckled as he pulled up his chair. "What is it?"

"I made a bundle. Not quite winning the Irish Sweepstakes, but nice enough."

Claire blew him a kiss. "How about Mumm's all around? Bubbles go with everything."

Sebastian raised his hand for the server. "Champagne? Well, of course."

Jean-Claude poked him. "A rich man? Ready to pay me back for that evening."

"Not when ladies are present."

Claire laughed and caught her breath. "Since when did you get all rich and proper?"

Sebastian cleared his throat and tugged his suit coat into place. "You are looking at a financial genius." He whispered toward the center of the table, so the others had to lean in to hear him. "The inflation in Shanghai."

Jean-Claude frowned at him. "What about it? We all know it's out of control there. The black market here isn't as bad."

He whispered, "I calculated it."

Jean-Claude chuckled. "You calculated something?"

"My dear friends, it is not merely the black market. The scale has tipped. As soon as most of the Americans and Europeans left after the war, I saw real inflation. I have an old source there, now in an unsavory trade. I simply compared prices there to here and found such a differential that I made a move in a currency purchase."

Claire began, "How—?"

He held up his hand to silence her. "The Nationalists control the currency. The government has printed bills as fast as it can to prop up their military spending. Some have it at eighty percent of the national budget. I think it may be more. Unsustainable. And the gold behind the currency has mysteriously fled to Taiwan. And perhaps some to New York."

Once the Champagne arrived and they had toasted each other, Sebastian rattled off his dinner order to the waiter. She only caught fragments but asked him to explain.

"The pinecone carp is wondrous. Fried in a U-shape with head and tail in the air. A sweet and sour sauce glazes it. Served for the table for us to pick at. Looks like a real pinecone."

"Was there another one?"

"Dezhou chicken. Boiled, then fried whole. More familiar taste, but so perfectly simple it is like a cloud. Waiter cuts it and serves at the table. But don't let the chicken head point to anyone. That's bad luck."

She winced theatrically. "Do we have to have the head on?"

"I'll speak to the man."

Claire reached for her newly filled glass and wondered about his source on the inflation data, because it was in sharp contrast to the official briefings. Not the time or place to ask.

Sebastian assumed an even thicker English accent, becoming a lecturing professor pointing a finger at Jean-Claude. "I merely worked the differential between last week and this week if I were to buy gold. What's left. Applied the maths classes I took in the dark ages to the differential. We're still stable here, so if I buy currency there for ten cents on the dollar and sell it here or buy investment-grade gemstones at a practical discount, I make money. You understand the plan?"

Jean-Claude motioned his theory aside. "Even gold and gems have changed in value."

"I take your point. From my extensive research on the matter, I know a Sheaffer fountain pen two years ago was worth a quick trip upstairs but now it can buy a week in a bordello."

Jean-Claude leaned toward him. "I always found it interesting that gamblers only brag about winnings and never report losses, even to their friends. Your true skill is in ordering food."

Claire asked, "You think Shanghai is slipping away?"

Sebastian dropped his cheerful face and whispered. "Mik closed his branch there, sold it all. Applied to Australia for entry."

Jean-Claude put down his glass. "No! When?"

"Last week. God only knows when it will get processed. There is a reception for the press at the Australian Embassy next week. What if we popped in and lobbied for Mik?"

The waiter arrived with their first course, a crab soup with a spicy finish. When Claire tasted it, she looked toward heaven and moaned. The next dishes arrived. Sebastian motioned for another bottle.

The rain seemed harder the next morning. At dawn, Claire drove south and pulled into a small lot. She read the faded Chinese signs: shoe repair, upholstery, appliances—all late openers. While the tubes in her Zenith radio warmed, she searched for any refugees who might have slept near the stores. Turning off the battered Ford, she put the earpiece in place and keyed: *Inflation higher than embassy claims. Shanghai falling faster.* Her journal listed Sebastian's dinner selections and said the restaurant was a true jewel, worth its weight in gold.

CHAPTER 16

Major Moretti locked his desk and was about to leave for the day when Sergeant Bowen hurried in holding a paper. "I think you'll want to look at this before it gets filed."

Moretti scanned the typed page. "When did this intel arrive?"

"Couple minutes ago. I took the call from one of our informants, typed it up while we talked. Thought you'd want to vet how far it went. Started as a standard black-market tip."

"Thanks. I'll run out there now, see if I can get any flesh on these bones."

Moretti scrapped his plans for a drink at the Grand's bar, pulled his .45 from the desk drawer, and drove to Badaguan District. The rain had drenched the city all day, but now the clouds gave way to the start of a violet sunset. Turning inland from Pacific Road, Shaoguan Road shimmered with the bronzed leaves of the cherry trees torn loose from their branches by the heavy rain. He braked hard at Ryan's home, blocking the driveway by the open gate. Ryan was in fatigues, with a holstered .45 on his hip. He shoved a flashlight into a wood crate in the Buick's trunk, then heard Moretti walking toward him.

"Where's the party, Captain?"

His shoulders dropped. "No party, sir."

He watched Ryan's hands. "Your weapon chambered?"

"Never is in town."

"How about you fold your arms while we talk, anyway?"

"Yes, sir."

Moretti lowered his voice. "Are you buying or selling on the black market?"

"You don't want to know."

"Actually, I do, Captain Ryan."

"It's cumshaw." Ryan held his breath.

"A bribe? For what?"

"You don't want to know that either."

"Try me."

"Ransom. I spread the word that I'd pay for Wilson, our downed pilot. Must have told twenty bartenders. Then I get a call. A case of Johnny Walker for the guy tonight. I needed more than I could buy at the base."

Moretti cut him off before he confessed to a crime. "Where is he being held?"

"The fisherman that pulled him out of the drink took him to his village chief. They are meeting me in a cove just past the border. South of where he ditched. I was on my way to hire a boat."

Moretti lifted the case from the Buick's trunk, put it in the back of his Jeep, and threw a tarp over it. "Get in."

Ryan spread his arms in protest. "Only some of it is black market."

"Shut up."

They rode in silence past the villas of Badaguan. Moretti sped along Pacific Road toward downtown.

"Come on! You can't take me in tonight. I'll turn myself in tomorrow."

Without warning, Moretti braked hard and veered left toward the marina. He parked at the edge of the dock and waved to the watchman. "Ryan! Grab the booze and follow me."

Moretti hurried down the dock and jumped aboard a small cabin cruiser tied to cleats fore and aft along the dock. Ryan took a cautious glance. Faded paint, name in Chinese on the stern. Unlike most of the marina's boats, this one had a dinghy tied to the forward deck, canvas over the cockpit, and a large rear deck. It could have been a commercial fishing boat in a prior life. Moretti unsnapped the canvas cover and exposed a perfectly maintained cockpit. Instruments gleamed, the two seats were clean and recently upholstered. He unlocked the cabin, threw down the canvas cover, and flipped the switch for the bilge fans.

"You sure you want to go up there, Major?"

"About as much as you do. Get the booze below. Loosen the lines while I finish blowing the bilge. I'll be right back. Gotta make a call and sign out."

Ryan carried the case down into the cabin. Faded cloth covered the bench seats on either side of a table. A large bunk nestled in the bow. Ryan pulled the canvas over the Scotch and went topside. The only sounds in the marina were the hum of the bilge fans, the light lapping of the water against the pilings, and the moaning of the rope bumpers rubbing the dock. The boat rocked when Moretti jumped aboard. He fired up the engines. The cloud of exhaust cleared before the dual engines settled into a throaty rumble. Moretti shouted from the controls. "Cast off!"

They cleared the marina at twilight. Once past the outer buoy, Moretti eased the throttle open until the bow rose, slapping the small chop, then leveled at full speed. Soon after, he cut the running lights. Ryan clutched the cowling with his left hand, anticipating a collision. He rested his other hand on the butt of the .45 on his hip. He continually scanned fore and aft for any sign of another craft, but only saw small sampans near the shore. No commie patrol boats.

Ryan pointed toward the sampans. "Think they'll get anything this late?"

"They seem to catch something all year, day or night. They really know these waters, what runs in what season, how deep to drop a net or a line."

Ryan relaxed slightly. "What a beautiful night to be in this god-awful mess."

"Yeah, just sitting between two mad dogs wondering which one will bite you first. Got a map on you for the meeting?"

"No, but I know it from the air. Got some instructions for when we arrive."

"Get the chart off the map rack below. Let's see where we are going."

Moretti brought the boat back to a cruising speed. Now, without the roar of the engines, the men found conversation possible without shouting.

Ryan looked at the chart and pointed to an outcropping. "That's it."

Moretti kept the boat at an easy cruising speed. He glanced at Ryan. "What were you thinking, taking on this mission all on your lonesome?"

"That it'd be a quick in and out. Safer than overland."

"You've got a wife and kid here. Right?"

"Yeah. Daughter. Beth, she's almost eight."

"God, I miss that age. Our girls are in high school. Whole different species now. Stella and I decided they'd be better finishing up there and getting into college without coming here. Tough call."

Ryan paused, discovering a new side of Moretti. "Where?"

"Maryland. Soon as they're out of the nest, we're retiring to the Keys. My tour's about up and my wife's arthritis doesn't appreciate cold winters."

"The Keys? In Florida?"

"Yup! I'm going to run a billfish boat. Happy to take money from rich business executives that need a trophy over their mantel."

Moretti slowed the boat to a crawl as they passed the point. He chambered a round into his sidearm before the cove. Ryan worked the slide on his gun as well and holstered it. He went below, put the case on deck, pulled out the flashlight, and gave the required signal. From shore, a light echoed the same pattern.

Moretti edged closer to shore and consulted his chart. "Supposed to be a sandy bottom, open cove. But I never trust these. Get on the bow and give a shout if you see anything or we get under ten feet." He flipped on the floodlights mounted on the roof of the cockpit. Ryan saw the clear water was obstruction free and gave a thumbs-up. Moretti edged fifty feet from shore before putting the engines to idle, but not anchoring.

Ryan said, "Can you help me untie the dinghy?"

Moretti pointed to the shore. "No need! They're coming out to us."

In the light of the quarter moon, Ryan watched a large rowboat move toward them. When it came into the circle of the boat's floodlights, Ryan saw there were two men, clad only in light shirts, on the oars. A small man in a black shirt held a rope at the bow. At the stern—a blond American in a flight suit. Phil Wilson.

When the rowboat nudged the boat's stern, the man in the bow threw a line that Moretti tied to the cleat. Ryan dropped a short rope ladder over the stern, expecting Wilson to board. Instead, the man in the bow scrambled barefoot up the wooden slats of the ladder and swung onto the rear deck.

Through Ryan's minimal Chinese and gestures, the pilot and the other two men came aboard.

Ryan grabbed Wilson's collar when he slipped on the first rung of the ladder, then hauled him aboard like a fish. He said something, but Ryan pointed to the cabin door. "Go below and wait for us there. Not a word."

He shoved the case of Scotch to the rear of the deck, expecting the men to take it and depart. When they just stared at it, Ryan shrugged and opened his hands. He then took out a bottle and showed it to the men. The tallest of the three men opened it, sniffed the amber liquid, then shoved the bottle at Ryan's chest, motioning for him to take a drink. He took a small sip, then offered it to the man as though they were seal-ing the deal. He took it, corked it, and dropped it to the case. The man opened a second bottle and handed it to Ryan.

Ryan fell back on his bartering language and asked if they thought it was bad. Without looking at Moretti, he said, "They think it might be poisoned." He tapped the case with his foot and said it was 'all number one good' in English and *dǐng hǎo* in Chinese.

The tall man crossed his arms, waiting for Ryan to sample the sec-ond bottle. And so, he did.

Ryan called back to Moretti, "Help me out! I can't pound twelve shots of Scotch."

Moretti went below and returned with a glass. "Pour some from each bottle into the glass and then take a sip. See if that does it."

After Ryan sipped from the glass, the three grinned and each took a long draw off a bottle, then offered it to Ryan, who declined. The shortest man picked up the case and balanced it on the stern rail until the other two were in the rowboat. Once the case was in the boat, the last man swung over the stern, and they rowed to shore.

Ryan offered the glass to Moretti. When he declined, Ryan took the glass below. Wilson stood, but Ryan motioned for him to sit again and handed him the glass.

Wilson downed the Scotch in one gulp. "Jesus! It is good to see you fellas. Where's the rest of the search and rescue team?"

"We're it. Where's your map?"

"Hid it in my boot. Then I had time to dry it out and burn it in the shack they kept me in."

"Good. Here's the plan. When we get to the redline, we're going to put you ashore and you're gonna be a 'walk in.' Got it?" Ryan looked at the pilot's wrist. "Where's your watch?"

"They took it."

"Okay. Here is your story. You've been ducking the Reds for a couple of days, sleeping during the day, moving at night, and living off the land. Traded your watch for food. It's barely after eight now, so you ought to be home by midnight. Follow the beach. I'll have some MP or Navy shore boat spot you."

"Why can't I go with you?"

Ryan took his shoulder. "We just traded with the enemy, son."

The blank stare frightened Ryan.

He moved closer to Wilson's face. "Let me be clear. I wasn't about to leave you as a hostage any longer than I had to. I wasn't about to wait days for some paperwork to get signed off and a search party mustered over the line. Got it?"

"Yes, sir."

Ryan pointed to Moretti. "And that guy. You've never seen him. Ever!"

Hunching over, Wilson began crying and whispered, "Thank you."

As they headed south, Moretti called below. "If he's hungry, there's some canned stuff under the sink."

Once Ryan was topside, he said, "Thanks, Major."

"Tony. I think you can call me Tony now."

Ryan pointed to himself. "Bill."

Once south of the redline, Moretti anchored, dropped the dinghy into the water, and Ryan rowed the pilot ashore. They stowed the dinghy and cruised home, running lights bright in the night.

Claire stretched and looked past the half-typed page. Stuck for words, she wandered out onto her balcony for air and inspiration. She glanced at the fishing boats bobbing in their usual pattern, then saw the running lights of a cabin cruiser turn toward the marina. The dock lights were on. She grabbed her binoculars.

Two men tied up the boat like it belonged there. The older man seemed to strain to lean over, the younger one looked like a pilot. Leather jacket. Sidearm. Moved like Bill, that boxer's balance and slim hips. For a fishing trip? Their faces were in shadows, the name of the boat obscured. It was the least attractive craft on that side of the dock. She'd be able to get its name easily enough.

On a whim, Claire telephoned the Ryans' home. Leon said, "So sorry, Madam Peters, Captain Ryan is not at home. Is there a message?"

Before she could answer, Peg came on the phone. "Claire, how are you?"

"Fine. Sorry to call so late, but I had a silly question for Bill about something at today's embassy briefing."

"Can I help?"

"Don't want to bother you. I'll ask him next time I see you both at the club."

Her journal entry read: *Late fishing off the dock*. She wondered what they caught and what her secret reader would make of her interest in fishing.

Hoping to clear her mind and find inspiration for her article, she started the shower. She frowned when the telephone jangled but hurried to answer it. *Who'd be calling this late? A source?* "Claire, here."

"I know you are *here*! I saw your light in the window. That's why I'm here, too." The accent, light laughter. He was taking liberties. She chuckled.

"Door'll be unlocked. I was about to step into the shower."

"Wait! I have hot food."

She chuckled. *Who else would have the brass to bring dinner this late?* "Sure. Come up." She dashed into the bathroom, turned off the shower, and ran a comb through her hair.

He called at the door. "Hello! Ready?" He held a brown paper bag in one hand and a bottle of Pinot Noir in the other as he elbowed the door shut. "Dinner."

She started clearing her desk, then pointed to the balcony. "I should get a table for out there."

"Why? We make a picnic." He grabbed a beach towel from the back of a chair and spread it on the balcony floor.

He opened the wine and left his corkscrew on her desk. She grabbed her two tumblers and sat beside him on the towel.

As he poured the wine, he said, "You need better glasses to honor the wine."

"Oh? You think you'll dine here again?"

"I am quite certain of it. Here." He handed her a wrapped box, a foot long and an inch across. Tearing back the gold paper, she saw four ebony chopsticks.

She examined the fine carving at the top. *Classic. Elegant. Heirloom.* "Beautiful."

"They are for you, even if you pretend to need a little practice." He tore down the sides of the sack and pulled the lid off a paper box of braised pork and noodles lacquered in a light sauce. The steam from the box carried the complex aromas of browned meat, the sharpness of ginger and garlic, and the richness of sesame oil. They shared gossip and story ideas as they ate. When the late-night breeze rose, her hair fluttered, and she shivered.

"Go to your shower." He stood, offering his hand to help her up. "I'll take the trash with me."

"Leave it there. I want your opinion on a piece I'm having trouble with." She pulled a page out of her typewriter and added it to two others. "Would you mind?"

The next evening, Claire was dancing at the marina club, doing her job, wishing for a quiet evening with Jean-Claude. When the local band stopped for a break, she took a fresh Tom Collins from the Navy Lieutenant who had invited her. She listened to the bar chatter weaving through his halting comments on the band and the weather. "Just over the line. Ditched a couple of days ago. Traded his watch for food. Phil walked in last night. Lucky son of a bitch."

He asked, "Ready for some dinner?"

She put the frosted glass against her forehead. "Could we get some air?"

He beamed. "Sure. My car's outside."

"How about a walk on the dock? That ought to cool me down."

"Okay, sure."

Claire motioned to the watchman that they wanted to walk down and back. Halfway down the dock, she pointed to a cabin cruiser in need of some paint. "Who owns that wreck?"

He laughed. "Not a Navy guy, that's for sure. Some Marine. Might be Moretti's. Heard he had a ratty fishing boat here." She translated the Chinese characters on the stern to herself. *Perfect Joy. Moretti? Met him*

*when I registered and tried him for quotes a couple times. A 'no comment'
type. Why would the head MP be out in his boat at night before Bill's guy
miraculously emerged? More than loyal to a fault. Bill had balls of steel to pull
that off. And with a cop!*

Claire pointed to a trim sailboat, a twenty-footer with fresh varnish.
"Bet that one belongs to a Navy guy."

"Yeah. Captain of the *Repose.*"

She laughed. "Well, rank helps, doesn't it? Ready for dinner?"

Her journal entry was brief: *Tonight, someone said they have flying fish
here. Could it be true?*

CHAPTER 17

November started with a cold snap and dry weather. Peg's last fitting for her dress was ten days before the Marine Corps Birthday Ball. Leon waited in the car when she picked up her gown. With it swaddled in tissue in a box three feet square, she struggled to get through the crowded sidewalk from the tailor's shop to the car. Once home, she asked Leon to bring the box into the house. Opening the kitchen door for him, Peg saw that Gerri had poured a glass of iced tea.

"Making a sandwich. Want one?"

Peg laughed and glanced at the clock. "Thanks anyway, but as soon as I put my dress away, I've got to run over and get Beth."

"That for the big dance?"

"Yes. I never had one made for me before. I feel like a princess."

"Can I see it?"

Putting the large box on the far end of the table, Peg opened it and pulled back the tissue. The gently scooping neckline showed a delicate gold embroidery against pale blue silk.

Gerri almost touched it but thought better of it. "That's real nice handwork."

"I thought it might complement the gold embroidery on each side of the blood stripe."

Gerri recoiled. "What?"

"That red stripe on their dress trousers. Commemorates the lives lost at a battle in the 1800s. I forget the details."

"JD don't have that gold on his dress up pants. It's a solid red."

Peg paused, wondering if her comments would create an added riff between them. "Is that the uniform with the white belt?"

She frowned. "Yeah, his blues."

"Well, there are two sets of blues. The white-belt version is like a nice business suit. That's the one that buttons all the way up the front. But the *dress* blues are like a tuxedo for a party. It has gold on either side of the stripe, buttons at the neck, and is open at the front so you see the red cummerbund."

Gerri looked confused and asked to see the rest of the dress. Peg removed it from the box and let the tissue paper fall to the floor as she held it in front of her.

"Oh, my gosh. That looks like a Cinderella dress. Long and everything. Is everyone going to be in a long dress?"

Peg sighed. This young woman was without a clue. "Yes. Floor length, covered shoulders, long gloves optional. Men in dress blues. All super fancy." She paused, thinking back to her first ball. She had been as nervous as she was making Gerri.

"So, it's not just a dinner dance?"

"No. It's all about the Marines and their rituals. Color guard, military music, introductions, speeches, toasts, a cake cutting. Finally, we get dinner and the dance." She laughed to make Gerri relax. "I know this sounds complicated, but Bill has a simpler version of the event: cocktails, ceremony, dinner, dance, then storm the local bars. Are you going?"

"JD was talking about it, but I don't know if he got tickets yet."

"Have him check with Bill first to see if his blues are okay. Better hurry. It is a celebration of their history and a silent pledge to continue its tradition of honor and valor. They plan these to a fare-thee-well, from what to wear, to who sits where, to speeches, music, and how they do the cake-cutting ceremony."

"Cake first?"

"No, only the ceremony. It's a birthday party for the Corps. They'll have an enormous cake. An honor guard brings it in. They cut it with a sword, then wheel it away. It gets served for dessert later."

When she listed the order of events in more detail, Gerri frowned and started fussing with her glass. Peg made one last effort. "If you go, at least be punctual. This is a big deal that has a set order and will go off like clockwork."

Gerri took her iced tea and sandwich, muttering a thank you. Peg watched her go and wondered if Bill could have them seated at a different table, then recalled how Betty, a captain's wife, rescued her before her first ball. She went after Gerri.

"Wait!"

Gerri turned.

"Look. If you are going and want me to help you, I can. If you want me to butt out, I'd be happy to. Just let me know." She picked up her dress as Gerri went upstairs.

Gerri looked over the tennis court as she ate her sandwich and wondered what in the world she had gotten into.

On the tenth of November, Peg dressed Beth in her best church outfit and had Claire stay with her in the living room while she and Bill dressed. Once they were in formal attire, they entered the living room, Peg on Bill's arm.

Beth stared at the transformation from parents into these storybook creatures. Bill winked at her. "What do you think of your mother's dress? Isn't she going to be the most beautiful lady there tonight? The best!"

Beth shouted, "She's really *dǐng hǎo!*"

Claire took several pictures of them standing by the fireplace to send to Bill's parents and Peg's father in their Christmas cards. Leon and Madam Tong came into the room to take charge of Beth. Peg grinned. "Claire? Do you have time for a couple more shots of all of us?"

Claire took several portraits of Madam Tong and Leon individually, together, and as a larger grouping.

Peg convinced Bill to leave home early to avoid standing in the chilly evening during the customary security check. As usual, Gerri and JD took a taxi. After she and George left their coats in the checkroom, Trudy glanced through the window to see JD helping Gerri from a cab.

Gerri took JD's right arm as they maneuvered toward the end of the line. Trudy nudged Peg and tipped her head toward Gerri. "Watch this."

"Really? I see more than enough of her at home."

"No. She's on his right, and they're approaching a full bird colonel."

Peg smiled as JD snapped a salute. His elbow nearly clipped his wife's cheek. She stumbled back and let go of his arm. Peg shook her head.

Trudy whispered, "Maybe someday she'll learn to walk on his left when he's in uniform."

Peg noticed Gerri offer a coy smile to the colonel. "About the time she learns it's better to stay in his shadow instead of making a spectacle of herself." Peg took Bill's left arm as they went to find their assigned seats. She sighed when she saw that the name card beside her was Gerri's and that Trudy and George were sitting across the table from them.

Peg was relieved to see that Gerri's formal was a light peach and modest. He wore his regular blues, as allowed in China, for junior officers.

As Gerri took her seat, she leaned close to Peg. "Thanks for the tip about the dress. I'd appreciate it if you kinda walked me through tonight. Up to the dancing part. I got that."

"Sure. Don't drink the wine when they pour it. Trust me."

She whispered, "Rotgut?"

"No. Save it for toasts, just a sip. Tell your husband how sharp he looks and just sit here for a minute."

Peg looked around and smiled at how spit-and-polish everyone was. Then she shook her head at herself. At some level, she hated these formal events, the ritual, the drinking, the private glass clinks to absent friends, the expectations, the scrutiny, the caste system that put officers in a ballroom and enlisted men in a hangar or mess hall somewhere else.

But she loved Bill in his dress blues. Poster-boy handsome, fit, even better looking than when they first met. Now he wasn't only her husband, but a good father to Beth and half his squadron, to hear them tell it. The event reminded her how much she had missed the fellowship of the wives in the years he was overseas, seeing how elegant they were at the ball, knowing all they did, of being a part of something larger, of something important, of something special.

Escorts in dress uniforms with swords formed two lines but remained at the rear of the hall. Once the guests of honor took their seats, the master of ceremonies tapped the microphone and instructed, "Please stand for the invocation."

A scuff of chairs and rustle of gowns, then silence. Sit, stand for introductions, sit again, stand for the escorts to enter.

Heels clicking against the hardwood floor, they entered as two columns, then stepped apart, turned, and presented swords. Men snapped to crisp attention as the color guard marched between the escorts. The band played "The Star-Spangled Banner" before playing the "Marine Hymn" with gusto.

The three-layer rectangular cake sat on a large trolley, pushed by two uniformed men. Gerri strained to see the eagle, globe, and anchor of the Marine Corps insignia drawn with colored icing on top. She caught Peg's glance and straightened up.

Two Marines marched behind the cake, one who had nicked his chin shaving; the other man's face was lined and weathered. Once again seated, Gerri forced her attention to the several speeches while waiting for the cake to be cut. Finally, the colonel approached the trolley with a junior aide tagging after him. The aide presented a deeply engraved sword to the colonel over his left forearm with a flourish worthy of a knight.

After the cake-cutting ceremony, the aide quickly returned the sword to its gleaming scabbard with a full load of frosting. Those close enough to see held their breath. Three squares of cake were plated. Gerri leaned over. "Hey, thought this was later."

Peg whispered. "Only for the oldest and youngest Marines on station and the guest of honor. Shush."

The master of ceremonies announced that dinner would be served.

"About time," Gerri muttered. Peg was relieved when the young woman did not reach for her wine glass when the steward filled it.

"Ladies and gentlemen, please stand for the toasts." The men came to parade-worthy attention, glasses in hand, their ladies beside them also holding glasses.

The colonel boomed, "To the President of the United States of America!"

All hoisted their wine glasses and, as one, replied, "The President." The litany followed, toasting the order of succession into the military, then the men of this command.

Peg watched as hapless newer officers drained their glasses too early and pantomimed the later toasts. Finally, the colonel said, "And to your ladies." Peg held her glass low so that Gerri would see she was not supposed to toast herself. With the last toast, they sat, dinner was served, and wine glasses refreshed.

After dinner, the band began with waltzes and sedate selections from Glenn Miller. After one dance, Bill and George motioned toward the exit and grinned as Peg and Trudy nodded agreement. Once the senior officers departed, jitterbugs broke out at one o'clock, formals be damned. The bachelors used the opportunity to continue telling tales at the bar. Gerri and JD lingered into the night, meeting other Marines who were not pilots.

Gerri pointed to a fellow spinning a story to several women. "Who's he? That Lieutenant."

"Some tank driver. I've seen him at the gym. Wayne Argos is his name. He probably could be a professional boxer if he wasn't driving a tank. He's that fast."

She took a long appraisal. "Bet they had to let out his blues for those shoulders. Just look at that."

JD hugged her waist. "I'd rather look at you."

The next morning, the Armistice Day celebration at the parade ground began with unwelcome cannon fire and parades of hungover troops. By noon, everyone had retreated indoors.

CHAPTER 18

The first week in December, five children celebrated their birthday parties together on a rainy day at the base movie theater. The twenty-four guests then played in the adjoining game room. Beth knew two of the other children. Sally, only one. Pin the Tail on the Donkey seemed to be the favored game while mothers traded ideas on what the best winter clothing options were and wondered if they could find Christmas ornaments at the base. The women hosted an ornament-making party the following week. Peg attended but neglected to mention that she had packed theirs.

When they got home, Peg asked Beth, "Don't you think it's time to get out our special Christmas ornaments for the mantel?"

"Sure. Can we get a tree?"

"That's your dad's department."

Opening the steamer trunk in the basement, Peg pulled out a shoe-box and handed it to Beth. "How about we take this upstairs and surprise your dad when he gets home?"

Beth held the box of ornaments while her mother eased the vases to the edges of the mantel. Beth unwrapped the tissue paper from the largest bundle. Grinning, she rang the silver bell like a town crier before handing it to her mother, who ran her finger over the engraving. "I love this cluster of holly, those spiky leaves, and little berries. Dad gave us this when you were born."

"Why? I wasn't born at Christmas."

"Because he said you made us a family. It was my mother's favorite."

"Can I ring it Christmas morning?"

"You sure can." Peg centered it on the mantel. Memories of her mother ringing the bell bloomed. Other memories followed: the pang, emptiness, that inability to confide her fears or celebrate her triumphs with her. Someone at the funeral said her mother's heart was just too big, and she was too good for this world. Peg tried only to remember the first part, and her mother's laugh.

As Beth unwrapped each of the smaller ornaments, Peg's stories layered on top of each other. The big snowflake—crocheted for Bill their first Christmas together, before Beth. A ceramic starfish with a jaunty Santa hat—Pensacola. The felt cactus dotted with sequins pretending to be a string of Christmas lights—Corpus Christi. The inch-tall plastic bottle of red wine, now glued in three places—Santa Barbara. All duty stations. None from the Christmases that Peg and Beth spent with her father in Rochester waiting out the war or Bill's year in China.

"Beth? You need to keep your eyes open when we're in town. We need a special China ornament." Peg often heard "travel light to go fast." She made that motto her own by spinning it into "traveling together, we'll go far." Now she had to do both.

By the second week in December, the hard edge of winter had arrived. Cloudy days gave way to sleet and a dusting of snow. Then three days of crystalline sun and a gentle breeze lured them outdoors. Peg took Beth to the street market to shop for small gifts for other children and a knitted hat. While Peg paid for the hat, Beth lingered at a woodcarver's stall nearby.

The older man sat slumped on a stool, elbows on his knees, carving a chunk of wood the size of a fist while waiting for customers. The folding table before him displayed carved birds—no larger than a baseball—all perfectly painted. Behind the birds were small bowls with open work at the rim, like lace. Peg stood behind her daughter as they inspected the craftsmanship. Beth pointed to a cylinder not over six inches tall, hidden in the shadows at the rear of the stall. When she smiled, he handed it to her. Once in the light, it became a replica of the blood-red pagoda at the end of the pier.

Peg saw Beth's interest in it and was about to bargain for it, as Bill had taught her. She stopped when Beth cobbled together sentences in Chinese. The wrinkled carver spoke softly to Beth. They gestured and passed the pagoda between them. He pointed at the fine detail on the top and grinned. It replicated the layering of the ceramic tiles topping the pagoda. He picked up a scrap of wood and a delicate chisel and demonstrated how those cuts had been made. Beth nodded enthusiastically, then asked him something that Peg did not understand. After some added discussion, he handed it to Beth and bowed to her mother.

Peg leaned over to Beth as she opened her purse. "How much?"

"Nothing. He gave it to me. *Lǐwù,* that's the word for gift."

Peg asked Beth to thank him in Chinese. Peg offered her appreciation by examining the fine craftsmanship and saying, "*Dǐng hǎo!*"

Beth held the carved pagoda with care while Peg selected other carved items to purchase. When they got home, Beth placed the pagoda beside the other ornaments on the mantel and said, "Don't tell Dad. See if he discovers it. Okay?"

Beth fidgeted through dinner, and after dessert, bolted for the sofa facing the fireplace. Peg nudged Bill to join Beth and whispered that he should ask about her new hat—and look at the mantel.

"Your mother told me you went looking for a hat today? Are you going to model it for me?"

Beth sighed.

He nudged her. "Well?"

Beth pointed. "Dad! Look! That's our China ornament!"

He hurried to the mantel and picked it up with care. "This is beautiful. Where'd you find this, Peg?"

"Beth did, at the carver's stall. She talked to him and somehow figured out that his grandfather carved it, and he kept it for good luck, but now he is going away and wanted it to be safe. Beth promised she would take care of it."

"Wow, what a marvelous story to boost the price! How much?"

Peg raised an eyebrow. "He gave it to her. Then I bought a few things from him for gifts. Really beautiful work."

Over the next week, Peg intensified her shopping efforts to secure the trimmings for the small pine by the tennis court that Beth had designated as "The Chinese Christmas Tree." The exchange ran out of the crinkly tin foil icicles, so she cut strands of ivory yarn she had set aside to trim the scarves she had knitted for Bill and Beth. Peg and Beth cut paper circles and colored them with crayons as ornaments. On Christmas Eve, they dressed the tree.

Bill woke before Beth, to his amazement, and made coffee before Leon came over from the bungalow. He brought a mug to the bedroom and waited for the aroma to wake Peg.

"Coffee? What a lovely way to start Christmas." She sat up, pulling her pillow behind her. Before she reached for the coffee, Bill sat beside her.

He whispered, "Merry Christmas, Sweetheart." He handed her a cloth-covered box. Removing the lid, she gasped at the carved jade pendant on a slim gold chain.

"Oh, Bill! It's beautiful."

He brought his shortwave radio into the living room and found a station in Shanghai that promised a Christmas program of carols and orchestral offerings. With this playing, he started the fire Leon had laid the night before. It was officially Christmas morning by the time Beth and Peg joined him. Still in bathrobes, the Ryans gathered around the fireplace. Presents opened, they threw the paper into the fire. Bill gave Peg a framed portrait of Beth that Claire had taken. Bill opened a box containing a silver money clip with a dragon engraved on it. He hugged Beth as he clipped it to the collar of his bathrobe. "It's perfect!"

"Dad! It's for your money!"

"Really?" he teased.

Beth got a new hat for church, a sweater, leather gloves, three books, and a new bookbag. Then, pulling on coats, they hurried to the garage, where Beth found enormous bows on a bicycle with a tag from her grandfather and a tennis racket from her mother.

Leon was taking the cinnamon rolls from the oven when they returned. He motioned to the living room. "Go. I'll bring a tray." As they warmed their hands by the fire, Leon brought carafes of coffee and hot chocolate and cups with a tray of rolls, plates, and napkins.

Peg grinned. "Leon, this is wonderful. Thank you."

"Would you like me to take a tray for them?" He motioned upstairs. Peg was relieved that Leon discarded the mangled language others used to humble him.

Bill said, "Thanks, but they left yesterday to be with some friends. But would Madam Tong like some?"

"She is away now, returning at noon."

Not knowing if Leon celebrated Christmas and not asking, Bill gave him a wrapped Timex watch when he came to clear the breakfast dishes. Leon slipped his battered timepiece off his wrist, stored it in his pocket, and thanked Bill profusely.

Near noon, Leon announced that Madam Tong was inviting them for tea and small cakes at four that afternoon. Once seated and served, Beth offered a flat box to Madam Tong with a grin. "Merry Christmas!"

"Oh! For me?" The older woman barely contained her smile as Beth urged her to open it quickly. Madam Tong teased Beth by folding back the paper with great care and exaggerated slowness.

Beth jiggled her feet. "Hurry!"

Once she had opened the box, Madam Tong read its gold lettering. "Ghirardelli chocolates! Oh, my! How could you know these are my favorite in the entire world?"

Peg barely had time to wonder if she knew of the San Francisco chocolate company or was merely being gracious before she offered a small confection to Beth.

Bill said, "Peg bought them in San Francisco for Christmas and somehow hid them from us. I guess she knew how special you are to us, even before she met you."

Tea refreshed and Beth's sticky hands cleaned by a wet cloth Leon brought to her, Beth told her about her presents and the red pagoda. Cups emptied; Leon removed the tea tray.

Peg reached into her pocket but stopped when Madam Tong chuckled. "And I have something for you, too." She presented Peg with a cylindrical package barely a foot long and five inches across, wrapped in red tissue paper. The older woman looked at Beth and teased, "Can you guess what it is? Does the shape suggest anything?"

Beth giggled. "It looks like a big sausage!"

Madam Tong laughed and motioned to Peg. "Just open one end."

Bill and Beth stared as she carefully pulled away the tissue and slid out a roll of fabric. Leon took it from her and unrolled it across the table.

Bill pointed at it. "Fantastic! How did you get a photograph of the city printed on cloth?"

Peg put her hand on his arm. "It's not a photo. Look closer."

They leaned over the image of Tsingtao. Four feet long and a foot wide, the intricate embroidery showed a panorama of the city. Somehow thousands of stitches of black, white, and shades of gray thread became a detailed representation of the city as viewed from the nearby mountaintop. The orderly streets of Badaguan, the sweep of the coast, the pier, and the web of rooftops in the older section. It was all there.

Beth pointed. "Look! There's our church. And the beach."

Peg put her hand to her mouth as tears welled. "You've given us your city. How beautiful."

Madam Tong smiled. "I thought it would travel better this way. But it deserves a frame."

Bill leaned over it. "The detail is astounding. This is a treasure."

After they had examined it, Madam Tong asked Leon to carefully roll it again.

Peg pulled a small box from her coat pocket and handed it to Madam Tong. "One more gift. I hope you will like it."

Before opening it, she smiled. "You know I will."

Silver gleamed as she placed the tea strainer on the table. Mother-of-pearl handle, a silver strainer suspended on a hinge over a silver bowl to catch the drips. Madam Tong showed Beth how it worked, tipping the handle to move the drip cup to the side. At the end of their visit, Bill made a show of thanking Madam Tong and giving Leon the rest of the day off. Peg looked askance but hurried across the yard as snow fell.

Hanging up her coat, she asked, "You gave him the day off? With Charlie out this week?"

Beth got the giggles.

Peg looked at her. "Okay. What are you up to?"

Bill took Beth's shoulders. "We are making dinner tonight. Leon's *dǐng hǎo* fried rice."

Beth shouted, "The best! *Dǐng hǎo!* Leon taught us how."

"When?"

Bill confessed, "When your monthly bridge group met at Maxine's. That was the only time I wished you played weekly, like many of the gals here. Claire conspired with me once when she took you and Jean-Claude to that jazz club without me. We've been working on this for months since you're usually here at night."

She laughed. "Is that a complaint?"

He laughed. "Hardly. We've sent some pretty good versions back with Charlie to the mission school, trying to get this perfect for you."

Peg shook her head and grinned at them.

Over the next hour, she perched on a kitchen chair and marveled at how her husband became a child and her child became an adult, trading laughter and stern admonitions randomly. Several fragments of shell remained in the eggs as Bill scrambled them with a dash of sweet sesame oil. Once the eggs cooled, Beth cut them into pieces. Soy sauce splattered on Bill's shirt when it exploded in the blazing-hot wok loaded with vegetables; the mixture filled the room with the aroma of its salty richness.

Somehow, they avoided disaster as they added the cut vegetables, the perfectly diced ham, and the scrambled egg, to the rice that Leon had prepared. Once the ingredients were combined and steaming, Bill tipped the wok for Beth to scoop the fried rice into a huge serving bowl. He chopped scallions into thin circles, which Beth then sprinkled on the steaming bowl, adding a fresh onion accent to the dish.

Now discovering that they had forgotten to set the dining room table for dinner, Bill shrugged and placed the beautiful aromatic dish in front of Peg. Beth grabbed chopsticks and forks from the drawer while Bill reached for deep bowls. They ate at the kitchen worktable, seated closer together than normal.

They laughed, spilled rice, and talked about other Christmases. How Bill's parents, who were much older, popped corn that Beth helped string on a thread, and how Grandpa Ryan knocked the angel off the tree when he tried to throw the popcorn string over it. Peg reminded Beth that her grandfather always put two marshmallows in their hot chocolate. Bill laughed while telling of the Christmas spent at his parents' home, how his mother made sugar cookies, and teased Beth about icing herself and his mother's cat, Blackie, while icing the cookies.

They talked about friends from the past, when they would see them again, and if Sally could learn to play tennis with Beth. No one mentioned Gerri or JD.

Peg complimented them for the third time on the fried rice and then asked why theirs did not clump together. Bill put the kettle on for Peg's tea and explained how Leon cooked the rice and cooled it on a tray, so it dried slightly.

Beth glared at her father. "Dad! Leon said that's his secret."

Peg said, "I promise not to tell, okay?" She enjoyed a cup of tea while watching Bill and Beth wash and put away all the dishes and pans.

Once finished, Bill casually said, "Beth! You never opened my present."

"What? I opened everything by the fireplace."

"But did you look in the bookcase beside the fireplace or on the mantel?"

She bolted to the living room and fanned through the books before finding an envelope under the red pagoda ornament. She held the envelope over her head, grinning, until her parents arrived.

Peg sat on the sofa, tucking her legs under her. "Go on!"

Beth ripped open the envelope. "Whales! Can we really go out on a ship and see them?"

"It will be a boat, not your big ship. When the weather clears. I told my friend, Tony, about you seeing the whales and he offered to take us out when they come here. How's that?"

Bill assumed the big hug meant she liked her present.

Two weeks later, Tony called Bill to report that the wintering whales were arriving. Bundled up and carrying a thermos of coffee and another of hot chocolate, the family arrived at the marina. Tony waited at the gate and led them to his boat.

He turned to Peg. "She's not much to look at, but she's sound as a dollar. Twin diesels."

Beth asked, "What's its name?"

Tony laughed. "Got me. Something's written in Chinese on the stern, but I never asked."

Once they spotted the whales, Tony pulled the throttle to idle and helped Bill and Beth get on the roof. From the sheltered cockpit, Peg watched Tony slide into the chair behind the controls, his smile fading. The easy purr of the idling engines blurred what Beth and her father were saying. Peg watched Tony adjust course.

He said, "Glad you could come out today. Special time for him."

"And Beth."

"Sure. He'll never have as many of these times as he wants. I'd give my right arm to have spent more time with my girls when they were little, but the war." He shook his head and looked away before saying, "The Chinese have a thing about whales. Say they brought millet, and that sustains life, to China. Don't ask me how. But that's what you and my wife do. You bring something that makes a family."

"Sorry your family didn't—"

"She couldn't. Her old man is sick, and she's taking care of him as well as raising the girls alone. Woman's a saint. Stella."

Peg let the engine hum cover his sniff.

He said, "I coulda dodged. I was a cop with a bum leg. When we talked about my volunteering, you know what she said? 'Go. They need you. I've got it covered here.' It was that simple for her." They let the silence rest between them until they heard Bill calling for them to help Beth down.

Peg said, "Thank you so much. Beth will never forget this."

"It's easier to pack memories than stuff."

PART II

1948

CHAPTER 19

The first week in February was brittle cold. Light snow flurries canceled Bill's weekend plans to drive his family to the bluffs north of town for a car picnic and possibly more whale spotting. Saturday morning, Peg dawdled over breakfast until Leon had taken Beth into the kitchen to help make a cherry pie from cherries picked and preserved last spring. She motioned Bill into the bedroom.

He grinned, reaching for her top button. "Now? Really? Great!"

She kissed his forehead. "Nice try. Listen. Claire told me there's going to be a big parade Monday night down Pacific Road. I'd like Beth to see it."

"Right. Lunar New Year. We got a security briefing about it. Should be a huge crowd. Not the safest place for a kid."

"I know. This is crazy, but I want to rent a room at the Grand Hotel. It's a once-in-a-lifetime thing. We can take some snacks and watch the parade from the balcony."

He took a deep breath. "That's going to be a pretty penny to see some tumblers and stilt walkers and a dragon."

"That's just it. There is going to be a huge dragon dance right in front of the Grand. Two different groups are performing. If we had to be on the street, I wouldn't ask."

"This is a big deal for you, isn't it?"

She looked directly at him. "This will give Beth a first-hand look at a big part of the Chinese culture. She'll remember it the rest of her life."

He crossed his arms and sat on the bed. Peg sat beside him. He put his arm over her shoulder. "If we're going to do this, we should really do it. How about I call George and see if they'd like to join us? And you can

175

call your friend, see if she wants to bring someone." He paused. "Does the hotel even have a room facing the street?"

She smiled. "One left. On the second floor. And they need a deposit by noon."

Grinning, Bill sprang into action. "I'll get the car. Tell Leon we're running errands and ask him to watch Beth."

Once at the Grand, Peg telephoned Trudy with the plan and swore her to secrecy. On the way home, Bill stopped at Claire's hotel. She was not there, but Peg left a quickly written invitation at the desk.

Monday, after Beth was at Trudy's, Peg told Leon of their plan and asked him to make some snacks to take with them.

He recoiled. "Snacks? No, Madam. I will attend to it. There are certain traditions to be observed." She protested but stopped when Leon smiled in his knowing way.

Bill arrived home from the base at four. Over Beth's objections, Peg dressed her daughter in warm clothes. "It's a surprise," is all she would say. Half an hour later, Leon drove them to the hotel.

Trudy, George, and Sally were in the lobby when they arrived. When Bill checked in, the desk clerk notified the manager. Bill extended his hand for the key, but the manager gave him a white envelope. "Your deposit, sir, if you will follow me."

Bill glanced at Peg as they passed the second floor. The girls giggled all the way up in the elevator, then ran inside when the manager opened the door to a penthouse suite. Two bedrooms and individual baths were past the sitting area. They had decorated the entire suite for the Lunar New Year. Red paper lanterns trimmed in gold dangled from the chandelier and each doorway. Red crepe paper draped the window frames and door to the balcony. Suspended above an ornate dresser was the mask of a dragon head.

Bill objected, but the manager handed him the key and shut the door. George stared. "Holy cow!"

Both girls rushed to the French doors and scrambled out onto the balcony. Peg and Trudy sped after them. At a knock at the door, Peg called, "That's Claire. Can you get it, Bill?"

He opened the door and stood back when he saw the manager, who handed him another envelope—this one on fine stationery—before wishing him a good evening. When the manager stepped aside, the red-coated servers positioned three carts along the wall and silently departed.

The first two carts held several domed platters, which were heated by candles, a glass bowl of tangerine sections, another of sweet rice balls, and a carefully stacked tower of peanut butter and grape jelly finger sandwiches.

The last cart held three bottles of white wine and a dozen bottles of orange soda in a huge ice bucket beside a carafe of hot chocolate and a tray of mugs. On the other side of the ice bucket stood two bottles of French Burgundy flanking a 1937 bottle from the Beaulieu Vineyard. George whistled and glanced at Bill in amazement. George picked up the bottle, read the label, and carefully returned it to the cart.

Peg took Bill's arm. "I only asked for some simple snacks! I mean, Leon mentioned having some traditional food. But *this!*"

Still in the doorway, Bill read the handwritten note silently, then most of it aloud. "We wish for you the most prosperous new year. To insure this, please enjoy our gift of traditional lucky foods. Dumplings and spring rolls for wealth, longevity noodles for happiness and a long life, steamed chicken and fish for increased prosperity, and most important, sweet rice balls for family togetherness." He looked up. "It's from Madam Tong."

Inside this note, there were two small red envelopes with "Beth" and "Sally" carefully written on them. Bill slipped these into his pocket per the instructions at the end of the note.

Trudy struggled to get the coats off the girls while staring at the room when Peg said, "Toss the coats on the bed for now. We'll need them out on the balcony later." They all heard the knock on the door.

Peg grinned. Claire wore a black wool coat, had a man on each arm, and her Kodak in one hand. Sebastian had become a tan bear in his cashmere coat. Jean-Claude, on the other arm, accented his black attire with a crimson scarf.

She shrugged. "Couldn't decide which one." She nodded to each as she introduced them. "Jean-Claude and Sebastian."

Peg said, "Welcome! Coats on the bed. Bill's about to open some bottles for the tall people."

Jean-Claude helped Claire with her coat and admired her pale green silk dress and matching heels. A shirtwaist design: a wide belt at her narrow waist, a full skirt, and a string of pearls in the open neck.

Sebastian surveyed the decorations and grinned. "Lovely! Show ought to start in about half an hour. Two elite clubs are in competition this year."

Claire tipped her head at him. "He's been here forever and is quite the historian. I thought he could enlighten us on the customs."

Sebastian harrumphed. "You are too kind to have us. Auspicious, all this." He eyed the girls staring at his hulk, made an effort to squat to their level, and smiled like a favorite uncle. "You know what auspicious means? Promising, favorable, conducive to success. Lucky! All this is to make your lives wonderful. To bring you good fortune."

Beth warmed to him immediately. "Really? How can this stuff do that?"

Ever one to tell the tale, he stood, removed his coat, and said, "Well, my dears, these red paper lanterns trimmed in gold are for wealth, good health, and good fortune. And! Do you know what year it is?"

Beth tentatively said, "Nineteen forty-eight."

"Ah! Correct in our Western world. But here, it is about to become the Year of the Rat!"

Sally cringed. "Is that bad?"

"It is a fine year to be born in or do business. One can adapt to new situations."

Across the room, Claire got on one knee to take a level shot of the girls being enchanted by Sebastian, followed by several candid shots of the adults by the wine.

Bill picked up a tall bottle from the ice bucket. Jean-Claude motioned for the opener. The Frenchman then presented the wine with a flourish. "A lovely Riesling from Alsace. Light enough to start and a fine compliment to the lighter dishes and seafood. And a fine pairing if there are spicy foods under those domes. The other two are French. A Chablis, steely bright, crisp and a Montrachet, lush and round. I'll open all three but suggest starting with the Riesling."

Claire joined them, winding her film, and asked, "Where did all that come from?"

"I worked in restaurants in Saigon as a boy. Learned from the sommelier."

She shrugged. "Who knew?"

As Jean-Claude opened the Riesling, Bill asked about the red wines.

Jean-Claude poured glasses as he said, "Both French Burgundies are excellent. I might suggest them for sipping after the meal."

Bill picked up the California bottle and showed it to him. "What about this one?"

Jean-Claude took it with care. "I have never tasted this, but the maker is perhaps the most famous in America. During the worldwide Golden Gate Exposition in thirty-nine, he won three of the ten medals for his Cabernet Sauvignon. That's who made this. How did you find it?"

"All this is a gift from Madam Tong."

His eyes opened wide. "Of the tea empire? You know her?"

Bill gave a wry grin. "She mentioned a tea business."

He laughed. "I do not intend to be rude, but I wondered how you could afford the thirty-seven Beaulieu. I've never actually seen a bottle of it. Just read about it."

Peg joined them. "Bill? Do you think this is a mistake, that maybe she sent it by accident?"

He glanced at the bottle. "We'd better check with her." As Peg removed the lids from the platters, the room filled with the sweetness of the sauces, of the richness of pork, and of the light touch of garlic and ginger.

Sebastian gestured to the spring rolls stacked like golden logs. "See that? Gold ingots! The Chinese say, 'A ton of gold,' when they eat 'em. Brings wealth." They all took one and tapped the ends together as though toasting, then took a bite.

Peg and Trudy made plates for the girls, sampling everything, and planted their daughters on the floor at each end of the rosewood coffee table. The adults brought their plates to the green velvet sofas.

Sebastian coaxed both girls into bites of all the "lucky food" before they fell back on the sandwiches. After he inhaled his food and finished a glass of Chablis, he tugged on his coat.

Claire called, "Leaving already?"

"Never!" Opening the balcony door, he shouted. "I'll send up a flare."

When he came in several minutes later, everyone scrambled for their coats. It astounded Peg to discover that heaters were placed around the rim of the balcony. The hum and buzz of the crowd below filtered up to them. Streetlights cast wide circles over the onlookers. Smoke from warming fires in old oil drums along the street wafted up in the frigid evening.

Sebastian looked left, his breath steaming in the night. "Watch, here they come." Mugs of hot chocolate in hand, the girls leaned against the high railing, straining to look down Pacific Road toward the distant booming of a drum and clatter of cymbals. When the huge wooden kettle drum on wheels turned onto Pacific, Peg saw it first. "There! Rounding the corner."

Beth leaned far enough over the railing that Bill grabbed her coat. Behind the drum was a slim woman clanging hand cymbals, followed by an older man slowly banging a large gong on a red cord.

Peg felt, as much as heard, the deep pulsing of the drum's marching cadence. Then a man in a red satin outfit with gold trim appeared. He held a ball the size of a beach ball on a pole high above his head.

Beth pointed. "It's like a Christmas ornament."

Sebastian chuckled. "It is the Pearl of Wisdom! Dragons always try to catch the Pearl of Wisdom. They want truth and wisdom, as should we all."

"Is he going to catch it?"

"Wait and see. There should be a dragon soon."

As the gold dragon rounded the corner and started toward them, Beth saw two men in red ruffled trousers managing poles that held the fierce lion-like head. As they continued around the corner, she then saw ten black-clad men, each about five feet apart under the center of the long serpentine body. Each man held a pole aloft, controlling a section of the gigantic dragon's round body, five feet across and fifty feet long.

Sally shouted, "Those guys in red pajamas in front are the dragon's front feet!"

Once the golden dragon had completed the turn onto Pacific Road, the pace of the drumbeat changed to a trot. Claire leaned over the balcony for a picture. Jean-Claude reached for her elbow.

Sebastian told the girls, "Watch the Pearl closely now." Soon the dragon became a living thing as its head bobbed up and down. The jaw snapped. The gold dragon slithered forward.

Trudy nudged George. "That thing must weigh a ton. Wonder what they stuffed it with? It's so round."

Sebastian said, "Hollow, in fact. Bamboo hoops. Lightest thing I could imagine. Allows them to be so nimble."

Now the gold dragon began a new move, following the Pearl weaving from curb to curb, the crowd shouting in mock terror as it slithered from side to side and lunged toward the crowd then the Pearl of Wisdom. As each segment echoed the head's movement, Beth squinted. Now the ball bobbed up and down. Chasing it, the dragon moved quickly from side to side, the massive puppet becoming a sinuous beast. Beth laughed and pointed. "It looks alive!"

Straightening out, the gold dragon moved forward until it was right under their window. Then it curled into a tight ball, reversed direction, and retreated.

Claire gasped. "Look! There's a red one coming up from the right."

Beth called, "Are they going to fight?"

Peg said, "A pretend fight."

The red dragon moved forward and did its sinuous dance under the window. Sebastian said, "It's showing off its moves and boasting its strength. Watch, it is going to retreat."

The drummer slowed to a walking pace.

Sally asked, "Is that all?"

Sebastian pointed at the gold dragon facing them, as the red dragon turned. "Now, it is about to get interesting. They are going to stare each other down for a bit. Let the dancers catch their breath."

Peg stood near Sebastian as he spun a tale to the girls. Snatches of history about the Han Dynasty, then the look of the dragon: horns of a stag, ears of a bull, tiger claws, fish scales, and the fearsome white teeth in that scarlet mouth! He leaned down and confided, "The dragon is in the clouds, and made of clouds. If you look hard enough when you are older, you might see other dragons."

Sally asked, "Even in America?"

He nodded. "Dragons can go anywhere and be anything when they are in their search." He stopped, waiting to see if the girls understood.

Beth said, "For the Pearl of Wisdom."

He beamed. "Precisely!"

Claire nudged Jean-Claude. "How did our Sebastian become someone's grandfather?"

He chuckled. "Even more astounding. He's drinking orange soda— for now!"

"The world is ending!"

The drumbeat changed again to a sprint. The larger cymbals crashed and clanged.

Sebastian announced, "The battle begins!"

Jean-Claude grinned when he put his arm around Claire's shoulder, and she leaned into him. Sebastian glanced at Claire to say something, then turned away.

Suddenly both Pearls of Wisdom sprinted toward each other. The dragons raced after them.

Beth held her breath expecting a collision, until both Pearls veered to their right, their dragons passing side by side. Then they faced each other again, and the battle continued.

The dragons passed each other again. But this time, they began a complex maneuver: the gold dragon passed under the red one's belly. The faster the kettle drum pounded, the more intense the serpentine twining became. One over the other. One under the other. The booming of the hand gong joined the drumbeat and clatter of cymbals. The two twined again, separated, and sprinted at each other.

"They're gonna crash!" Beth shouted. As they barely passed each other, they slowed, coiled into a neat ball, and settled to the street near their own Pearl of Wisdom. The drumbeat slowed, then stopped. The cymbals continued while the man with the hand gong went into the middle of the street and stood between the sleeping dragons and clanged it ferociously.

The men abandoned their poles and collapsed on the side of the street, panting, their dragons now mere tubes of fabric devoid of magic. The Pearls of Wisdom lay on the sidewalks, their tenders now flat on their backs.

Sally pointed at a woman passing a sack among the bystanders. "Look! They want to get paid."

Beth glanced at her father. "Can I give them some money?"

Bill pulled out his silver money clip and counted out a few American banknotes. "I'll do it." Jean-Claude added some high-denomination Chinese notes.

Sebastian pulled a handful of notes from his wallet. "No need for you to go down, dear boy. It's brass-monkey cold down there, and I'm off to fresh adventures." Sebastian took the money from Bill and shook Peg's hand. "I cannot tell you when I have had a more enjoyable evening. Thank you so much."

When he opened the door, two hotel bellboys entered, removed the food carts, the three empty bottles of white wine, and wheeled in a cart with hot chocolate, coffee, tea, and slices of chocolate cake.

Peg asked, "You'll come back for dessert, won't you?"

He tipped his head toward Claire at the end of the balcony. "I fear I would be a third wheel tonight. Well, I'm off."

Once on the street, Sebastian made their donation, saluted toward the balcony, then ambled into the crowd. Beth and Sally waved at him.

Bill asked Jean-Claude to open a French wine. He poured a little and handed the glass to Bill. He tasted it and rolled his eyes. "Is this as excellent as I think it is?"

"She is a generous woman. Should be incredible with chocolate cake."

Claire sat beside Jean-Claude on a sofa and sipped. "This is decadent."

Trudy poured hot chocolate for the girls. "At the very least!"

When Bill delivered the red envelopes to the children, Beth asked, "What's this for?"

"It's from Madam Tong. If you get money tonight, you will get more in the coming year."

Sally said, "Neat!"

They ripped open the envelopes and examined the Chinese bank notes.

Jean-Claude asked, "And what do you intend to do with your new fortune?"

Sally thought hard, then blurted, "Buy a Chinese doll!"

Beth bit the edge of her lip. Claire asked, "Any ideas?"

"A book. But I don't know which one I want now."

Jean-Claude smiled at her. "What are the books you enjoy?"

"Stories about different places and people. Like *Pippi Longstocking* in

Sweden. And *The Little Mermaid* in Denmark. And *The Secret Garden* in England. Daddy reads them to me and does voices. His Wizard of Oz voice used to scare me when I was little."

"Have you been to the English bookstore in town?"

"Sometimes, but usually, my grandfather sends new books."

At nine, Bill walked George, Trudy, and Sally to the lobby and put them into a waiting taxi. When he returned, he saw that Beth was dozing on the sofa. He picked her up and took her to the smaller bedroom. Peg pulled covers over her without waking her to change into her pajamas.

As Bill shut the door, he whispered, "I figured she'd get to sleep about tomorrow after all the excitement and chocolate. What'd you do, slip her a glass of wine?"

Peg chuckled as she sat on the edge of the sofa beside Bill, tucking her legs under her and smiling at Claire on the other sofa. She frowned when Jean-Claude stood. "I hope you both will stay. There's plenty of time for more wine and conversation."

Jean-Claude opened the second bottle of Burgundy—to Claire's delight—and shared Sebastian's slice of cake with her. Tales of favorite foods, silly school pranks, and favorite books and films rubbed away any memory of the war or concern about the city falling.

Jean-Claude seemed lost in thought. Claire nudged him. "Where'd you go?"

"Wondering if there is a translation of *Le Petit Prince* into English. Probably as *The Little Prince*. Small book by a Frenchman, an aviator. Takes place in the Sahara. A downed pilot meets a traveler arriving on an asteroid. They debate nature or science in the most humorous, no, the most thoughtful, manner."

Claire looked at him anew. "A children's book?"

"I think it is a fraud to call it that. It only appears to be a child's book, but any age can read it. If they don't have it, I could translate it for her. Perhaps interest her in the French language and her travels to other lands via the magic of books."

Firecrackers popped sharply along the street. Bill looked toward the bedroom door, expecting Beth to emerge. Jean-Claude laughed. "How did it become so late? The noise wards off the evil *Nian,* which emerges at midnight."

Claire finished the last of her wine. "Well, guess it's safe to go now." After the exchange of "Happy New Year" wishes and hugs all around, they left.

Peg checked on Beth. "Out like a light, still."

Once in bed, Bill held her close. "Is this what you wanted?"

"More than I could have imagined."

That night, Claire woke before Jean-Claude, watched the sunrise, and wondered why Sebastian had Australian pound notes in his wallet. Her journal entry would have to wait until much later in the day.

CHAPTER 20

The Thursday before Easter, Trudy and Peg surprised the girls by declaring Friday their Easter school holiday. Only on the drive home did Peg tell Beth that George had rented a mountain cabin as a surprise and that the Franklin family would be gone during the three-day weekend.

When they got home, Beth ran into the kitchen, math lessons in hand, announcing she didn't have school until Monday. Leon opened a tin of sliced apples and reached for the sugar. "No lessons? Want to watch?"

She pulled a chair out from under the worktable and sighed as he put a large bowl on the table. "Sure."

"What's that long face all about?"

"Sally won't be here for Easter. And the math lesson is hard."

He measured out the pie spices and glanced at her while Charlie washed dishes. "Sometimes doing something else can clear your mind and make tasks easier. Want to help?"

"Okay. But just a little. It's gonna take me forever to get these figured out."

He pointed toward the sink. "But for now, wash your hands and then stir the apples until the sugar and spice are all over them. Think you can do that?"

"That's easy." She did as she was told and picked up the bowl. "That's a lot of apples."

"Enough for two pies. Your mother is taking one to her friend Maxine tomorrow morning." He began rolling out the pie dough on a floured corner of the big worktable and pretended not to notice when a slice of apple hit the floor.

"Leon? When are the trees going to be pink?"

"You mean the full blossom? In a few weeks if the weather cooper-ates. If you look closely, you can see the little buds on ours."

Beth let the spoon clank against the bowl as she finished and put it beside Leon. "Mom says you know about antiques. Is that right?"

He slid the dough into the pie tin and started rolling the second ball. "Some."

"Do you know about rings, too?"

"Some."

"Could you help me look at a ring and see if it's fake and ask how much it costs?"

"You want a ring? Did you ask your mother?"

"I can't. It's for her. We saw it when we were in town, and she said she loved it but wouldn't spend that much on herself, but I don't know how much it really is. They won't let me go into town alone, and Dad's busy, so I thought you could take me."

"Let me think about it while I finish the pies."

"Okay." She climbed up on a stool and watched him.

He glanced at her. "Do you think Madam Tong might like to have tea with you this afternoon?"

"I'll go ask her."

That night, JD was unusually silent during dinner. Gerri picked at her food before letting her fork clatter on the plate. "I don't know why you think going up in the hills to kill something is a good idea."

"It's a boar hunt. I'm never gonna get a chance like this in the States."

"Maybe that's a good thing, ever think of that?"

"Come on. It's just a couple of days."

She snapped. "Three days! You're gonna be gone tomorrow and the entire weekend! If you're gonna take leave, we coulda gone somewhere for Easter like up to that pretty mountain place."

"I'll be back in time to take you to dinner at the club Sunday night. How's that?"

Gerri pouted. "In town? A fancy place. It's Easter, you know!"

Bill hesitated, then asked, "Think the weather's gonna hold?"

JD scowled at Bill. "The guys I'm going with have done this before. They know what they're doing."

Bill glanced at Peg.

Gerri pointed to Bill. "Listen to him, will ya? It's a dumb idea to roll out there in the woods if the weather's bad."

"He never said it's going to be bad."

She folded her napkin and dropped it on the table. "He as much as said so. Don't you ever listen to anyone but yourself?"

Beth followed the bickering as though it were a tennis match.

Peg sighed. "Anyone for pie?"

Gerri pushed her chair back. "Thanks anyway." JD followed her upstairs and slammed their bedroom door.

After dinner, Peg trundled Beth off to her bath as soon as possible.

That night, Bill held his arm across the bed as she got in. "Come here. What are you so riled up about? You were jumpy as a cat during dinner."

"She's making me crazy."

He said, "Tell her."

"What? That she's rude and drinks too much when they go out and is still disrespectful to Leon."

"Bet she knows that already." She crossed her arms. "I hate being civil to her, but I can still hear my mother. 'She's a guest in our home. You don't tell off guests.' And she's right."

"She's a renter! They *rent* from us. At least they are paying their way now."

"Yeah, some for food. Couldn't they go rent someplace else? If she'd quit spending his paycheck on cocktail dresses and jewelry, they could."

"There isn't housing, Peg. Believe me, I check at work and call church all the time. Refugees who can afford it are twenty to a room downtown. Besides, it won't be forever."

She groaned. "It's going to seem like it."

He laughed.

She flung her pillow at him. "Stop that!"

Friday morning, Beth woke to JD and Gerri screaming in the living room and the slamming of the front door. She dressed herself and waited in the kitchen for Leon to arrive. Over breakfast, she grew increasingly distracted and cranky.

At ten, Peg took the pie to Maxine. Beth spread three pages of math problems over the dining room table. When Gerri walked past her toward the kitchen, she paused and looked over Beth's shoulder. "What's that?"

"Stupid homework for next week. Sally's gone, and I'm stuck here, so I may as well do it."

"Looks like multiplication to me."

"Well, it's hard."

She sat beside Beth. "Always is at the start. Can I see?"

Beth slid the pages in front of her. Gerri looked over the problems and sat back. "Okay. I see what they're getting at."

"You do?"

"Sure. This is easy. Multiplication is nothing more than a slick way to add numbers fast. That's why you memorize your multiplication tables. Do they have you doing that now?"

"Yeah, but it's hard."

"Just at first. I know some tricks. Want me to show you?"

Beth sat straighter. "Sure."

"You up to your tens yet?"

"Like ten times something?"

Gerri said, "Yeah, those are easy. Just add a zero. But how about the nines table?"

"That's harder."

"You know how to subtract?"

Beth huffed. "That's easy."

"Okay, for the nines, think of the tens and subtract nine from the total. So, ten times nine is?"

"Ninety."

"Minus nine is?"

"Eighty-one."

"And so is nine times nine."

"Oh, yeah."

"See a pattern? But that's for starters. When you memorize it all, you can do it in a snap, and get it all right. Hey, I got an idea. You gonna be here a while?"

"Yeah."

After pouring her iced tea, Gerri returned to quiz Beth. A few minutes later, Leon brought her an old abacus. "Thanks, Leon. Beth, this is a Chinese adding machine. Let's use it to do some multiplication."

"Can you do that?"

"Yes! In a shop, I asked the lady that added up my bill to show me how it worked. It's fun."

For the next hour, Gerri used the beads to illustrate the multiplication tables, then invented problems and slid the beads from the ones column to the tens column and into the line of beads representing the hundreds and even thousands. Beth slid the beads slowly at first as she went through her multiplication tables. Their game picked up speed and accuracy. By the time Leon interrupted them to offer lunch, Beth had completed her homework and was playing with the abacus. She and Gerri laughed and created math problems for each other. After lunch, Gerri retreated upstairs to read her movie magazines.

When Beth discovered that Leon was going out, she never went to Madam Tong's as she said she would. She talked Charlie into abandoning his kitchen duties and taking her into town in a rickshaw. She sat forward in the seat so she could see past the tall sides of the rickshaw, like she did when her father took her for rides.

Traveling on Pacific Road just past the marina, Beth saw her father's Buick heading toward the house. She leaned over as if to tie her shoe. But Bill saw her, turned the car around, and honked at the rickshaw. As usual, the rickshaw-coolie pulled to the edge of the road to let the car pass. When the Buick pulled to the side of the road ahead of him, he stopped.

Bill slammed the car door and ran to the rickshaw.

He glared at Beth and ignored the cook. "What are you doing out here?"

"Going to a store."

"Where's your mother?"

"Out somewhere."

"Get in the car."

"What about him? I promised to pay."

Bill fished a few bills out of his pocket and told the cook to take the rickshaw home.

Scowling in the front seat, arms crossed, Beth was silent as her father started the car. "How'd you do it?"

"Do what?"

His knuckles were white on the steering wheel. "Give them all the slip?"

"Mom's still out. Leon went shopping. I never went over to Madam Tong's."

"Don't you think she'd be worried if you were missing?"

She looked down and squirmed. "I guess, but I never told her I was coming."

"Do you think that was okay to duck out?"

"Probably not, since you're so mad."

"I'm not mad, but I'm disappointed and relieved you are safe. I want you to apologize to Madam Tong for not keeping your word and to Leon for leaving. You need to be good to your word if people are going to trust you. And to the cook for getting him in trouble."

"He didn't know better."

"He should have. When we get home, you can go to your room and think about why I'm disappointed with your actions today. Your mother and I will discuss this and decide on your punishment."

"Can't you make me miss a movie on Saturday?"

"Why? So, you don't have to think? Nope. I want you to understand why this was wrong."

She knotted up her fists. "Are you going to tell Mom?"

"No! You are. We don't keep secrets."

"I can't tell her."

"Why?"

"Because I was going to see how much a ring cost for her Easter present to match the jade thing you gave her for Christmas, and nobody would take me. She saw it when we were in town and loved it. She wouldn't ask how much. It's perfect for her, Daddy. Just perfect! But you are too busy. Leon's too busy." Her tone shifted. She spread her arms theatrically. "Obviously Mom can't!" She sat back and crossed her arms again.

Bill swerved off Pacific Road into the marina parking lot and stopped the car by the club door. "I'm gonna call home and tell them you are okay." She did not leave the car. "Come on."

Marching into the club, he parked Beth in a booth in the empty bar and ordered two Coca-Colas in bottles with straws. He used the phone at the end of the bar to call home, picked up the two sodas, and slid one to Beth.

"I'm not thirsty."

He sat across from her. "Drink up."

After a few minutes of not looking at her father, she muttered, "Thanks."

"Sure. Think you can straighten up and fly right?"

"Yes, sir."

"Good. Now you are going to give me the full story. From the start."

When they arrived at home, Bill asked Leon to serve an early dinner, knowing that his daughter would not keep her secret much longer. Beth prodded her mother to hurry to the dinner table and then got the giggles.

"What's that all about? It's not even six! You think it's Easter already?" Beth squirmed as Bill pulled up his chair. "Okay, Beth!"

"Mom! Put your napkin in your lap!"

Peg shook her head and reached for the folded linen, then noticed the bump. Carefully pulling back the cloth, she put her hand to her mouth. She looked first at Bill, then Beth. "What have you two done?"

"It's the bunny! He's early!" Beth shouted.

"Happy Easter, Darling." Bill gave her a peck on the cheek. "Open it before Beth explodes."

Peg's eyes clouded as she tried on the ring. "Oh, my." She blinked as she modeled it for Beth. "This is simply amazing."

"The jade matches the one Daddy got you for Christmas. Same color exactly!"

"It certainly does. Thank you." She reached over and held both of their hands, struggling to find the words.

CHAPTER 21

The hunters braked when the rutted road became a deer trail. Wayne and JD got out of their Jeep and walked over to Sam, Ben, and Richard, still in the other Jeep.

Sam said, "Get your gear."

Wayne pointed east. "Hey, there's a tank track about a half mile that way from an incursion about six months ago. Doubt if it's grown over by now. Why don't we take it?"

Sam laughed. "Or we could ask the General if we could borrow the Marine Band to announce our arrival."

Wayne shrugged off the comment. Half an hour later, they found a grove of oak trees that looked plowed. JD pointed. "Pigs did all that?"

Ben said, "Yup. Wild boars ain't pigs!"

Sam pointed to a rocky outcropping a couple hundred feet above them. "We'll overnight up there where there's nothing to interest them." They shared set-up duties at twilight and ate cold rations, then settled into their bags under a cloudy sky.

At dawn on Saturday, Ben lit a can of Sterno to heat their breakfasts. Breaking camp, Sam checked the others out on the weapons and led them along the outcrop into a valley. As they trekked north, signs of the hogs were obvious. Rooting at the edge of a meadow. Droppings were fresher. It was late afternoon when they came upon a grove, dense with oaks and littered with acorns.

Sam said, "This here is a cork oak patch. Boars love these acorns. Since this is the next patch up from where they ate yesterday, I figure it's a prime spot to set up a blind and wait for them to get hungry."

JD asked, "Think they'll come this late?"

"Maybe. But I think it best if we make camp on that bluff, anyway. JD, stay with Wayne and me. Richard, go with Ben. We'll all set up a blind up there so there's no chance of a crossfire. Going to be a rock scramble on the way up, so empty chambers until we're in place."

JD whispered to Wayne, "I thought we'd go after them. Hunt them down."

"Easier to let them come to us."

They followed Sam up a crumbly dirt face at the base of the bluff. Richard lagged, poking at the bark on the oak with his K-Bar. "They really make corks outta this stuff?"

Before Ben could answer, a thrashing in the underbrush made Richard turn. "Run for it!"

Three boars, each barely smaller than a Jeep, charged into the grove, snorting. Dry leaves and twigs crackled under their hooves. Ben chambered a round. He took aim, but Richard sprinted into his line of fire, blocking the shot.

The first boar clipped Richard, who flew over the boar's back and landed badly. The other hogs ran past Richard directly toward Ben. He took his shot, felling the first of the three boars. The others veered into the underbrush as their leader pitched onto his shoulder and let out an unearthly howl before it shuddered and was still.

Richard moaned. He had flipped to his back and pulled his knee to his chin. Sam and Ben held their rifles at the ready, expecting a charge from the thicket as Wayne and JD knelt beside him. Wayne said, "Ankle's all fucked up."

Sam came over, still watching the underbrush. "How bad?"

JD said, "Bad."

Sam looked at the tilt of the swelling ankle. "Broken for sure. Gotta carry him out. Where's that tank track from here?"

Wayne pointed east. "About a mile that way. If you get him there, I'll drive up." Still on watch, Ben sidled up, glanced at the ankle. "Yup! It's a pack out."

Richard moaned and pointed to the boar. "Can't we take any of it? Seems only fair."

Sam laughed. "You are one tough mother, aren't you? Want us to take it or you?" He looked at Wayne. "Think you can make it to your Jeep before dark?"

Wayne said, "If I run."

Ben stepped forward. "Nobody goes alone. The Reds are still probing the perimeter."

Wayne said, "Got a better chance of running into a smuggler than a Red."

"Either way, take your pal and keep your head on a swivel going down. Get as close to your Jeep as you can tonight. You can't use the headlights, so get up to the tank track at first light. Otherwise, we'll be lugging him three days from now."

JD turned to Wayne. "Can we merge gear and go light?"

Wayne scanned the dark clouds coming from the north. "Yeah. I think we can beat the rain."

But they didn't.

An hour later, the light faded. The mist became sleet. Drenched through, JD curled himself into a ball under a tree to escape the chilly rain. Wayne pulled him up by his collar. "Get the hell outta there. Ain't you ever heard that lightning hits trees? Same here in China. Come on. We passed some caves on the way up. Not deep, but enough for shelter."

Within twenty minutes, they came upon cliffs with pockets of erosion at the base, some as deep as ten to fifteen feet. The entrances were three to five feet high, and less than five feet wide at the base.

"Grab the light and see which is deep enough and not something's lair. Be careful."

JD found one that was ten feet deep but under five feet high. After he had thrown several rocks into it and flashed his light around, he shouted for Wayne. "Think I got one!"

Wayne hurried to it and fanned his light around the cave. "Better than any I found. Go in and open two rations. I'll cut some branches with my K-Bar. Easy enough to cover the opening and hold in some of our body heat after dinner."

JD swept together a pile of dry twigs and leaves from the floor of the cave. He was about to light it when Wayne returned with heavy pine boughs in each hand and blocked the entrance. He flipped on his flashlight and left it angled against the wall. "Stop. We gotta eat 'em cold. Reds could smell the smoke for miles. That's why he used Sterno to heat breakfast, not wood."

The storm had soaked JD. He leaned against the cave wall and pulled his knees in tight as he spooned the cold beans and franks in as fast as he could. When they finished, Wayne held out his palm for the empty tin. JD's hand shook as he handed it to Wayne.

"Use your web belt and holster for a pillow and wrap up tight in your poncho. Get against the cave wall. It's still got some heat from the day. I'll tuck in on the other side of you. You'll shake off the chill soon."

After stowing the trash in his backpack, Wayne crawled near JD and killed his flashlight.

"You good?"

JD muttered, "Sure. Night."

About ten, Wayne woke to JD shaking violently. "Are you okay?"

"Cold. Need a Saint Bernard with a keg of brandy."

Wayne flipped on his flashlight and dug in his pack. "No such luck. Here. Chinese version of Life Savers. Chew a couple."

While JD unwrapped the candy, Wayne vigorously rubbed his legs and upper arms. "I'd tell you to do some jumping jacks, but you'd hit your head."

"Yeah. That's all I'd need. Thanks, it's getting better."

Wayne pulled his poncho over himself and motioned to the candy. "Finish 'em up."

JD shoved the wrapper into his pocket and pulled on his poncho. "Jesus, I'm never going to get warm again."

"Shut up and get some sleep. Sugar'll kick in soon." Wayne snuggled in behind him and wrapped his poncho around them.

Near midnight, JD woke, his right arm numb. He shifted, then felt Wayne's hardness pressing against his back. He chuckled and pulled the poncho tighter.

Wayne moaned. "You awake?"

"Half-freezing."

"I can get your blood moving."

"Jumping jacks?"

He started massaging JD's upper arm, then his chest. "You getting wood too?"

JD didn't answer, but his body said yes. *Why him? Why now? Is it want, or the cold, or the fire in my crotch?*

Wayne's deep massage worked down JD's chest to his belly. He let his hand rest on JD's belt buckle. Waiting. JD put his hand over Wayne's. A moment later, he pushed it aside, paused, then released the clasp.

The first time was fast. First JD then Wayne. Their heat overcame the cold. Then they explored each other. Wayne's bulldog physique and thick thatch on his chest and belly contrasted to JD's sleek muscles under fine hair. Calloused hands running over JD's lean muscles. Bristles against his neck. Touching. Then sorting out the tumbled clothes, pulling on pants, Wayne buttoning JD's shirt, helping him into his jacket.

Hours later, JD woke with a start and slid out of Wayne's embrace. He sat up. Still dead dark in the cave. He crawled toward the faint light behind the branches and stood in the open. Trees were still dripping.

As he peed, he watched the fingers of fog rolling through the valley and wanted a cup of coffee. Did he dream a wet dream of Wayne's hands on his body or want it or do it? Stone sober, he struggled to sort out the night. But his body remembered.

When he returned, Wayne had broken camp and put their packs at the mouth of the cave. He swept branches over the prints of their bodies in the dry red soil. Divots from knees and boots and elbows. Swirls from their sleeping embrace. All a memory now as he scattered the branches.

JD slung his pack over his shoulder, like it was any other Saturday. "Morning. Let's go."

When they arrived at the Bismarck Barracks late Saturday afternoon, they discovered the sick bay there was closed. Wayne said, "I'll take Richard to the *Repose*. JD lives in town, and I'll need to drop him off, anyway."

After they helped their injured buddy board the hospital ship and were back in the Jeep, JD tried to ignore the pressure in his shorts. Three minutes of baseball scores failed to diminish his desire. *Shit. I'm not a teenager.* This was new, and the lust was fresh.

Wayne glanced at him. "Time for a drink?"

"Looking like this and smelling like hell?"

"I know a place."

"A quick one."

Cresting Chungshan Road, passing the churches, Wayne veered into an alley near the tailors' row. He braked by a green door and dug in his jacket pocket for his door key. "It's a postage stamp of a place, but it's all mine."

"How'd you find it? Heard that was impossible."

"Don't ask."

Once inside the dim entryway, JD blinked. Wayne kissed him, pressing him against the door with his longing.

When Wayne dropped him at the curb Sunday morning, their hair was still wet from their shower. JD hoped his wife had gone to brunch with some of her girlfriends. He heard the kitchen door slam and Gerri calling his name.

"Yeah, it's me." He bolted upstairs, stripped quickly, and left his crumpled clothes on the bathroom floor. The water hadn't heated when he slid under it, wetting his hair, shivering.

She opened the bathroom door, drink in hand. "How's my boy doing? How was hunting?"

"Great. What's up?" He soaped quickly.

"They just left with the kid. Easter church ought to go on forever. I thought we might fool around."

"Uh. Sure. I'll be out in a sec."

She picked up his filthy clothes and dropped them into the hamper.

CHAPTER 22

The June day was warming as Beth dawdled over her cereal. Peg checked her watch. "Get moving. Trudy's going to be here soon."

"No lessons today! It's Saturday! Why do I have to go over there?"

"We have things to do if you want your birthday party to be fun."

Beth listened to the clatter behind the kitchen door. "What's Leon doing?"

"None of your business. Finish your cereal."

"Can I take my dishes to the kitchen?"

"Not today! Go wash up."

As Peg put Beth into Trudy's car and watched them drive away under the shade of the cherry trees, she felt a sheen of sweat on her upper lip. *Not another scorcher, please!*

She followed the yeasty sweetness of the cupcakes into the kitchen. "Smells wonderful."

Without interrupting his work racking the cupcakes, Leon said, "Extra vanilla is my secret."

The bell at the street gate rang. Leon told Charlie to keep working, let in four day-laborers, and led them down the driveway. Soon, the tennis court became a party venue with a stage on one side of the net. They had arranged tables and chairs on the other. A long buffet table was situated against the back fence. When he returned to the kitchen, Peg asked, "The food?"

"Everything is ready. Baked beans, potato salad, all ready. Hot dogs and buns from the commissary are ready for Captain Ryan to cook over the charcoal brasier." He added, "Stage is ready for the record player for the games. And Madam Tong has a surprise for your guests."

"What is it?"

He tipped his head and raised his eyebrows.

She laughed. "I get it. It's a surprise."

"Should I set up a bar outside?"

"No. Just the lemonade. Two big pitchers. I'm going to spike one for the grown-ups and make the kids pink lemonade."

About one, a donkey cart with a steamer trunk blocked the driveway. A stocky man held the donkey's harness while a young boy pulled the bell chain. Leon motioned them into the driveway and helped the man move the heavy trunk into the garage.

At four, the guests began arriving, girls in dresses, boys in play pants, all bearing gifts.

Peg's friends from church soon engaged the children in a series of games. Then the guests sang songs that blared from the record player. While the children played, Peg made her way around the adults with pitchers of lemonade. Leon brought the bowls of potato salad and baked beans to the table while Bill manned the grill. She caught snatches of conversation between two mothers as she refreshed their glasses. "Growing like weeds."

"It wouldn't be so obvious if there were actual stores for them."

"The tailors are fine for a church dress, but I wouldn't pay them for play clothes."

"Look at them. Half the boys are in high-water pants, and most of the girls are wearing hand-me-downs that are too long."

"No point in hemming them. I only baste them up."

"True. I don't want them to look like ragamuffins in the snapshots."

Peg noticed Andy Anderson by himself with an empty glass. He smiled as she held up a pitcher. "No thanks. Just dropped by to see the birthday girl and leave a gift."

"That was sweet of you. How's Maxine?"

"Says fine, but her legs are killing her. She swears she's as big as a watermelon."

Laughing, Peg shook her head. "Summer seemed twice as hot in the last days before Beth arrived." Peg took his arm. "If you need anything, call me. That last couple of weeks can seem awfully long." Peg hoped the *Repose* didn't go out to sea.

He whispered, "Bill said you've delivered babies. If—"

She nodded. "It's going to be fine."

Andy gave her a bigger hug than Peg expected. "Thanks for the invite."

Major Moretti arrived in uniform, holding a small gift box. "Hey, Bill! Sorry I'm late." He wandered over to the table with gifts and returned to help Bill grill the hot dogs.

Peg noticed Gerri standing in the shade at the far end of the tennis court. JD stepped in behind her, handed her a pink lemonade, and wrapped his arm around her waist.

"Lemonade? I want another martini."

"Later. We had enough to coast for a while."

She put her hand on his muscular forearm, and said louder than necessary, "Damn, babe. You've really been working out, haven't you?"

"What'd you think I was doing at the gym, just whistling Dixie? I gotta have the strength to wrestle that pile of iron in the sky."

He nuzzled the back of her neck. "Hey, this ought to be something. Musical chairs! Look at them, half the kids have lost their front teeth. Looks like a bunch of hillbillies."

Claire's arrival interrupted Peg's thought of throttling Gerri right there. "Looks like I'm in time to help."

Peg handed the pitcher of pink lemonade to Claire. "Top off anyone. The pink is for kids. I spiked the other one. I'll hang on to it."

Bill called for everyone to get their food. Once the diners finished, Leon and Charlie brought out trays of cupcakes. Leon then escorted Madam Tong to the chair reserved for her. Peg asked what she would like to eat. She smiled. "Just a cupcake and a lemonade." Peg whispered the choices. Madam Tong grinned and pointed to the pitcher in Peg's hand. Beth pulled her chair beside Madam Tong's. Claire slipped to the edge of the stage to capture the show with her Kodak.

Leon stepped onto the stage, led everyone in singing "Happy Birthday," and then announced, "Ladies and gentlemen, please help yourself to dessert and take a seat. The entertainment is about to begin." When he clapped his hands, a man and three shoulder-high children, a boy and two girls, sprinted onto the stage. All wore matching red silk pajamas with gold dragons embroidered down the trouser legs. The children bowed forward until all three were walking on their hands around the front of the stage, distracting attention from Leon and the man moving a trunk.

When the man clapped his hands, all three jumped to their feet. The boy brought him two dinner plates from the trunk and the man tapped them together. The crisp ring proved they were porcelain. He juggled them before spinning them on long rods above his head.

Leon pointed. "Now for gymnastics!" After setting down the rods and plates, the man reached for the boy's hands and pulled him into a handstand above his head. Behind them, the girls shed their bulky pajamas, revealing cotton pullovers and tights. "The rings!" Leon shouted. The adults applauded and several children moved closer to the stage as the girls lifted rings the size of barrel hoops and did a series of contortions, weaving the rings over their bodies and pulling their arms and legs through the center in intricate patterns. Several children pointed at them, eyes wide, mouths open.

Leon and the man dropped the tennis net to reveal a thick wire between the two sturdy poles. The two girls pulled large paper fans from the trunk and hurried to opposite posts. The older daughter took small, careful steps across the length of the tight wire and returned. Then she and her sister each walked the wire until they met in the center. Each stood on one foot and extended the other in mirror images. They turned and took mincing steps toward the end post; the fans fluttering for balance. In unison, the girls gave a shout, dropped their fans, and did back flips off the wire. Claire captured them at the height of the dismount and again on landing with their arms above their heads.

Beth clapped and started to say something to Madam Tong but paused. The older woman was wiping her eyes with an embroidered handkerchief, her lips pressed into a tight line. She saw Beth and patted her arm. "It's nothing. Just a memory." Unconvinced but not knowing what else to do, Beth watched the boy become a rubber man, bending backward until he grabbed his own ankles and walked a few paces.

Before the performers left, Claire took Beth's picture with them. When Peg told Beth that Madam Tong had arranged the performance, Beth raced back and gave Madam Tong a hug as large as the ones she reserved for her grandfather.

As the guests milled about, leaving, Gerri leaned over to JD and whispered, "If you was that limber, you could suck yourself."

"Hush, you'll get us in trouble with the schoolmarm." He blushed and hugged her closer to him.

She laughed. "What's she gonna do? Keep us after school?"

"I'm serious. She could kick us to the curb in a heartbeat."

Gerri chuckled. "That's not gonna happen. She's not gonna do anything to embarrass her hubby." Gerri and JD retreated as the guests left and the cleanup began.

Peg walked Madam Tong to her bungalow. "I cannot thank you enough. She will remember today forever."

She patted Peg's arm. "It is a wonderful house for entertaining. We often had garden parties in the spring. In summer, my husband would convert the tennis court to a dance floor and have a band at the far end on a raised stage." She laughed, then pressed her hand to her mouth. "Once he had it wrapped in dark canvas. He made it into *the* speakeasy bar we had visited in Los Angeles in '32 during the Olympics. You know, when we were there, I went to the beach, Malibu beach, it was called. I saw the Pacific Ocean and thought that if I got on a boat, I could sail to my front door. Once Leon has it back to being a court, would you like to play a game next week?"

"I'd love to. Thank you again."

Claire joined Charlie and Leon in gathering the plates and silverware on trays and drying as Charlie washed the dishes while Leon supervised the removal of the stage. Once the only remaining chore was drying the dessert plates, Peg excused Charlie and Leon with profuse thanks. Bill popped into the kitchen. "All gifts secured. What else can I do?"

She whispered, "How about keeping the birthday girl out of the kitchen? Something's up with Claire."

Bill invited his daughter to a story in the living room. She grinned and followed.

Peg shut the door and let the silence linger in the room. Claire was drying the last plate when she motioned toward the living room. "How did you know?"

"Know what?"

"You made it sound so simple when I interviewed you on the ship. 'Met Bill. Got married.' How'd you know Bill was the one?"

Peg took the plate from Claire, added it to the tall stack, and smiled, "Because he *was*! Still is." She watched Claire fussing with the wet towel. "Oh my God! It's Jean-Claude!"

Failing to look innocent, Claire sputtered, "What?"

"Oh, come on! I expect the room to catch fire when you two look at each other. What do you want? Some sign from above? Permission?"

"Peg. I have a life, and—"

"You *had* a life, but that was yesterday. What do you want your to-morrow to be? Every day you have that choice. That's the question I ask myself, and it always comes back to Bill and Beth and our family. However, wherever!"

Claire looked at the ceiling and blew out a plume of invisible smoke.

CHAPTER 23

JD picked the downtown club for their evening out, away from their usual crowd. The local Chinese band played off-tempo while the singer mangled a version of Perry Como's "Prisoner of Love." Gerri groaned and sucked up the last of her second Tom Collins after dinner. JD glanced at his watch and nursed his Canadian Club and Seven. Not even nine yet.

She put her hand on his arm. "You ready to go? I'm tired of hearing the lousy band and those old hens go on about whose kid pooped green today and who's teething or where they are going to retire. It's like all the life got sucked right out of 'em."

He choked on his drink and put his arm around her shoulder. "Honey, even if they bore you stiff, you gotta be social with these women, and kiss up to the older ones, so they'll tell their hubbies what a delightful couple we are."

"Who cares what they think? We're not gonna be here forever."

"Look, if you want me to get promoted so we'll have more money, you gotta play the game."

She crossed her arms and frowned.

"Baby, I'm serious. When I get promoted, we'll be doing more parties. How much they like you reflects on how much they like me. And if three guys are all up for promotion and there's just one slot, guess who has a leg up?"

"The guy whose wife gets along best with the Colonel's wife?"

"You got it, Baby. I do a damn fine job, but so do other fellas, so a little pillow talk from the Colonel's wife can make a big difference in *our* career."

After a deep sigh, she said, "If it means that much to you."

"It does. It really does."

"Then I'll sign up for the book club since I don't know how to play bridge."

"Bet they'd love to teach you."

"Can't I just start with the book club? That's like going back to school and having homework."

"Sure."

A week later, JD dug through the closet for his Hawaiian shirt after Gerri reported that the bar at the marina club offered a Saturday-night luau. When they arrived, the bar had been transformed from its nautical theme to something between a Hawaiian dive bar and a high school prom. Crepe paper leis hung over the framed pictures of ships at sea or planes in combat maneuvers. They draped smaller versions of the same leis around the necks of everyone who entered. The thrum of ukulele music was incessant.

Men wore untucked Hawaiian shirts over their usual slacks. Those who had been in Hawaii had coconut shell buttons on cotton shirts. The local versions had plastic buttons and rayon fabric. Women had enough time to have their tailor make something resembling a muumuu for the older women or a sheath in a Hawaiian print for the younger ones.

Besides the usual items, the buffet offered shredded Kalua pork, spareribs in a sweet marinade, chicken in rice, and shrimp cocktails.

JD was nursing a beer at the bar when Wayne slid in beside him. "Hey."

"Hi." His grin grew with his slow turn toward Wayne.

"Going stag tonight?"

"Naw. Waiting for the ball and chain. She's coming in as soon as her book club breaks up. Two in the afternoon to whenever they end, which means closer to seven or eight if the Colonel's wife is pouring or holding court, lecturing them about something, or planning some event with her captive audience." He put down his empty bottle.

"Still doing her monthly coffee thing?"

"Yeah. Got two nights a month for sure."

"Nice work." Wayne lit a smoke with his Zippo.

The barman asked, "What's your pleasure?"

"How about a CC and Seven, lots of ice?"

JD shoved his empty bottle across the bar. "Make it two." When the barkeep pulled the bottle of Canadian Club off the shelf, Wayne placed a small box of matches on the bar. "Take it."

"You know I don't smoke. Gerri gets all crazy about it."

He lowered his voice. "Just put it in your pocket. Now."

JD watched the bartender in the mirror making the drinks and slid the matchbox into the pocket of his loose slacks.

"It's your key to our place."

Wayne grinned as Gerri came into the bar looking for her husband. "See you around, pal." As Wayne walked past Gerri, JD looked at one, then the other, longingly. Gerri saw his half-smile and gave him her best hip swing as she stumbled into him. "Hi ya, Handsome."

"Been drinking, Beautiful?"

"Martinis. She made the biggest pitcher of martinis. Great ones."

The bartender delivered his drink. JD lifted his hand. "And a Coke for the lady."

"But I want a martini."

"After we get some food."

Once his wife's soda arrived, JD took their drinks to a table for two. "Let's hit the chow line before it gets too crowded. Hawaiian ribs tonight."

"Sure, Baby."

Sunday morning came too early for Gerri. JD had to nudge her several times before she moaned, "Another five minutes."

"Come on, Baby. We got the brunch this morning."

"Can't we skip it? My head's two sizes too big."

"You know the plan. Wash up and get ready." JD was shaving when she toweled off and downed two glasses of water and an aspirin. The morning was already muggy despite the fan clicking overhead.

He watched Gerri rooting in the closet and wondered if Wayne was going to be there. Then he knew the stirring, the tingle, the warmth of a pending erection. "Gonna grab a fast shower. Won't be a minute."

Gerri took two hangers from the closet and thrust them at him. "Which one. Halter top or the blouse?"

He randomly pointed to the white one, pulled fresh boxers from the open dresser, and escaped to the shower.

When he emerged in his boxers, she had dressed in loose turquoise trousers of a nubby raw silk and a white halter top that accented her ample cleavage.

"New slacks? Kinda tight at the ankle, aren't they?"

"Harem pants. Supposed to look puffy. They're in the latest fashion magazines. The Colonel's wife, Maggie! She said I could call her Maggie. Anyway, she said I should find my own 'color profile.' She took me to her tailor in town and picked out the fabric herself. What could I do?"

He sighed dramatically. "How much?"

"Two bucks. She said it would have cost at least fifty at Bergdorf's."

"Where's that?"

"New York or D.C. I forget. She goes on and on about stores and restaurants in the States, what I should wear or buy or do or say. Says I should build my wardrobe and accessories here where it's cheap, and they'll be exotic when we get back home."

"Why's she adopting you?"

"She says I remind her of herself. Says I have 'promise.' And thinks we make a fine-looking couple."

"What's her angle, Babe?"

Gerri shrugged in a way that emphasized her cleavage. "I'm just doing what you told me to."

JD laughed as he pulled his new light blue sports shirt from the wardrobe. The square cut flattered his slim build. The fabric was why she'd bought it for him.

"Love that fabric. Wish they had it where they made these slacks."

"Harem pants," he corrected.

As the taxi drove along Pacific Road, JD rolled down his window. "Jesus. I'm gonna sweat to death by the time we get there. Can't you crank down your window too?"

"We're about there. I can't go in there with my hair in a toss, looking like we just got out of bed."

The cabbie gunned the engine and swerved around a rickshaw-coolie trotting near the side of the road. Gerri clenched her jaw, looked out the side window. When the driver stopped at the Edgewater Mansions Hotel, she said, "I thought brunch was at the club in town."

"Moved to the Edgewater. Some Washington bigwigs showed up. We need to look casual but be spit and polish. Okay?"

"Don't lecture me on how to act. I get enough of that from the Colonel's wife."

"You mean your buddy Maggie?"

"Knock it off."

"You first."

JD whistled as the taxi stopped behind a shining Cadillac from the embassy. He offered Gerri his arm at the steps.

She snapped, "Aren't you the fancy one?"

"Don't want to disappoint Maggie."

"It's Margaret, and you can't call her that. She hasn't given you permission yet."

"Where'd you get that load of crap?"

"She's got a book on how to do stuff."

JD stopped at the doorway of the banquet room.

She tugged at his elbow. "Come on. What's the holdup?"

Without answering, he steered her toward the head table. "Mrs.

Stanford, I wanted to express my appreciation for the interest you have taken in Gerri's wardrobe. I think she looks stunning in these new harem pants." He spun his wife off his arm with the twirl he used to end their dances. While the women at the table examined both the cut of the pants and Gerri's figure, the men enjoyed the innocent shrug she gave at the conclusion of the twirl.

The Colonel's wife offered JD the smile of a proud parent. "Oh, call me Maggie. My pleasure entirely. It was the least I could do. Your wife brings such a fresh perspective to our book club."

Gerri tipped her head in a practiced modesty.

JD bowed slightly to the table. "She is something, isn't she? Well. We best leave you to enjoy this lovely day."

As they moved off, Gerri took his arm. "You little charmer."

He pulled out a chair for her so that she had a view of the water while he faced the room. "Looks like it's the usual Officers' Club gang. Most of them stuck with their kids. Bet they eat and run. Probably to the beach." He glanced at the crowded bar. Wayne and a man in a golf shirt were chatting.

JD smiled at her and asked, "What's your fancy?"

"How about a Ramos fizz?"

He stood. "I'll get it for you. It'll take forever if we wait for someone to take our order."

"Take your time. I love watching the sailboats."

JD shook a few hands and slapped a guy on the back on his way to the bar. He stalled, shifting from one foot to the other while waiting for the server beside Wayne to pick up his damn tray and move along.

Sliding into the gap the server had left, he ordered loudly, "Hey! A Ramos fizz, no rush, and a CC and Seven while I wait." JD leaned hard on the gleaming bar top as though willing his elbows into the mahogany. *Come on, Wayne, turn around. Tonight? I'll pawn her off on someone.*

As though Wayne had sensed his desire, he turned. "Hey, JD. Meet Jerry Farmerton. He's the golfer."

JD reached out his hand and gave a hearty shake. "Saw you play when you were an amateur. Never seen a swing like yours. Power and finesse all at once."

"Thanks."

"Wish I could have seen you at the Atlanta invitational last year. Read that you gave 'em a run for their money."

"Hey, what else could I do against a master like Jimmy Demaret? You play?"

"Bit rusty. Spending more time in the air than on the course." JD laughed, not mentioning the fact that the pro had finagled a 4-F deferral from service yet played in the tournaments immediately after the war.

Wayne slung his arm over the pro's shoulder. "This old boy is out here with the D.C. contingent, some congressmen with their wives. Trophy hunting for some antiques and collectibles."

JD forced a smile. "Wow, that must be swell."

Wayne continued, "And he coaches Truman on his putting game, which is horrible. We're going to shoot eighteen tomorrow morning and have dinner tomorrow night." As the pro shook hands with the other men at the bar, Wayne pulled JD aside. "Says he's looking for a club pro in a year when he expands his business ventures. Saw me play in the amateur circuit. I'm getting out about then and might have a shot at it, if I make an impression."

"But I . . . we."

"Not now. See you later."

"When?"

"Later!"

When Wayne walked away, JD moved down the bar to where Bill was waiting for a drink and chatting with other pilots. "About a week ago, we were on a routine flight. I was all braced for that standard test-fire of the Brownings." Bill mimed pulling the trigger on the stick. "Then nothing. That silence was chilling. I looked down at the control stick, squeezed again, confirmed trigger movement, and swore. Empty. Some clown didn't load my guns. I was flying naked."

Andy took over from there. "Bombing run was fine, and no interdiction came our way. When we landed, Skipper was cool as a cucumber. He jumped down and opened the ammo hatches. That was when he blew. He started running for the crew shed. I really thought he might kill someone."

"Then what?"

Andy said, "Cool as ice. He looks at the crew chief, says, 'You will be on the field to load ammo in each plane personally until I am transferred out of here.' The guy answers back."

Phil picked up the story. "When he gave Skipper some lip, he put his hand on the butt of his .45 and the guy shut up. When he realized his crew had sent a pilot up unarmed, there was a wet spot on his trousers."

Andy pushed in and shouted. "And it got bigger and bigger!"

The bartender delivered the Ramos fizz. JD refreshed his drink and carried them to the table. "So, when's your next big thing with Maggie?"

"Book club next month. Next week, there's a 'hail and farewell' coffee. I think that's every month too."

He looked at the boats and said absently, "Sure. Hail to the new arrivals. Farewell to those leaving."

"So, I'm stuck for two nights a month with that old cow."

"I'll try to go to the gym those nights, so our schedules match."

Gerri sat at the back of the well-appointed living room, listening to the Colonel's wife go on and on to the assembled wives about their contribution to the morale of the men, particularly the bachelors. She chuckled. *Those boys are having the time of their life living high on the hog here.* Watching the older woman, Gerri wondered if she'd always had this power or if it grew as her husband rose in the ranks. She thought she should have her own title, but maybe "the Colonel's wife" was it.

Margaret began, "We all know that a month away seems like a long time, especially since the Navy's hosting the buffet and soft drinks for the Fourth of July beach party. But our boys are going to want some homemade snacks."

After a grueling thirty minutes of detailing party assignments and expectations, Margaret sighed. "Well. I'm thirsty. Any of you gals want to join me in a martini?" Without waiting for responses, she motioned the houseboy to mix up a pitcher.

As most of the women left, the Colonel's wife said, "Thank you all. There is no better reminder of home than our work. And isn't that what we are all about, making our fellow wives welcome and caring for our menfolk, who are keeping the Red Menace of communism away from America?"

The four ladies who remained with Gerri accepted a drink and chatted about shopping discoveries and small social events. One complained her husband kept firing anyone she hired, so she was always training someone how to cook or mend or clean to her standards.

After the others left, Margaret looked at Gerri and refreshed their drinks. "You're new to this all, aren't you, gal?"

"Well, yes. We just got married."

"You really outta get your own copy of *The Navy Wife*, my dear."

"Not unless it's a romance!"

Laughing, almost spilling her drink, Margaret said, "Hardly! It's an Emily Post for the wives. How to address ranks, protocol, attire, table settings. All you ever need to know to support his position, the service, when to present your card, and how to manage a Navy household."

"But I'm a Marine's wife!" she said, feeling the alcohol. "Don't gimmie that line about the Corps being a part of the Navy."

"That's precious. He's a charmer, but if you intend to help his career, it's a must."

"Why?"

Margaret smiled. "I have a gold Bulova that you've been admiring all night. You have a Timex. If you want him promoted, you make a difference. Don't let anyone tell you any different. Like it or not. Smile at these meetings, volunteer, and stand taller at the parties. And read the damn book!"

"Yes, ma'am."

Margaret spoke with practiced care, hiding the drinks she had already downed. "Do I hear a bit of the South when you talk?"

Gerri giggled. "Sorta comes out when I drink. North Carolina."

"That's hardly South. My people are from Atlanta. Now that's 'bout as South as they come."

Gerri finished her drink and offered to take the accumulated glasses to the kitchen.

Margaret brayed. "Leave 'em. That's what we got servants here and coloreds back home for, girl. You get on and have yourself a fine evening with your handsome hubby."

CHAPTER 24

On the Fourth of July, Gerri dressed before JD even finished showering.

He said, "Hey! Why're you rushing off? I thought since it was a holiday, we could have our own fireworks this morning."

"Sorry. The boss lady wants us there early. It's all planned to a gnat's ass, so maybe she wants us to polish the grains of sand or some other shit. She's beyond belief. If I didn't love you so much, I'd quit her stupid meetings in a heartbeat. Or just shoot her."

"I checked out a Jeep for the weekend. Want me to drive you down and meet you later?"

"No, she's got drivers picking up her slaves on this side of town." She glanced at her Timex. "Gotta run."

Later, when he saw Bill in the kitchen, JD asked, "Taking the family to the picnic?"

Bill filled his mug with coffee. "Thought we'd go about eleven, so the kids don't fry. Should be a scorcher."

"See you all there. Oh, if you're planning to bring some beer, don't let Margaret catch you. Gerri says she declared it a dry party."

Bill laughed. "Fat chance."

Once the beach umbrella and a sturdy canvas chair were in its shade, Margaret took to her throne. As her "girls" arrived, she dispatched them to any random task that occurred to her. Gerri looked around. She was used to the beach, the roped boundary of the swimming area, the float, and the lifeguard stand.

Today was different. Already a man with binoculars was on the stand. They had roped off a new smaller area for wading. There were two patrol boats offshore. *No Chinese were going to wander into this party. Not on Margaret's watch!*

When the two Navy commissary trucks arrived, Margaret clucked over each table that was taken off the truck and pointed to a shaded area well away from the water for the coolers of soft drinks. As the men from the *Estes* unloaded iced bins of potato salad and steam trays for baked beans, and crates of buns and hot dogs, she pointed and directed the setup, even though the messmen had instructions from their superiors.

After the men put several five-gallon insulated water jugs on a sturdy picnic bench, Margaret sent Gerri to have a water jug taken closer to the wading area. Families had claimed the long rows of picnic benches with attached seats. Beach bags, light overshirts, or towels marked territories by ten a.m. They added folding chairs to the line of weathered wooden seats along the planked boardwalk. Mothers placed faded beach chairs close enough to the wading area to dip their toes in the water while watching their children. Six-year-olds inside the wading area floated on opened life jackets laid flat like rafts. They would roll off, laugh, and splash each other.

Most of the bachelors clustered around the volleyball net. A few wore Bermuda shorts and untucked shirts. Guys who'd had duty stations in Hawaii wore their colorful original Hawaiian shirts featuring hula girls and pineapples. Others wore the local versions featuring Diamond Head or hibiscus flowers in neon shades. A few men wore their green fatigue tees and swim trunks.

Gerri nudged another of the wives. "Nurses from the *Repose*! I can tell by their suits. See those gals in the one-piece Jansen swimsuits, the coral and navy ones? They're younger. The older gals want the Cole designs by Esther Williams. Got a lot more support and cleavage. It's all for the men. They want you to look like you are jailbait until you're thirty. Then after that, who cares? By then you're married or a career hag."

At the end of a game, JD waved to Gerri, who smiled and tipped her head to Margaret. JD grinned at her. Wayne trotted from the parking lot to the net and asked if he could substitute in on the opposing team. A winded sailor waved him in and wandered off to grab a beer from the unauthorized ice chest in the trunk of a nearby car.

After winning that game, Wayne said, "Thanks, guys. Gonna catch a swim before they open the chow line." As he passed JD, he whispered, "Meet me at the float."

Gerri saw that the volleyball game was ending and stood. "I'm gonna go see JD for a minute."

He grabbed a Coke and joined his wife. He took a sip and gave it to her. "Here, Babe. I'm going for a swim, wanna come?"

She raised her eyebrows and glanced behind her. "Can't. Besides, I'm not gonna be looking like a drowned rat when we eat. Go cool off—you're sweating like a horse."

JD took a running dive into the water, skimmed the surface like a skipped rock, and stroked hard. He felt it. The way his suit pressed against his dick. Feather light, shifting, stroking. Warming.

Wayne was alone, lounging on the canvas deck of the float when JD arrived and hung onto the side. Wayne glanced at the swimmers near shore and said, "Go around to the far side." He made a smooth dive and came up near JD. "You don't have to avoid me. It was just volleyball!"

"I'm sorry. I don't—"

"Don't what? Don't like me? Not at all?"

JD paused, not sure if Wayne was teasing or sincere. "Sure. Yes. I like you. More than that. It's complicated. I can't see you whenever."

Wayne was beside him, their shoulders a foot apart, but legs touching under the water. "Why? Because you're married? How does that change what you feel?"

"It doesn't, but . . ."

Wayne chided, "Worried about how you act around me? Is that it? Think someone might notice?" His foot stroked JD's leg.

JD faced him and tilted his head as if to kiss him.

Wayne pulled away. "Jesus! The Navy's got patrol boats out there with binocs."

JD held on to the float with one hand. The other found Wayne's flat belly and then pressed against his hard cock.

"Christ! Now I'm gonna be out here for an hour." Wayne laughed, pushed off, and briefly floated on his back, his trunks bulging.

JD smiled. "I'll fix it."

From her shaded chair, Margaret noted the latecomers. The Ryans and Franklins. Mothers held their daughters by the hand. Fathers juggled beach blankets, folding chairs, and umbrellas. Behind them, Claire carried three beach bags. Margaret lifted her sunglasses to inspect Claire. The sun hat, linen trousers, and long-sleeved blouse were all the exact shade of lime green. The outfit was straight out of *Vogue*.

She nudged Gerri. "Who's their guest?"

"Peg's reporter friend, Claire. They do some orphanage thing together. She's been over to the house a couple times to develop film and print pictures in Peg's darkroom."

"Reporter?"

"*Ladies' Home Journal*, I think she said. Never read it."

"Introduce me as the day goes along. Why don't you go help them set up? Then come right back."

Margaret watched Claire for a moment before turning to the shoreline. Slim mothers splashed with their toddlers in the ankle-deep water. She reached into her beach bag for her cigarette case. Black enamel. She allotted herself four cigarettes a day. This was her last, and it wasn't yet noon. Her lighter looked like a Dunhill with its crisp, upright design and the striker bar on the edge. A clever imitation, a deeply engraved dragon encircled it. That's who she was. A silver lighter in a sea of men with Zippos.

She chuckled and put the flame on the cigarette. Women and children, mere accessories for the military. Families dispatched into harm's way to appease politicians and take the pressure off the calls to bring the fellas home. The draftees were being winnowed out now. Going home and getting jobs. *Thus ever*, she thought. *Duty and honor for some, just a shitty job for others.*

A few minutes later, Gerri came back into the shade. "Boiling out there. Need a Coke?"

"No, thanks." She buried her cigarette stub in the sand and watched children splashing each other. The older boys, high schoolers, raced each other out to the float and back, falling winded on the sand. A couple of strong swimmers who had been at the float left it when the boys crawled onto the float. The swimmers approached the outer rope with the floats and swam parallel to it.

Near the picnic benches, several younger girls were playing tag, kicking up sand, and squealing as the next one became "it."

Bill shouted to Beth, "Race you to the water!" They took off, and both did splashy racing dives and came up laughing. Beth stood on her father's shoulders and yelped when she dove off into the water. Bill laced his fingers together. She held his shoulders and put both feet into his hands. He launched her well above his head. She flipped and landed with a splash.

A scream near the game of tag cut Beth's laughing short. Sally had tripped, fallen, and tangled in a folding chair. Bill motioned Beth to shore.

"Mommy!" Sally's scream morphed into sobs. She sat in the sand, holding her cheek, and howling.

Margaret pointed toward the commotion. "Gerri, go see what that's all about."

By the time she arrived, Trudy had a handkerchief pressed against Sally's cheek. Peg raced over to them. Blood speckled the front of Sally's bathing suit and soaked through the handkerchief. A nurse in a blue swimsuit dropped to her knees beside them. "I'm from the *Repose*."

Trudy said, "It's bad."

The nurse gently lifted the cloth. "A couple of butterfly bandages should close it. It's not deep enough for stitches."

Peg said, "I can do it at the house, or we can take her to the ship. It's okay. I worked in a doctor's office during the war."

George skidded to a stop as Trudy said, "Your place! It's closer."

Peg grabbed her purse from the blanket. Bill and Beth ran toward her.

Looking up, Peg called, "Sally cut her cheek. I'll patch her up and be back for you."

Bill took Beth's hand. "Roger that."

Claire was at the far end of the beach when she saw Peg and Trudy running to the car with George carrying Sally. She ran toward them as the car drove away. She joined Bill and Beth, who were toweling off at their blanket. Bill shook his head. "Kids. One thing or another, bless 'em."

She decided not to ask when she saw Beth looking after the car as her mother sped from the parking area, then glanced at Bill. "I was going to shoot some pictures of the party. Do you think Beth could join me?"

He looked at his daughter, who nodded. "Sure." He reached into Peg's beach bag and pulled out the Hawkeye camera. "Don't forget this."

Claire sat on the blanket and dug deep into her bag for her camera. When she pulled out a Kodak Medalist, Beth asked, "Where's your square one?"

"The Rollei? I only use it for work. Kodak's better for quick action shots, like your birthday party. Here. Look." Bill watched as she handed the camera to Beth. He hadn't really noticed it at the party.

"It's heavy!"

"About three pounds." Claire took the camera back and held it to her eye, showing Beth how the direct sighting worked.

Beth asked, "You don't need to look down?"

"No. And it takes the same film as yours."

"Six-twenty?"

"Right, but I only get eight prints off a roll."

Beth laughed. "I get twelve!"

"What do you think would be unusual to take a picture of? Let's find something different from the usual beach party pictures."

Beth stood and slipped her camera strap over her neck. After making a full circle turn, she stared at the men setting up the buffet line of food and drinks. "Them."

Claire pointed, and they walked in that direction. "Perfect. You don't see that every day. I was also thinking about the guys playing volleyball."

Beth grinned. "Because they're cute?"

Claire laughed. "Could be."

"Aren't you hot in that shirt?"

"Not really. But I'd sunburn something awful if I were in a suit now."

"Because you have red hair like Sally?"

"You're so smart." Claire watched the girl and wanted to scream the truth. *I didn't burn before Nagasaki.*

Colonel Stanford walked past them and handed his wife a tall glass. She frowned. "Lemonade?"

"With a light splash, dear. Thought you could use it."

She smiled. "Supposed to be a dry party, Darlin'. Kids and all." She tipped her head to the empty chair beside her as she took the glass. For a moment, they were silent, sitting in the beach chairs under an umbrella. She took a sip, then leaned down and brushed sand from the hem of her loose linen slacks.

She sighed. "They're all so young and so much is ahead of them. It's hard to remember we were once their ages. Could be our kids if we'd had any."

"How many of these parties have we been to?"

"Too many or just enough. Hard to tell some days." She sipped. "It's about over, isn't it?"

"Our time here? Yes. If Washington can't shit or get off the pot, Mao will push us into the sea. Until then, we carry on with this puppet show of having families in the middle of a civil war, pretending it is another lark."

Margaret watched the Negro messmen in their bright whites delivering the last of the trays for the buffet. Navy. She thought it was better when all the help was from the Philippines. Before the coloreds. Maybe it was the war that changed it. Or did the Philippines get some independence that left the sailors shorthanded? She pointed at the messmen. "Think the Corps is going to have them in the mess someday?"

"Probably. Rumor is that Truman's going to integrate the services."

"It's an election year. People say the damnedest things. You wouldn't vote for him, anyway."

An hour later, Peg parked the Buick and hurried to where Bill, Beth, and Claire were in the umbrella's shade. "She's all fixed up, more of a scare than anything. But she wanted to stay at home."

Beth asked, "Can I go see her?"

"Now? Don't you want to stay for the food?"

"No. Leon's is better."

Bill glanced at Peg and shrugged. "Your call."

Peg made a face and said, "Okay! Let's blow this joint!"

Claire helped ferry their gear to the car and accepted their invitation to spend the day with them. Once in the car, she reached into her bag and gave Peg a small square envelope. "It's an invitation from Jean-Claude. I'm just the messenger."

Peg blushed. "How sweet."

"He loved your family. Open it."

Peg carefully peeled open the envelope. "Bastille Day?"

"Sorta the French Fourth of July. He promises the best fireworks ever! And kids are welcome."

She slid the note back into the envelope. "This is so kind, but we don't speak French."

Claire laughed. "It's not a fussy thing at the embassy. We rented the dining room at my hotel for a buffet before we trundle out on the rocks to see the fireworks. Please! He promised that a lovely girl, about Beth's age who speaks English, will take Beth under her wing."

Peg glanced at Bill, who smiled and said, "Sounds great. Count us in."

CHAPTER 25

Margaret watched the Ryans depart with that redheaded woman, then resumed her command of the event. "About noon," she muttered.

Her husband nudged her. "Are you really going to stick to your schedule and make this a military operation? It's a holiday."

"Wind's coming up, don't want them eating sand. Besides, wives always have our schedules."

He winked. "Just don't make them march in parade formation."

She shook her head and laughed as she motioned for Gerri. "Hun? Go tell the lifeguard to blow his whistle and wave 'em all in for lunch. Then go tell them to start the chow line. That's a good girl."

Gerri thought this was about as useful as telling the sun to rise, but she did it anyway, calling up to the sailor in trunks who wore a Shore Patrol white helmet. She walked to the first station in the hot food line and eyed a messman while the other stations were still being set up. "Lady over there says to serve ASAP."

Messman Fred Tanner looked up from sweating over a steam tray of baked beans. "Yes, ma'am. Soon as I can."

Minutes later, the line formed, everyone holding mess trays. Fred hurried to fill the designated section on the steel trays. A couple started arguing at the back of the line. One lady yelled for her kid. "Timmy!" A man shouted for the boy. *Typical confusion for these events,* Tanner thought.

He dipped into the pot without looking up to hurry people along, not wanting any complaints from some officer's cranky wife. When the next sailor greeted him, he looked up and something past the man's shoulder caught his eye. Something orange flashed in the small chop. After filling another tray, he saw the orange life vest and a blond kid bob up before disappearing behind the next wave.

"Kid's out there!" He dropped the full ladle on the sand, pushed through the line, and sprinted toward the water.

The little boy slipped under and came up sputtering. He flailed toward the life jacket, now out of reach. Fred had stripped off his overblouse and flipped away his shoes by the time he hit the water. His powerful strokes propelled him to where he last saw the boy. Now the orange jacket—floating free. Panting, Fred grabbed it, shoved it underwater, and used its buoyancy to lift himself above the chop. He spun in every direction. Nothing. Empty sea.

Whistles on shore. Both patrol boats blew clouds of exhaust behind them and were coming at full speed toward him, but they were over a hundred yards away. Three Marines in trunks and T-shirts bolted after Fred, but he had outdistanced them. The sailor who had been the lifeguard mounted the tower again, put the binoculars to his eyes, and swept the area around the orange dot. He shook his head.

The Colonel, now on his feet at the base of the tower, shouted, "Keep looking! Scan upwind of the jacket." The parents hovered beside the stand, frantic.

The lifeguard started a slow sweep again. "Got him!" He jerked his arm into position to guide the boats. He blasted his whistle, watching the cook's white T-shirt swirling against his dark skin. Fred saw the lifeguard pointing.

He twisted in the water. Seeing nothing on the surface but trusting the guide, he let go of the life jacket, sucked in two deep breaths, and speared down. He kicked and pulled a wrenching breaststroke, pushing deep into the murky water until he collided with the sandy bottom. Saltwater stinging his eyes, he swam along the bottom, jerking his head in both directions.

The sandy bottom gave way to the rock pile that calmed the sea.

Boulders the size of Jeeps piled against each other fifteen feet under the surface. He kicked toward them, praying the rocks had not trapped the boy.

Lungs aflame, he pulled himself over the top of the boulders and down the far side. His ears seared with pain.

He blinked.

Light shafted through the murky green water. He saw a flash of yellow just under the surface.

Trunks.

The boy floated, hunched like a jellyfish. Fred slammed his hand into a boulder to turn and kicked hard. He torpedoed up, grabbing the boy's elbow, and launching him out of the water. The child was limp.

Floating on his back, Fred laid the boy on his chest and pressed his fist under the boy's small rib cage. Nothing. His weight pushed Fred underwater. He kicked and surfaced, legs trembling, failing.

The wind shifted. He saw the life jacket. But the boy was still limp.

Fred wrapped his right arm around the boy, pressed the small back against his own chest, and hugged him again as hard as he could, with all his strength and all his hope. Water exploded from the child's mouth. He started coughing, crying. Fred dipped under and bobbed back up.

The boy thrashed. "You're okay, son. Relax!"

Strength deserting him, Fred side-stroked toward the orange jacket and grabbed hold of it.

His left calf cramped. He winced. He was breathing hard and had to pull in air between his words. "Son! Grab the jacket. Not gonna let you go! Okay?"

The boy nodded.

"Keep your head real high."

Fred bobbed beside him, legs cramping. *Gotta keep kicking. Life jacket won't hold us both.* "Atta boy. Boat's coming for us."

The roar of the motors grew louder. They were closing fast.

The first patrol boat cut power and drifted close to Fred and the child. A sailor at the stern threw a life ring on a line a few strokes ahead of Fred. He hooked his arm through the white ring while still holding on to the boy.

The sailor in the stern leaned down. "Timmy! Give me your hand." Two swimmers closed in on them and helped hoist the boy from the water. A sailor pulled Fred aboard.

Fred crumpled into a ball, watching others take care of the shaking child.

The patrol boat sped to within a few feet of shore where several Marines had waded out to meet it. One carried the boy to a blanket at the shoreline where an off-duty nurse examined him there. As a Shore Patrol Jeep sped toward them over the sand, the boy's parents knelt beside him, touching his shoulders, the mother weeping.

Fred pulled himself up and slid over the side of the boat—into waist-deep water—and stumbled. Two Marines grabbed him by his elbows and helped him to shore. Another one wrapped the discarded shoes in the messman's shirt and handed the bundle to him.

The nurse pointed to Fred as they were loading the boy and his parents into the Jeep. "He's going to the *Repose* too. Make room."

The Shore Patrol driver sped inland, around Signal Hill, to the wharves. Timmy's parents rushed him to the sick bay. The hospital ship's sentry stopped Fred and denied him entry for being out of uniform. He walked—wet and barefoot—a quarter mile to return to his bunk on the command ship *Estes*. He showered and dressed before reporting to sick bay on the *Repose*. Once there, he took a seat in the waiting area.

A few minutes later, a nurse brought him to a small examination room and opened a folder. She read the cover page. Without looking up, she asked, "Tanner?"

"Yes, ma'am."

She glanced at the patient seated on the examination table, wearing fresh cook's whites, holding a dishtowel packed with ice around his left hand.

"Burn?"

"No, ma'am. Jammed my middle finger. I can close my hand, but my middle finger doesn't come back up unless I help it with my other hand."

"Let me look." The ice clattered when she put the wet towel into a basin.

She placed her palm under his, then examined each of his fingers. "I'm not finding any break or dislocation, so let's see what works and what doesn't. Can you lift each of your fingers off my hand, one at a time?"

He was able to comply. "Now slowly make a fist and open it. Stop if there is any pain."

He closed his fist, but when the middle finger stopped short of his palm, she said, "That's enough, now straighten your fingers."

When the middle finger remained down, she made a more careful examination. "The good news is that you don't have a rip in the ligament or tendon. If you did, you couldn't have pulled your fingers up. But your middle knuckle is going to be swollen for several days. The tendon and ligaments are going to need some rest to let the swelling subside."

He coughed. "Am I gonna need a cast? I don't want to miss work."

"You in the kitchen here?"

"No, ma'am. On the *Estes*."

"We'll see what the doctor says in a minute, but you'll probably get it taped and a changed duty order." She made notes on the chart.

He glanced briefly at her nameplate. "Rosetti?"

"Like the poet."

"You really Italian?"

"Parts."

"What other parts?"

"Dad's folks were from Sicily. Mom's from the islands."

"Hawaii?"

She shook her head and laughed. "Virgin Islands."

"In the Caribbean." He guessed.

She laughed at his tentativeness. "It is part of America, you know?"

"I do now."

She stood back. "I saw you in church, didn't I?"

"Probably."

"Why'd you always duck out before the recessional?"

"Not too sure how welcome a dark face is there. Navy's fine with me making their food and manning a battle station during war, but not sitting down with 'em to eat or pray. Don't need to rile anyone up."

"Okay. Mister—"

"Tanner. Easy enough to remember. I'm tanner than you."

She chuckled. "Why don't you just go to chapel in base?"

"Other guys go to the chapel over at the Bismarck Barracks, then work out or play some basketball, but I go into town. Walk around. Try new food on my own."

"Sounds wonderful. Nurses go everywhere in clusters, shopping or to a club. Like a covey of quail."

He laughed. "There's this beautiful park, the Seashore Park, just around the point from the Edgewater Hotel. Been there?"

"No."

"It's got this beautiful big *pailou*. Birds on top."

"What's a *pailou*?"

He grinned. "Guess you'll have to come find out for yourself."

She stopped at the sound of heavy footsteps on the linoleum. She picked up the chart and resumed making notes.

When the doctor entered, he asked her, "Finished here?"

"Yes, sir. Middle finger, middle joint. I don't think it's torn, a simple hyperflexion of the tendon. In place of a cast, I'd recommend buddy-taping the ring and middle fingers above and below the middle joint to allow the swelling to subside while he remains on duty."

The doctor examined Fred's hand. "Good. Modified duty for two weeks. Tape it up. Give him a roll of tape and show him how to do it, so he's not in here every day."

"Yes, sir. Review two weeks from tomorrow? Monday the eighteenth?" He took the completed chart from her, initialed her summary, and tossed it on the examination table.

She rummaged through a drawer and found a roll of adhesive tape. Tearing off two strips, she put one above and one below the knuckle to join his middle and ring fingers.

Anna finished taping the fingers and handed him the roll. "Keep it as dry as you can. Retape as needed. You're off dishwashing but can still do most of your job."

She picked up his file. "What's the name of the park again? I might go there some Sunday. After church."

When Anna checked the sick bay appointment calendar and saw Fred's name on the schedule in mid-July, she juggled patients with another nurse to see him. She looked at his taped fingers. "How's it been?"

"Feels pretty good."

She clipped the adhesive tape between his fingers with blunt-ended scissors, bracing his fingers as she removed the tape. She examined his skin for any deterioration or fungus. "Fingers look great. We usually see some erosion if you are in water frequently."

"You warned me about that. I musta gone through ten miles of tape since I wash my hands all the time."

"Well, it was worth it. Slowly make a fist for me." He did and winced. "That's enough. Now extend." The middle finger had an improved range of motion. "You're right on schedule. For the next two weeks, tape when you are working hard, lifting. But off duty and sleeping, go without the tape and slowly test your motion. I'm changing the restriction. If it gets worse, see me."

He laughed. "Unless I see you first. Sorry, that was my sister's usual goodbye to me. The way you said it reminded me of her. Sorry."

She laughed. "No need to apologize."

"The only time she wanted to be around me was when I was cooking up some barbecue. Then she glued herself to my side."

"Fancy yourself an excellent cook?"

He grinned. "Sure do. Planning to open my own place once my hitch is over. You?"

"Looking for a career here. Navy's done right by me."

"I might see you in Norfolk. That's where my sis still lives. She's going in with me on the restaurant."

"Think your food's that good?"

"Sure! Cook all kinda food the Navy don't serve."

"Won't you be out of practice?"

"No. Got me a cold-water walk-up here where I cook. Make take-away plates for the other colored boys on the ship when they're in town." He whispered, "Be mighty pleased to fix a plate for you sometime."

Hearing the crisp heel strike against the ship's linoleum, she finished charting and pulled a fresh roll of tape from a drawer. She made a quick notation on a memo pad and handed it to him. "Back to restricted duty, sailor. Give that to your boss. Make a follow-up appointment."

"Thank you, Lieutenant Rosetti."

She whispered, "Anna."

The following Sunday, she saw him leaving church. She smiled, remembering his description of the park, and wondered if it was indeed the tranquil escape from the frenetic activity of the city. As she walked downhill to Pacific Road, she stopped at several makeshift stalls and bought a small necklace to send to her niece. At the waterfront, she took a rickshaw to Seashore Park, half-wondering if he might be there. After paying the coolie, she wandered toward the park entrance, enticed by lush plantings and mature trees.

She stopped to admire the tall ornamental gateway. It resembled the crimson gateway she had seen at the entrance to Chinatown in San Francisco. But unlike that garish one, they made this of pale stone, capped with moss-green tiles. Two smaller openings flanked the center opening, which was ten feet high. And Fred was right. There were real-istic porcelain birds, perhaps doves, taking flight from the ornamental roof. Several doves cooed somewhere past a small bamboo grove.

The crunch of gravel underfoot stopped near her. He said, "Hoped you'd be here."

She pointed at the gateway. "So that's a *pailou!*"

"Yup. Join me?"

They walked to a bluff overlooking the bay. She waited for him to say something, but only heard the breeze teasing leaves and the distant birdsong. He pointed to a bench. They sat in silence for several minutes before he asked, "You hungry?"

"Sure. You bring a picnic expecting me to be here?"

He chuckled. "Did once."

"Sorry."

"No need. Ate it all myself. I could get us some street food."

"I thought you offered me a home-cooked meal."

"You sure?"

She smiled.

He pulled a small paper out of his pocket and gave it to her. "I keep a few of these to give to the cabs or rickshaw-coolies. If they can read the Chinese, fine. If not, I had a guy spell it like it sounds in English. Seems to work fine. How 'bout I meet you there in about an hour? That'll give me time to go through the market stalls. Get something fresh."

She held his arm. "Fred?"

"Yeah?"

"Why didn't you tell me you jammed your finger rescuing that boy?"

He laughed. "My finger didn't care how I did it."

As planned, he met her in the alley and had her go ahead of him upstairs.

She smiled when she entered his room. It smelled like Sundays when she was a child, of strong soap and newly fried bacon. The room was simple, but neat. The single bed along the far wall had a light blanket on it, pulled tight in the Navy way. Beside it was a bookcase with several books, a few plates, glasses, and a small box of silverware. On top was a shortwave radio, softly playing big band music.

By the door, a two-burner stove held a frying pan and a saucepan that was steaming. A battered ice chest sat on the counter. The window to the right had a gauzy lemon-yellow curtain fluttering with the cooling breeze. A small table with two mismatched chairs sat under it.

To the left, she saw a pale blue shower curtain covering a narrow alcove. "Even got a shower! I'm impressed."

"Don't be. It's just a toilet."

"I'm still impressed. What're you making? BLTs?"

He pulled two plates from the bookshelf and set them beside the burners. "No. Bacon is for a wilted spinach salad. Boiled eggs for it too. Gonna put a nice snapper fillet beside it and have us a fine lunch."

Without asking, she found forks and glasses on the bookshelf and set their places at the small table. He tossed a large handful of spinach into the hot bacon fat, then plated the greens a minute later, topping them with bacon crumbles and diced egg. Then he slipped a large fillet into the hot pan and let it sizzle before flipping it.

"Got beer and water in the ice chest. Beer for me."

Bringing two beers to the table, she sat and watched him put down their plates.

She smiled. "Wow! This is lovely. I expected some barbeque."

"Short notice. I slow-cook my BBQ meats. Works the sauce into 'em better. Cheap joints slather it on at the end."

She took a bite and rolled her eyes. "You gotta put this on the menu! It's wonderful."

They ate with ease and chatted about favorite foods, then exotic items they had sampled in China. They tried to one-up each other and laughed.

Halfway through, Fred asked, "How'd you get to be a Navy nurse?"

"Short or long story?"

"I got time."

"Always wanted to be a nurse, but figured I'd end up teaching, because I could get into that school. Then the war comes along and there's a shortage of nurses. They started the Cadet Nurse Corps, and on that application, I didn't need to check a box for Negro or white, which was lucky since I'm some of each. Thanks to Mrs. Roosevelt, they just looked at us all as humans, which was good, since my father says we're all more of a Heinz 57 than we know."

"Wasn't that program to fill in for the nurses who had joined up?"

"At the start, we were only stateside. Then, when the Navy started losing its wartime nurses, they took on some of us. I jumped at it."

He grinned. "I'm glad you did. Tell me about your Heinz family."

"Well, my folks are from New York. Dad's mom, my Nana, was right off the boat from Italy. Built like a fireplug. Ge-maw was from the islands. Dark as ink. Came north as a maid. My mother is a cup of cocoa. And me, I came out light."

He smiled at her. "Yes, you did."

"But you saw."

"I hoped."

Suddenly, Anna stopped with her fork inches away from her mouth. She listened again—moaning. She got a silly grin when she heard a deep male laugh. "Is that what I think it is?"

He leaned toward the window. "Sounds like it. Sorry, never happened before."

She pushed back from the table, stood up, and reached for the curtain. "Wanna take a peek?"

Laughing, he pulled aside the gauzy fabric, looked across the alley into an open window, and whispered, "Jesus!" He reached past the curtain and shut the window.

She glared at him. "What'd you do that for?"

"It's a couple of guys! Ain't Chinese either."

She giggled, "Seriously?"

"Guys from the picnic. At least one of 'em."

"Which one?"

She edged the curtain aside and glanced across the alley. He whispered, "Don't look. Navy doesn't want them together, doing whatever, any more than an officer and a messman can sit down together, let alone you being so light and me dark as dark can be."

She sat. "So what? It's a standoff. What are they gonna do, tattle on us having lunch?"

"Two white guys? They can say anything. MPs gonna believe them over anything I'd say. You know that. Anna! That's the way of the world now."

CHAPTER 26

The heat settled like a dome over the city. Some days, relief came as a light breeze from the sea. Madam Tong invited Peg for tea on such a day. She poured without her usual comments about the tea or polite small talk. "Peg, it is time to speak plainly. I hope that is not presumptuous of me, but in the year that you have lived here . . ."

Peg froze. *A year! Their lease was only for a year.* "Is it about the lease?"

The older woman laughed. "Not at all. I told your husband that you are welcome to stay if Leon or I am here. Although we never expected you to be here this long, there is no need for change in our agreement."

Peg took the cup from her, silently.

"I wanted you to know that I will remove the important paintings and art from the main house next week. Over the following weeks, I will exchange the furnishings for less expensive replacements. To any visitor, it will appear as a redecoration, not an exit. But that is what I am preparing for."

Peg asked, "What can we do to help?"

"Ignore it. Treat it as an old lady's whim. I doubt if that couple upstairs would notice, as I will not be changing their rooms. It is time to move anything of value."

Peg nodded and asked, "Where will you go if they—"

"It is only *when*. We are a country of farmers, peasants living at the barest survival level. Mao has promised them land reform, meaning they could go from what you call sharecropping to becoming landowners. A promise of comfort. A heaven on earth. We have few cities, but those are where the educated and wealthy live. They supported the Nationalists. But this is the difference." With her hands, she made a balance scale,

238

weighted clearly to one side. "I will go to Shanghai next week for a few days to arrange our business interests there."

Peg paused longer than necessary over her first sip. "Then what? Move to Taiwan?"

"And join the Nationalists and bankers hiding there on that pitiful island, thinking they can get back a China that never was? No, thank you!"

"Then where? Shanghai?"

"Why? It will fall after Tsingtao."

"How do you know that?"

She laughed. "I read tea leaves. Our value is the strategic port. You can abandon us in a moment. But Shanghai is where your wealthy American oil companies have invested deeply. You won't let those go as easily—but Shanghai will fall."

"Then where will you go?"

She smiled. "Our business interests are extensive. We have other homes. Perhaps Ceylon or another of our tea-growing areas for a while."

Peg took a long sip. "Is there anything Bill and I can do? Provide a recommendation for your immigration to America?"

She shook her head. "Kind offer, but no. Your country only allows just over a hundred Chinese to enter each year. I am certain those slots are long gone. But for Leon, it is different."

"How so?"

"He is an American citizen."

Peg's cup rattled as she tried to balance it on her knee. "What!"

Madam Tong laughed. "He is my son. He was born in San Francisco."

Peg felt as if time had stopped. How could Leon, part of a tea empire, be serving them breakfast and managing his own house for them?

The older woman continued, "We live in two worlds and need two faces. But I assure you that even without Beth's discovery of his excellent English months ago, when he read to her, you and I would be having this conversation. We have grown to trust and love you as family."

Peg blinked back tears as she reached for her hand. "Leon is going to the States?"

Madam Tong patted it and sat back in her chair, struggling to continue. After she dabbed her eyes, she said, "San Francisco or Portland. He hasn't decided yet. We have businesses in both places. Perhaps I may join him. Someday."

"I am confused."

She smiled at Peg's candor. "My family exported tea for over a century before I was born. My husband's father started his import business in San Francisco after the big earthquake. He ran a laundry before that. But that earthquake changed everything."

Peg tipped her head, trying to understand.

"My husband became what they called a 'paperboy' back then."

"He delivered newspapers?"

She laughed. "No. Birth records burned in the fire. My father-in-law was smart enough to register my husband as having been born there. He was only ten years old in 1906. Suddenly, my husband was born in the city and became a citizen, as did his father, who listed his birthplace as Sacramento. I have no shame in telling you this now because both are now beyond any risk."

She refreshed Peg's tea. "The city was half gone. The pier where coffee and tea had been unloaded from ships had vanished, as had the major import houses near it. My father-in-law seized the opportunity to start his own business. From the rubble came a new life."

"But how did you ever meet?"

"My family needed a new importer. We had offices in Portland and San Francisco, so we continued exporting to Portland while San Francisco rebuilt. My father-in-law went there to learn the trade, taking his family with him. They imported tea from us. Tong tea was famous, even then. That's why I held onto my name. Leon carries his father's name."

"What is it?"

"Chen. Leon's real name is Chen Tu. His first name, Tu, means fast learner or intelligent, which he certainly is."

"I've heard you and Beth call him Tu, but thought it was a term of endearment or a nickname. But I am still confused. If the Chinese couldn't come to America but Mr. Chen could travel to China and back, how did you get into America?"

"After a federal court ruling in 1915, the exclusion law exempted merchants, so he applied for a merchant visa for me as a tea exporter. Tu was born in November 1915. After our business together became successful and he saw how hard it was going to be for Tu living in America, he wanted us to live here. For us. He thought of it as a resort, like Cannes or Saint-Tropez. And he was right! We loved it here and traveled to the West Coast annually for business."

"Do you think he knew this day would come?"

"He was wise, but not a fortune teller."

"But you and your son will be apart."

"He is a grown man and a chameleon. Tu could pass for one of Mao's country people as easily as he passed for your butler. He can stay here longer than I could."

"The thought of being separated . . . ."

Madam Tong reached over to Peg and held her hand. They sat in silence as Peg suddenly felt her own mother's absence afresh.

Despite the heat and humidity that night, she needed Bill to hold her.

He listened as she told him of her conversation with Madam Tong, of Leon being American, her son, and his plan to go to the U.S. to manage their tea empire. Peg continued, "And she is packing up the good stuff starting next week. She says we are to tell Beth she's redecorating."

"She'll see through that."

"Well, you've had us moving things back little by little for months. First, the special purchases here, the big porcelain serving platter with the crimson dragon on the rim, bolts of silk, the ginger jars, our extra winter clothes, and the silver tea service, all wrapped up in blankets. Then the extra clothes and books and the carved rosewood end tables you found before Beth's birthday. We only have our winter clothes and a few odds and ends left. Maybe a crate worth. What's changed?"

He took a deep breath. "Couple weeks ago. Battle of Yanzhou. It's no secret, but the papers barely covered it. Let me piece it together for you. Fighting was over the central portion of the rail system, which had been going on for months. Mao's got control of the railroads now and is pushing the Nationalists into Tsingtao and Jinan. He can move troops and supplies. The Nationalists can't. The campaign was grueling."

"How bad?"

He whispered, "I hear over 60,000 Nationalist troops. Mao's troops are only a day's drive away. They are at our backdoor. But it's a holding game."

When the phone rang, he swore and hurried to the hall to answer it. A few minutes later, he came back to bed, grinning. "I told Andy to stay home next week. Mother and *daughter* are doing fine."

Peg sighed. "I'm glad the *Repose* was in port."

Bill was silent for a while, then asked, "Say, your friend Claire? Where was she during the war?"

Peg leaned against his shoulder despite the heat. The fan rippled her nightgown. "Why are we talking about her?"

He persisted. "Any idea?"

Peg sat up and flapped the front of her nightgown. "New York, I think. She mentioned some newspapers, but I can't recall the names."

"Nothing in D.C. or military?"

She frowned. "Where is this going?"

"She pulled a Medalist out of her purse when she took Beth to get some snapshots at the beach while you were patching up Sally. That camera was only issued to the government. Think she might have had it at the New Year's party or Beth's birthday, but I didn't pay it any mind. She distracted Beth nicely with it, but left me scratching my head. Where'd she get it?"

"Dad said the Medalist had a second version with a flash for the public."

"No. It was the original. Same model I've seen used by military correspondents and some intelligence officers."

"I'll invite her over to develop film again. See what develops." She laughed at her own joke, then Bill tossed his pillow at her.

CHAPTER 27

Mikhail was late again. Claire had dressed for the party at the British Embassy and was fidgeting over her Chablis.

Sebastian grinned when the door opened, revealing the tardy Mikhail. "So pleased you could join us." He lifted his empty glass. "As you are a round late, I offer you my appreciation for subsidizing our evil ways when David presents our monthly accounting."

Mikhail stood before the two seated members of the Booth Club and spread his arms. "I have an announcement. My daughter is getting married to a wonderful young man. They have known each other for over a year. He has become a member of our family both at worship and around our dinner table." Mikhail dropped his arms. "Where is Jean-Claude? I wanted to tell you all at the same time."

Claire adopted Jean-Claude's French nonchalance with a toss of her hair. "Embassy party. I'll let him in on the best news of the year."

Sebastian peppered him with questions, but he held up his palms. Claire stood and hugged him. She raised her eyebrows. "And how long have you known without telling us? It takes time to find a wedding gift!"

"She made me promise not to tell until it was all fixed. So much paperwork. The American Embassy. Rabbi. Medical clearance. It's been a swirl. And Arina has been floating on air for weeks, in joy for Katia and despair of losing her. But as a couple, they are two boots to a pair, that well-suited for each other."

Claire nudged him. "Who is he?"

"Jacob is a doctor in the American Navy."

Claire hugged him again. "Doctor Stein! I've met him. He's wonderful."

"His family lives in San Diego, in the lower part of California. He showed me on a map." His eyes brimmed. "She'll go there now as his wife, live with his people. He swears we will visit each other."

Claire asked, "What can we get them? Her trousseau? Clothes for America? Can I help?"

He laughed. "No. I appreciate your offer, but the details are all taken care of. However, we would be honored if you all would attend the reception after the wedding."

"At your synagogue? Or here?"

He laughed with a robustness she had not heard in weeks. "No. The nurses on his ship have arranged it. Mrs. Goldstein, the German lady who owns that boarding house on the beach. She's providing German and Russian delicacies. And of course, Chinese food."

Claire hesitated before asking. "At her place?"

"No. Reception hall. Just up Chungshan Road, about five minutes away. It's near the orphanage where they met. It's next Sunday, September fifth."

She grinned. "Wonderful." She blew a kiss to Sebastian. "Gotta run. Congratulations, Mik!"

CHAPTER 28

Six months after ditching his plane at sea, Phil Wilson twisted, not yet awake, tangled in sweat-soaked sheets.

Water to my waist, I look up. The canopy's back, but I'm not floating up. Tethered to a dead pile of iron. Twist free of the shoulder straps. But now I am floating ass up, head down. The blue devil is dragging me under even deeper. Ears pop.

Last of my breath escapes.

Then, I see it. The fucking radio wire leashes me to the plane.

Tug! The wires suddenly breaks. I'm free! Spit out like Jonah.

My shoulder shook. Shark!

Kick it away. Heel hit it.

Free.

Up.

Up to air.

Up to the light.

Then it hits my shoulder again as I follow my bubbles to the surface.

Then I hear it.

A woman.

Eleanor?

She held his shoulder. "It's okay. It's Saturday. You're not flying today."

Wet pillow. Wet cheeks. Not at sea. Safe.

She reached out again. Wrapped her arms around him. Her warmth against his back, safe from his flailing, calmed him. Pushing past moments of weakness, of shame.

"You okay now?"

How could he tell her he would never be okay again? That part of him had died. How could they live without his flight pay? If he wasn't a pilot, who was he? What could he do for a living?

She held him until the shaking stopped, until the sweat dried, until he could breathe again.

Phil lifted his watch off the nightstand. Three. Later than the usual visitations.

She looked at him. *Christ, how long can we put up with this madness? How long can he keep flying with only two hours of proper sleep without killing himself or one of his buddies?*

Pulling the cord on his pajamas, she held him until he was hard. Once he became the man he wanted to be, she straddled him.

In the morning, she put the empty Canadian Club bottle in the trash, made pancakes before he woke, and kept them warm for him in the small oven in their apartment.

She was frying the bacon when he came into the kitchen, a towel around his waist, his crew cut wet and spiky. She smoothed his hair, smiled, and gave him a kiss that elicited a grin. He took the pan off the burner. "Happy Saturday. We got a squadron party tonight." He pulled the cord on her robe.

She smiled back. "Someone feeling his oats?"

"Rather be feeling you next to me."

She pulled his towel away and leaned into him. His response pleased him. He was back.

They were ferocious in bed, each conquering fear masked as passion.

When it was over, he fondled her breast tenderly. "How'd I ever get so lucky?"

She kissed him. "Gonna need another shower, or those boys will know how we fiddled away the morning."

"Let 'em, so they know I'm the luckiest son of a bitch on Earth."

She lifted to one elbow. "The dreams—"

"Everyone has dreams, Ellie."

"Not like yours."

"I'm fine."

She didn't want to lose the morning, so she grinned at him. "Finer than frog's hair."

"Right. Think the bacon survived?"

"Let's go see."

The cars started parking along Shaoguan at six. Men did not come late when Bill hosted a squadron party at his house. Once he set the date, Peg coordinated with the wives to avoid duplicates of the heavy appetizers. By default, the host provided the first round and the unmarried pilots brought extra booze.

Given the potential for loose lips when the men talked "business," Bill excused Leon from the party or cleaning duties. At five, Leon and Beth went to Madam Tong's bungalow to play records and dominoes. Sally joined them at six.

As couples arrived, the platters and bowls populated the dining table. Peg had made a huge cheese and salami tray. Trudy brought cocktail franks in barbecue sauce. Others offered bowls and platters, and soon the table held ham and cheese finger sandwiches, meatballs floating in tomato sauce, cold shrimp and hot sauce, a crab dip, pots of pimento cheese and a deviled ham dip sat beside a bowl of Ritz crackers, deviled eggs, brownies, Rice Crispy squares, and a coconut cream pie.

After they inhaled the food, the squadron members split into three factions. At nine, most of the single guys headed out for a club, with Gerri and JD joining them. Phil and Eleanor Wilson left in the chaos, heading for home. The remaining men refreshed their drinks and circulated between a raucous game of pool and more civilized discussions of flying and politics in the living room.

Women congregated in the kitchen. Peg put the kettle on for Lipton tea from the commissary and brought out a bottle of white wine and another of brandy. As they collected the platters and bowls, the variety of patterns became clear. In shifts, between chatting and sipping, the women washed and dried the dishes.

As Trudy dried a platter with a gold band at the edge, she asked, "Whose is this? It's beautiful!"

Patty laughed. "Arturo said I could 'buy whatever china I wanted in China.' His big joke."

"Wow, that's great."

"You know 'three moves'—"

Several women finished the saying, "—'are as good as a fire.'"

"Well, we did it in just one move! We got all the household goods packed up for storage and followed the mover out to the main road. Then we watched as he missed the turn and flipped the truck into a ditch. He was okay, but it burst into flames. I am not kidding."

"How'd you ever—"

"Fortunately, I'd already sent what I needed to stay at my folks while he was over here."

Trudy asked, "Where'd you find it? It's lovely."

"There's a little antique shop. Not much to look at in front, but he's got a big back room filled with crates of dishes, silverware, and crystal glasses he bought from the rich folks leaving town. I'll get the address if any of you are interested."

Looking around, Patty asked, "Hey. Where's Eleanor?"

Maxine held a soapy dish and said, "Ellie and Phil ducked out with the singles crowd. They don't seem like they're at parties much these days."

Peg put a fresh pot of tea on the worktable. "She said he was feeling tired."

Patty asked, "Did she leave her dish? I can drop it off tomorrow."

Peg shook her head. "She slipped it into a paper sack and took it with her. Guess she was planning on an early evening."

On the drive home, Eleanor watched Phil and wondered if the other pilots had nightmares that slashed their nights to tatters and if their wives ever wondered if their marriage would survive.

A week later, when Phil was gone for a few days to Shanghai, she haunted the bars in the off-limits part of town. Sailors and drunks, smelling of incense and beer, rolling out of dim doorways, bumped into her frequently.

They ignored her at the Cherry Club and the Prime Club. She left the dime-a-dance joint immediately.

Finally, at the Lucky Seven, she came in at last call and nursed a brandy and soda until she was the only customer left. The bartender approached her table and wiped it down. "Need to wrap it up." She raised her glass and threw back her drink. As she stood, she purposely swayed into him.

He blocked her fall with his body and righted her. "Steady there. I'll get you a rickshaw or do you want a cab? You aren't walking home like that."

"Didn't think I could get a buzz tonight. Got some troubles."

He flipped the wet bar towel over his shoulder. "You looking for someone or what? I ain't seen you here before."

"Can't sleep. Man troubles."

He motioned toward her wedding ring. "Hubby doing you wrong? That why you're boozing?"

"Can't a lady have a drink?"

"Sure, but are you interested in something stronger?"

"I might be. Will it make me sleep?"

"Like the dead. Ever heard of opium? Go to an opium den. You can sleep there."

She huffed and pushed at his shoulder. "He'd know if I'm gone. And if I brought it home, having all that stuff in his house, he'd beat me, either way."

"What about *maduk*? Ever try it?"

She frowned and sat back down in the booth, hard. "What?"

"It's a mix of opium and tobacco. Smoke it in a regular pipe or cigs. No lamps or opium pipes to give it away. The heat from the tobacco is enough to work the opium."

Then, per her plan, she got testy, baiting him. "I don't believe you. I've never heard of it."

"Want a sample to see if I'm lying?"

"I can't do it here. Gotta get home. He'll be back later."

He took her glass to the bar and placed it in the sink. Just when she thought he'd been bluffing, he opened the cash register, removed the drawer, and pulled out a hand-rolled cigarette. He handed it to her. She took it. Both ends were twisted tight.

"Open the one end, make it like a cigarette. It's gonna smell awful, so burn some incense."

"How much?" She suppressed her smile.

"Nothing tonight. If you come back, I can introduce you to someone."

Mission accomplished.

CHAPTER 29

As had become their custom, Fred left church and was at his apartment by one on Sunday afternoon. Benny Goodman's music filled the room when Anna arrived shortly after three. He turned down the radio.

"Sorry I'm late."

He smiled. "Glad you made it. How about an early dinner of some stir-fry, or did you fill up on cake?"

"Always got room for your cooking. Wish you coulda come to the reception. Katia was beaming."

He popped the caps from two beers. She took a sip and told him all about the reception while he chopped green beans and fresh mushrooms, and made a sauce of minced ginger, sesame oil, soy sauce, and rice wine. She smiled when she realized he had already boiled, cooled, and lightly oiled the lo mein noodles.

As he minced several cloves of garlic, he said, "Funny thing about this kinda cooking. It's all prep, then it cooks up in a second."

She looked at the collection of bowls holding the many ingredients. "But you got all these dishes."

He sliced scallions at an angle for a garnish and asked, "Can you light the fire under the fry pan?"

"Sure."

While the pan heated, she set the table with forks and called back to him, "Okay if I open the window?" He clicked off the radio. As he flash-fried the ingredients in the order he learned from watching street cooks, the small room filled with rich spiced scents. When he brought their steaming plates to the table, he grinned.

"Oh, my gosh! This smells even better than it looks."

He teased, "You saying there's something wrong with the way it looks?"

She shook her head, took a bite, and rolled her eyes. "You sure you don't want to open a Chinese place when you get home? This is fantastic!"

"Nope. Got my plan. Gonna be lively music and the best ribs in all of Norfolk."

"Why music?"

"I watch you. Seems to me you love your music about as much as my cooking. Guess other folks might too."

"Might be. Ever learn to play an instrument in school? Clarinet or trumpet?"

He laughed. "Why those?"

"Seems like something you might pick."

The breeze fluttered the curtain. "Nope. No band where I went to school. We were lucky to have books in Norfolk. Hand-me-downs from the white schools. Some had a list of eight or nine students' names inside the covers. Some of 'em so old, you'd wonder if the Civil War was still going on. Or the 'War of Northern Aggression,' as they called it."

Anna leaned back and watched him as he shook off old memories.

She took a drink. "This is such a relief from the ship, just talking. Like sitting on a stoop at home with a neighbor."

"I never imagined you'd come up for lunch that first time."

"Neither did the Navy!" She giggled.

He tipped his head, then cautiously pulled back the edge of the curtain.

She chuckled. "What now? They back at it like rabbits?"

He smirked and let the curtain drop. "Not yet." The voices from the alley caught her ear. She reached for the curtain. He motioned for her to be quiet as he stood at the side of the window and peeked into the alley.

Now she heard it.

The argument was a swirl of Chinese and English. Words tangling over words. Escalating to shouting. She went behind Fred, looking around his shoulder. A thin man in a Hawaiian shirt motioned for the rickshaw-coolie to leave, fanning him away with one hand while holding a paper sack in the other. The ragged man pointed to his rickshaw, waved his arms over his head, shouted, and held out his hand.

The green door to the row house across the alley burst open, clattering against the tin siding. A brick of a man in green fatigues ran into the alley and grabbed the rickshaw-coolie by the shoulder. The coolie twisted free and stumbled back. He kept yelling and pointing at the thin man.

Wayne shouted over the man's outrage, "What's going on, JD?"

"Wants a second fare. He can go to hell."

JD walked away, but the man grabbed the back of his loose shirt. As JD spun, the sack ripped. A paper box fell against his chest splattering a deep mahogany sauce onto the cobblestones. JD grabbed the man's shirt and cocked a fist.

Wayne wedged between them, his back to JD, shouting, "For Christ's sake, go inside! I'll pay him off."

Wayne faced the fuming man and reached into his side pocket and pulled out a fistful of bills wrapped in a rubber band.

Seeing the wad of money, the coolie lunged for it. Wayne pulled back, turning to his right. The coolie grabbed the K-Bar from Wayne's belt. He pointed the tip of the knife at JD, who stumbled backward. The coolie lunged at Wayne like a fencer, jabbing at him, motioning for the money. Before Wayne could react, the knife glanced off his rib and found his belly.

He doubled over as he fell, landed on his side, and rolled to his back, motionless.

The ragged man scooped up the bills from the filthy street. In the horrid silence that followed, Fred saw the thin man turn and sprint away from them, into the maze of alleys.

Anna started for the door. "God!"

Fred grabbed her arm. "You can't."

"Have to!"

She wriggled free and ran down the stairs, Fred on her heels, and sprinted toward the bleeding man just as the coolie brushed past her. Fred spun and took off after him.

She dropped to her knees and searched for a pulse. Nothing. She tried his neck. Her head swimming, she put her palm down for balance as she tried to stand. Blood was spreading downhill toward her right hand. Her fingers were suddenly wet.

Fred returned, winded, grabbed her elbow, and helped her up. *Blood on her hand. Her shoes are clean. No footprints.*

"Come on!"

Holding her shoulders, he steered her to his door. She leaned her forearms on the kitchen sink, head down, catching her breath.

He washed her hand in the sink and let the cold water run until it was clear, then had her wash her hands twice more. He guided her to a chair and inspected her knees, a snagged stocking, still no blood. Her shoes were still clean. The hem of her dress, too.

He faced her. "Get back on the ship as fast as you can."

"We saw—"

"Something we can't do nothing about." He grabbed a cloisonné vase. "Here! Take it. I bought it for you in a shop across town. The card from the shop's still inside. Go to the ship and brag about the great deal you got on it there. That'll put you far away from here."

She took the vase but stalled.

He pointed to the door. "Nothing we do can change any of this, except keep you the hell out of it. Now go!"

After she left, he discovered a dark spot in the center of his shirt. Blood? From the coolie when he'd grabbed him? From washing her hands? He pulled his shirt free and blotted the browning stain with a wet cloth. It wasn't coming out. The sauce! He ran his finger through the remains of the stir-fry on his plate and smudged the brown sauce on his shirt as he heard a siren in the distance. He sprinted down the alley away from Chungshan Road.

That night in Badaguan, Peg stretched as she came into their bedroom and started to change for bed. "She's sawing logs."

Bill pulled back the sheet and slid into bed. "Busy day!"

"Sorry you couldn't go to the wedding reception with us."

"They're rotating out some of the older planes. We're getting eight new and a couple of almost new Corsairs. The crew chief and I had to verify all the maintenance orders and that all the parts were changed before I released them for flight."

"Ready now?"

"Almost. Tell me about the reception."

"It was wonderful. Joyous. Claire helped Beth line up some shots. And the cake! I think Beth had three pieces."

"Sounds like she had a ball."

"She did. We stopped for an early dinner at the club in town and she seemed moody. That's why I wanted your opinion. Did she seem out of sorts when you got home?"

He nodded. "Do you think she overheard anyone talking about the infantryman that got stabbed?"

"No. I didn't hear about it until Trudy phoned after we'd come home. Beth started getting fussy during the reception. The cake seemed to distract her there, but she was not herself when we got home."

"Odd. She rarely holds back if she's pissed about something."

"She was so excited to take the pictures of everyone."

He propped up on one elbow as she slipped into bed. "Maybe she was jealous that you had the good camera or that Claire's work got all the attention?"

"No. I asked her, and she said somebody got into a shot. Spoiled it, so she wanted another roll. She's still cranky that I didn't allow it. We'll see how she is in the morning."

"Let's find something to distract her. What's up with your pals? Isn't some kid about to have a party? Seems like there's one every few weeks."

She smiled at him. "Kid's movie tomorrow night. Want to go?"

"If it's all the same. I'll finish writing up the reports."

She let out a small chuckle. "Got it. A little peace and quiet never hurt. Either of us."

"Thanks." After a moment, he said, "Think she needs a new challenge?"

"Should I cut back on my time at the orphanage? When I started going there, the city was alive, and it seemed the right thing to do. Be the good American. But it has changed, we're swamped. And I feel different about it. I can't say why."

"Try, Honey."

She swallowed hard. "I'm really trying to sort it out." He held her closer, and she continued, "It's harder there now. It should be easier to quit. But I want those kids to have a family but know that most won't. Two sisters came in a couple of days ago. There was something special in the way they cared for each other, knowing they were all they had in the world, just tore at me."

"I'd say it's natural. You're an exceptional mother, and those orphans need all the mothering they can get."

"Some days I wonder if I am sacrificing time with Beth so I can help other children."

He gave her a squeeze and laughed. "Oh, Sweetheart. You and Trudy are running a school for Beth and Sally. You go to all the events with other mothers so she can be around other kids. She understands that those children are in need and sees how you are helping Maxine with her baby. Those are huge mothering lessons." He leaned back and grinned. "Seeing the two kids together, did that get you thinking about another baby? Beth's already eight. That's getting to be a big spread between kids.

Like we talked about, she'd be a great older sister—"

"Thank the Corps for her being an only child! Sending you all over hell and gone."

"Well, I'm here now!"

CHAPTER 30

Major Moretti hurried past the Duty Officer at six a.m. Monday and went into the bullpen to put on a pot of coffee. He smiled when he saw Sergeant Jackson on the phone and handwritten statement sheets already in the basket for typing. A fresh pot was stinking up the room. He filled his mug slowly. His guys should have enjoyed their Sunday and come in at eight, but here they were. Call it jungle drums or the grapevine. Somehow, they always knew what to do. Fast-tracking the information, they'd follow leads when they were fresh and finish the paperwork later.

Sergeant Ripley came in with a fistful of papers, pulling his tie loose, looking like the Chicago detective he'd been before the war. "Got yesterday's liberty logs and the check-in sheet from the SPs at the gangplanks for both ships. Put in a request to Marine HQ for duty rosters for Sunday afternoon, twelve hundred to eighteen hundred hours. At least we'll know who was not in town."

Sergeant Bowen ran in after him. "Just left the *Repose*. Doc narrowed it to sixteen hundred, plus or minus half an hour, medically. But says to use the call to the Shore Patrol as the latest. Says it was fast and more like a punch to the gut."

Ripley said, "Okay. The call was at sixteen-ten, barely after four. No name or info offered, just 'a Marine in the alley needs a medic.' A guy. Rattled. Street sounds, so probably a pay phone somewhere. That's it. Sunday afternoon. Couldn't have been a worse time. Weekend shore leave, a wedding reception, some doings at the marina."

"Folks were scattered like chickens all over town. And half of 'em drunk. Anything else from the doc?" The coffee seemed bitter to Moretti.

259

Bowen said, "He released the knife to me. I logged it in. Says to expect his written report in a few days, but the knife wound killed him. Knife's a Marine issue."

Moretti watched Bowen. "Prove it."

"First, it has the stacked leather washer handle design the Marines use. Navy K-Bars have a plastic handle, so it won't rot at sea. Second, his knife wasn't in his leather sheath on his belt. Third, a serial number scratched on it matched his dog tags."

Shaking his head, Moretti smirked. "A real Sherlock move there. Great! A Marine gets killed with his own knife. Let me see the transmittal request for the print run to D.C. before you package it all up."

"Sure thing, boss."

When he sat at his desk and started reviewing the notes, he grinned. *You can call these guys sergeants and pay them crap, but they stack up with the best of the big-city detectives I've ever met.*

Monday was a goat rope. Rumors scattered as far as his three investigators could travel. By five, Moretti had twenty-some pages of typed statements on his desk. Ripley came in holding a stack of paper. "Boss! I finished matching the liberty log to the sentry logs. Everyone allowed to be off the ships came back." Before Moretti took the pages, his telephone rang. He motioned Ripley to stay. After the call, Moretti said, "Lieutenant Colonel Mathis set a briefing at nineteen hundred."

Ripley said, "We'll be in the bullpen if you have questions."

Twenty-three minutes later, he returned the typed interviews to the bullpen.

Bowen, Jackson, and Ripley looked up when Moretti stood in the doorway.

"Nice work. Let me feed it back and see if I'm on target. Lieutenant Wayne Argos called a drill on Sunday morning because of some sloppy work in the field during a rainstorm the week before. It pissed off his unit to miss a down day, or the start of the annual Marine-Navy football game. He was as demanding of himself as others. Spit-and-polish, even in the field."

Bowen cleared his throat. "Usually. One Marine reported Argos said he intended to change in his room at the BOQ because his laundry delivery was late, so he didn't have his spare fatigues in his gym locker to clean up before going into town per usual. He told another guy he had no time to change. Had to get something before a store closed."

Moretti fanned through the reports again. "Wearing dirty fatigues was out of character for the guy." Moretti's shoulders slumped. "Need to see what was in the gym locker and at his quarters."

Bowen leaned back in his chair. "I did 'em both, sir. Writing it up now. Someone said he played basketball at the Y, so I checked there too. No lockers there. He usually brought a gym bag. For a neat guy in the field, he collected lots of local stuff. Had a footlocker at the BOQ jammed full of carvings, mostly ivory or rosewood. A couple of silk scrolls. Everything is small and of high value. All very classy. Stuff you'd decorate a mansion with or sell to an antique dealer back home. Nothing kinky. But the ivory looked old enough to be on the antiquities list of contraband. No clue how he planned to smuggle it home."

"Good work. Oh, can one of you remind Graves Registration that we'll need to keep all his belongings here? We'll make the release to the family after the investigation is closed."

Jackson raised his hand. "On it, sir."

"Thanks. Anything interesting in that bag?"

"Standard ID and stuff. Got a key. Loose in his pocket with some change. I'd like to check it out of evidence and see what a local locksmith could tell us about it."

"Do it."

Bowen asked, "What do you make of the uniform thing? Why'd he lie about something as dumb as where to change?"

Moretti said, "Just one more question in the bucket. What'd you get from the scene, Ripley?"

"Not much of value besides the knife. Torn bag of food on the ground nearby. Ribs in dark sauce. Gotta be from that day, or something would have eaten it overnight. Maybe he just got back from a food run and the guy figured him for some money and followed him into the alley."

Moretti asked, "What else?"

"A shirt button, under him, civilian, not military. Who knows how long that was there? We didn't bag the usual alley crap that looked like it'd been there forever. Bone scraps, some dog shit."

"Thanks, guys. Good work. Anything else I should know before seeing Mathis tonight? Shore Patrol begged off since the victim was a Marine."

When Bowen's phone rang, he cupped his hand around the mouthpiece. Several fast exchanges. Hanging up, he said, "Duty Officer on the *Estes* said the sentry saw a guy with a messy uniform. Stain on the belly. Sailor made a joke about him being a sloppy eater, spilling soy sauce on himself. Signed back aboard at sixteen-twenty. After hearing about the Marine, the sentry told the Duty Officer and amended the log. I asked him to get the shirt, book it with us, and give us the amended log."

Jackson grinned. "Interesting. He boards ten minutes after the SP gets that call."

Moretti held up his hand. "I'm not throwing it out at tonight's meeting without more."

"Meeting here or the Colonel's office?"

"Mathis booked the big conference room upstairs for nineteen hundred. Commander Li is coming from the city police."

"Just you two?"

"Yup. Going to grab a bite first."

Jackson said, "Check your desk before you go up. We'll leave anything new there."

Moretti gave him a thumbs-up and left the bullpen but was still close enough to hear Bowen say, "Booked the conference room? For three people? What a dick."

Moretti left his office five minutes before the meeting, although it was just an elevator ride to the top floor of the hotel annex. It was as pretentious as calling the cluster of cops on the first floor the 'Joint Operations Sino-American Police'. When Moretti arrived, he ignored the dented conference table and mismatched chairs. The room had once been a penthouse for dignitaries or the honeymoon suite before the war, and the wallpaper boasted palm trees and rickshaws that seemed overly festive for the matter at hand. He looked over the bay. The ceiling fan barely moved the humid air.

Lieutenant Colonel Mathis rushed in, in full uniform, swagger stick under his arm, as if he were a British General in the Punjab. Moretti glanced back at the sea. *When did riding crops become swagger sticks?* That useless status symbol of exotic wood with silver fittings at both ends. Some had the eagle, globe, and anchor, others featured a dragon. Mathis let his stick clatter on the table to get attention.

Just as bad as the "ring-knockers" from the Academy, clicking their rings against their ever-present coffee mugs, reminding everyone how special they were. Same stunt. Same clatter and chest pounding. Moretti forced himself to look at Mathis, ignoring the accessory.

Mathis checked his watch. Commander Li had taken his seat beside Moretti when Mathis barked, "Where's the Navy in this briefing?"

Moretti said, "They deferred to the MPs for any added investigation since the victim was a Marine."

"Didn't they have a suspect? Some messman?" Mathis lit a cigar. The cloud barely shifted.

Moretti was being blindsided. "Sir, they gave us the sentry logs. They showed the return time of any personnel. Just before I left my office, we got a call from his ship reporting that a messman had a stained shirt-front. Named him. That's it. Returned to his ship with a spot on his uniform. Maybe blood. Maybe soy sauce, for all we know. We asked them to bag the shirt and get it over to us. Not much to make him a suspect."

Mathis frowned. "What is this? Some kind of Mexican standoff? I got a suspect and you're not interested? Hell of a mess."

Moretti tapped the table. "I think it's flimsy—"

Mathis cut him off and glared at Commander Li. "Can your guys put him near the stabbing?"

"The major asked me that. So far, we have no witnesses to the attack or anyone reporting a sailor being nearby."

"So, nobody can tell me where he was in the city? In his whites, on Sunday. A colored sailor in uniform!"

Li declined to answer as Mathis grew more agitated.

Mathis pointed at Moretti. "What can the lab here do? Can they tell if that boy had the victim's blood on his uniform?"

Moretti said, "When we got the info about the shirt, we asked the Navy to confiscate it. No word back on that yet. But that's pointless, anyway."

Mathis boomed, "And why is that?"

"Even if it is blood, they both had the same blood type. I checked their files. All he has to say is he 'cut himself' if it isn't a food stain. Cooks get cut."

"I've got a *potential* suspect. And you both tell me you have shit."

"It's early," Moretti said. "We'll see if D.C. can pull any prints off the knife. Expect a two- or three-week turnaround. Until then, it's an open question."

"I'm not letting him off his ship to disappear. Got it? So, you tell his captain that I want him in custody in the brig ashore or confined to quarters on his ship."

"Based on what we have, I'd feel better if they confined him to his ship."

Standing, Mathis started for the door. "Fine. Just so you *feel* better. Let me know when you get the report on the prints or anything on that shirt."

"Count on it, sir."

After Mathis left, Commander Li stood.

Moretti stood quickly and offered a quick bow to the man. A courtesy that he rarely extended, but this man, this Oxford-educated warrior attempting to be a peacekeeper, this man merited it. "Let me apologize for—"

He brushed the comment away with his uncommon grace.

When they left, Moretti took a taxi to the *Repose*. He went to the sick bay waiting room.

About eight, a doctor in pale green scrubs called his name. "Oh. Sorry, I didn't recognize you, Doc."

"Not my Sunday-go-to-meeting attire. But it was an emergency. I had to set a compound fracture. It was so bad that I needed some wire to hold the mess together."

"Thanks for the preliminary info you gave my guys."

"Not at all. Report's in for typing now. I'll have it walked over to you as soon as I sign off on it. Come in. I'll give you the highlights."

"Appreciate it."

Moretti followed him to a small exam room. He leaned against a table while the doctor plopped into a chair.

"Long day?"

"Long enough. The deceased—"

"Lieutenant Wayne Argos."

"Yes. My report must call him the deceased, but I will take your point. He was a man, a Marine, and I don't forget that either. Wayne was right-handed. He carried his sidearm there. His K-Bar was on the left hip. Both logic and the scabbard's placement on his utility belt confirm that. I released his effects to your investigator."

"Got it."

"Here's my impression. Someone facing him used their right hand to pull his knife from its sheath. The incision is across Wayne's body, a right-hander's customary angle of attack. Your arm is stronger going toward your center than away. I've seen more of these gut cuts than I ever wanted to from battle. Most of 'em we can stitch up in surgery, thankfully.

But a battlefield wound is usually more orderly, practiced, than a street fight. Lower in the belly to avoid hitting a rib. This guy just nicked it. Training is to open an intestine so if you missed the aortic artery, infection finishes the job. This entry was higher."

Moretti said, "But lethal."

"Indeed. Severed the aorta, here." He pointed to his solar plexus. "That's the primary artery from the heart to everything that's important. Bled out in a matter of seconds, not minutes. I couldn't have saved him if I'd been five feet away."

"So right-handed, not trained. Or the guy was in a hurry. Any defensive wounds, a scraped knuckle or anything?"

"Just a small scuff on his ear, probably from the fall."

Moretti asked, "Robbery?"

"That's your business. Stabbed in an alley, Sunday afternoon. Might expect a guy to have a bankroll on him to pick up some trinkets, or a girl. Healthy, but for that wound. Had to open him to confirm the damage. Want to look?"

"No. But I will."

Moretti went back to his office to make a quick note of his discussion. A message from Bowen was on his blotter. "Navy sending shirt in a.m. BUT the sailor did what they train cooks to do—bleached and hand washed his shirt immediately. No joy!"

CHAPTER 31

Tuesday, Gerri woke at five when JD bolted out of bed. Groggy, she looked outside. The sun touched the top of the pines by the tennis court. She tried to open the bathroom door, but he pushed it shut.

She yelled, "Hey! I gotta pee!"

He pulled the bath towel away from his face and called, "Use the one downstairs." He moaned dramatically. "Still got the trots something awful." When he heard her leave, he dug in his travel kit for eye drops and returned to the toilet. *The drops took the red out after a bender.* But he'd have to stop crying first.

When she returned, she tapped again. "Open up! Got you a soda to settle your stomach."

"Leave it on the dresser. I'll get it when I can."

He sat on the toilet, sobbing into the towel. When he heard her in the bedroom, he moaned and flushed occasionally.

Gerri dressed and brought up toast and Pepto, leaving them beside the soda on the dresser. "JD? I'm going downstairs. I'll tell Bill that you're still sick, so he won't wait for you."

When Leon came in to make coffee and then breakfast for the family, it startled him to see her. Gerri asked, "You got any tricks to help him get better besides Pepto? JD has the Tsingtao trots. Started yesterday."

"*Dootze-tung* can be bad. Eat plain rice. Drink lukewarm tea with sugar. Wet towel on head. Wash hands!"

Gerri was making tea and Leon was boiling rice when Bill, in his flight suit, came into the kitchen for coffee. "Early flight. JD get eight hours of sleep?"

She shrugged. "He was up all night."

267

Bill poured his coffee without looking at her. Without the required sleep, JD couldn't fly, even if his gut settled down. Now they were short one on a recon mission.

JD was pale and slept most of Tuesday. Gerri nagged her husband to see a doctor. He brushed her concerns aside and ate small, bland meals. He didn't fly until Friday.

The next week, while JD packed his flight bag, he glanced at her, still in bed. "What does your book club think about that guy getting stabbed last week?"

"Oh, Margaret's all up in arms. She heard about it the next day and called all of us. Wants the colonel to have MPs escort us when we go shopping. Thinks the killer was a refugee."

"Why? Was it a robbery?"

Gerri grabbed her robe. "Guess so. Want some eggs? I got some cheese at the commissary and can make you a real French omelet. She showed me how. They were in France for a while before the war, attached to the embassy in Paris. Says I'm as good as her French cook."

"You hanging out, making omelets with her?"

"No. One book we read had some French food in it. She took a class there in French cooking. 'Cuisine,' she calls it."

He closed his bag. "Bet that was fun."

"She says there's a hundred kinds of cheese there. Can you imagine?"

"Nope."

"You know, Leon's not the only one around here that knows how to cook. Can I make you one now?"

"Another time, Baby. I'm flying today. I can't pull to the side of a cloud and take a dump."

"Such talk."

"How come you're getting so high and mighty?"

"Just want to be refined. Margaret says . . . ."

He forced a smile as he grabbed his flight bag. "You're doing fine. You getting close to her is a real step up."

She followed him downstairs, gave him a hug at the door, and watched as he backed the borrowed Jeep onto the street. He waved as he shut the gate.

A mile out of town, he pulled to the side of the road, draped his arms around the top of the steering wheel, and sobbed.

CHAPTER 32

Two weeks after Moretti's men sent Wayne's knife to the FBI, Bowen rapped on the open door of Moretti's office and waved a Teletype sheet as he entered. "They got matches on two of the three sets on the K-Bar blade!"

"The cook?"

He handed the flimsy paper to Moretti. "No. Both were Marines. Wayne Argos, infantry and John David Summers, aviation. At the top of the blade, there was a clean thumbprint on one side and index on the other, but not in the registry. Smudges on the leather handle."

"Know anything about Summers?"

"Pulled his record. A flyboy. No mention of him in any of the interviews by city police or us. No incidents in his personnel jacket. Married, living in Badaguan."

Moretti frowned. "Bit pricey for a lieutenant, isn't it?"

"Shares a house with another family."

"Before I invite him in for an interview, why don't you try to figure out where they could have run into each other, on or off duty? See if there is some connection, so I'm not interviewing him cold. And let me know who he's rooming with."

"Sure thing, boss."

Three days later, Moretti had JD brought to his office late in the afternoon. Once seated, Moretti smiled. "I asked you here because the duty roster showed you as off duty at the time that one of our servicemen died from an attack in town. I'm sure you heard about it a few Sundays ago. We are looking for witnesses who might have seen anything to assist us in figuring out who might have assaulted him."

JD stalled. His neck seemed to color slightly. He put on a frown suggesting deep thought, then he smiled. "Was that the day of the football game, the Baby Rice Bowl out at the Bismarck Barracks? Navy against Marines."

Moretti nodded.

JD grinned. "Yeah. I went to the game."

"Meet some friends there?"

He shook his head. "I didn't plan it. Came in late and sat by myself."

"Remember the final score?"

"Navy won. Game was boring, so I went over to the gym and did some weights."

"Go there often?"

"Couple times a month, sometimes more. Gotta stay in shape."

"Ever box? Use the timing bag?"

"No."

Moretti watched him as he asked, "Do roadwork?"

"You mean go for a run? Sure. Like in basic."

"Was Argos your running partner?" Moretti waited to see if he asked who Wayne was.

He stammered. "Partner? No. We'd do some roadwork or spot each other on weights if we bumped into each other. Nothing planned."

"So, after you left the football game and gym, where did you go?"

"Home. I was home at sixteen hundred, or a couple minutes earlier, but not much. You can ask my wife. She got home about the same time from her book club. She was tired, so I made us a couple of sandwiches, ham and cheese with mayo and mustard. Loves lots of mustard on her sandwich. We ate upstairs, casual."

"You live alone? Just you and your wife?"

"No, sir. We live with Captain Ryan and his family out in Badaguan. Has a wife and kid."

"See them when you got home?"

He shook his head. "They went to some kid's birthday party or a wedding. We fooled around, if you get my drift, so we didn't go downstairs that night."

"How about we take it from the time you got up?"

"That Sunday?"

Moretti tapped on his notes. "Same day, Sunday. What time did you get up?"

"Gee. Seven or seven-thirty. I was off duty that weekend, so might have slept in a little longer."

"Have breakfast?"

"Yes."

"Lunch?"

"Not there. Thought I'd get something at the game."

"Go anywhere in the morning?"

JD smiled. "Nope. Hung around the house until about eleven when she needed to finish some book for her club. Has a regular reading room. Shuts the bedroom door, parks herself in a chair that catches the breeze, opens her book, and gets lost for hours."

"What was it?"

"What?"

"The book. It's title."

He frowned. "I don't remember. Is that important?"

"Just interested in finding a new book to read."

"I'll ask her the title and get back to you."

"That won't be necessary. I'll ask her myself."

JD's mouth opened. Moretti waited. JD swallowed. "Is that it?"

"For now."

Moretti stood and walked him out. JD faltered slightly when he saw his wife, neatly dressed, in the lobby. He smiled at her. "Want me to wait for you here, Babe?"

She asked Moretti, "Is this going to take long?"

"Shouldn't."

He gave her arm a gentle squeeze. "Why don't I meet you next door in the Grand's bar when you're done?"

"That'd be nice."

Moretti motioned smoothly with his arm. "This way, if you please."

Once seated, Gerri crossed her legs and arranged the hem of her light cotton skirt modestly. Moretti watched her, waiting, wanting to be wrong about her husband.

"I am trying to put together the pieces on a Sunday over two weeks ago when a serviceman was assaulted. Your husband helped me a lot, but I think you might fill in some gaps I still have in my understanding of that day."

"When that Marine died?"

"Yes. Did you know him?"

"JD said his name was Wayne when I asked him if he knew the guy. He drove tanks, so we didn't really run in the same circles."

"Did you ever see him at the Officers' Club?"

"Which one? JD usually goes to the club by the boats. It's closer to our house. But I don't remember anyone named Wayne hanging around with us."

"Could I show you his picture?"

She paused, then trusted him not to show her a dead man. "Sure."

He slid an eight-by-ten black-and-white head shot of a square-jawed Marine. She picked it up, searched it, and then handed it back to Moretti, shaking her head.

"Now, about that Sunday, can you tell me how your day went, what you did, who you saw?"

"Sure. We got up late, seven-thirty or eight. Later than usual since he had the day off. Had breakfast. It was hot in the house, so we ate in the garden, under the shade, on cute iron benches. There are side tables for the plates and things. Leon makes a good cup of joe, let me tell you. They trained him right."

"After breakfast?"

"I got my nose in the book. I hadn't finished it and had book club at two. That's fourteen hundred for you guys."

"I use both. My wife hates the twenty-four-hour clock. Said you were stupid if you couldn't tell day from night."

Gerri relaxed and laughed. "Is she here?"

"No. Unfortunately."

"Oh, I'm sorry to hear that."

"So, you are in a book club. Is that the one Colonel Stanford's wife hosts?"

She beamed. "Yes, it is."

"She gave us a list of who she remembered being there that day. Would you be kind enough to look it over and tell me if that matches your memory?"

She took the typed sheet, read it, and handed it back. "That's our group. I remember Betty missed that meeting. I don't know why. Maybe she thought the book was too hard to read. Anyway, the list is right for who was there, as far as I recall. Oh, and everyone arrived on time."

Moretti asked, "Can we go back a bit? Did you have lunch?"

"Gee, I don't think so. I just finished the book and got dressed right before Nancy picked me up."

He smiled. "How was the meeting? Did you all enjoy the book?"

"I think they did, but I thought that Somerset Maugham went on and on about stuff in the tropics that was dull. Maybe because he's English. Anyway, she made a gin and tonic to start us off like we were English."

She looked at her hands in her lap and paused. "I didn't like it and said so. But half the women there didn't like them either. Too bitter. So, she made a big pitcher of martinis. Well, they were a hit, so she made a second one. Nancy had to go, but some of us overstayed our welcome. We usually end about four, but I thought it was really late when one hubby came to get his wife. He was steamed. She hadn't come home yet. They live near us, and he offered me a lift. I was in no state to trust a taxi."

"Very responsible. I wish others were as wise."

She offered a strained smile. "Sort of snuck up on me."

"What time do you think you got home?"

"I was afraid JD was gonna be mad at me, since I thought it was dinnertime, about six. But he said it was just four or four-fifteen, I think. He offered to make us some sandwiches. I changed clothes into something cooler, dropped my dress in the hamper, and saw that his shirt was messy. He musta spilled his lunch on it, so I ran it under cold water so the stain wouldn't set on his favorite shirt. Charlie, he's the cook and houseboy, never pays attention to the laundry like that, washes everything together."

"You spotted his shirt? I think that's what my wife calls it."

"Yeah. I want him looking sharp. It's his party shirt, he says. Were you there at the Fourth of July beach party?"

Moretti paused before answering. "Yes, I was."

"That's the Hawaiian one he wore to the picnic. It is the real deal, cotton. Got it in Hawaii, not a cheap local one."

"You've got a good eye for fabric."

"I worked in a mill in North Carolina before I met him. That shirt's gonna be good as new."

"Going back, you changed into cooler clothes, then what?"

"He was a sweetie, made us a couple of sandwiches, and brought up some beer."

"Didn't you eat with the Ryans?"

She cleared her throat. "We don't eat together much anymore. The kid, you know. Different interests and schedules. Anyway, I was half in the bag and starving. So, we ate upstairs."

"Remember what kind of sandwich he made?"

"Sure. Peanut butter and jelly. Said it would settle my tummy."

Moretti tried not to frown as he asked, "And then?"

She cleared her throat. "I sorta passed out. I guess the beer put me over the top. Woke up in my clothes. He teased me about it, but he's so forgiving and supportive. Encourages me to take part in events with the other wives. He's not like some other husbands. And having Leon and a cook, I don't have to do dishes or laundry or much of anything, so I have time for the clubs and meetings and stuff."

"That must be very nice." Moretti watched her. *Did she not mention or remember "fooling around" as JD so delicately put it, or did he lie, or take advantage of a drunken wife?*

She smiled. "It is. We enjoy our time together now even more than we did when we were first married."

"That's wonderful. Wish everyone was as happy as you two. Oh, just for my information, do you recall the book your club discussed that day?"

She smiled. "*The Razor's Edge*. Not new, but it's supposed to be swell. And I said his name wrong. It starts with a letter. It's W. Somerset Maugham."

"Thank you for clarifying."

She smiled. "Is that all?"

"Yes. I don't want to keep your husband waiting. Enjoy your evening." She hurried to the Grand Hotel.

When JD saw her, he stood. "How'd it go?"

"Nice guy. Seemed more interested in my book club than anything else."

She tapped her fingers on the bar top while waiting for JD to order her drink. He drained his in short order.

Neither of them noticed Claire as she passed through the bar into a back room and closed the door. Once there, she discovered only Mikhail had arrived.

He stood, and she hugged him. "Thank you for the honor of being allowed to photograph them before the ceremony. Your daughter was so beautiful."

"She always is. But then I am her father." He shook his head. "California. She'll be a world away. I think Arina feels it already. She took her shopping today and is having them to dinner tonight."

"Where are the fellas?" She looked at her watch. "They're never this late."

"Not coming tonight. I told David to wait on our drinks until I knew if you would be here."

"Where are they?"

"Out trying their magic on my behalf. They both have sources we will never know about. They are trying to find a way for us to get to Australia, but the situation is shifting day by day."

"What's the latest?"

He motioned for her to sit and slid in beside her. "Ever been to Tilanqiao District in Shanghai?" She shook her head. "It's like a Noah's Ark for Jews from all over Europe, and Russian Jews like us. Twenty thousand at one count. I hear it's close to full panic. They are filling up the quotas."

Claire tensed. *After the Holocaust, the losses, the displacement, how could they bear this new horror?* She took a breath and resumed her cover. "Now, there's a human-interest story." She laughed. "Who am I kidding? All my rag wants from me are fashion and food stories."

"Truman recognized the new State of Israel a couple months ago. We applied there too."

Claire touched his arm. "But your shop in Sidney?"

"Fifteen years I've rented there, done business, but it is not enough!" He shut his eyes for a moment, then said, "However, our Katia is safe. She's leaving next week. My daughter. A married woman."

"Let's drink to their happiness. Just us."

He chuckled. "A short drink to a long and happy life. I'll tell David."

CHAPTER 33

The woman's voice startled Moretti when he answered his telephone. "Miss?"

"I'd rather not say."

He frowned, reached for his pen, and noted the time at the top of a legal pad. "How may I help you?"

"I'm only going to say this once, so please don't interrupt me. Okay?"

"Agreed."

"The sailor you have confined to his ship did not do it. You have the wrong person in custody. I saw it. The Marine got stabbed. I heard an argument and looked down. The man had just opened his door in the alley. The one with green paint on it. Another man in a Hawaiian shirt was by a rickshaw. I guess the coolie wanted more money for the fare."

She went silent and Moretti feared he had lost her, but she continued, "That's a guess. I couldn't really hear them—except their tone and gestures. Anyway, they were kinda shoving each other then he dropped a sack and turned to punch the coolie. That's when the Marine in fatigues stepped between them and pulled out a big wad of cash. Like he was going to pay off the coolie. That's when the coolie grabbed the Marine's knife."

Silence.

Moretti listened hard for any sound in the background and wondered if she had abandoned the phone.

She whispered, "The coolie stabbed him. He grabbed the money and ran away." Anna stopped, put her hand over the phone's mouthpiece as the PA system on the ship issued the usual double click before an all-hands announcement.

Moretti heard the first click and wondered if she had ended the call. "Miss?" He plugged his other ear and strained to hear the muffled sound. Unclear. Where was she? The click. He'd been on enough Navy transports to expect a shipboard announcement.

"Yes. I'm still here." He checked his wall clock again. A minute before two. If she were aboard, they should ring four bells at two in the afternoon. *Stall.*

"May I ask a question now?"

"Yes."

"What was the rickshaw passenger wearing?"

She snapped, "Told you! Hawaiian shirt! And tan slacks, not uniform khaki. Skinny guy."

Moretti took a chance. "You could be anyone paid to call me. If you want me to believe you, meet me at Seashore Park. Tonight. Eighteen hundred sharp. I'll be the old guy in civvies nursing a Coke on a bench." A bell struck in the background as she hung up.

He ripped the paper off the yellow pad and folded it with care. He put it in his back pocket. Before he checked out for the evening, Moretti went into the locker room and changed his uniform shirt for a light blue short-sleeve shirt with a square tail he left untucked. He pulled a Coke from the fridge in the duty room and took a rickshaw to the park. The twenty-minute ride let him think through the complications arising in the case. A witness that might show up—or not. But she might have the solution. She might be real. He was halfway to the Badaguan District when the coolie stopped at the park.

He sat on a stone slab of a bench facing the entrance. His back hurt, and he wished there were chairs.

Late summer brought the greens in the park to their fullness. The seaside humidity held the scent of jasmine close enough to be cloying. If she showed, it should be soon. He wedged the top from his soda bottle with an opener on his knife and leaned forward, elbows on his knees. At the sound of a scuff in the gravel, he looked up. A nurse, still in uniform.

He would have expected the caller to have changed into civilian attire to blend with the wives and civilian ex-pats who floated through the park. But not her. He stood.

"Major Moretti?"

"Yes. Please have a seat. I just opened the bottle; would you like it? I only used it to identify myself."

She shook her head. "Would you like to walk?"

Moretti smiled. "That would be nice."

"Nicer on your back as well. Looks like it's giving you trouble."

"A Navy nurse. I suspected it from your call."

She pointed to her rank insignia. "This is the first reason I wanted to meet privately."

Moretti nodded. *Fraternization. A crime. Navy nurses are officers. Cooks are enlisted. I could charge them on her statement.*

She watched his eyes. "Never have we compromised the chain of command. Never! We spent some time together, talking about going home and cooking. He wants to be a cook and have his own place in Norfolk. I want to keep my career."

"You know what your testimony would do to that?"

"Yes."

"You love him that much?"

"No. We're just friends. But I couldn't live with myself if they tried him, let alone convicted him of a murder he did not commit. Better he spends two years for fraternization with an officer than life in Leavenworth."

"And your career?"

"Prison, dishonorable discharge! Goodbye to my chance for any nursing job in the States."

"And you would risk this?"

"I am not a dishonorable person. Even if a court martial—"

"Not so fast! You saw the coolie take the money from the Marine in fatigues and stab him. Is that your testimony?"

"Yes. But he stabbed him first. If you need me to write it for you, I will."

"No. What happened after you saw this and from where?"

"From Fred's apartment. The kitchen window faces the alley. It's above a tailoring shop. We had just sat down to eat lunch when we heard the commotion. Like I said on the phone, there was an argument. Then the coolie stabbed him. We ran down to help. He was dead by the time I got there. Didn't have a chance. The coolie ran up Chungshan Road, toward the church. Fred chased him."

"And after you saw he was dead?"

"I think I froze. There. Fred came back. Sweaty. I had blood on my hand. He helped me wash up. He told me to sign back aboard my ship ASAP. I did. I haven't seen him since."

"Did you see any blood on the sailor's uniform?"

"I don't know. If there was, it coulda come from helping me."

"How is his apartment situated relative to the men and the door of the other apartment?"

She reached for a small stick beside the pathway and drew a simple diagram in the gravel. "Here's Fred's. Theirs was across the alley and down a door or two."

"Could I tell from the alley which room was Tanner's?"

"Yes. It has a yellow curtain."

"And you will testify to what you observed?"

"Yes." She scuffed away the memory in the gravel.

Moretti paused, then asked, "Why couldn't he catch the man pulling a rickshaw?"

"The coolie left it in the alley, ran like hell."

Moretti stopped. "Chekhov said the task of any writer is not to solve the problem but to state the problem correctly."

"What does that mean?"

"Deduction is like writing a play. Once you find the right question, much of the rest just falls into place."

"You are looking for a pattern. Like assessing symptoms that lead to a diagnosis."

Moretti smiled. "I guess it is. It also means that I'm uncertain you need to be a part of this yet." He took the folded paper from his pocket and handed it to her. "My notes from our telephone conversation. Let me do some more work and get back to you. Please do not leave port without telling me, personally. No messages."

"Thank you."

"We'll talk again."

"But I haven't told you my name."

Moretti pointed to her name badge and smiled. "You sure you don't want the Coke? I'm not gonna drink it."

She took it from him. "Thanks."

"Go on. I'm gonna be here a while."

A minute later, he saw her give the Coke to a ragged kid leaning against a wall before she flagged down an empty rickshaw.

The next morning Moretti called Bowen into his office. "Was there a rickshaw in the alley when the Shore Patrol arrived? I didn't see it mentioned in their report."

"When I went to pick up the log, we shot the shit about the scene. There's always something left out of a report. Rarely matters. He didn't mention a rickshaw."

"Just thinking, there are usually several in that area and maybe somebody saw something."

"Want me to talk to the local cops?"

"No. Had a wild idea. How about the key? Any info?"

"Locksmith says it's Chinese made, common in the older business district, not the newer parts of town."

Moretti clasped his hands behind his neck. "Book it back into evidence yet?"

"No."

"Grab it. I've got an idea."

When they left the office, the air was rancid from coal smoke and the stink of low tide. Bowen asked, "Going back to the alley?"

"Yup."

"Let me guess. You plan on trying every door in a six-block area?"

"No, just a couple."

In the alley, the rain had erased any sign of the violence. Moretti saw the door with the green paint and glanced across the alley, scanning the second floor. A yellow curtain. *Clear view of the crime scene. More support for her story.* A crumpled paper blew past Moretti as he reviewed the doors on both sides of the alley. He held the key beside the green door.

Bowen frowned as Moretti tried the handle. The door opened easily. The two men stared at each other. Moretti closed the door, locked it, tested the door, and then unlocked it. He called up the stairs, "Anyone here?"

Silence.

Moretti stepped inside. "Just a quick look, then I'll call Commander Li. Stay there."

He stopped at the top of the stairs. The one-room apartment was neat. Bed. Hot plate. No pans or dishes. There was no stove or refrigerator. No food. A bottle of brandy on the counter. A uniform on a hanger in the bathroom. He squinted to read the name tag. *Argos.* For a moment, Moretti was silent, wondering what life the man had lived and who he could have become.

Bowen called, "His place?"

As Moretti came down the stairs, he nodded then locked the door. "Let's go meet with Li. Do a chain of evidence, turn over the key, and let him do whatever the Chinese landlord is going to need to let us jointly look over the place, and recover any of his belongings for his family."

"Sounds good, boss."

CHAPTER 34

Jean-Claude and Claire arrived in the lobby of the Grand separately, carrying their raincoats.

"Early," he said.

"On time," she said.

He laughed. "Can't stay long. Might have an informant on the gold transfers."

"Still chasing your tail?"

"Perhaps. Would you be interested in joining me?"

Sebastian sat scowling over an almost-empty glass of gin and tonic as he waved a small piece of paper at them. "Mik won't make it tonight. Some contract meeting. David just passed me the note." He stood and proposed trying a new restaurant.

Jean-Claude raised his hand in apology. "Sorry, just time for a quick drink. I have a meeting in an hour."

Sebastian raised his eyebrows, looking at Claire.

She patted his shoulder. "Another time."

"Well then, I guess I am solo tonight. Might just run down a new angle on the refugee story." Sebastian maneuvered out of the booth, finished his drink, threw his raincoat over his arm, and stomped away.

Jean-Claude turned to her. "We should eat before going to that bar. I know a place."

"Fancy?"

"No. But we need to hurry."

Five minutes later, she smiled at his understatement. The rain clouds were building as they arrived at the foot of the pier that led to the red pagoda. A man squatted by a steel plate over a charcoal burner that looked like a big tin can. Slices of pork on slivers of bamboo floated in a tub of dark sauce by his feet. Thin fillets of raw fish were in another tub of what looked like seawater.

Jean-Claude motioned for two portions of pork. It sizzled on the steel while the man scooped rice into two paper cones. He pulled the sizzling pork strips off the sticks, balanced them on the rice, and drizzled dark sauce on both servings. Claire took four chopsticks, barely more than splintered wood, from the tall tin can beside the man's feet and followed Jean-Claude to the seawall.

She held out a pair of chopsticks for him. "Smells wonderful. What are the chances of getting *dootze-tung?*"

"Slim if you leave the chopsticks on the seawall." She dropped them and took the cones he thrust at her. He pulled a cloth napkin from his coat pocket. Unwrapping it, he stuck a small metal fork into each of their cones. "His food is wonderful, but his utensils are risky."

Spreading his raincoat on the seawall, he motioned her to sit. She asked, "You always carry these?"

"Usually just one fork. Besides, you showed that you had mastered chopsticks at our first meal. That's why I gave you the ebony ones. You deserved them." *Is he testing me? Teasing? Had my skills from Ceylon come back too easily?*

Claire tasted the meat. "This is delicious!"

He grunted agreement.

She watched him eat, his focus, the way his hair fell to the side. *Am I getting too comfortable with him? Are my questions too probing? I'll back off tonight. Make it about someone other than him. Think about it when I'm alone.* "How'd you ever take a chance on that guy's cooking?"

"Sebastian knows his food." He tipped the cone for the last of the rice.

She finished and folded the paper cone. "Why his interest in displaced persons? It's a story, yes. But he's making it more."

"It's not new. Remember, he lived in India. Loved it. The partition, you know, splitting the Hindus and Muslims into two countries, making the new Pakistan. You followed it in the news?"

She nodded. "Right after I arrived. I had just met you all."

"He put on the face for you. It hurt him deeply. He says over fourteen million people were displaced. More than reported. You must have seen the pictures in *Life*."

"Margaret Bourke-White's. Of course. Heartbreaking. People with nothing more than a sack of belongings walking to a new life. Evacuating to the unknown."

"For Sebastian, it is more than that. He feels it will cause a break in the nations and people he admires that will last many lifetimes."

"Maybe it is more of a story than I saw. Am I too focused on what my delicate ladies at home want to read, not what they should know?"

"Just follow the news. Let others decide." He checked his watch. "Bar's across town. What you call a dive."

"Is it worse than the Double Star?"

He pretended to think for a moment. "Only the beer is safe. In a bottle!"

"Sure. Let's go."

Claire waited in the dim booth facing the bar while Jean-Claude went to get two bottled beers, Tsingtao brand preferably. The Lucky Seven wasn't a place where she would trust a draft beer in a smudged glass. His meeting wasn't for another ten minutes. Hopefully, no one would notice them as reporters in the fog of cigarette and cigar smoke.

As Jean-Claude reached across the bar for the dripping bottles, a stocky blond woman came through the front door and walked directly to the far end of the bar. She hoisted herself onto the stool and took off a damp scarf. Not a place the bartender would notice or serve quickly. She seemed in no hurry. She dug in the purse on her lap and placed a pack of Camels on the bar top. *Waiting for someone, or anyone, to offer her a light?*

Claire had crawled through enough dive bars with Jean-Claude running down his stories to know that the Lucky Seven was not a place for unescorted women, let alone some woman who looked like she belonged in *her* article on baking muffins. But there she was. Not smoking her cigarettes. Not drinking, either. The hem of her raincoat opened, exposing the skirt of a floral housedress. Barely five feet tall, she had an extra thirty pounds on her, mostly south of her belt. Claire thought she knew the face from the *Anderson*. Married. Her hair was shorter now, lighter. Tight curls almost hid her face. "Blondie" until Claire found her name if she became interesting. *What the hell was Blondie doing here?* Claire slid to her right in the booth so she could watch her over Jean-Claude's shoulder when he returned.

He handed a dripping bottle to her across the sticky table, sat, and watched the door. "Lost in thought?"

She was quiet for a long time. "Thinking about that guy who was killed."

"Not something for your readers. Besides, no one is talking about it. Can't get information from anyone."

"Wonder if this guy you're meeting tonight has anything for you."

He chuckled. "My last two leads had nothing but fantasies of how Chiang moved gold from the treasury. Not worth the drinks I bought them. At least it was safer here in town than going north like I did for a story—"

"Just before I met you, at the embassy briefing." She laughed, thinking back to her first impression of him. "Are you certain that my being here won't scare him off?"

He stifled a chuckle. "*Au contraire.* We may attract men wanting to meet you. I would not blame them."

She shuddered theatrically. "These guys?"

"I would protect you." She looked into his eyes and knew he would. He slumped back and nursed his beer, comfortable in their silence.

A man in a brown leather coat, rain still on the shoulders, rushed past their booth and stood beside Blondie, facing the bar. Thin. Not quite six feet. Wordlessly, he pulled a pack of cigarettes from his pocket, blue. Gauloises. French. He put them on the bar beside the Camels, watching the bartender, not Blondie, while he did so.

Claire took a slow sip of her beer and watched him pocket Blondie's Camels. He hurried toward the door. Now she saw his face. Chinese. High cheekbones. He shaved his hair on the sides but left it too long on top to be military. Blondie slid the Gauloises off the bar into the purse on her lap.

Claire watched Blondie leave and shook her head. That was the sloppiest handoff she had ever seen. However, Blondie just got promoted to interesting and now needed a name. Peg knew almost everyone from the ship, at the orphanage, moms and dads through birthday parties, her charity drives for the enlisted boys at Christmas, and embassy secretaries through bridge games. Claire fussed with the label on the beer bottle and decided she would drop by Peg's this week with a new photography magazine for Beth.

After the second beer, Jean-Claude looked at his watch. "He's over an hour late. Stay or go?"

The tip of her head said "go."

They walked through the drizzle toward the center of town. After they passed a small laundry and hole-in-the-wall food place, he veered into an alley, pulled her into a doorway, and kissed her. "Want to know why we always meet in your hotel?" He opened a weathered door. "This is where I live. One room. Stinks of garlic most nights. Shared toilet. There is a book for you, but I keep forgetting it. Want to come up?"

She laughed, "Sure." *Worst line I've ever had thrown at me. And now, of all times, when all he had to do was look at me and I feel fifteen again.*

The place reminded her of the tenements along the waterfront in Ceylon. *Firetrap, hovel, no doubt roach infested and smelling of garlic and armpit.* He grabbed the book and flipped the light switch, surrendering the room to the bugs.

That night, after Jean-Claude left her hotel room, Claire fanned through an out-of-print history of Mao's early years, washed their tumblers, and tried to imagine what could fit into a paper cigarette packet to trade for something of equal value and size. *Cigarettes? A pile of gems for what? Other gems. A small brick of gold. For what? No, too heavy for that exchange.* She decided not to drive herself crazy and went out to the balcony to examine the fishing boats through her binoculars. Nothing. They were really fishing. Nets and lines. A good haul, judging by the baskets that were filled. *But what the hell was in those cigarette packs on the bar?* Nothing to key on the Zenith tonight, but she made a note in her journal. *Blondie had smokes at the Lucky Seven.* It was enough of a time tag if she ever needed it—and gossip to add to her journal if she didn't.

CHAPTER 35

Late in the afternoon, Moretti shut the bulging case file shut and reached for the telephone. Getting a busy signal, he slammed down the handset. He leaned back in his chair with his hands clasped behind his neck and watched the ceiling fan. He dialed again.

"The Ryan residence," Leon said.

"This is Tony Moretti. Is Bill there?"

"Please wait, sir."

"Thanks."

Moretti listened after the phone clattered on the hall table. Moments later, Bill said, "Hey, Tony. What's up?"

"You busy?"

"Nope. Just got home."

"Wondering if you could do me a favor."

"Is this an official or unofficial one?"

Moretti sighed. "Guess it depends on the outcome. I need to follow up on something and talk to Leon."

"Wanna come by here?"

"This is on the QT."

"Sure. It's quiet here now. Leon said Peg and Beth went to a movie. Think JD and Gerri are off somewhere, probably drinking. Come on over."

Leon hurried to the gate as Moretti parked his Jeep on the street.

"Evening, Leon."

"Captain Ryan is waiting for you, sir."

"Did he tell you I wanted to talk to you?"

"Yes. As you wish, sir."

Bill met them at the front door. "Want me to make myself scarce, or can I listen in?"

"Suit yourself."

Moretti motioned for Leon to sit on the sofa in the front room. Leon looked at Bill for approval. At Bill's nod, he sat formally. Bill leaned against the fireplace.

Moretti took out a small notepad from his rear pocket, opened the cardboard cover, and sat in the armchair facing Leon. "I want to clarify some events on the day of the Marine's death in town. I'm only looking for potential witnesses, not accusing anyone."

Leon nodded slowly.

Moretti continued, "I understand that on Sunday, Mrs. Summers has a book club."

"Yes, but only on the first Sunday of every month."

"Thinking back to the last book club Sunday, do you remember what time she got home after the meeting?"

"Could you excuse me a moment?"

"Sure."

When Leon returned, he carried a handful of pages. He looked at the second page. "No dinner here that night. During the day, there was a reception. Captain Ryan was at the base. Madam Ryan and Beth ate somewhere in town. I don't make dinner for the others unless they ask. Sometimes together. Sometimes not."

"What are you looking at?"

"My plan. Menus, how many for what meal, party plans, so I know what to buy, schedule for our cook." He folded the pages. "When I finished in the big house, I went over to Madam Tong's bungalow about six. That's where I have my room."

"Did you hear anyone come in after six?"

"No. We were playing some records. I would not have heard the gate. I really don't know what time anyone in the big house got back."

Moretti looked up from his notes. "Did you make sandwiches for anyone that night?"

"No. But someone did. It might have been Miss Beth. There was a smear of peanut butter on the counter in the morning."

"Do you do the laundry for everyone?"

"No. Charlie, the cook, does it after the amah quit."

"Do you check his work?"

Leon said, "I make sure all is proper on hangers and put back in the right closet."

"And if there were a stain or a rip, would he fix it?"

"No. He would tell me when he gets it from a hamper. I'd see if I could get the stain out or fix it or if it needed to go to a tailor."

"Did you need to fix any clothes that Sunday or the next time you did laundry?"

"Yes. Right after the reception, Madam Ryan told me that Miss Beth's white dress had chocolate frosting on it. She changed Miss Beth's dress and went out to dinner. I fixed it right away. Came out with a second wash and lemon juice. Monday is the usual laundry day for clothes. Tuesday for sheets and towels." He paused. Moretti let the silence linger. Leon frowned, then said, "Charlie showed me a shirt on Monday. Put wet into the hamper. Very wrinkled. And the bottom button was missing. I put on a new one."

"Bill's shirt?" Moretti tested.

Leon shook his head and pointed upstairs. "His."

"Uniform?"

Leon shook his head. "Loud. Sporty."

Moretti paused. "What kind of button did you put on it?"

"Dark brown, like the buttons on the shirt. Not the same button that looks like wood, but a close match."

"I'm sure it is." Moretti closed his book and stood. "Thanks, Leon. You should not discuss our meeting with anyone. Understand?"

"Yes, sir."

"Oh. Is the shirt up there now?"

As Leon nodded, Moretti stood, pulled a sealed envelope from his pocket and said, "Let's take a look."

When they returned to the living room, Moretti thanked Leon and stood by the fireplace watching him depart. He folded the torn envelope in thirds and sealed it in a fresh one. After making a note in ink across the sealed flap, he sighed.

Bill motioned to the billiard room. "About ready for a drink?"

"Nice idea."

"Name your poison."

"Anything with ice. It's going to be a tropical night."

"Whisky soda, tall?" When Moretti smiled, Bill said, "I'll be back in a minute. Leon doesn't fill the ice bucket unless we are having guests."

"So, I'm not a guest?"

"You are family now. Get your own damn glass."

Moretti laughed and followed Bill to the kitchen, where he pulled two tall glasses from a cabinet and took an aluminum ice tray from the refrigerator. He pulled the lever, and the ice crackled. Bill filled the glasses and handed Tony his.

Back in the billiard room, Bill poured an inch of Seagram's in his glass and handed the bottle to Tony, who did the same. Capping the bottle, Bill took the siphon with a wire cage and whooshed the carbonated water into both glasses.

Tony asked, "Living room or outside?"

"Outside. There should be a breeze by the tennis court."

Once settled, Tony ran his hand over his thinning hair and said, "I still don't get it. Something's not right, but I can't crack the nut."

"What's the problem?"

"Wayne had a key in his pocket that we traced to an apartment near where he died."

"Not too uncommon for guys in the BOQ or on a ship. Have their own rat hole of a place to catch a little privacy."

"I'll give you that. But his apartment is a puzzle. City cops think it was a love nest, but no rubbers, no leftovers from hookers. No trash. Not even dust under the bed. Clean as a whistle. No chow or drinks other than a bottle of brandy and two glasses. One had his prints. Who knows?"

"Someone does. So, where are you right now? Talking it out might help connect the dots."

"If I file what I have now, two fine people are looking at a potential discharge and federal prison if they tell the truth. I figured JD for a liar, perhaps even an accomplice in some scheme, but not a killer. But there is a killer who is going to walk away free as a bird because I can't arrest him without exposing the other two, even if I could find the man. And all I can do is put JD at the scene and charge him for making a false statement for saying he was home at four with Gerri."

Gerri looked up from her book at the sound of her name. *Is someone calling me?* She glanced down at the tennis court.

Bill asked, "How do you know JD was in the alley?"

"His missing button. The buttons on his shirt matched the one from the scene. Leon replaced it right after the event. And there is the sauce his wife washed out. It all fits."

Bill paused and took a long drink. "What'd the sailor say he did that afternoon?"

Moretti shrugged. "They never asked him officially, just confined him to the ship. I think JD and Wayne were up to something."

"So, why were they meeting there?"

Moretti lowered his voice. "Good bet they were involved with each other."

Bill pulled back and frowned. "You're thinking he left his boyfriend to die in some alley and set up his drunken wife as his alibi? I thought I knew the guys in my squadron! But now! Christ, you're saying he might have killed the guy. I want him out of my house tonight."

"He didn't kill him."

"What? You put him at the scene."

"My witness says a coolie did it. Robbery."

Bill snapped, "Why would you believe him?"

"Her. If her name goes in this investigation, she's out of the Navy and looking at prison time."

"Why would she do that? Blow a bright and shining future."

"Because she thinks doing what is right is more important than living a bright and shining lie."

Bill shook his head. "Whether it's JD or a coolie, the cook is in deep shit because he had a messy uniform."

Moretti took a slow drink. "That he cleaned immediately. My boss says that smear is enough to put him in the brig now and convene a court martial. But I disagree."

"Right, so if your witness has to testify, she will exonerate her friend, but then they both land in deep shit."

"His story of spilling lunch on himself isn't flying with my boss."

"I see why this is driving you crazy. When do you have to file the case?"

"Yesterday. I'm stalling and getting a shitload of pressure to wrap it up."

"Should I kick him out of the house?"

"He's not the killer, and she's rough as a cob, but trustworthy. Maybe Gerri will make the first move."

She looked up from her book again. Pushing the curtain aside, she recognized Moretti.

Bill asked, "How's that?"

"I don't think she's gonna put up with his shit once she figures out that he's the kinda guy that eats corn dogs at the county fair, if you get my drift."

Gerri closed her book and sat, biting her lip.

CHAPTER 36

Several days later, Gerri thought about the picture Moretti had shown her. Then she realized she had seen the man at the Fourth of July party with JD. She took a taxi to the Provost Marshal's Office and asked to see Major Moretti.

He motioned her to the chair beside his desk. "Nice to see you again, Mrs. Summers. What can I do for you?"

"Can I look at that picture again?"

He pulled the investigation folder from the bottom drawer, opened it carefully facing toward him, and removed the eight-by-ten of Wayne's face, used on his ID card, not the crime scene photographs. "Is this what you wanted to see?"

"After I thought about it, I saw him. I'm sure of it. He and JD were playing volleyball against each other at the Fourth of July beach party. Then they went for a swim. I lost sight of them. That was right before that kid almost drowned. I guess I forgot seeing him, what with all the hubbub."

"Thank you. I can check the roster for the party."

"Was he a big guy? Broad shoulders?"

"Yes."

"I think we saw him at the Birthday Ball." She blinked hard and took a deep breath. "Another thing. I asked Margaret what time I left after the book club and drinks that day. She said it was about six. So, I couldn't have been home when JD told me I was."

"Thank you for clarifying that, Mrs. Summers."

She stood to go before the tears she felt welling spilled down her cheeks.

Moretti hurried past her to the door. He paused before opening it. "I don't think he is the killer."

She took a rickshaw home. The sea air and beauty of the coast helped clear her mind. She wiped away tears as she approached Badaguan and called for the coolie to stop short of the house so she could collect herself. She let herself in through the gate and hurried to the front door. Beth was reading a magazine on the living room sofa. Gerri plopped down beside her. "What do you have there?"

"The new *Popular Photography*. Claire came over and gave it to me. She wanted to ask Mom about some lady that was on the ship with us. She couldn't remember her name."

Gerri looked at the magazine over Beth's shoulder. "You guys really like to take pictures!"

"Yeah. It's fun."

"Hey, Beth. Can you do me a favor?"

"What?"

"Go into the kitchen and grab an ice cube tray and meet me in the pool room."

"Dad calls it the billiard room, even though it's a pool table. There's a difference, you know."

"Sure. Can you just get it?"

Beth marched into the kitchen and, without disturbing Leon or her mother, pulled an ice cube tray from the freezer and left. Peg glanced at her and shook her head.

By the time Beth arrived, the tall glass Bill used for martinis held a generous pour of gin. Gerri topped it with a splash from the green bottle of vermouth. "Just in time. Thanks." She took the tray from Beth, pulled the lever, and dumped the cubes into the pitcher.

The girl picked up the long bar spoon. "Can I stir it?"

"Sure, kid."

Peg came around the corner, frowning. "What's going on?"

Beth smiled and stirred. "We're making martinis, right?"

Gerri handed Peg the ice cube tray, took the pitcher and two glasses, and stomped upstairs.

A few minutes later, JD came home and hurried upstairs to change out of his flight suit. When he walked into the bedroom, he spotted the pitcher of martinis on the table beside the window and grinned. He poured both glasses. "Nice surprise."

She watched him take a sip and put his glass on the dresser. "You were with him when it happened, weren't you?"

He looked away, picked up his glass, and spilled some. He faced her, his voice shook. "I didn't hurt him. A coolie argued with me, wanted me to overpay for a ride. He stepped in to stop him."

She looked out the window and was quiet for the longest time. She wiped away silent tears and said, "Greater love hath no man than to give up his life for another."

"What?"

She stood and faced him. Her voice was flat. "That's what the Bible says. He saved you, didn't he? He must have been a good man to do that. It coulda been you."

He stared at her, tears forming, then nodded once.

"I've known something was up for a while."

"How?"

"It's not important."

"But you never said anything."

"What could I say? Ask you why being with that guy was more important than being with me? Why'd I have to go to that dumb book club or volunteer for crap, so you'd have free time to sneak away to be with a man? What do you want me to do now, throw a plate at you and scream? Call you names? Slam a door? Walk out? What would any of that change?"

He reached for her.

She pulled away. "Were there others?"

"No. I don't know how it started."

"I don't care."

"Do you want a divorce? I'll do whatever, but you can't tell anyone. I could go to jail."

"Right now, I don't know what I want."

"I can move to the BOQ and find you a hotel until I can get you on a plane."

"To where? We don't have the money for airfare, and I'm not about to gin up some lie about a family emergency so that Uncle Sam can fly me home."

"Let me explain."

She held up her hand. "You can lie to yourself all you want. But you will not lie to me. Not anymore. Look, it's Friday. You're not flying tomorrow so you can suck down all the martinis you want. I'll bring a sandwich for you later. Maybe even a peanut butter and jelly *to soothe your tummy!*"

He pointed toward her untouched martini. "Have a drink and calm down."

She picked her book up from the table. At the door, she called over her shoulder, "You're sleeping in the other room starting tonight, so get comfortable. We'll talk tomorrow, away from here. Got it?"

As Gerri came downstairs, she saw Beth cocooned on the living room sofa, looking at a page of contact prints with a magnifying glass. She used a grease pencil to put a slash over a shot she did not like.

Gerri sat beside her and picked up a photography magazine.

Beth pursed her lips then said, "You're not supposed to have me help with grown-up stuff."

"You are right. I'm sorry. I'll apologize to your mom in a minute. What are you doing?"

"Looking at contact sheets. That's what you call these small pictures. I get to pick out my favorites from the wedding reception. I want to give them some for a present."

Gerri took the magnifying glass that Beth offered. "They are a pretty couple, aren't they?"

"They looked happy. And the cake was really good. Chocolate."

Bill came through the front door in his flight suit. He kissed his daughter's head. "Hi, Gerri. What are you two doing?"

"Helping her pick the best pictures from the party."

Beth looked over her shoulder. "Mom said I could give Miss Katia three blow-ups for a present."

"That's a great idea. Where is your mother?"

Without stopping her inspection, Beth said, "Kitchen."

Bill smiled at Leon and gave Peg a hug. "What's with the scene of domestic tranquility out there? Gerri—"

"Is probably blitzed upstairs by now."

"What? No. She's helping Beth in the living room with some photos."

"Bill! She had Beth stirring a pitcher of martinis! I wanted to talk to you before I killed her." Leon, head down, continued working.

Bill looked out the window for a moment, lost in thought. "Did you print all the film from the reception?"

"No. Beth is still cranky that I'm making her choose a few to print from her contact sheet of the negatives."

He turned but she touched his shoulder. "She's marking them with a grease pencil. You need the clean negatives."

"Show me!"

"Now? Can't it wait until after dinner?"

"No! I need to see them now."

Peg frowned, then they hurried to the garage, descended the stairs to the basement, and flipped on the overhead lights, then the white light in the darkroom.

Bill smiled when he saw how well she had arranged her darkroom to include Beth. Under the red safelight was the large table that held the developing trays. Peg pushed a stool under the table with the enlarger. Several notebooks and a metal box holding the undeveloped photo paper were on the lower of three shelves. She pulled out a notebook and flipped it open beside the enlarger. "We developed the film and made contact sheets. No prints yet. Here are the negatives from the reception." She handed Bill a large magnifying glass. "What are you looking for?"

"Something in the background that Beth might have caught by accident."

"What?"

He squinted at the last two frames, tilting the film strip toward the light. Mikhail Karpov was about to shove a large piece of cake into his mouth. But in the blurred background across the street, there were two men.

"How hard would it be to make a print of this right now?"

"Mix all the chemicals and delay dinner for one print? Let it dry? Couple of hours. Why? Why don't I just put the negative in the enlarger and we can get a better look that way?"

"Sure."

As she slipped the strip of film into the carrier of the Kodak enlarger and turned on its light, Bill closed the door. Peg killed the overhead light and brought the negative into focus. Bill examined it and hugged her.

Black and white were reversed in the negative. In the foreground, cake eating. Behind that was a blurred sailor, his dark skin was white and his white uniform black. A man, dressed in rags like a rickshaw-coolie, ran in front of him. A scarecrow in gray tones.

Bill shook his head. "That's it! The sailor's alibi! I'll call Tony. Invite him for dinner. You can make a print or give him the negative, whatever he wants."

Peg looked at him as if he had lost his mind. "What's this all about?"

"I think Beth just solved a murder investigation—and saved several careers."

CHAPTER 37

When Peg and Bill returned from the basement darkroom, Gerri was waiting in the kitchen. "Peg? Can I talk to you for a minute?"

Peg watched Bill go into the hall to telephone Tony, then steered the young woman into the dining room, closing the door.

After a deep breath, Gerri said, "JD and I are splitting up. He's leaving."

"Why?"

"I know you know JD was a suspect. I saw Major Moretti over here talking to Bill the other day."

She whispered. "Gerri, JD had nothing to do with that man's death."

"But he was there, and he lied to the cops. I think he loved the guy and lied to himself. Maybe I could work past that, but he lied to me. And I can't make that right."

Peg watched her, waiting for the tears, but there were none. "You sure about this?"

"I thought being married was a fun way to get out of a mill town and have an adventure, go to China for free. I saw you on the ship over and thought how boring marriage must be, since you had to drag a kid halfway around the world. Then I got it. You do what you want to do. This is the life you want. Never really thought I had choices until now. I want to apologize for being a pain and want you to know I'm going to be better around Beth. And with him gone, I'm gonna cut way back on the drinking."

Peg pulled out two chairs and motioned for Gerri to sit beside her. "You're young. You're learning. It's okay."

302

Gerri pressed on. "Well, not soon enough. He just left. Going to the BOQ. And I'll be on my way as soon as I can. You think Leon could help me find a cheap rooming house or hotel until I can get a boat back? For half the rent we're paying you."

Peg leaned over, laughing.

"What's funny? I'm flat busted."

"Gerri, here's a secret. You've never paid rent. Not from day one. Sometimes we'd get money from JD for part of your food, but only after Bill got on him."

"But he said . . . oh hell. Just another lie so he could be the big man and throw money around. So here I am spending like we got the world by the tail and thinking you're pissed at me for my freedom. But all the while, I was a freeloader." Tears cut a path down her cheeks. "I can sell some of the jewelry and make good on what we owe you."

"No need. You're welcome to stay here until you go back to the States."

"I couldn't."

"I don't think there's a better choice. Go wash your face for dinner."

"I think I'll make a sandwich for tonight. I don't know how I could face Bill."

Peg said, "Just for tonight."

Detained by a last-minute meeting, Moretti arrived after Peg put Beth to bed. Once he saw the image from the enlarger, he leaned against the table. "Fantastic! Just what I needed to end this."

Turning on the overhead light, Bill asked, "How will you explain how you put this together? The sailor never copped to being nearby."

Moretti grinned. "I was over here and saw your pictures. Happy accident. Then I'll ask the sailor if that's him."

Peg asked, "You want the negative, or a print?"

"For now, only three prints. Keep the negative safe here in case we need a different chain of custody on it. How soon?"

Pointing to the door, Peg said, "Tony, go try to beat Bill at pool while

I make them. It's going to take some time."

After mixing two whisky sodas and a coin toss, Moretti broke for their first game, sank one and missed the next.

Bill chalked up and asked, "Anything I should know about why you're late?"

"Boss pulled rank and called an emergency meeting so some jerk could give a pep talk on Operation Beleaguer. Ought to be called Operation Shitshow."

Bill missed a bank shot and stood back.

Moretti chalked up. "We'd repatriated over a half a million Japanese and Koreans that were in China. Protected coal trains so the Chinese would have heat in the winter. Brought shiploads of food so they wouldn't starve. Operation Thankless."

Bill sank the last ball and left his cue stick on the table. He picked up his drink and stared at the table. What could he say, even to a fellow Marine? *Mao won. It's just mopping up now.* "When does it end?" he asked.

"When there's not a penny left to take off a dead man's eyes." Moretti lowered his voice. "We'll be gone soon enough. You're not downtown much, but it's changing. Local cops have thrown up their hands. Just waiting for the next regime."

Bill put his cue on the wall rack. "When?"

"Who knows? But if you have anything you want to send home, now would be a great time to start before they ration shipments."

"Peg's been shipping stuff for months. She even sent back a length of silk fabric for Beth's wedding gown. How's that for planning? Fifteen years early!"

Moretti handed Bill his cue to place in the rack. "I'd get it down to a suitcase each and be ready to walk away from the rest. Ask Madam Tong if you can borrow any of her basics. She staying?"

"I don't think so. Not sure what her plan is."

"Leon?"

"He's a man of many talents, most of which he hides. I'm sure he has a plan."

Moretti said, "Not going to be easy for the Nationalists to leave, according to the bulletins coming into my office."

Bill paused before asking, "And you? Where are you going next?"

He finished the last ice cube in his glass with a crunch. "I'm one of the lucky ones. I got to raise my girls between the big wars. Second one's about ready for college. Got a year left on my hitch, so wherever they send me is fine. My wife still wants me to come home. Ain't that something after all I've put her through?"

"Still dreaming about the Keys?"

"Damn right. Figure I could make a business there. Plenty of good years ahead."

Bill smiled. "Want some pie?"

"Sure. And a cup of coffee too?"

They left their glasses in the kitchen sink. Bill filled the percolator with water, scooped grounds into the basket, and put it on the stove. He cut a slice of cherry pie for Moretti.

Once the coffee brewed, Bill brought the percolator to the table.

Halfway through his dessert, Moretti asked, "How's Phil Wilson these days, fully recovered from ditching the plane last year?"

"Why do you ask?"

"Got a question about him the other day. Can't say more. How's he looking?"

Bill paused for a long sip of coffee before answering. "A little lighter. Some days it's like he's not sleeping well, but he's sharp at briefings, his pre-fights check out fine, he's on his targets. Haven't seen much of him or Eleanor except for squadron parties."

"Okay. Thanks."

Peg came in with three damp prints and spread them on dish towels on the counter. "These will be dry enough for you to take in a few minutes." She glanced at Bill and cocked her head. She knew that set of his jaw. "You okay?"

"We're fine. Just chewing the fat."

Moretti said, "I'm surprised that Madam Tong hasn't left by now. She's got the resources to make a run for it. Look at this mansion."

Peg said, "Leon's the one I worry about."

Bill said, "Yeah. Someday, he will vanish. Crafty fellow. Can't figure out why he's still sticking around."

Moretti clapped Bill on the shoulder. "For a smart guy, sometimes you astound me."

"Why?"

"Haven't you figured out he's staying to protect your family? The guy's like a mama bear around your wife and kid."

CHAPTER 38

When the weather was random in September, the weekly meetings of the Booth Club grew sporadic. Claire never knew who was going to show, but she was always there. Their fellowship became as important to her as their information had been at the beginning of her time in China.

She smiled when Jean-Claude arrived, carrying a small parcel. He slid it toward her. "For me?"

"Temporarily. It's for Beth. *The Little Prince*. My order finally arrived. Can you give it to Peg next time you visit?"

"She'll love it. Any word on our colleagues?"

He shook his head. "That look."

Taking on an innocent pout, she asked, "What look?"

"Your 'question' look. You always arrive with a question."

"Do I?"

He smiled. "Always. Shall I have David make Manhattans today for a change?"

"Sounds perfect."

When Jean-Claude returned, he slipped into the booth beside her. "Ask."

"I wonder what they really think of us in town. Are our guys just a bunch of drunken kids playing the black market, or are we saviors—the only thing between them and the Red Menace?"

He shook his head in disbelief. "You still think in nation-to-nation terms like it is some football game. It is more like chess. They have taken the countryside, pawn by pawn, moving toward the cities. Now the castles and bishops are falling."

"Sure, the smaller ones."

"Look at a map instead of trusting those briefings! Mao's almost to the water's edge! Tsingtao is a port the communists need. Then Shanghai. That big industrial and financial prize is next."

Claire looked at him. The intensity in his eyes frightened her. She barely dared to whisper, "And then what?"

"We go on to the next part of life. I have an offer for a position in Saigon."

She felt her gut clench. She sighed when Jean-Claude looked away, giving her a moment to gather herself. David delivered their cocktails. She took a sip and looked at the glass. "I thought you were taking the Paris desk."

"Who told you that?"

She forced a half-smile. "Can't keep a secret in this town. Even if it's not true."

The door banged open as Sebastian rolled in, peeled off his wet coat, and plopped down beside her.

She asked, "Is Mik joining us?"

He looked at his watch. "He's usually on time if he can make it."

Jean-Claude stood. "I'll call his shop, see if he's working late."

Claire said, "Hold on. We need to talk. What can we do to help Mik and Arina get out of China?"

Jean-Claude shook his head. "They may have waited too long." He pulled a slim notebook from his back pocket. "Here's the latest from the Australian Embassy briefing yesterday. Australia has already accepted 15,000 Jews and promised slots for another 100,000 Displaced Persons during the next year and a half, but many will be from Europe."

Watching him, hopefully, she asked, "Where do Mik and Arina fit in?"

Jean-Claude closed his notebook. "I know they've applied to Israel, 5,000 spaces there. Australia will have a thousand at a time in transit to elsewhere. Some ships bringing DPs from Europe might take the

Shanghai DPs to Israel or Italy. And France is opening."

She pushed her hair back. "It's a game of musical chairs, not solving a thing."

Sebastian added, "Unless you have some anchor, the Aussies are not interested. A relative, a business, or a unique skill like a doctor."

Claire said, "What about his shop in Australia?"

Jean-Claude shook his head. "He rents. I asked him the price for the building. It is more than they have." He motioned them closer. "It seems Russia's getting interested in the exiled White Russians here. Some are relinquishing their Soviet passports and applying for 'stateless person passports.' Their embassy is having some people leave their Russian passports 'on deposit' to return if they have a change of mind."

She frowned. "I don't understand."

Jean-Claude shook his head. "Don't you see? It's a brilliant way to slip Soviet agents in with the real DPs all over the world."

The door opened. Mikhail rushed in, then stood at the edge of the table, coat dripping, hands in his pockets. He pulled out an envelope and held it overhead, catching his breath.

Claire asked, "Katia?"

He shook his head. "No, from Ravenswood, my landlord in Sidney. Helped me frame the Australian pound note from my first sale. Hung it on the office wall upstairs years ago." Tears coursed down his cheeks. "He took it down." Mik caught his breath. "Just sold the shop to me. For a single pound! Can you believe it? This is the deed."

Jean-Claude grinned. "You own property!"

Mikhail shook his head. "I consider it a down payment, but yes."

Claire jumped up and embraced him. "Australia! When?"

"We go to the embassy tomorrow with this. Then, who knows?"

Sebastian lumbered toward the door and bellowed, "Champagne to celebrate!"

Mikhail caught his arm. "None for me tonight, dear friends. Arina will be home soon, and I need to tell her the news."

Sebastian grabbed his coat. "Then another time. I'll take my libations elsewhere. Let me walk you out." He gave an overhead wave to Claire and Jean-Claude. "I am away!"

She stared at the cherry in her Manhattan to compose herself. "It's winding down, isn't it?"

"Any day now. Nationalists here can't stop it. Too many refugees in the city. They'll support Mao when it comes down to it." She took Jean-Claude's hand. "You'll be at your Saigon desk by the time they all pull out, won't you?"

"Join me. You can write there."

She shrugged. "I barely interested my American readers in China. My editor's most lavish praise was for my column when the military wives attended a class on Chinese cooking."

"Hardly the geopolitical matters you discuss with us."

"I have learned so much from you and Sebastian. You opened my eyes."

"Then Washington should be ever the more grateful."

"What?" She took a sip, stalling.

He held up his hand. "Don't deny that you were toying with us. I watch you at embassy parties. You pretend to accompany Peg and Bill or your Navy friends, make them comfortable with your manners. Only sometimes talking to the deal makers, but always within earshot—always listening. You are too damn smart to be writing 'How to Cook a Fish in a Wok' stories."

She adopted a theatrical look of shock. "You saw it?"

"I read everything under your byline, even if you never wrote it. You're too clever for those stories. I wondered what you really wrote, as well as who reads it."

Searching for a turn in the conversation, she chuckled. "Well, nobody's even seen my journal. My political and personal perspective. I think that might find a publisher. Not in its current form, however. Mere notations and abbreviations, but if written in full—"

He smiled, wanting to believe her.

She nudged him. "Dinner?"

"It's pouring out there. I'll have David find us something from the menu. We can eat here while you tell me about your journal."

He took her grin as a "yes" and suggested the hotel's classic *escalope de veau avec pommes frites*. During a leisurely meal, they shared ideas for books or articles and publishers that might be interested in their independent work.

As they were finishing coffees after their meal, the door crashed open. Sebastian returned, hair dripping. Shucking off his wet coat, he plopped on the edge of the booth. A trail of rancid sweat, beer, and cloying incense overwhelmed his usual lime aftershave.

Claire waved her hand to fend off the fumes. "What's got you in a lather?"

"Just filed a scoop."

Jean-Claude winced. "Where have you been the last couple of hours?"

"Ping Kong Tung Lee's."

"The whorehouse? I didn't think you'd lower your standards."

"Strictly research. Saw some Marines, flight mechanics I recognized from the airfield. Wrong time. Wrong day. I made my way to the bar and overheard that they'd done a tune-up on everything with wings and rotors and then got the afternoon off. Then one says this is their last chance to 'wet their willies' because the squadron is moving out, 'Pronto.' That was his word. I stood the lads to a round to wish them well."

Jean-Claude laughed. "Brilliant research. Where and when?"

"Shanghai? Whenever 'pronto' is."

"You're misreading the tea leaves, Sebastian," Claire said.

Looking offended, he asked, "You have a better source?"

She played coy. "There could be someone at ComNavWesPac."

Jean-Claude asked, "Is that even a word?"

Sebastian whispered to him, "She means somebody in his cups at the Officers' Club."

She forced a laugh. "Just reporting! He wouldn't have invited me to dinner on Wednesday if he were in Shanghai, would he?"

Sebastian tipped his head. "Point taken."

Jean-Claude said, "And your aviation fellows, they'd be in lockdown, wouldn't they, if evacuation were imminent?"

Claire responded, "Makes sense. Impose a curfew so the boys didn't go wandering off on a bender or to a whorehouse when they need 'em."

Sebastian muttered, "Bastards. Having a joke on me? Think I should pull the story?"

Jean-Claude laughed. "I would."

Sebastian stood and launched himself toward the phone in the lobby, returning a few minutes later.

Jean-Claude finished the last of his coffee and asked, "Then what's this week's story?"

"The classic puffery. 'In the Orient, the questions outnumber the answers,' or 'It remains to be seen if . . .' then fill in the question. Clichés work. Editors love them because they shorten the copy. But then I find comfort that tomorrow my immortal words will line a bird's cage or wrap a greasy portion of fish and chips in a hamlet back home."

Jean-Claude suddenly grabbed his raincoat and said to Claire as he left the booth, "Wait here. I'll be back."

Sebastian sighed as he leaned against the table. "Going to miss you all—this has been the most fun in a long time. He's off to Saigon, you know. Offered me a desk this morning, but those days are over once I file my last dispatch from here. Tired of chasing lies and liars."

Claire blinked away the thought of Jean-Claude in Saigon. She forced a smile. "Retiring? Buying an estate in the Highlands and breeding show dogs?"

"Australia! Accepted months ago. Commonwealth, you know. Didn't need to mention it when Mik was on eggshells. Thinking about Sidney, or perhaps Brisbane. Both lovely spots for a writer. I think I'll post myself somewhere near Mik, now that he's got the green light. And you?"

She sighed. "Stateside, I guess, then we'll see what's what."

Sebastian glanced at his watch. "Say good night to the lad for me, will you? You will stay in touch."

"Yes. Never know when or where I might show up."

David came in, collected the coffee cups, and asked, "Anything else, Miss?"

"I'd love a carafe of water."

When David returned with the water, he paused.

Claire looked up, "Yes?"

"I was just informed that the manager is no longer willing to run a monthly accounting for this group. I dissuaded him from imposing his new rule tonight, but—"

She smiled, reaching for her purse. "Thank you, David, for everything. I'll settle the bill now. Including our dinner."

Jean-Claude rushed through the door ten minutes later, out of breath. She pushed a glass of water toward him. "What was that all about?"

"Ran up the hill to look at the ships, their smokestacks. Nothing. You are right." He gulped down the water. "If this was the evacuation, they'd be firing up the boilers and moving out to sea. But no. Nothing to report. We're still here."

He put his hand on hers.

Claire reduced her keyed message from her car in the pouring rain that night to the barest essentials: *loose lips say imminent departure to Shanghai, not supported by actions on the ground; Russians may insert spies as Displaced Persons.* Her journal wondered at the duality her life was becoming, but not in so many words.

CHAPTER 39

Moretti had a spring in his step when he passed the sentry at the gangplank of the *Estes*. Rain tugged at his trench coat as he climbed the gangplank. Showing his credentials to the ship's Duty Officer, he requested an interview with Messman Fredrick Tanner.

Half an hour later, the two sat across from each other in a cramped room. "Sailor, I am Major Moretti, head of the MPs here. Your name's Fredrick Tanner?"

"Yes, sir. This about that Marine who got killed?"

Moretti's voice was crisp. "I have a couple questions to ask. I do not want you to tell me your version of events or explain anything or answer in any way other than a yes or no. Offering a false answer *when interviewed* is a court martial offence. Clear?"

Fred paused, wondering about the emphasis. "Yes, sir."

Moretti reviewed the skimpy report and returned it to the large envelope. Navy did a slap-dash job and gave it to him a week later. *During the interview, they never asked him about his stain, just if he killed the guy. Never asked if he knew anything about it. Piss-poor interview.* He pulled out a blank page and unclipped the pen from his pocket. He noted the time and date at the top of the page. "For simplicity, I will not repeat the questions the Navy asked before, so only answer mine with a yes or no. The interview begins now. Understand?"

"Yes, sir."

"Were you on leave the Sunday when the Marine, Lieutenant Argos, was stabbed in the alleyway just off Chungshan Road?"

"Yes, sir."

"Did you stab him?"

"No, sir."

"Was your shirtfront *wet* when you signed back on your ship?"

"Yes, sir." Fred pressed his lips together. Moretti knew he wanted to say more.

"In the *interview*, did the Navy ask you about it?"

Fred paused and considered the question. "No, sir."

Moretti made a quick notation. He put his pen down and pulled an enlargement from the envelope under his stack of paperwork. "I would like you to examine this photograph. In a minute, I am going to ask if that is you chasing a Chinese man up Chungshan Road shortly after the attack. Take your time."

Tanner's frown shifted. Moretti wondered if he knew Anna had been his witness, or feared for her, or if he just wondered what the hell was happening.

Moretti asked, "Through looking at it?"

"Yes, sir."

Tanner braced his shoulders.

"Well, is that you?"

"Yes, sir."

"Now, as *briefly* as possible, please tell me why you were chasing him."

Fred started, but stopped himself, crafting his response with care. "He stabbed the Marine. I was trying to catch him."

Moretti finished his notes quickly and slid them with the photo back into the envelope. Clipping his pen in his shirt pocket, he said, "Interview's over."

Tanner frowned, trying to understand why the major was asking questions in that odd way. He closed his eyes, knowing what she had done for him.

Moretti stood and shook Tanner's hand. "Hang in there, son. This will soon be over. But do not discuss our talk or anything about the case with anyone. And I mean anyone."

"Sir?"

"Yes?"

"That's it?"

"As far as I am concerned, it's just paperwork now. But can I ask you a question?"

Tanner nodded.

"Why didn't you just change your shirt at your apartment?"

"I cleaned up before she visited. Everything was at the laundry."

Once he left the command ship *Estes*, Moretti started for his office, then walked to the hospital ship *Repose*. He asked the Corpsman on duty in sick bay to see Nurse Rosetti with a follow-up question about an injured man.

When she entered the waiting area, she froze, staring at Moretti. She composed herself when he quietly asked, "Is there a place where we can talk?"

Taking him into an exam room, she leaned against the door and bit her lip.

Moretti whispered, "He'll be out in a day or so."

She slumped, taking deep breaths. A moment later, she stood taller and waited for Moretti to give her a lecture. When he didn't, she said, "Thank you. You won't have to worry."

"I know. Take care of yourself." They shook hands.

When he arrived at headquarters, Moretti rushed directly to the bullpen. "How'd you like to put a ribbon on a case?" They all looked up. "Just interviewed the sailor."

He took the enlarged photo from the envelope and put it on Bowen's desk. The others hurried to look at it.

Bowen asked, "Is that Tanner?"

"Yup, chasing the killer."

Ripley pointed. "Looks like a rickshaw guy."

Bowen said, "But there wasn't a rickshaw in the alley when the Shore Patrol got there."

Ripley smiled. "That's China for you: If it ain't nailed down, someone's gonna take it. Especially now."

Moretti put the photograph back in the envelope. "At least we know the sailor didn't do it. I got his statement that the coolie did, and he confirmed the picture was of him chasing the guy. It's a city police matter now."

Ripley said, "Even better, you get to tell Mathis to stick it."

Smirking, Bowen reached for the phone. "You want to call a briefing tonight at nineteen hundred? I can book the big conference room."

Moretti chuckled as he closed his office door before calling Mathis.

CHAPTER 40

Moretti finished cleaning the boat after a good Sunday out on the water. Fish were biting, and the weather cooperated. Twenty minutes later, he stopped his Jeep a few doors from Bill's home to gather his thoughts. *How many times have I been here?* The pink cloud of spring blossoms had long passed. The rain had washed away the carpet of browned petals covering Shaoguan Road weeks ago. When Moretti rang the street bell, Leon frowned at the interruption; he was starting dinner. Once he saw the major, he opened the gate and walked to his Jeep.

Moretti leaned against the hood. "Bill said you wanted to talk to me."

Dry leaves skittered across the street.

"It's about your boat. Would you be interested in selling?"

Moretti paused, surprised by the directness of his question. "Possibly." The dance had started, the haggling and negotiating.

"How difficult would it be to teach me to drive it?"

Moretti thought for a moment. *What's he really asking?* "Easy once you leave the harbor. Docking takes some practice. Navigating away from shore and handling it in a rough sea is not simple."

"What is the distance it can travel?"

He grasped Leon's intent. "In a calm sea, three-fifty or four hundred miles. Shanghai is about four hundred miles to the south. You could put a couple of fuel drums on deck to be safe."

"Could you show me how to run it?"

"Sure. Wouldn't be hard if all you wanted to do was follow the coast south." Moretti considered the risks Leon was taking by staying even another day. "We'll find a time to take her out this week."

Leon accepted the three large fish that Moretti thought looked like

318

sea bass. After Moretti left, Leon filleted the fish for dinner in place of the chicken he had planned.

After dinner, Beth curled up on the sofa against Bill's chest. He opened *The Little Prince*. Peg and Bill had previewed it together, fearing a pilot ditching in the desert may frighten her, but loved the story and its illustrations. As Bill read to his daughter, Peg recalled something Claire said when she dropped off the book. *Do you see what you believe or believe what you see? It's going to be important soon. We'll need fresh eyes.* At first, it sounded like a comment on photography or the book, but now Peg wondered what she really intended.

The phone rang. After a moment, Leon entered the living room, motioning Bill into the hallway. "Please pardon my intrusion, but Major Moretti said it was urgent."

Bill picked up the receiver. "Thanks for the fish we—"

"There's a problem with one of your guys."

Bill stood taller. "Who?"

"Phil Wilson and his wife got arrested. Picked her up at the embassy this afternoon and arrested him at home a few minutes ago."

Bill leaned against the wall. "Why?"

"You know what Shanghai Sally or *maduk* is?"

"Tell me."

"Opium mixed with tobacco so you can smoke it in a regular pipe."

"I don't like where this is going."

Moretti continued, "Naval Intelligence got a tip about her trading with a dope dealer. Then she shows up at the embassy for something. When they did the usual search of her purse, they find a classified mission map. She starts boo-hooing and says she needed the *maduk* so Phil could sleep."

"What? That makes no sense." He whispered, "He looked fine, and the maps are under lock and key until they're issued to us. Old ones go into a burn bag."

"He didn't take a new one. He bribed a Nationalist kid to give him old ones with the mission markings. Eleanor traded 'em for dope."

Bill's fist clenched on the phone. "Damn it!"

"When it went from drug dealing to treason, they took it out of my hands."

It took all his will not to ask the questions he knew Moretti couldn't answer. "Thanks for letting me know."

"Act puzzled when your pilot is absent tomorrow. Maybe call the MPs to go to his house and check on him."

"Will do. Thanks."

He pulled the receiver away from his ear but heard Moretti. "And Bill?"

"About hung up on you, sorry."

"Wanted you to know Leon bought the boat. I think he's got a plan."

"Thanks, Tony. That's a relief."

Bill returned to the living room and forced a grin when he saw Peg and Beth waiting for him. He was about to take his daughter to the Sahara Desert and introduce her to a pilot and a visitor who rode an asteroid to many planets. Thinking about espionage, betrayal, and deception had to wait.

That night, Peg snuggled close to Bill as he stared at the ceiling. She whispered, "You're a brilliant father. You always know exactly what Beth needs, how to help her stretch her wings. It's like you have a sixth sense on how she's doing and what she needs—"

Bill slammed his hand against the mattress. "Then why the hell couldn't I 'sense' that one of my guys was in trouble?"

Peg paused for a moment. *Bill needs me now more than he needs my news.*

She sat up. "What? Tell me about it."

CHAPTER 41

Peg moaned when the alarm clock on Bill's side of the bed clanged. Ten minutes later, she squinted at the light from the bathroom. "Early mission?"

"Go back to sleep."

"Thanks for putting Beth to bed last night."

He pulled on his flight suit. "Sure. Base called after you both were sawing logs. Last-minute decision to ferry some Corsairs to the *Rendova*. Weather's going to be perfect for trying out the new Chance Vought landing gear on the planes they rotated in. Should reduce the bounce. Red and I might be out there overnight if the weather somehow goes stink or we need to make a couple of runs each. Didn't hear how many planes we're moving, but only a few of us are carrier qualified."

She sat up. *She'd heard them at parties whispering about their carrier landings, calling the Corsair the Widow Maker.* Ice shot through her veins. *Cockpit too far back to see over the hog nose.* Her breath grew shallow. *Landing gear they called a kangaroo for the way it bounced over the arresting cables.* She felt her scalp tingle. *He's testing it for them.* Through the edge of nausea, a word came to her. *Duty. No, double duty. He was already flying double-duty after Phil's arrest and Art's transfer, putting it all on his own shoulders.* She got up and gave him a long hug, knowing there was nothing she could say. Holding her breath.

He kissed her. "Go back to bed. I'll grab coffee at the base."

Right on schedule, Leon drove Beth to Trudy's. When he returned, Peg drove the Buick to the orphanage. The day soon became overwhelming. Severely undernourished children of all ages arrived. Medical exams, bathing, clothing, and feeding the newcomers took priority over lessons and games. The older children fed the younger ones to free the adults to attend to the new arrivals. At noon, Peg saw the nurse return to the small medical office and tapped on the partially open door.

Without looking up from writing in a chart, Anna called, "Come in and have a seat."

Peg remained in the doorway. "Could I have a minute? Buy you lunch at the Grand."

She closed the chart and pointed to a chair. "Sorry. Can't today. I'm swamped. I'm going to grab a quick sandwich at the snack bar at the Y and eat it on the way back."

"It's freezing out there!"

"Got to clear my brain. These new case files are going to take hours. We're swamped."

Peg motioned her to stay seated. "Ham on rye or chicken salad?"

"Ham will buy you five minutes in the park."

Twenty minutes later, when Peg waved a sandwich wrapped in waxed paper, the nurse picked up her coat and followed Peg out to the street. "Peg?"

She pointed into the park. "Let's find a bench."

They passed several older women with quilted jackets who were doing a slow tai chi in perfect unison. A giggling cluster of small boys in shorts and knee socks ran past them, playing a version of Hide and Seek. They were dressed well, not like the children in rags on the edge of town.

Two small girls wearing red satin pajamas and light coats were playing. One had found a feather and tossed it into the air and the other tried to catch it as it spun down. The two giggled as they played. Anna nodded, saying, "Love 'em. Making something out of nothing."

Peg took a handkerchief and quickly wiped soot off the bench before they sat. While Anna started on her sandwich, Peg watched the girls. *Women's work. Making something out of nothing, indeed. That's what we do. Make babies. Teach them to be human. Make strangers into friends and a community. Lovers into a family. Weaving a future out of hope. Invisible.*

Indispensable. Not like the boys, just chasing after each other.

Anna gestured with her sandwich. "It's so smoky these days. Like living in a chimney."

"I've stopped taking Beth outside unless the air is clear."

"From more refugees cooking jook over coal fires. Ever had it?"

"That watery rice porridge? No."

"Local health briefing says that's about all they're eating out there now. Jook with a salted fish head if they're in the money."

"Why? It's faster to cook a pot of rice than overcook it to make porridge."

"Bowl of rice feeds one, same rice in a jook fills more bellies." Anna touched Peg's arm and said, "Okay. Spill. What's really going on? Just between us."

Peg lowered her voice. "What are you hearing about measles in town?"

"Not much. I'll ask at our next meeting with the city health office."

"When's that?"

"Why the rush?" Anna took a big bite.

"I need to know!" Her voice cracked.

"Beth?"

"No. She's fine or I wouldn't have come in today. So are her playmates, but there's a rumor of measles in the refugee camps."

"Thinking about quitting the orphanage?"

"I am wondering if Beth and I should leave now."

Anna crumpled the waxed paper and scowled. "The Corps will not look kindly on dependents folding their tent. It's not like you to overreact."

She took the sandwich wrapper from Anna as they stood. "There's a slim chance I might be pregnant. I know how measles in the first trimester could harm a baby. The birth defects."

Anna adjusted her cap without giving Peg their usual quick hug. "Or miscarriage. I'll drop by the city clinic on my way back to the ship and see what I can find out today." She took Peg's arm. "Don't even go back in there today. We might have a case already."

"Thanks," she told her friend—and now confidant. "Call me?"

Peg pulled the Buick to the curb in front of the Franklins' house and tapped the horn. Instead of Beth hurrying out after her lessons, Trudy appeared at the door and waved for Peg to come in. Peg abandoned her warm car.

Trudy took Peg's coat. "You're early. Everything okay?"

The two friends went into the kitchen. Peg changed the topic. "Girls behave today?"

"Lessons went well. We finished early, and I let them play cards. It was Crazy Eights a few minutes ago. They could be playing poker by now."

Peg forced a laugh.

Trudy slid a cup of tea to her. She frowned as Peg stared at the wall clock, its cloth-covered cord looping up to the outlet in the ceiling. "Peg?"

"Sorry. Hard day at the orphanage. Lots of new intakes." She looked at her hands for a moment then caught Trudy's eye. "Trudy?"

"What is it?"

"If anything happened to me here, you'd care for Beth until Bill or my dad . . ."

"Nothing's gonna happen to you. Of course I would, like you'd tend Sally. It's what we do. Where's this coming from?"

"I don't know."

Trudy whispered, "I'm getting edgy, too. George says some nights, the 'heat lightning' we hear is mortar fire west of the city. But the embassy says everything is still peachy."

Peg let out a deep breath and leaned her elbows on the table. "Bill says to trust what people *do* more than what they say." She glanced at the door. "Sometimes, it's what they *don't* say. When I was at the embassy dropping off our absentee ballots, I didn't see the usual notice calling for volunteers to set up Thanksgiving dinner. Did you?"

"No, now that you mention it."

"And at the base, there's nothing about the Birthday Ball. Last year, they were selling tickets by now."

Trudy said, "Taking planes out to the *Rendova* makes no sense if they are going to be defending the city."

"Exactly. I figure when we get the word to leave, we'll need to go fast. But it's making me crazy. It's on everyone's mind, but nobody's talking about it."

Trudy said, "Agree. Good thing I sent our last trunk of stuff to my folks yesterday."

"Leon's taking ours tomorrow. So, you see it like I do."

"Truth is, most of the gals here are packing on the sly. Everyone's just pretending everything is okay. Heck, considering that you, me, and most of us are used to packing to move across the country in a couple of days, getting ready for an evacuation shouldn't be too hard."

"Except for managing the kids and doing everything at the last minute."

"Right. Look around. All the bridge groups got too busy to meet. No secret there are lots more crates at the wharf lately that aren't military." Her shoulders slumped. "What're you gonna do? Protect your family by getting ready to leave in private or blab about how the mission has failed? That's a slap in the face for our husbands."

"Why? They're doing their damnedest! It's the guys in D.C. that ought to wake up to what's happening." Peg pressed her lips together until she had calmed. "After Leon dropped Beth here this morning, I packed my suitcase and arranged her closet and dresser so I can fill her things in minutes. Figured tonight I'd organize the bathroom, get the toiletries and the first aid kit ready for the field bag after she's asleep."

"That sounds like a good plan. I better pack when Sally's at your place."

"Trudy, I know you aren't going into town much now, but it has really changed. Refugees fill the side streets near the orphanage, and scavengers are picking through the garbage as soon as it's dumped. Leon drives us more frequently now, for safety. I can ask him to bring you to our place whenever you want to come over."

"But we're just a couple of streets away! It's wonderful exercise, unless the air's rotten."

"I know. But Bill and I agreed. No more taxis or rickshaw rides. Sticking close to home unless Leon is with us."

"You think Gerri has a clue?"

She sighed. "Don't know. She's a homebody now. Gerri says JD's working on getting her on a flight soon. I can tell her to get packed for that." Peg finished the last of her tea, stood, and put the cup on the counter. "Can you and Sally come over for dinner?"

"Can't tonight. Promised Sally we'd cook dinner together. Might be pancakes or French toast."

She bundled Beth into her coat and drove home.

Peg was picking at her dinner when the telephone rang. She left Beth and Gerri at the table without waiting for Leon to call her.

Anna said in a low overly calm voice, "It's starting slowly. But the rate of transmission via airborne exposure is about ninety percent, not to mention direct contact with open sores. They're living on top of each other out there—"

"So, the rumor's true."

"A few cases in the refugee shantytown on the west side. The local health authorities are trying to quarantine the kids. Fat chance that'll work. I'd expect a generalized outbreak within the next few weeks. We'll need a new protocol at the orphanage."

"What should I do, isolate here?"

Anna continued with an urgency. "Look. We were supposed to leave port for an exercise next week, but that's canceled as of an hour ago. They are diverting a troop transport from that exercise to come here. Something's up. Bill might get some info on the incoming ship."

"Seriously?"

"I think you need to consider whether to evac by plane or ship, but keep in mind that both have issues."

"Like what?"

"If you're sharing air with anyone contagious on that plane from here to Guam, you are at a serious risk of contracting measles. Ditto the next legs of the hop home."

Peg leaned against the wall. "If we use surgical masks?"

"Better odds, but that's a long flight in a closed cabin."

"And on a ship?"

"You could isolate in sick bay. No contact with Beth. Bill would need to mask and gown if they'd even let him see you. Sorry. Wish they had a shot for it, like influenza."

"Me too. Thanks."

"Oh, Peg? One more thing. Get the pregnancy test, then stay home. If you're expecting, it's like the Marines say, 'Eat the apple and fuck the Corps.' Your family comes first."

"Thanks." She blinked back tears as she dialed the orphanage.

When Peg returned to the table, Beth was telling Gerri about seeing whales from Moretti's boat in the spring. At bedtime, Beth recounted the day's American history lesson quickly as she changed into her pajamas and slipped into bed. Peg went into her own bedroom and pulled a heavy Hudson Bay blanket, a wedding present, from the trunk at the foot of her bed. As she arranged it on Beth's covers, she said, "It's going to be chilly tonight, even with the furnace on. I want you to be toasty."

Beth rubbed the colored bars at the end of the white wool blanket in order: green, red, yellow, and indigo. "It's pretty."

"A gift from your grandmother before you were born. It's special. Almost as special as you."

Peg sat beside her, both propped against pillows and each holding one side of *The Little Prince*. Occasionally, Peg stopped reading and pointed to a word to see if Beth knew it; sometimes she had her daughter take over for a sentence or two. Once Beth was asleep, Peg organized the bathroom and medical kit for a rapid departure.

The wind picked up and sent blackened leaves off the cherry trees tapping against the windows. Peg wondered if the gusty wind and rattle of the branches would wake Beth. The fall weather made wild swings between the pretense of summer and the threat of winter. But now, after two days of falling temperatures and a dusting of snow in the afternoon, the weather had gone bad.

Once in bed, Peg shivered while trying to read. She hurried to the closet and grabbed Bill's flannel shirt to use as a bed jacket over her pajamas. She plowed through the first three chapters of the novel Gerri said her book club loved. Gusts outside rattled her bedroom window, crackling as dried leaves and twigs hit it. She sighed, grateful that between Bill and Leon, the place was a fortress. The walled compound and the barred windows on the ground floor were the most forbidding in the district. Still, the creaking of the trees and scuffing of leaves in the compound bothered her.

Attempting a new chapter, she heard Beth muttering. A dream? An earache? She put the book aside and got out of bed.

Beth screamed, "Mommy!" at the snap and crash of breaking glass. Peg smelled the stench of garlic and old smoke before the cold air from the broken window hit her. The shaft of light from her bedroom lit Beth, kneeling on the edge of her bed, holding a blanket beside the gaping hole in the window.

A hand from outside grabbed for the blanket but fell short, the bars restraining him. His face distorted, grasping, pressing his shoulder between the bars. A young man. Chinese face. Beth yelled at him in Chinese.

Peg screamed, "No!" Beth dropped the blanket. Peg pulled her away from the window, screaming at the man to leave. Floodlights suddenly flared across the yard as Leon sprinted toward them, shouting.

The thief pulled back, his right elbow twisted, trapped between the bars. Tugging to break free, his jacket snagged on the glass. He jerked to free himself.

In an instant, the shattered glass sliced through his thin quilted coat. He shrieked in pain, twisted, and screamed when the jagged glass dug deeper into his forearm.

Peg picked Beth up as though she were still a toddler and ran into the hallway. Kneeling beside her, she glanced over her daughter's shoulder into the bedroom and saw a dark line of blood snaking down the wall. Leon was behind the man.

Peg searched Beth's wide eyes and pale face. Fear, not shock. Peg led her into the living room. After turning on the lights, she wedged her daughter into the corner of the sofa, held her shoulders, and examined her face. "Did he grab you? Any glass hit you?" When Beth shook her head, Peg wrapped her daughter in the lap robe from the back of the sofa and held her. Both breathing hard, hearts hammering, trembling.

Gerri rushed to the top of the stairway, pulling her robe around her. "What's the racket?"

Peg gasped for breath. "Robber! Broke Beth's window. Leon's got him. Outside."

Without hesitating, Gerri hurried down the stairs to Beth. "You okay, Sweetie?"

Peg said, "He was trying to take her blanket."

Beth whispered, "He was cold."

Leon shouted from the kitchen door, "Call the police! Tell them to hurry. He's bleeding bad."

Peg stood. "Beth, stay with her."

Gerri asked, "Want me to call?"

"No. Not yet."

The thief had passed out under the floodlight by the kitchen door, dark blood pooling under his arm where the jacket had torn away. Not even twenty, she guessed. She grabbed a kitchen towel, folded it, and pressed it against his sliced jacket.

"He's still losing blood. Needs stitches. Stay here, I'll get my kit."

Then she glanced into the living room and shouted to Gerri, "Watch her!"

The young woman took Beth's hand. "We'll be upstairs."

Rushing to the bathroom, Peg grabbed the medical kit. All the lights were blazing in the kitchen when she returned. A reddish smear crossed the floor from the back door to the laundry room.

Leon had somehow hoisted the young man onto the long metal table used for folding laundry and held a tea towel against the man's right forearm. The bloodied jacket was crumpled in the deep laundry sink with several tea towels that had been used as compresses. The man's frayed undershirt and trousers were a light cotton. Lack and want radiated from the intruder. He struggled to sit up.

When he saw Peg, he stopped struggling but was still fearful. Leon explained in Chinese that she would help him.

After a brief inspection, she said, "Put more pressure on the wound. And push here, under his armpit. Keep him flat." She had Leon lift the compress and return it quickly. She rolled up the sleeves of Bill's shirt, filled a large pitcher of water, and put an empty soup pot on the floor under his arm.

"Tell him after I clean the wound, I'll put on Mercurochrome to stop infection, stitch it, and then bandage it."

The man's terrified gaze darted between Leon and Peg. He frowned and struggled again. After Leon shouted at him, he stopped and watched Peg thread a curved needle and place small forceps and tweezers beside it on a dinner plate next to them. She poured alcohol on the plate to sanitize her tools, then pulled on latex gloves.

"Hold the pot under his arm while I pour water over the cut." When Peg nodded, Leon pulled away the compress and picked up the pot. She poured the water over the wound and used tweezers to pull out bits of his quilted jacket from his flesh. The sharp scent of the alcohol masked the musky, wet-dog smell coming from the young man. The cut began bleeding again. Leon started to replace the compress, but she motioned him away. "Let it flush for a moment."

Fresh blood dripped from his arm into the large pot. The young man squirmed.

"Open the bottle of Mercurochrome and pour it over the wound. Tell him he will feel it." The patient twitched and clenched his jaw as the sting of the antiseptic penetrated the deep cut. The reddish orange stain saturated the wound, ran down his arm, and across the back of his right hand, dripping into the pot.

Placing her fingers on either side of the gash, Peg evaluated how deep a stitch she would need to make. "Open the BFI powder and sprinkle it over the wound." Leon's hand shook as he sprinkled it from the small can. He jumped when a branch broke outside and slammed against the door.

Peg said, "Tell him this helps stop the bleeding and keeps infection away."

He translated, then asked, "What is it?" as she picked up the curved needle in one hand and the forceps in the other.

"Stands for bismuth, formic, and iodide. Been around since the First World War."

The depth of the gash alarmed her. The slice went well into the muscle and required more than a skin-to-skin closure, or it would pucker and fester.

Peg held the needle where the boy could see it. "Have him hold still, or it will get worse. I'll go as fast as I can."

Starting on the right side of the gash, she drew the curved needle through the skin into the flesh and up, leaving a tail on the surgical thread. She repeated the deep stitch on the left before drawing the sides together and tying a surgeon's knot with one hand, looping the thread around the end of the forceps. One down.

Leon watched her work. "That knot. I've never seen—"

"Triple loop on the first throw holds it while you do the second, so you can pull it tight without the skin puckering."

She listened to Leon calming the young man, not understanding his words but knowing the tone while she kept silent for the remaining twelve stitches. Once finished, she stretched her back and dropped the needle and forceps into the alcohol bath on the plate. She found a gauze pad in her kit, balanced it on the closed wound, then cut adhesive tape to hold it in place. She stared at it. Not satisfied, she pulled a roll of gauze and wrapped it around his arm.

"Help him sit up slowly. Keep him on the table." She looked at Leon. "Tell him to keep it dry for a week, at least. Change the bandage if it gets wet. He can cut out the sutures in seven to ten days, then clean it and bandage it again."

Leon told him, knowing the young man could not do much more than try to keep it dry. And that was a maybe. When he finished, Peg said, "He can't wear that filthy jacket."

"I'll find something." He told the man to stay there, waited for Peg's nod, and left quickly. The young man's head slumped forward on his chest, and he breathed deeply. He held on to the edge of the table with both hands.

In a few moments, Leon carried in a worn work coat. He helped the man put it on and saw Peg staring at her patient. In contrast to his ebony hair, his pallor was startling.

"He's not looking well. Ask him when he ate last."

Leon reported it was the day before. "There's rice pudding. See if he'll eat some. I'm going to check on Beth." As she passed Leon, she held his arm for a moment. "Thank you, Leon."

Beth's lip quivered when she saw her mother in the doorway a minute later. "I'm sorry. I didn't want him to get hurt, just have the blanket. He was so cold."

Holding her daughter, Peg said, "You did nothing wrong."

The girl sniffed. "Could you give him a blanket?"

"Sure. I fixed his cut. He's going to be fine. I'll be right back."

Peg quickly changed into slacks and a sweater and found an old blanket in the linen closet. She folded it into a tight bundle on her way back to the kitchen, then placed it beside the man, who was finishing the rice pudding. "Leon, tell him he can have it." A moment later she asked, "What should we do with him? Let him go or drive him to the refugee mission at church?"

Leon and the young man had several fast exchanges. The man wanted to leave on foot. He clutched the blanket to his chest and bowed deeply to Peg before Leon walked him to the gate. She leaned against the closed door and tried to gather herself.

When Leon returned, carrying a bucket, mop, and a large brown bottle of disinfectant, he said, "Several limbs of the old cherry tree outside the wall cracked and fell. He must have used them to climb into the courtyard. I'll stand guard until morning, after I clean up. Safer to keep her upstairs tonight. She shouldn't remember her bedroom that way."

Peg hurried upstairs and motioned to Gerri. They stepped into the hallway, where Peg whispered, "I'll be back after we do some cleanup."

Gerri said, "No. Stay with your kid. I'll go help Leon. Listen. With that broken window, you'd freeze your tail feathers off down there. I got fresh sheets on the bed, so why don't you both turn in up here? I'll grab a blanket and sleep on the sofa next door when we're finished."

Exhausted after her adrenaline had ebbed, Peg nodded. She held Beth and wondered what Bill would say about the girl's generosity, Leon's bravery, Gerri's help, the young man's need, or how she managed the situation.

And the baby.

CHAPTER 42

Peg woke with a start: Beth beside her, upstairs, the room bright. Then the memory exploded—the shattering glass; Beth, Leon, the intruder; the stench of garlic and the rusted iron smell of blood. She took a sharp breath, sat up, and took another to quell her nausea.

She studied her daughter, curled and making puppy sounds under a tangle of covers. In response to her mother smoothing the surrounding blankets, Beth moaned. Peg whispered to her. "Go back to sleep. You're upstairs and everything's fine." She hurried downstairs, dressed quickly in fresh slacks and a turtleneck, and opened the door to Beth's bedroom, expecting chaos.

Other than the broken window, there was no sign of last night's terror. But the room had changed. The bed was now on the far side of the room. The dresser was under the broken window, perhaps hiding the stain on the wall. She shivered when the winter wind swirled around her.

She pulled the door closed, sat on the bed she and Bill shared, and wept. *It could have ended so differently. How could I think about outwitting Mao's army when I barely managed one intruder?* Deep breath. *Beth's safe upstairs. Bill's due back today. Madam Tong and Leon are here.* Deep breath.

After pulling on a heavy sweater and washing her face, Peg needed tea and toast to calm her stomach before Charlie scrambled eggs for Beth and the smell sent her stomach into a cyclone. She padded silently down the hall but stopped at the doorway to the kitchen. Gerri was reading *Thunder Over China*. She closed the book when she saw Peg. "How's Beth?"

"Still sleeping. Where's Charlie?" Peg asked.

334

"I had Leon fire him this morning. Leon's doing dinners. I'm covering breakfast and lunch."

Peg slammed her palm against the counter. "What? You had no right!"

Gerri stood at the stove and struck a match. The gas popped to life. She slid the teakettle over the flame. "Nobody made you the boss of the world."

"No, but this is our house. Bill said you could stay here when you had no place to go. Then you just stayed and stayed."

Gerri leaned down and adjusted the flame, then faced Peg with her hands on her hips. "Look! I know you think I'm some hick that doesn't know up from down. But I do. I see you're in a family way and don't want to tell anyone yet."

A wave of nausea hit. Peg leaned against the counter.

Gerri said softly, "Bet if I fried an egg now, you'd be in the bathroom for an hour." Without waiting for a reply, she sliced two thick pieces from a loaf of white bread Leon had baked the day before.

"So? What do you want, Gerri?"

"Me? Nothing. Have a seat. I'm gonna make some sugar tea and dry toast for you. That's how you are going to be starting your days for at least a month. If you want to eat alone before the kid's up, fine. If you want to chance it if she wants fried eggs and sausage, fine by me. Let me know when you're going to tell everybody. Until then, my lips are sealed. And I'm cooking." Gerri pulled a ceramic teapot from the cupboard. "You want green tea or Lipton's?"

"Green, please. I'm confused."

"About what? I'm the oldest of eight. I know what morning sickness looks like a mile away—and what food can calm it down. Charlie and Leon are guys. What do they know?"

"Why are you helping me?"

"Because I can. Maybe it's time you let someone help you for a change. I've learned more from you than I ever would from that book the

Colonel's wife made me read. She's a taker, like JD. You're a giver. That's all I really need to know about a person."

"I'm sorry, Gerri."

"For what? Putting up with us? We got off on the wrong foot, but I'm not as bad as you think. I'm just different. And I sorta lost my way with all the shiny stuff JD was throwing at me. It never occurred to me he wasn't pulling his weight. We barely knew each other when we got married, but I thought it might work. Then some days were harder than others. Sometimes I drank too much."

"I'm sorry we had that argument."

"Yeah. I shouldn't have had the kid help me make drinks. But, damn, she did a great job."

"I treated you like a child."

"That's who I was. When I got questioned about my husband killing that guy and, you know, the light went on. It scared the hell out of me." The toast popped. Gerri put two pieces on a plate and cut the toast on the diagonal. "Take small bites."

"Thank you."

The young woman grabbed the kettle as it whistled, poured the steaming water into the teapot, and pushed the sugar bowl over to Peg. "It'll be ready in a couple minutes."

They both jerked at the sound of hammering. Gerri laughed and held her hand to her chest. "That's Leon. Said he had some wood in the basement to cover the window. At least it'll keep the cold out until he can get it fixed proper."

Beth wandered into the kitchen, hair tangled, barefoot, rubbing her eye.

Peg scooted her chair back and opened her arms. "Come here." Beth slid onto her mother's lap as if she were a three-year-old and pushed her head into Peg's shoulder.

Gerri turned toward the door. "I'm gonna get dressed, then make breakfast for Beth and me when you're through."

Peg nodded to her and hugged Beth. "We'll have quite a story to tell your father, won't we?"

"Mommy? He got hurt real bad, didn't he?"

She said slowly, "He cut his arm, and I fixed it. It is going to heal. He said to thank you for the blanket." Peg smoothed Beth's hair. "After breakfast, do you want to stay home or go to Sally's for your lessons? We had a big night, so if you want to stay home, that's fine."

"Is Leon going to be hammering all day?"

Peg forced a chuckle. "Never know what he has up his sleeve."

Beth hopped down. "Then I want to go tell Sally about last night."

"Good. Let Leon fix the window. He might need to move some furniture and we don't want to get in his way. I'll grab your clothes and be right back."

When Peg went to the driveway to warm up the Buick, she saw Gerri holding the ladder while Leon cut the last of the broken limbs from the cherry tree. He hurried down the ladder and reached for the car keys. "I'll drive Miss Beth."

Peg said, "Thanks, but I can."

He held out his hand. "Captain Ryan said—"

Peg relinquished the keys as her daughter emerged from the house.

As soon as the Buick left, Madam Tong appeared beside the house and motioned Peg to come out of the chill and into her bungalow. Once inside, she asked Peg to follow her to a small alcove. *An apartment kitchen? No, more of a laboratory.* The older woman said, "Before we talk, I thought you might enjoy seeing how professionals test tea. A diversion from last night. And I need your opinion."

Narrow shelves ran across a little work area fitted with a gas burner and small sink. The top shelf held a row of pint-size lab beakers. Below that, at eye level, a dozen glass jars each held loose tea. It resembled the Chinese apothecary shop in town.

Madam Tong silently busied herself. With scientific precision, she placed the beakers on two scales by weight, added loose tea from two different containers and water after she took its temperature. As she set a timer, she said, "To compare things properly, you must have a controlled sample. Just like your laboratory work in college."

"How did you know about that?"

"Your husband told me about your awards, your offers to do medical research, to challenge yourself. How you walked away from that to marry a pilot."

"I didn't marry 'a pilot,' I married Bill. He was a senior, studying architecture. The war came. Plans changed." She stopped and adjusted her story. "You've seen how committed he is to us. He feels the same about America. He found something more important to him than building buildings."

"And you?"

"My family can be anywhere."

"You expect much from Beth. College?"

"If her grades are good enough and we can afford it. We've started saving already."

"Good. Please, make yourself comfortable. I will bring these in when they are ready."

Peg marveled at the transformation: a worn sofa, cheap tables, and reproductions of Chinese scrolls on the wall. She tried to get comfortable on the lumpy sofa, then forced a smile when Madam Tong brought a tray with four small Chinese teacups, not the delicate English ones she had expected. She placed the tray on the table, then sat beside Peg. "The left two are yours."

"Should I taste one before the other?"

"As you wish." Madam Tong picked up the end cup and inhaled as she sipped, slurping, making the noise they had cautioned Beth not to make.

Peg stopped her cup inches from her face. "Is that how I should taste it?"

The older woman laughed. "It takes some practice, but you can try it or wait for the tea to cool."

"I'll let it cool a bit." Peg sipped each tea, one after the other, then again.

"Which do you prefer?"

"Similar, but this one."

She grinned. "My newest blend. Calming for expectant or anxious people. I thought you would be the perfect taster, given your condition."

Peg laughed. "First, Gerri guesses and tells Leon to fire the cook. Then Leon tells you! My protectors. But Bill doesn't know, yet. And we'll want to tell Beth together."

Madam Tong shifted closer to Peg. "Let me come to the point. I know you are concerned about safety, especially considering the intruder. First, a guard from our old warehouse begins tonight." Peg started to say something, but Madam Tong's raised hand silenced her. "Second, Leon and I have completed the transfer of our business offshore. It is all settled now."

"Considering Taiwan?"

"No. I've decided on Ceylon. Leon's off to San Francisco or Portland, where we already have offices." The older woman paused before asking, "May I request a candid opinion? What do you think of Gerri? I've rarely even said hello to her, but Leon has formed an opinion of her."

Peg paused to really consider the question. "I think in her time here, she has grown a lot. Basically, a kind and decent girl with rough edges that hid it. At first, I did not trust her to be around Beth. But she changed. Helped with her lessons several times. Quite the math wizard." She laughed. "Even borrowed an abacus from Leon to explain something Beth didn't understand. When she told me she'd worked in a mill, and her dad's store, she neglected to say she was their bookkeeper. As I got to know her, I asked why she married JD when she barely knew him. She'd quit her mill job when they told her to run a second set of books. I think that had to do with her wanting to get out of town however she could. How she managed that mess with JD took grit and courage. Integrity.

And she could not have been more helpful last night."

"Leon told me. Thank you. And now, about the house. All completed, at last. A Swiss family will have ownership, but only when it is vacant. They already have a relation with the communists and the Nationalists, so whatever happens, someone will welcome them. Banking is always welcome." She pulled a small box from her pocket. "I wanted you to have this for Beth when she is old enough."

Peg opened the simple cardboard box and found a pendant of green jade on a gold chain. She smiled. "It is lovely. She will treasure it. Thank you."

"And for you." She pulled a cheap box from her other pocket but held it. "However, I want you to understand this gift is not yours, but for you to administer for college educations: Beth's and the baby, and then for other young women. At Beth's birthday party, those girls walking the tight wire moved me. The way they walked—mincing, tiny steps, needing fans for balance." She stopped herself and looked at Peg. "My grandmother had 'lotus feet' and walked that way. Her feet were bound when she was younger than Beth. Folded over, bones broken, over and over for two years. All to make her more 'beautiful' and marriageable. That was the only future they could imagine for her."

A tear slid down Peg's cheek. She closed her eyes. *The rocking gait of the bent, old women in the market—like bowlegged cowboys on a bender. The small feet, the ever-present cane, the pain. Now I know why.* She blinked.

Madam Tong continued. "That was the old China. They crippled her for life. This elegant woman, who could have been anything, maimed by loving parents. She transitioned into a modern world with grace and instilled in my mother and me the need for women to be independent. And this begins with education."

Peg received the box and opened it. A circular pin the size of a quarter was paved with pale green stones and glittered. Every stone was set in its own pronged nest. She stared at Madam Tong, speechless.

"The stones are not the original chipped glass that was in that inexpensive setting. But for your travels, put it with Beth's play jewelry."

"They almost look like emeralds."

She watched Peg's realization and smiled graciously. "They are. A special shade. There used to be mines close to here. Exhausted hundreds of years ago. So, the stones are quite rare now. Almost no one would recognize them."

"I don't know if I can accept this."

"You must." She laughed. "In China, it is rude to refuse a gift. Besides, you don't know what it is if you bought it from a street vendor. You could always have it appraised once you return home, but there is no need to do so now."

Peg paused, knowing the emeralds that she now held were antiquities that were illegal for foreigners to remove from the country, but she also knew the stones could pay for Beth's college and change their life. Weighing their value against the cost of the deception, she whispered, "I can't."

"Really? I will leave soon. You must decide now. We will not be having this conversation again."

Peg put the lid on the box and handed it back on open palms, with head bowed, an offering, a supplication. When the older woman took it, Peg looked up and smiled. "I'll give you my father's address. You and Leon can find us through him until we get settled. You both mean so much to us." Peg studied the empty teacup. "How soon?"

"Tomorrow? A month? Leon can stay longer. I think I should tell Beth today."

CHAPTER 43

Beth settled into her usual place beside her mother and fidgeted when the adults failed to have tea, as usual.

Madam Tong smiled at the girl. "I have been telling your mother how much I have enjoyed getting to know you as a family. But that makes what I have to say now even harder. It has come time for me to say goodbye to Tsingtao and to you, our new friends."

Beth shrank into her mother's side. "Can you come with us?"

The older woman smiled and patted the seat of the shabby over-stuffed chair for Beth to sit beside her, as she did when they read to each other. Putting her arm around Beth, she continued. "No, I am afraid not." Beth sniffed. Madam Tong pulled her closer. "I will need to leave quickly. But I couldn't leave without giving you a last hug."

"Can you come visit us sometime?"

"Possibly. In the meantime, we can write letters to each other. I have seen how well you write, and you have interesting things to say."

"Where will you go?"

"An island called Ceylon, to start. America, someday."

Beth was quiet for a moment, then asked, "Can I keep the stamps from the letters you send?"

She laughed and gave the girl a long hug. "Of course. I shall try to find interesting ones to send to you. Why don't you go help Leon in the kitchen? Tell him what you want for dessert tonight."

Beth ran back to the main house, her expression cloudy. Peg said her goodbyes with a tearful hug and paused outside the bungalow. Memories flooded. She took a deep breath and wondered how she was going to console Beth. First the intruder, now losing Madam Tong.

As soon as Peg opened the kitchen door, she saw Leon's face and heard Beth crying. Hurrying to the bedroom, Peg held her daughter until she had calmed. "I know. I'm going to miss her too. But she said you could write."

"Okay."

"Say, since your father's going to be home late, what if we developed that roll of film you took at the squadron baseball game a couple of weeks ago? He'd love to give some of your pictures to the guys."

Beth asked, "Can we have Claire come over too?"

Peg marveled at her resiliency. "I'll call her now."

Claire canceled an afternoon interview and arrived at four. By six, they had developed several rolls of film and broke for a fast dinner of ham sandwiches and Beth's favorite macaroni salad while the film strips dried.

Peg avoided the rich salad, finished first, and said, "Why don't you have dessert while I get the trays set up? Come down when you finish."

After her mother left for the darkroom, Beth poked at her chocolate cake. Claire watched her for a moment before saying, "It's really nice of you to have me over tonight."

"Mom's trying to make me happy."

"Are you sad about something?"

She looked at her cake and said, "Madam Tong is going away."

"Is Leon staying?"

"I guess. And Mom sent some of my stuff to Grandpa's. So maybe we're gonna go too."

Claire forced a smile and finished her cake. "I'm sure your mother has a brilliant plan. Hey! You know what I do when I'm sad?"

"What?"

"I can't let sad thoughts push out happy ones, so I think about 'what's next.' Can you think of something we can do tonight after we print your shots of the baseball game?"

"Cards, maybe."

"Sure. Eat up. I don't want to keep your mother waiting."

About eight, Leon rapped on the door to the darkroom to announce that Captain Ryan was on the telephone.

As soon as she dropped a print into the rinse, Peg dashed upstairs and grabbed the telephone from the hall table. "Bill?"

"Hi. We're at the wharf. The tender brought us in from the *Rendova*. Any chance you could pick us up at the main guard gate?"

"Sure. Just you?"

"George. Is there a problem?"

"Nope. Be there in about twenty minutes."

Peg called for Leon to watch Beth, hurried to the darkroom, and clipped Claire's last print with the others on a line to dry. She calmed Beth, who wanted to go with her, argued the keys away from Leon, and offered Claire a ride to her hotel.

Claire grabbed her purse. "Thanks anyway. I've got the Ford. I'll pick up the prints tomorrow. Say hi to Bill for me." As they walked to the gate, Claire noticed Peg stop and catch her breath. "You okay? You were looking a little shaky down there."

"Sure. Drop by tomorrow for your prints. I should be home all afternoon."

Claire pulled off Pacific Road into the seashore park. Once she saw Peg's Buick pass, she retrieved the Zenith from the trunk. After locking her doors, she keyed: *Dependents preparing for departure. Shipping crates for freighters increasing. No planning for usual events. No sign of military or embassy extraction plan. Other sources suggest rebel infiltration of city is increasing with refugees. Recommend staging air transports for civilian evacuation flights ASAP.*

Bill hopped into the car beside Peg and kissed her while George tossed their flight bags into the trunk. She glanced into the rear-view mirror at George lounging in the back seat.

During the drive back to the Badaguan District, she told them how she and Trudy had the last of their valuables on their way to the States, were secretly packing suitcases for an evacuation, and that they were keeping the girls in the dark.

When Bill gave her a questioning glance, Peg said that it was for everyone's well-being and safety right now, if the girls don't know the plan, they can't tell anyone, and they won't be afraid. She finished by saying she and Trudy decided that, when the time came, they would meet at Peg's house and leave as a group. The men listened to the details of the plan, both realizing their wives had developed it in their absence. Then she announced, "And we've even come up with our coded alert. If either of you call Trudy or me and say that you'll be late for dinner and use the word 'skedaddle,' Trudy and I will have the girls and our bags at our house, all ready to go."

They dropped George off at his house, then drove toward home. Bill frowned when she took a side street and shut off the car. "What's going on, Peg? You've been chattering nonstop. Is Beth okay?"

"Yes. We all are. But this can't wait until we are in bed alone. Last night, we had an intruder get over the wall and break a window. Leon got him and the window has a temporary cover on it. Madam Tong hired a night watchman."

"And?"

"What?"

"What's the other part?"

She took a deep breath. "It was Beth's window. The bars kept him out. He was trying to get a blanket off her bed. She was handing it to him when I came in. Unafraid. He cut his arm on the glass. Needed stitches. But Beth didn't see any of that. Gerri stepped in, kept her upstairs, and helped Leon clean up the mess."

"That settles it. You both are going on the first plane out of here. They are reorganizing the squadron. When we leave here, George and I both have orders for stateside. We can get Trudy and Sally on the flight with you now."

She took his hand. "It's not that easy. Remember, before you left . . .

when I said you were a good father?"

He frowned. "Sure, but—"

"I was trying to tell you something, but we ended up talking about Phil's arrest."

"Sorry." He watched her.

Peg rushed, her words tangling together, telling him about the dangers of measles in town, modes of transmission, the recycled air on a plane, about sick bay on a ship being safer, and finally—that—he might be a father again.

Bill's eyes filled with tears as he held her. Grinning, he pulled back to look at her. "A baby! How can you be this amazing?"

She laughed. "I think it was a joint effort."

He kissed her and whispered, "Just when I thought I couldn't love you more, you pull this stunt." He looked to the side, thinking, then asked, "How do we tell Beth?"

"More a 'when' question. It's early still."

"Who knows? Have you been to a doctor?"

She put her finger to his lips. "Too early for the test. At first, I thought I was late from all the craziness, then I recognized the changes in my body. Gerri guessed, told Leon, who told Madam Tong."

"Trudy?"

She shook her head. "Not before I told you! I'll call her in the morning."

He grinned. "We can tell Beth first thing tomorrow. She's going to be a terrific big sister."

The next day, the news delighted Beth. Peg's quick call to Trudy was greeted with joy and followed by their daughters giggling to each other on the phone. Beth told Leon stories about what she and the baby would do together as he sorted the clean laundry. When Claire arrived after lunch, Beth opened the gate for her and announced that she was going to be a sister before Peg caught up with her.

Claire grinned and knelt by Beth. "Fantastic! You are going to have such fun with the baby."

Peg handed Claire the prints in a brown clasp envelope. "Guess you heard the news."

"Congratulations."

Peg sent Beth back into the house. "Wanted to tell you last night, but Bill deserved to get the news first."

"Leaving soon?"

"When he gets orders or if he can book passage for Beth and me on the *Mitchell* when it arrives in a couple of weeks. I don't know if you heard, but there is a measles outbreak, and I could isolate in a cabin. Leaving on a plane . . ."

"Close quarters. I got it. Let's have lunch before you go."

That night at dinner, Beth was quiet as she stirred her peas into her mashed potatoes and ignored her parents.

Bill watched her. "What's on your mind?"

"I don't see why she has to go away."

Peg looked to Bill to answer her. He cleared his throat. "She and Leon are going to new homes, like we will."

Beth looked at her mother. "Remember when we left Grandpa's? How he made a special dinner for us?"

"Yes. Do you think we should invite Madam Tong and Leon to dinner?"

Beth grinned. "Sure, we can make it super special, like Christmas, with a roast beef and everything. But Leon can't cook it. He's gotta be a guest."

Peg forced a smile. "Remember the written invitation from Madam Tong for tea when we got here? Why don't you go write one? I'll help you in a minute."

Once Beth left, she whispered to Bill, "How the hell can I cook a roast without tossing my cookies? Can't we take them out?"

Bill said, "We'll think of something."

The next morning, Bill woke Peg with a cup of hot sweetened tea and a big grin.

She sat up. "What are you smiling about?"

"Dinner. I'll have Leon hire back Charlie and a cleanup helper. You don't go near the kitchen. He can supervise, then be a guest. And I think we should invite the Franklins, Claire, and Jean-Claude. The table has had ten chairs around it the whole time we've been here. Let's fill them up for once. Make it a big deal."

She mirrored his grin. "You're really something. What about Gerri?"

"Sure. She's become a different person in the past few weeks. I'd be happy for you to invite her."

Peg penned a formal invitation from Beth to Madam Tong and Leon. Although invited, Gerri declined and offered to help in the kitchen and then play with the girls after dinner.

Madam Tong's written acceptance arrived that afternoon. Leon and Peg discretely designed the menu. He negotiated his part in the event, overseeing the kitchen and serving soup and dessert from the sideboard while Bill would carve at the table. Bill shopped at the commissary for the roast beef and in town for the few local vegetables that were available. Leon and Gerri worked well together that afternoon.

At Leon's detailed instruction, Gerri unpacked the last of the treasures Madam Tong intended to ship and set the table with the formal silver service: knife, dinner and dessert forks, regular and soup spoons. She balanced small knives on bread plates set at an angle to the forks, then filled and set silver salt and pepper shakers, the size of dice, at each place. Then she arranged the dinner plates, dessert plates, and soup bowls on the sideboard.

When she thought she was through, Leon arrived with three silver candelabras for her to fit with fresh candles and place along the center of the table while he arranged the Waterford glasses—water, white, and red wine—at each place. He then cut small evergreen branches and artfully arranged them between the candelabras, offering both a visual representation and the scent of a Christmas tree.

Leon brought the Spode platter, soup tureen, coffee cups, and serving dishes to the kitchen and told Gerri how to arrange the roast—surrounded by roasted potatoes and carrots—to facilitate Bill's carving and serving at the table. He made a point that he wanted to portion and serve the cherry pies he had made that morning.

After working together until five o'clock, Leon relinquished control of the kitchen to Gerri and Charlie. The Franklins arrived a few minutes early and made themselves comfortable in the living room.

At six precisely, Jean-Claude and Claire rang the gate bell, each holding a bottle of red wine. Expecting them, Leon opened the gate, wearing black trousers and his usual gray coat. After showing them to the front door, Leon went to the bungalow, changed jackets, and escorted Madam Tong to the front door and knocked. Beth opened the door and stared.

Leon—in a tuxedo. Madam Tong—on his arm in a mink coat.

Bill and Peg stood behind Beth, invited them in, and Bill took her coat. The older woman had a jeweled comb in her hair. A simple string of pearls accented her royal blue sheath. Leon presented their hostess gift to Peg, the 1937 Beaulieu Vineyard wine they had returned to her after the Lunar New Year party in February.

After cocktails for the adults and apple juice for Peg and the girls, dinner was served. Madam Tong and Leon had become guests in their own home, dining in its elegance for the last time.

CHAPTER 44

The first Sunday in October, the book club started late. Once the members had settled, Margaret said, "I'm sure you all are going to miss the Birthday Ball this year as much as I am, but we wives are nothing but flexible, aren't we? Just too much going on. Bertha and Patty told me they will leave us next week. Hubbies transferred to Shanghai, and they're heading home. Anyone have other news before we talk about the book this month?"

Gerri stood. "Thank you all for welcoming me. I learned a lot from all of you and wanted to come by and say thanks before I left."

Nancy asked, "JD get his orders?"

Forcing a smile, Gerri said, "No. But thanks again." As she left, she overheard Margaret ranting about Truman and urging a vote for Dewey.

Leon held the car door for Gerri and ignored her sniffles on the way home.

Tuesday, when the young woman's suitcases were at the front door, Beth asked, "Where are you going to live now?"

"Well, first I'm going to see some people in Reno. That's in Nevada. Then I have a job lined up in California. You be a good girl for your folks, like I know you will." She leaned down and gave Beth a hug.

Peg walked Gerri to the car while her daughter stood at the front door and shouted, "Bye!"

The next morning, Leon reported that Madam Tong had taken a private plane from the small municipal airport to Shanghai at dawn and from there, a steamer would take her to Ceylon.

On Friday, Peg finished the morning lessons at the dining room table and listened to both girls whine about the slushy snow from the early storm—too cold to play outside but not cold enough to make a snow-man. When the telephone rang, she met Leon in the hallway.

He handed her the receiver. "Captain Ryan."

"Could you take the girls to the kitchen and start lunch?" As soon as he left, she said, "Hi, Bill."

"Peg!" His voice was deliberate, crisp. "Listen! I gotta *skedaddle*. Dress warm—it's going to snow tonight. There's sleet out at the field already. I'll be another hour here before I can leave."

She closed her eyes and took a deep breath. "Guess I better invite Trudy over for dinner if you are going to be late."

"Okay. And pack Mister Smith too. He can't fly with us, but he might want to go for the drive."

"Bill? When are the others going to know? The wives?"

"Embassy and HQ are announcing in about twenty minutes. Why?"

"The phone tree! I want to alert them now. But . . ."

"Do it!"

She steeled herself. *Evacuation by air.* Despite knowing she had gauze surgical masks hidden in her purse, the result of talking with Anna, Peg's knees still buckled. Leaning against the wall, she whispered, "Bye." She dialed Trudy. No answer after eight rings.

Peg hurried to the bedroom, where she spun the combination lock on Bill's metal briefcase. Her hand trembled. It took three tries to line up the numbers. She carefully removed the Smith & Wesson from its leather holster, checked to confirm that it was loaded, and returned it to the unlocked briefcase on the top shelf. Available, but out of Beth's reach.

Catching her breath, she dialed Trudy, who picked up on the fourth ring. "Tru, this is Peg."

"Hi, just got home. Can I call you in a bit? Need to change. The rain's gone to snow."

"No! Get. . . *skedaddle* over here. Now! Like we talked about. You are having *dinner* with us! We'll call the others from here."

"Oh, Christ! I'm on it."

"I'm sending Leon to pick you up."

"Thanks, bye."

Peg checked on Beth. She and Sally were giggling as they made sandwiches under Leon's supervision. Peg rushed to her bedroom, pulled her packed suitcase from under the bed, and then filled Beth's with clothes and her camera. Grabbing her field bag, she swept through the bathroom, shoving their toilet kits and first aid pack into it. She said a silent prayer and tossed in her purse. She left the bag in the hallway and tried to catch her breath.

Peg forced a smile as she passed the girls eating at the dining room table and went into the kitchen.

Leon asked, "May I make you something? A sandwich? Tea?"

She held his shoulder and whispered, "I need you to drive over and pick up Trudy. It's an emergency."

"Has the time come?"

Peg nodded once.

He grabbed his heavy jacket from the hook and hurried for the door.

Peg looked at the kitchen clock, guessing how much time she had to do a last review. Despite her obsessive orderliness during the prior few weeks, she needed a last sweep. A little over an hour. She rushed into the living room. Mantel emptied. Leaving *Thunder Over China*, she grabbed *The Little Prince* and dropped it into her field bag. *Claire!* She rushed to the telephone. Dialing Claire's direct line, Peg gasped when she answered. "Claire!" Peg fought to keep her voice down. "It's starting. The evac. I know I shouldn't tell you, but—"

"You won't be my source. Did you get passage on the *Mitchell*?"

"God! I wish, Bill tried, but it was all booked, but at least he gets to fly with us. The Franklins are going with us. Gotta go. Be safe."

"You too."

She slammed down the phone and hurried toward the girls.

CHAPTER 45

Peg settled the girls into a game of cards in the dining room. She closed the door before moving their two suitcases and her field bag out to the front stoop. She started to lift Bill's heavy seabag, then dragged it. When Leon pulled the Buick into the driveway with Trudy, he left the gate open. Peg met them outside. The snow was falling harder.

Trudy hugged Peg, then grabbed her arm. "The girls?"

"Clueless, so far."

Leon pointed to the luggage on the steps. The snow was collecting on them. "Is that all?" When she nodded, he grabbed two suitcases and sprinted for the Buick.

"Heard anything else? Anything from the embassy?" Trudy asked.

Peg said, "No. And we're not supposed to clog the lines calling there, either. I guess we're still on to evac by plane."

Trudy frowned. "You don't think the boys are having a laugh on us? Gonna come in with big grins and say this was just a drill?"

"Wouldn't that be wonderful? Either way, this counts as three moves. Evacuation is as good as a fire!"

Leon loaded their other bags. As he slammed the trunk lid a Jeep skidded to a stop in the middle of the snowy road. Bill and George jumped out.

Both Marines wore their wool winter uniforms and leather flight jackets. Holstered .45s were on their web belts. A dusting of snow clung to their shoulders.

Leon shouted as Bill sprinted past him to the house, "All packed!"

The wives greeted both men with fast hugs inside the front door.

Bill whispered to Peg, "Beth?" She pointed to the dining room, then he asked, "Smith?"

"Still in the briefcase."

At the sound of voices, Beth opened the dining room door and saw the determination on her father's face as he rushed past her, still wearing his jacket. She knew something was happening, something the adults wouldn't put a name to, something dangerous. Her heart pounded and her mouth tasted like tin. Trudy shouted, "Come on, girls! Grab your coats!"

Sally looked up from her cards as Beth yelled, "Hurry!"

Bill put his revolver in the pocket of his jacket and ran to the living room.

George and Trudy each had a child by the hand and were running toward the car.

Bill slammed the front door and took Peg's arm as they hurried down the slippery steps, then ran for the Buick. George sat behind Leon, Trudy beside him with Sally on her lap. Bill helped Peg into the back seat. Beth crawled onto her lap. Bill slid into the front seat as Leon shifted into reverse.

A Ford blocked the driveway, its horn blasting. Leon braked just before ramming it.

Claire jumped out of the car, left it running, and sprinted toward the Buick. Bill raced back to meet her. She thrust two brown envelopes at him. "Passage for the lot of you on the *Mitchell* if you can get there in time. If not, go on the plane. You're still booked. Pacific's blocked near the Edgewater. MPs said to go inland over Signal Hill to the wharf. Don't ask."

She turned. He grabbed her wrist, pulled her to his chest, and whispered. "Thank you, whoever you are. Be safe and look us up when you can."

She smiled. "How'd you know?"

"The camera. There weren't many like it and you were always where the action was."

"Kiss the baby for me." She sprinted back to the Ford and peeled away. He shoved the envelopes inside his jacket.

Bill slammed his door and shouted, "We're going to the wharf! Claire got us passage."

Peg leaned past Beth and called to Bill, "*Mitchell* is full! How'd she—"

He shrugged and turned on the radio. Music. He twisted the knob to find the local English language station, hoping for news. After a static burst, a man's British accent made an announcement for a church rummage sale. He turned it off.

Leon sped up Shaoguan Road, then took the corner too fast. Tires skittered on the snow, clipping the curb before he slowed. "I'll get you there. I know my city." The windows fogged; the defroster was useless until the car had fully warmed. Bill and Leon rolled down their windows. The women held their children tighter.

As the car slid through corners, Beth sat taller to see where they were going. Sally started whimpering. Trudy pulled her daughter into her chest and rubbed the girl's back. She wanted to hold George's hand, but he was gripping his holstered pistol.

Leon sped toward Signal Hill, knowing the harbor was just past it. When the road made a hairpin turn, he slammed on the brakes to avoid ramming the barricade: two overturned cars. The Buick went sideways.

A lean young man raced to the stopped car and put a pistol to Leon's head.

Beth pointed at him and shouted, "*Bù!*" Her "No!" startled him, and he paused.

Peg saw the orange Mercurochrome stain on his hand and pulled Beth to her.

He recognized Beth and Peg, then took a second look at Leon. In rapid Chinese, he told Leon to go back and try a parallel road one up from Pacific.

Leon made a fast turn. As the man aimed the gun at the side of the car, Beth grabbed her mother's arm. "Mommy, that was the man—"

He fired two shots over the roof of the car. Trudy screamed as he laughed for the benefit of his comrades.

Leon ignored the man's directions and sped down to Pacific Road. "My boat!"

Bill clapped his shoulder. "Yes."

Leon veered into the parking lot and skidded to a stop. All four doors opened at once.

Peg gagged at the smell of scorched rubber. She handed her field bag to Beth. "Can you carry it?"

"I got it."

While they unloaded their baggage, Leon sprinted down the dock, jumped into his boat, unlocked the cabin, and started the fans. He raced back to the car, passing George, who was carrying a suitcase and his sea-bag. Trudy had a smaller suitcase in one hand and Sally in the other as they hurried down the snow-slick dock.

Leon pulled the key from the Buick's ignition and dropped it and the house key into the ashtray. As the Ryans started down the dock, Leon smashed the glass of the empty watchman's shack, gaining entry to make a fast call. He checked the trunk, slammed the lid, and sprinted back to fire up the boat's engines.

Bill helped Peg onto the deck before loosening the bow line. The rear deck now held four fifty-gallon drums welded together and bolted to the stern.

As Peg and Trudy seated their daughters at the small table in the cabin, Bill and George shoved their suitcases beside the drums and dropped their heavy sea bags in front to secure the luggage. Bill motioned George to go below.

Beth looked at her shaking friend and shouted over the engine, "This is the whale boat! Don't worry. It's a good one."

The blue cloud of exhaust still lingered when Leon told Bill to cast off the bow line and jump aboard.

Bill slid into the cockpit seat across from Leon and shouted, "The car? Will it be okay there?"

He laughed. "Not for long. The Swiss banker who bought the house wanted an extra vehicle. I told his man to collect it at the marina. It's all theirs now!"

As the boat picked up speed, snow pelted the windshield and clotted in its corners. Leon peered around the windshield. The snow was like needles against his face. The boat jolted against the chop while Peg and Trudy tied life jackets on their daughters. Leon powered past the harbor's buoy and went out a hundred yards before turning. Bill pointed closer to shore.

Leon shouted, "No! Low tide. Tell them to hang on." Snow slid off the roof onto the rear deck in clumps.

When Bill shouted into the cabin, Peg and Trudy held the girls even tighter as the boat shuddered and skidded, slamming through the choppy water. George braced in the hatchway.

When the boat lurched, Beth laughed. "It's like a roller coaster! Look, Mommy. We've been to all those places."

Peg looked past Beth out the window as they sped by the bathing beaches and the rocky promontory of the Edgewater Mansions Hotel, where Claire had thrown a huge going-away party for Jean-Claude the previous week and racked up the largest bar tab Peg had ever seen.

Through the curtain of snow, she saw the wide Chungshan Road cutting up the hill from the red pagoda, past the splash of daffodil yellow of the orphanage, past their church, and the steeples of the Catholic church, all disappearing in the snow. She briefly shut her eyes, and it all came back to her. The clatter of carts and the buzz and hum of haggling on market day. The scent of fresh cantaloupe, the suffocating stench of charcoal fires, and the sound of the gongs and cymbals of the dragon dance, firecrackers, and laughter. Forcing back tears, she held tight to Beth, remembering the pink cloud of cherry blossoms and the aroma of Leon's cherry pies fresh from the oven. The special cherries of Shaoguan.

"Hold on!" Bill shouted as they made a hard turn to port to go around the spit of land sheltering the harbor. Moments later, the boat canted hard to starboard and straightened, entering the calmer water of the bay.

They sped toward the three docked ships. Shore Patrol sentries at the end of the wharf moved their rifles from guard position and aimed. White flecks peppered the water ahead of them.

Bill yanked back the throttle and screamed into the cabin, "Warning shots. Our own guys are shooting at us! The fuel drums must look like a bomb!" Leon froze at the wheel.

"George! Get up here! Lose your cap!" The sentries on the wharf twenty feet above the water shifted their aim from warning shots to sighting on Leon. George scrambled up to the deck. When the sentries saw his red hair and their Marine uniforms, they lowered their rifles. Bill motioned Leon to steer a hundred yards past the ships to the lower gas dock. He handed George his transit papers.

As Leon let the wind bring his boat against the dock, Trudy climbed on deck and reached down for Sally. Bill dropped into the cabin, helped Peg and Beth up the steps. Once alone, Bill slipped his Smith & Wesson into the back of the food locker. George jumped off the bow with a line and tied it off.

On deck, Leon smiled at Beth. "Safe travels, Miss Beth. And you, Madam."

Peg hugged him. "Our home is yours. You have my father's address. Let him know where you are."

Bill clapped Leon on the shoulder and let his hand remain. "Leon. Best to you! Hope you don't need it, but I left a gun in the food locker."

Once they were on the dock, George pointed through the cabin's window to a maroon leather suitcase. "That yours, Peg?"

Before she could answer, Leon responded. "No. It's mine. I'm going to Shanghai!"

Bill cast off the lines and held the boat to the dock only by its railing. "Thanks for everything you did for my family. I'll never forget it." He shoved the craft away from the dock. Leon made a clean turn, waved, and pushed the throttle to full.

The two families raced toward the small cluster of sailors stationed at the foot of the gangplank. The guard quickly glanced at George's papers. At his nod, a sailor grabbed their suitcases and rushed up the slush-covered gangplank. Trudy took Sally's hand and followed him while George hurried after them carrying his seabag. As Bill stuffed their transit documents back into his jacket, a sailor grabbed their suitcases, and another took Bill's seabag as Peg and Beth rushed to Bill's side. Bill saw a battered Ford skidding to a stop at the guard gate fifty yards away. Claire bolted from the car and sprinted down the wharf, waving her press pass at the stunned guard, who looked at the redhead in a fur coat in amazement.

Peg shouted over the deep throb of the ship's engines. "Claire! You made it!"

She held her camera aloft. "Not this trip. I'm just getting a story."

The ship's horn blasted four times, the "getting underway" warning to other craft and obliterated what Peg called to Claire.

Bill boosted Beth to his hip and took Peg's arm. They made it up the first few steps before they heard a shout from the wharf over the rumble of the ship. They turned.

Claire shouted again, "Bon voyage!" She braced against a piling, focused her Kodak Medalist, snapped the picture, and pulled her camera away from her eye. She grinned and waved through the falling snow.

Once the Ryans were on deck, the crew raised the gangplank.

As the *Mitchell* pulled away from the dock, Peg put her hand to her heart and bowed to Claire. She returned the gesture, then hurried back to her car.

Flakes fell thicker and stuck to the deck. Peg held on to the wooden rail, sucking in the frozen air, trembling. With Bill and Beth on either side, the Ryans pressed together as one until they lost the city and the red pagoda behind the gauze of snow.

Bill whispered to her, "Sweetheart. Time to get out of your wet things and down to sick bay."

She pulled him closer. "I need a minute." She knelt, brushed the snow from Beth's hair, and held her face. "Remember how we talked about how I've got to stay away from anyone who might have the measles to keep the baby safe?" The girl grabbed her mother's hand. Peg waited until Beth nodded. "Good. Well, I'm going to a special room on the ship now to take care of the baby, just like your father's going to look after you all the way back to America."

Beth was teary-eyed and held tighter to her mother's hand. "Can I visit?"

"I don't know yet. Take care of your daddy for me." She kissed her daughter's forehead.

Beth took her father's hand. "Okay."

Bill began to say something, but Peg interrupted him. "Go on now. I want to feel the wind on my face a little longer." She smiled and gave him a kiss to last until San Francisco.

EPILOGUE

1948-2005

EPILOGUE

*L*ife printed the photograph of the Ryans on the gangplank above the headline, "The Last China Marine." But they were not truly the last. A few dependents joined the throng of airlifted civilians after the *Mitchell* sailed. Marines remained in Tsingtao for months to protect American nationals and then redeployed to Shanghai as that city fell into chaos.

Peg's baby was born healthy and beautiful. Soon after Ruth's first birthday, Bill was flying Corsairs in Korea. When they were older, Beth joked that Ruth should have "Made in China" tattooed on her foot.

Claire married Jean-Claude in Saigon and changed her name to Grace DuPont. Their book on the emergence of the conflict in Viet Nam and their sequel on the American involvement in that civil war became required reading in diplomatic circles. When the couple covered the Paris Peace Talks, her photo of the signing of the accord at the Majestic Hotel in 1973 was a finalist for the Pulitzer. Grace, however, took greater pride in their three adopted children.

Sebastian sailed to Shanghai to cover the story of the Displaced Persons and emerging aid agencies in December 1948, aboard a ship variously called the *Jiangya* or *Kiangya*. Most agreed that they rated the ship for 1,189 passengers, but the manifest recorded 2,150, and there were at least 500 added stowaways. He was one of the 700 survivors when the ship hit a Japanese mine some 50 miles south of Shanghai. "A greater disaster than the *Titanic*," he wrote in the introduction to his award-winning chronicle.

Mikhail and Arina Karpov became Australian citizens. They visit San Diego every few years to see their daughter, son-in-law, and grandchildren.

JD left the military and opened a crop-dusting service in Kansas.

Gerri managed the accounting department in the San Francisco office of Tong Tea, which Chen Tu established as the company's corporate headquarters.

Fred Tanner opened a successful restaurant in Norfolk, Virginia, with his sister.

Anna Rosetti completed her career in the Navy. Upon retirement, she became a consultant to nursing homes in the Midwest and an elder care advocate.

Madam Tong was the oldest of the one hundred and thirty-two people taking their oath of allegiance to the United States as citizens in 1955. The caption under her picture in the *San Francisco Examiner* called her Mrs. Chen. The Ryan family—Bill, Peg, fifteen-year-old Beth (who was as tall as her mother), and six-year-old Ruth—were in the background beside Chen Tu (who Peg continued to call Leon). At a celebratory lunch at Fisherman's Wharf, he regaled Ruth with stories of Beth's escapades in China.

While the others enjoyed dessert, Peg and Madam Tong strolled to the end of the wharf, arm in arm. Madam Tong pointed. "China's just over there, you know." Peg hugged her shoulder. Madam Tong whispered, "You recall those emeralds you refused?"

"Of course! The most generous—"

"Their value increased substantially since 1948. I sold them last year in Hong Kong and formed the Greenstone Trust for college

scholarships. Your daughters will be the first of many recipients if they apply."

Tony Moretti's 1957 Christmas card from Florida included a note in his precise handwriting, "Fishing is great. Whale watching included! Hope you can make it again this year!"

Peg and Bill retired in Southern California. Trudy and George moved three houses down from them a year later. When the couples met for bridge or dinner, conversation often drifted to their China days. On a whim, Peg and Trudy launched an outreach to other Marine wives who had been in Tsingtao. Their occasional luncheons grew to a "Tsingtao Remembered" gala attended by more than a hundred China Marines and their wives.

Peg and Trudy remained friends for more than half a century—celebrating the successes of their children and mourning the passing of their husbands. Their daughters last saw each other in the spring of 2004 while visiting Trudy in hospice.

Summer 2005

Beth tapped her cell phone after the first distinctive ring. "Hi, Mom."

"Honey? I know it's short notice, but can you drive me to an appointment this afternoon? Leave here about one?"

"Sure. Which doc?"

"Not a doctor, thank goodness." She heard Beth sigh. "Wear tennies and a jacket."

Beth knew not to waste time asking more, despite the day being shirt-sleeve warm for March. Willful and kind at the same time. She'd never figure her out. Not in a million years. Then she leaned against the wall, wondering if they had even one of those million years left to

annoy and adore each other.

"Sure. Dinner out somewhere on the way back from wherever?"

"We'll see."

"Okay. I'll be in front at one on the dot."

The attendant in pink scrubs helped Peg from her wheelchair into the passenger seat of Beth's SUV. Wearing her old tan golf club windbreaker and light blue slacks, the older woman still looked like she could beat Beth on the first nine holes if it hadn't been for that car T-boning her a few years ago. Beth waved. "Thanks, Rosa."

The attendant smiled and shut the door.

Beth started the engine. "Where to?"

"The marina."

"Why?"

"You'll see."

Half an hour later, Beth eased into the driveway of the public parking lot at Sunset Marina and drove toward the sportfishing dock, hunting for a parking place near a sidewalk. Peg pointed at the owner's lot. "Go to eighteen. It's up a few spaces. By the gate."

"Mom! Those are reserved."

"I know."

Beth pulled into the slot but left her SUV running. "Seriously!"

"Shut it off. We're going for a boat ride."

Beth shook her head as she pulled the light wheelchair from the hatchback. As she helped Peg into it, the light caught her mother's jade ring, now loose on her finger. She kissed her mother on the top of her head.

The breeze carried the iodine hint of kelp from the nearby beach. As Beth pushed the chair across the parking lot, Peg pulled a dark blue-and-white checked scarf out of her pocket and tied it under her chin.

A stocky man in his forties on the dock jogged toward the gate and held it open.

"Walter, this is Beth." Peg looked over her shoulder at her older daughter. "He's the new volunteer chaplain at my place. Nice man."

He took the handles of the chair from Beth and nodded toward a thirty-foot cabin cruiser. "That's her. Going to be a good afternoon to take her out, light clouds, calm sea." He winked at Beth. "She's all warmed up."

Peg said, "Takes families out to scatter ashes at sea."

He laughed. "Not today. Sorry for the late invitation, but I only got word this morning that the super-pod was along the coast."

"Mom?"

"I told him how much we enjoyed seeing the whales off Hawaii and in China." She cackled. "And about our boat ride with Leon in '48! Just enjoy the ride. Nobody's shooting at us this time. And there might be whales."

"I'm sorry that Ruthie's out of town with her kids. They'd love this."

Walter eased the wheelchair down the ramp from the dock to his boat. After bracing the wheels next to the bench seating, he pulled the ramp onboard and helped Beth step down onto the boat's rear deck.

He loosened the stern line and left it looped around the rear cleat. Handing the line to Beth, he said, "Hang onto this while I drop the other line." He jumped from the dock and stepped into the cockpit. Beth dropped her line, and he eased the boat into the channel. Beth sat down beside her mother.

Past the breakwater, he steered south and sped through the calm water. Peg slid her scarf back, so it circled her neck. "I love how the air feels different on the water, even this close to land." She leaned over to Beth. "You were such a good sailor. I wish you'd been older to remember it all."

The wind snapped at Beth's ponytail as she shouted back, "I still can't get over your courage taking a kid over there!"

Peg flicked her hand as if shooing away a bug. "Don't bother with all that nonsense. Our family was together. We had a good time."

"It was the best, Mom. *Dǐng hǎo.*"

Her mother chuckled and patted Beth's hand. "*Dǐng hǎo!*"

The wind swirled Peg's short white hair into a dandelion puff. She smiled, holding Beth's hand, and watching for whales.

AUTHOR'S NOTE

As a child, I sailed to Tsingtao, China, as a Marine Corps dependent on the USS *General A.E. Anderson* and returned to America on the USS *General William Mitchell*. I grew into adulthood seeing Marine wives not only as military spouses and mothers but as remarkable and independent women. I attended reunions of the Marine wives who became my mother's friends in that remote outpost. Many were as close as sisters. Their stories of life in a war zone, quiet courage, love, loss, and mutual support inspired me to discover *why* the U.S. military was in China in the middle of their civil war and *how* these remarkable women thrived in that environment and began their lifelong friendships.

Primary research sources included interviews with the women and men who were there, their children, hearing family stories, reading letters, diaries, listening to voice recordings on shellac disks, and watching home movies. Documentary research included Navy or Marine Corps mimeographed directives on disintegrating newsprint and the fading carbon copies of typed materials on transparent onionskin paper; State Department correspondence and unclassified embassy dispatches; Department of War and the subsequent Department of Defense directives.

Secondary interpretive resources included contemporary newspaper and magazine articles and the retrospective and analytical works of historians. The families, archivists, and librarians making these resources available have my undying gratitude.

This novel is a blending of memory, fact, and imagination, which occasionally required the compression of events. The men, women, children, and their stories in this novel are pure invention. More can be found about my other books at www.SharonOLightholder.com.

ACKNOWLEDGMENT

I have had the good fortune to have thanked all who contributed to the content of this book in person. Some thanks were given decades ago over tea and letters, telegrams or a beer and home movies. More recently, friends, readers of my prior novels, and others in the San Diego writing and military communities offered encouragement when this book was in its earliest stages.

My editor, Laurie Gibson, brought a clarity, precision, and heart to my early drafts. Stephanie Larson (www.StephanieLarsonDesign.com) designed the wonderful cover. The multiple contractors supporting Albedo Press brought it all together beautifully.

As always, thanks to both my sister, Maureen O. Shanahan, and her husband, Dennis F. Shanahan, M.D., COL USA retired, for support and encouragement beyond the call of duty.